A Power Older than the Gods Lies in Mortal Hands

"What do you see?" she asked.

Captain Thoster said, "A whole lot of nothing. So?"

"I see a world ready to be plucked," replied Nogah. Japheth tried to ignore her squishy, lisping inflection to Common, like she was trying to suck the marrow out of a bloody bone with each word. "I see a world crying out for new direction. A world where those who align themselves properly will be rewarded with riches beyond their wildest dreams. What do you say to that?"

"I see that every time I pull alongside a merchant ship and demand the contents of their hold," boasted Thoster.

"Baubles compared to what I offer." Nogah sniffed.

"What exactly *do* you offer?" asked Seren.

But Power Comes with a Price.

ABOLETHIC SOVEREIGNTY

ALSO BY BRUCE R. CORDELL

BRUCE R. CORDELL

ABOLETHIC SOVEREIGNTY BOOK I

PLAGUE of SPELLS

Abolethic Sovereignty
Book I
PLAGUE OF SPELLS

©2008 Wizards of the Coast, Inc.

Cover art by J. P. Targete
First Printing: December 2008

9 8 7 6 5 4 3 2 1

ISBN: 978-0-7869-4965-6
620-21770740-001-EN

U.S., CANADA,
ASIA, PACIFIC, & LATIN AMERICA
Wizards of the Coast, Inc.
P.O. Box 707
Renton, WA 98057-0707
+1-800-324-6496

EUROPEAN HEADQUARTERS
Hasbro UK Ltd
Caswell Way
Newport, Gwent NP9 0YH
GREAT BRITAIN
Save this address for your records.

Visit our web site at www.wizards.com

Dedication
For Dee

Acknowledgments
Susan Morris, John Staab, Phil Athans, Rich Baker

CHAPTER ONE

28 Tarsakh, the Year of Blue Fire (1385 DR)
Starmantle, Dragon Coast

The storm blew in from the east.

The storm's leading edge spread wide to shadow the Dragon Coast. It dripped cold rain and threw a pall across the sun. Behind this sullen herald churned the storm's bruised core, rumbling with elemental rage.

Rain, hail, and freezing winds burst into the port city of Starmantle.

In the first moments of the downpour, city dwellers attempted to go about their business. But the rain came stronger, and the chill deepened into an out-of-season wintry onslaught. Even sailors used to nature's fury dashed for cover. People exclaimed in shock and discomfort as needle-sharp sleet sought cracks in roofs, walls, and clothing.

The streets rapidly emptied. A man skidded in fresh mud and fell. A street merchant struggled to pull down the awning of his cart against the rising wind that tried to tear it away. Broadsheets and trash cavorted through the air. The fishy smell of the port town was overwhelmed with the tang of the thunderstorm.

A short woman holding a blue shawl over her head stumbled and nearly fell when her boot slid on rain-slick paving stones.

Raidon Kane reached out and steadied her. She nodded thanks, then hurried away, still seeking shelter. She and Raidon were alike, both caught out in the sudden, freezing deluge without a cloak.

Raidon returned his attention to the narrow cobbled way at his feet. The rain and sudden chill made the paving stones more than slick—in some places moisture and the plunging temperature conspired to spin icy traps for the unwary.

He frowned, one hand shielding his eyes from stinging rain. He wondered from where the winter storm had come, so far into the reign of Greengrass. His voyage across the Sea of Fallen Stars had seen mild days and cool nights. When he'd made landfall earlier that day, a balmy spring sun smiled from the east.

Raidon's fare for passage had required that he help the crew wrestle its cargo of iron ingots, spell-preserved cream, and Rethild-weave silk onto the pier. He'd sweated and labored with the others under a wide sky bereft even of haze. And now, freezing rain, hail, and possibly snow?

Raidon pulled a silver chain from beneath his shirt. The stone of his amulet dangled from it. A leafless white tree was etched into the stone, surrounded by a field of heart-breakingly pure blue. The symbol was the Cerulean Sign. Overlapping inscriptions so small they could easily be mistaken for texture covered the remainder of the amulet in a language he didn't know.

The stone warned him of aberrations and distortions of the natural order by dropping precipitously in temperature.

In the wind, Raidon could barely feel his hands, let alone whether the stone was colder than the air. Yes, it was chilled, but in warning? Or because the wind whistled with the bite of a frost giant's breath?

He squinted at the symbol through a flurry of ice crystals, looking for any discoloration in tree or border, or for any change in the tiny script crabbing the stone's remaining surface.

The Cerulean Sign betrayed no change. The blue of the border was as startling and sky bright as ever, while the tree at the center glimmered white as a star. Which meant the sudden onset of inclement weather wasn't due to aberrations.

The Sign's lack of response didn't rule out any of a host of other malign possibilities, of course. It was entirely possible some wizard or priest of the natural world was casting foul-weather rituals with a nefarious end in mind.

But Raidon's amulet wasn't keyed to respond to such mundane possibilities. Evil born in mortal hearts, no matter the depth of its wickedness, was of a lesser order than the abominations he watched for. Whatever the weather's origin, he judged it beyond his concern.

He released a relieved sigh.

A who-knows-how-long delay to ferret out and dispatch some local monstrosity was not in the offing. His schedule would not be disrupted. His daughter, Ailyn, expected to see him in Nathlekh in just five days, and he had vowed not to disappoint her again. She was too young to understand the long absences required by his ever wider searches.

Raidon slipped the amulet back beneath his shirt.

The amulet was a family heirloom left to him by his mother, a fey woman of Sildëyuir. In the years since he'd taken up the birthright, he'd walked much of Faerûn looking for some trace of her. He'd found hints, stories, and long-stale traces but never his mother or even her grave.

Instead, Raidon discovered a terrible peril. A danger too few recognized to actively resist. Except for him, with the aid of his mother's amulet, a relic Cerulean Sign.

A cruel gust of wind cut through his reverie.

Zai zi, it was cold! His silk shirt offered next to no protection. A late-season snowstorm was well and truly begun. Even if birthed by nothing more than nature's random temper, the storm blew with a cold that was becoming dangerous.

Down a side street, he spied a wildly swinging placard in the shape of a white boar, with a flagon emblazoned upon it. Maybe someone inside would be willing to part with a cloak thicker than his own silk jacket. At least he could take a moment to warm up and perhaps wait out the freezing wind and icefall.

Raidon entered the tavern. The place was nearly filled with patrons who'd had the same idea as Raidon. A great fire burned in the hearth, and warm mead was being served at half price.

The tavern's layout reminded Raidon of a pub he'd visited in Amn a few years ago. He recalled how his amulet had become as ice against his chest when he talked to the pub's proprietor. Something foul lurked nearby. That night, the proprietor tried to brain him in his sleep with an iron chamber pot.

Thanks to the amulet, Raidon had been expecting trouble. He had punched the proprietor's sternum, breaking it, while simultaneously sweeping his attacker's legs, knocking the man to the floor. Examination of the proprietor with the aid of his amulet showed him to be in the thrall of a mind flayer, an aberration out of the deep earth scheming in the sewers below the city.

Raidon shook his head to clear the memory. Nothing like that was occurring here.

He sat down at the end of one of the long common tables. The half-dozen men and women already seated ignored him.

A server came up, a teenage boy with unkempt hair. The boy glanced at Raidon, then said, as if asking a question, "We have West Lake Dragon Well?"

The boy had correctly teased out his human Shou ancestry from his fey blood.

Raidon smiled his gratitude and nodded. He added, "Please bring me a pot. I would love to sample your West Lake Dragon Well."

"Very good!" The server scampered off through the crowd.

Both Starmantle and Westgate had seen a flood of Shou across the Sea of Fallen Stars from Thesk and points farther east along the Golden Road. Both cities strove to become the destination port of choice for the immigrants. This rivalry was just one more avenue through which each city sought to capture the trade moving across the sea. The custom provided by the constant influx of Shou was considerable.

All of which meant that Raidon could now anticipate enjoying a cup of fine tea in a tavern that ten years earlier likely was known only for its mead and ale. Times change. Thankfully, the locals had figured out the quickest way to a Shou's heart was through a proper tea service.

The boy returned soon enough with an oven-fired clay pot and a mismatched, slightly cracked teacup.

Raidon suppressed a frown at the presentation and even managed to tap three fingers on the table in thanks. He poured a cup, sipped.

Ah, yes. The warm brew was indeed West Lake Dragon Well, if just so slightly stale. The green tea's growing popularity was well deserved. The boy held out his hand, "A silver, then?"

Raidon nodded and paid the profligate price. Tea was one of the few luxuries he allowed himself.

Ailyn loved tea too, despite her mere five years. He'd last seen her three months earlier over steaming cups. She'd giggled when he pantomimed burning his lips to show her to be careful. Three months was too long for a father to be separated from his daughter. It was nearly a lifetime for a child that age.

When he'd rescued her in Telflamm, she was just one year old. When he'd found her, the girl's natural family was already dead, killed and consumed by a nest of creatures who wore their victims' skins to secretly stalk Telflamm's alleys. Ailyn had been spared only because she was too small to bother with.

After Raidon wiped out the nest, he found her lying quiet in her crib. The girl had looked up at him, catching his gaze with blinking eyes the color of the sea. He lifted her out of the enclosure, and she fumbled at the front of his jacket with her two small hands. "Don't worry, little one. You're safe now," he'd promised.

But even as Raidon said those words, he wondered how they could be true. He knew the girl had no remaining family. He'd saved her life—now the child was his responsibility. The child finally managed to get a hold on his jacket and gripped it.

In the end, Raidon adopted her.

But he couldn't set up a home in Telflamm. Even though he'd cleaned out the nest of skinstealers, the city yakuza had marked Raidon Kane as an enemy to be killed on sight for a past offense against a crime boss. So he took Ailyn west across the sea, becoming one more Shou immigrant hoping to build something new for himself and his child south of the Dragon Coast. He'd settled in the city of Nathlekh, whose Shou population was burgeoning. With the gold he'd accumulated during years of fighting aberrations (and liberating their hoards), he'd established a household staffed with trusted nannies and guards. Ailyn always cried when he left to continue his search, but he always brought her a gift on his return.

He pulled from a breast pocket a small bell. Its handle was mahogany, and the bell was wrought mithral. The clapper was stilled by a leather tongue. He'd purchased the bell in the Sembian city of Selgaunt. When he'd tested it, it had sounded with a pure, joyous note. Ailyn would love it. He smiled, anticipating her reaction, and returned it to his pocket.

Raidon took another sip of tea and noticed a white-haired woman. The woman's locks were pulled into a single long braid down her back. She sat nearly opposite him at the common table. Several patrons were gathered around the woman. The woman gazed into an irregularly shaped piece of yellowish crystal on the table before her.

Small sparks of light began to swirl within it, but the woman stared resolutely forward. Her tight mouth turned slowly into a frown. Finally, she broke visual contact with the stone. It immediately went dark. Raidon recognized the crystal as a prophesier's crutch—usually used as a prop by those who fabricated rosy-sounding futures in return for payment.

Raidon's young server stood at the woman's elbow, his duties apparently forgotten for the moment. Raidon heard him ask over the inn's hubbub, "What do you see, Lady Mimura? Will the storm soon pass? We're waiting on salt; do you think the salt ship will make it by morning?"

The woman glanced up and around, surprised to see the attention she'd gathered. She stood, gathering the crystal to her bosom. With her free hand, she gave the boy's head an absent-minded pat.

"Mistress? Are you well? Will the weather let up tomorrow?"

The woman shook her head, her frown still in place, a look of confusion and concern in her eyes. She muttered, "Something. I can't say. Somewhere, beyond our ken, a great crime shudders toward conclusion."

"A crime? What, do you mean a burglary? A murder?" demanded another patron.

She shook her head and replied, "I don't know." As if in a daze, she left. The briefly opened door sent a new chill into the room. Despite Raidon's belief that the woman was merely a local fakir, he covertly checked his amulet again, just to be certain.

It remained pristine.

Some time later it seemed the storm was waning, but a cold rain still lashed Starmantle's streets. In the interim, Raidon purchased a knee-length woolen coat from another patron.

The coat was black, with golden yellow piping at the cuffs and along the hem—quite striking, really. The coat would be useful against snow and cold, but Raidon guessed it would be soaked through in an instant in the ongoing downpour. More important, he doubted caravans would depart the city that afternoon or evening in such weather. The monk planned to travel the final miles swiftly on horseback or wagon as a hired hand on a merchant caravan. Not today, seemingly.

Raidon asked for a room to wait out the storm.

Though usually a heavy sleeper, that night he dozed fitfully, troubled by the pounding of the rain on roof tiles and window panes.

He opened his eyes to light leaking through shutter cracks. Sleep had apparently finally claimed him, though he recalled no dreams. Grogginess weakened his resolve to get an early start. But the rain's patter was gone, and the howling wind too. He bounded from the cot, finished his ablutions, and descended to the common room. After a quick bite of cold pork, Raidon exited the establishment, tying the sash of his new coat.

A coat he was happy to have. White frost covered every surface, and his breath steamed in great fluffy billows. A strange calm held the frigid air, and dawn's advance was tempered with a whitish blue hue. An unusual acrid smell, like that of burnt metal, suffused common urban smells.

The odor reminded the monk uncomfortably of when he'd witnessed a demonic aberration rip a sword in two with unearthly strength. The sharp, caustic smell was the same the metal gave off as it was pulled in two. It was the smell of something breaking.

Raidon made it to Starmantle's principal gate without delay. Hardly anyone was up and about. Those who were awake idled in the streets in small, awkward groups. They looked east, murmuring into the oddly tinted sunrise.

A two-story caravanserai hunkered just outside the city walls. Already merchants marshaled horses, wagons, drivers, coach hands, and guards. Trade did not wait upon strange colors in the sky or odd smells, for which Raidon was grateful. In his travels, he'd learned how to move swiftly around Faerûn, taking advantage of the continent's vast network of commerce. Through its use, he wasn't saddled with horses or travel coaches of his own to care for. Many caravan captains knew him by reputation, if not by sight, and were happy to have Raidon Kane's company on dangerous routes.

The half-elf entered the trade house and shortly accepted a commission to escort a trade company heading to Nathlekh after first skirting the Long Arm Lake's northwest edge. In return for loading and unloading, as well as serving as a caravan guard in a pinch, Raidon would make far better time than he could afoot. Pay was part of his contract, but the tidy sum he'd amassed cleaning out aberration lairs dwarfed anything a merchant lord could tempt him with.

They set out in four tarp-roofed wagons, each pulled by four horses, as well as a couple of outriders behind and ahead. Raidon volunteered to ride behind, keeping an eye out for bandits. A couple of squabbling goblin bands had lately encamped in the eaves of the Gulthmere Forest, the monk knew from his most recent trip. The creatures were cowardly in small groups, but en masse they represented a real threat.

The caravan chief lent Raidon a spirited horse to ride rear

guard. She told Raidon its name was Tanner. Raidon sat on the steed, waiting for the caravan to pull ahead. Tanner was a fine beast, unhappy to see her fellows pull away, but he calmed her with low words and pats.

The monk was stroking Tanner's mane when an odd noise distracted him.

The thudding beat of hundreds of wings against the still air pulled his gaze upward. A great flock of crows, their black silhouettes skating swiftly across the morning sky, flew out of the east. The flock didn't veer or hesitate. It swiftly overtook the caravan then passed it, flying arrow-straight into the west. Raidon squinted into the distance, looking for a pursuer—perhaps a griffon or a small dragon? No. Only the rising sun. A sun as blue as the eye of a storm giant and as devoid of heat as an advancing glacier.

Blue? What—

A cacophony of shrill calls and screams broke from a copse of sheltering trees to the south. A mob of stunted figures in patchwork armor dashed forth. Some brandished spears, others axes. Goblin bandits! Raidon estimated twenty at least. The one leading the charge dwarfed the rest and was shaggier.

Caravan guards tumbled out of the wagons, buckling on scabbards and fumbling cords to unstrung bows.

Raidon sawed on the reins, turning Tanner back toward the wagons. He spurred her into a gallop. Tanner responded, collapsing the distance between her and the creature leading the charge. The leader stood nearly seven feet tall. Coarse hair poked from the joints in its armor. Daggerlike fangs filled its gaping mouth. In one hand it wielded a broad-headed battle-axe, in the other a severed human head by the hair. It whirled the head like a flail. This was no goblin.

Raidon hijacked a portion of Tanner's momentum as he vaulted from the stirrups. He dived at the shaggy bandit leader, hands forward as if anticipating a plunge into the sea. His foe swung its axe around, missing Raidon by several hand spans. The monk's reaching left hand touched the soil near the leader's foot. Raidon snagged the creature's nearest ankle with his right arm, hugging it close to his chest as he tucked into a roll.

In less time than it took to make a single revolution, an awful, meaty snap rang out. The half-elf loosed his hold and concluded his roll, allowing the maneuver to bleed away his speed in just three revolutions. Back on his feet with hands ready, he saw the shaggy bandit leader on its back, one leg splayed to the side at an obscene angle. It continued to scream, but no longer in challenge.

The remaining goblins, composed entirely of the smaller, greenish breed, stumbled to a halt. They looked down at their chieftain, then back to Raidon. The monk stared them down, knowing he could intimidate the goblin rabble with a confident stance. The goblins' greenish skin seemed to shift, flickering and brightening under his scrutiny, until it was blue. Not only their skin, but their equipment, the ground they stood upon, and everything else.

Was he hallucinating?

Uncertainty turned to alarm among the goblins. They pointed and spoke excitedly in their debased tongue. Raidon cocked his head. He couldn't understand their language or why their frightened pointing wasn't at him.

Raidon shifted his stance so he faced the sunrise.

The oddly chill sun was gone. Instead, the horizon was on fire.

Blue fire.

From beyond the horizon's rim, a pillar of azure fire with a fat crown tumbled toward the sky as if intent on piercing heaven's vault itself. The ravening pillar's crown was molten sapphire, and unleashed a fiery catastrophe in its wake.

Raidon gaped with all the rest, his focus lost in the apocalyptic image.

Was it some sort of demonic assault? Or had the monstrosities he hunted—the mind flayers, the aboleths, the beholders, the skinstealers, and all the other deformed and formless hordes—finally combined their efforts to find and ambush him? He fumbled for his amulet, his hands trembling with uncharacteristic haste.

No. It was just as when he'd checked it yesterday. The amulet remained warm to the touch, its image unblemished. Its serenity indicated aberrations were not responsible for the catastrophic skyline. That knowledge offered no comfort in the face of what was the most incredible display of destruction Raidon had ever witnessed.

Raidon let the amulet drop back against his chest, a groan on his lips as he looked to the south. A second fiery pillar clawed up over the jagged edges of the Orsraun Mountains, small in the vast distance. Whatever was happening, more than just the Dragon Coast was caught up in it.

Tanner shuffled sideways, snorting. Some of the goblins dashed toward the edges of the Gulthmere, but most stood rooted, comrades in fear with the caravan guards. All stared in mute incomprehension at the chaos in the east.

A shimmering wall of disrupted air raced over the lip of the horizon and down across the plain toward them. Within that wall, blue flames licked and cavorted. The wall stretched north and south as far as Raidon could see, and reached up too, miles beyond his comprehension.

Wild creatures tried to outrun the advancing wall of fire; bounding jackrabbits, sprinting deer, and a lone wolf stretching its stride in a desperate bid for escape. None could outrace death. The oncoming wall washed over them, burning each to ash.

Bandits and caravaneers alike cried out in a single voice as panic grew. Scrambling, pawing, screaming, they turned west, already running, some falling in their fear, only to be trampled by their companions.

Raidon felt himself reverberate with the mob's panic, but he held himself back, mentally searching for his vaunted focus. If his end was imminent, he didn't want to perish in a moment of failed self-control. He spurred Tanner west. "Run," he murmured into the neighing creature's flicking ear. "Gallop as never before!"

The horse ran. She strained forward, shivering with her effort. She easily overtook the goblins and men fleeing afoot. Next she pulled past the other mounted caravan outriders.

A moment later, the oncoming front enveloped them.

A shrieking gust of air punched Raidon from Tanner's saddle. He saw the horse stumble and go down, but he was already past, spiraling through air flickering with fiery blue streamers. He twisted his body into the wind, trying to mimic his mid-gallop tumble from the saddle moments earlier.

The bare earth began to steam. The haze hindered Raidon's ability to judge his roll. He fell, out of control. Something hard cracked his left elbow. The snap vibrated through him, and his left arm went as loose as a rag doll's. His training temporarily shielded him from pain, though he already felt signals he couldn't long ignore gathering at the edge of his mind. His roll concluded in a flopping, painful heap. He came to rest in the lee of a larger boulder. The outcrop shielded him from the tornado-like wind.

He blinked into the torrent, trying desperately to comprehend what was occurring all around him. Raidon wondered if he wasn't within the belly of chaos itself. The wind's screech was so loud he was partly deafened. Blood trickled from one of his ears.

A woman lay just beyond the ravine that ran along the road. Raidon recognized her after a moment: the caravan chief. The roadside ravine, like his boulder, offered partial protection from the roaring wind. The woman struggled to rise from where the shock front had tossed her. Blood soaked one side of her face. She saw Raidon behind his boulder and reached.

Then she caught fire and screamed. Blue flame wreathed her in an instant. The eldritch flame burned brightest in her eyes and open mouth. Raidon cried out in sympathy and in fear, but he couldn't hear himself. A nimbus of cobalt flame sprouted from the woman's back as if she unfurled fiery wings, but before Raidon quite understood what he saw, the woman burned away to ash.

Then the pain from his inelegant fall shuddered through him. Tears further clouded his vision, but he recognized the dim shapes of caravan wagons as they tumbled by on each side, blowing and bounding along in twenty-foot hops, spinning and breaking into ever smaller fragments each time they struck the ground. He saw trees too, and horses, men, loose cargo, and goblins, all held in the wind's fierce grip. The boulder he sheltered behind continued to divert the displaced air, but he felt a terrifying force plucking at his garments and exposed skin, as if eager to embrace him once more.

A goblin smacked onto the leading face of Raidon's boulder. Its mouth was open in a soundless scream, for it was aflame like the caravan chief. But the flame wasn't consuming it; instead, the fire seemed to grip the goblin in a form-changing spell, one gone terribly awry.

When the goblin's head came off, Raidon gasped. But when the detached head began to pull itself toward the monk on suddenly elongating, blue-burning hair, Raidon's already tottering mental equilibrium shattered. He bellowed in full-throated alarm. Raidon kicked at the grotesque head. It bit at him, slavering. The tentacle-like hair tried to wind around his leg. But Raidon's kick was true, and the awful, animate body part sailed out into the surge and was gone.

The boulder began to shudder to a new resonance. Raidon squinted. Was it beginning to glow? No, it was losing opacity, and light shone through it. The stone slowly faded from dark, dirty brown to a glasslike consistency. He clutched the boulder desperately. It remained solid, though its new transparency allowed Raidon an unimpeded view directly back toward the shock wave's origin.

The land shuddered and flowed, tossed and lapped, as if water, not solid earth. Crystalline spokes sprouted, their tips slowly revolving as they pushed ever higher until a madman's lattice squatted on the horizon. Even as Raidon's mind tried to grasp the structure's skewed, unsound geometry, the lattice began to evaporate.

Then his boulder sloughed away. The half-elf dived toward the ravine, but a passing streamer of blue fire caught him squarely through his chest, like an arrow fired from a divine bow.

Time's passage slowed to a trickle. Raidon's momentum drained away, and he hung suspended by nothing save fiery pain. Something tugged at his neck. His amulet fell up and away into the sky as the links of its chain flamed blue and melted.

He strained, body and mind, reaching for the glinting stone. He couldn't afford to lose it! It was more than the Symbol of the Cerulean Sign; it was the only tangible effect left to him by his mother. His finger tips brushed its fleeing edge. The normally cerulean blue surrounding the white tree changed, as if infected with the blue fire.

"No!" he yelled into the timeless moment. He saw the amulet, like its chain, begin to flare. A moment later, it dissolved as it fell upward.

Left behind was an image of the symbol surrounded by a roil of insubstantial glyphs. He continued to reach anyway, straining against the temporal pause. If he could just touch the lingering glow of retreating energy, perhaps . . .

As if responding to his desire, the remnant flared. Its upward trajectory slowed, then reversed. The disembodied symbol slashed back down, striking Raidon's chest. Fire burned through his new coat and consumed it in an instant. The symbol's cerulean blue now fully matched the cobalt blue of the surrounding calamity—a subtle change, but enormous for what it implied. Not that Raidon was permitted any more time to think. The insubstantial symbol seared into his body, his mind, and his very soul.

All faded to blue, then to nothing.

CHAPTER TWO

Ten Years After the Spellplague
The Year of Silent Death (1395 DR)
The Depths of the Sea of Fallen Stars

The sea coach veered toward the wall, then sawed away just as abruptly. The gargantuan nautilus shell shuddered and nearly collided with stone. Braided kelp reins strained as the beast pulling the conveyance through the inky water attempted to shake free of its harness.

Nogah was lightly tethered to the sea coach's deck at the open mouth of the nautilus. To the eyes of a surface dweller she seemed bloated, but no more so than any other member of her amphibious race.

Nogah's finely scaled, webbed hands pulled sharply on the reins that stretched down into the murk. Some of the cords were attached to the whiskerlike barbels of the beast pulling the sea coach: a catfish the size of a small whale.

With the reins so attached, Nogah could steer the great fish up, down, left, right, or in any combination of directions. Now she pulled back on all the reins at once, sharply enough to inflict pain.

The creature's great flukes ceased their agitated movement. The fish drifted in the center of the vertical vent, waiting for either food or the next tweak on the reins. In the absolute darkness of the water-filled shaft, Nogah could only dimly make out the outline of the great beast, even with her keen, water-adapted sight. They were already far deeper than her kind were ever meant to descend.

The titanic catfish was rapidly becoming a troublesome liability for her expedition. The fish was not happy about being directed to swim so deep, so far past the bottom of the Sea of Fallen Stars, straight down a drowned earth vent whose depth was unfathomed.

But the beast would serve. It had to. Failure was not an option for Nogah. If she failed, her status as a senior whip of the Queen of the Depths and Sea Mother would come into question, and the few kuo-toa who still followed her would reject her aberrant teaching and return to the traditional dogma of the majority. Nogah would become a wanderer, declared heretic by the other whips. She would likely be hunted for sport and possibly vengeance. Nogah had her enemies. They worked even now toward her undoing back in the shallow city of Olleth.

With one hand still grasping the reins, she pulled her pincer-staff from its holster and rapped sharply on the nautilus shell behind her tether post. The mammoth shell's winding interior was large enough to hold pockets of air, capable of serving as living space for six additional kuo-toa, though only she and one junior whip inhabited it. The few who retained enough respect to have accompanied Nogah on her journey of discovery remained in Olleth. She had set them to propagandize the expedition, lest her enemies sink her reputation while she was absent.

Curampah, her junior whip, slithered out of the opening, his bulging, silver-black eyes blinking a question. She had sponsored his study and apprenticeship to the Sea Mother's worship, and he owed her direct service, regardless of his opinion of the expedition's worthiness. This close, the tingle of electric affinity all whips shared danced on her scales.

"Curampah, what ails this beast?" she asked, tiny bubbles escaping upward with each word. "It fed according to its usual schedule, yet it continues to balk."

"Daughter of the Sea," he replied, using the honorific due her, "if I may, you have urged it downward past its span of strength. It grows weary. Even with the protective prayers enclosing us, some hint of the growing pressure beyond leaks inward. Can't you feel it, Nogah? I can, and it wearies me. My dreams are troubled."

Nogah allowed her translucent, inner lids to half close, blurring Curampah's image. It was her conscious look of calculation, useful for cowing subordinates. It made them wonder if she would respond civilly or curse them to a literal, painful death.

The junior whip trod precariously close to disrespect. She knew to what he referred, and to lecture her about it was insolence, should she choose to view it as such. Even with the fortitude provided her by her connection to the Sea Mother, a fortitude that Curampah's fledgling association couldn't hope to match, she sensed the unrelenting grip of the sea. Beyond her magical barrier, it obstinately tried to crush them—catfish, nautilus shell, and scales—in one final spasm.

But she would not sing poison into his blood or cause his heart to explode, which he also knew. She had too few resources to throw away subordinates without greater cause than simply reminding her of unpleasant truths.

Under such conditions, any other senior kuo-toa whip would turn back or find another way downward.

But her tenacity was born of divine decree, or so she chose to believe.

True, no direct communication had occurred between her and the Sea Mother or any of the Sea Mother's exarchs . . . but what of her dreams? She knew the Sea Mother wanted something of her, something the divine being was somehow unable to articulate directly.

A frightening thought! If something prevented the Sea Mother's clear communication, it must be a dire threat indeed! At least, so Nogah interpreted the signs. Others, untroubled by dreams, declared Nogah unstable.

Despite the risk of being outcast, she persisted in her claims, describing how her visions revealed a taint welling up from a near-bottomless trench, a hole in the earth where none had been before.

And hadn't she been vindicated with the discovery of a newborn vent's existence? And how else could she have predicted its location in the dim, uncharted depths?

Despite her successful predictions, or perhaps because of them, Nogah remained alone in her conviction that the Sea Mother had revealed the cavity for a reason. She was convinced the newly opened vent must be plumbed, and no argument could sway her. The other whips of the Sea Mother told her the cavity was just one more altered feature of the landscape left in the Spellplague's wake a decade earlier. By every estimation, this particular seafloor vent numbered among the least remarkable of the changes wrought by the Weave's collapse. When compared to whole kingdoms erased, continents rearranged, plaguechanged monstrosities, floating motes of water and land, renewed contact with Abeir, and the real threat that the Sea of Fallen Stars would drain completely into the Underdark . . . yes, this particular vent seemed a minor issue. The kuo-toa were more concerned that even the celestial and infernal realms themselves still fluctuated. The Spellplague had chewed through earth, stone, magic, and planar boundaries as readily as through fallible flesh. Empty, drowned crevices that apparently led nowhere were judged a waste of attention.

Thus, the senior whips decreed Nogah's plan would divert resources that could be better used elsewhere. Threats to the people were always gathering. The Weave's failure, combined with the ongoing realignment of the celestial dominions, put even the Sea Mother at risk!

Nogah growled. As if her current task were not meant to stem just such a threat! Hadn't the Sea Mother directed her on this venture through her strange silences, as if urging Nogah to investigate the mystery? The other whips were blind. Always decisive, Nogah committed to the exploratory dive despite the consensus building against her, and before that consensus solidified into official directive. She used up the last of her favors to gain the use of this fabulous sea coach, its harnessed beast, and a leave from her duties in the city of Olleth.

Now here she was, miles below the seafloor in the vent she'd first glimpsed in dreams. The strange flavor of the water all around her seemed to promise grim consequences to those who failed to heed its warning. The odd scent seemed to go hand in fin with the interference that made communion with the Sea Mother difficult. Nogah took it as further evidence the Sea Mother wanted her here, to investigate that which lay at the shaft's nadir.

Nogah's translucent, third eyelids snapped open. She decreed, "No, we shall push on. Time grows short. The . . . taint? The . . . hindrance grows stronger each day we fail to discover its source!"

Curampah merely nodded. Perhaps her junior whip did not share Nogah's sense of urgency. She guessed Curampah preferred the majority opinion in the kuo-toa ruled city of Olleth. Not that what he thought mattered. The beliefs junior whips harbored in their secret hearts were unimportant. Their duty was only to obey. Curampah would do as she commanded.

Nogah twitched the reins, and the great catfish surged straight downward once more, jolting the coach. The immense nautilus shell descended through a sudden rush of silvery bubbles born in the thrashing wake of the fish's wide tail.

Nogah woke to her name voiced in air. Splinters of the dream faded, the same dream she always had, of the Sea Mother beckoning to her from across a vast gulf of sea-fine particulates and rushing water, warning her, warning . . .

She lay in her crèche within the inmost chamber of the spiral nautilus.

A voice, Curampah's, said again, "Nogah, Daughter of the Sea, wake!"

Blinking toward full awareness, but not yet stirring her limbs, she said, "I am awake. I . . ." She could still hear the groaning water from her dream. The walls of the shell moaned and vibrated, as if being squeezed. Had they struck the vent wall? Nogah mentally checked the status of all the divine rituals she'd applied to the sea coach.

The subsidiary rituals of maintenance and protection lacing the nautilus's shell were intact. The bubble of air trapped within the coiled corridors of the shell was stable and fresh. The magic that maintained the equilibrium between air and water was firm. She mentally expanded her examination of the ritual prayers underlying the sea coach and was relieved to find the enchantments holding the catfish also remained active. The protective prayers warding off crushing pressure seemed intact, but . . .

"Mother preserve!" The linchpin charm was half unraveled! The groaning noise was precursor to the nautilus shell's collapse.

She lurched upright, her webbed hands already tracing the runes necessary to renew the prayer. She worked quickly, invigorating the lines of divine force required. A heartbeat later, the frayed linchpin was repaired. But how could it have failed so precipitously?

She looked at Curampah. "Explain," she commanded.

"Daughter of the Sea," he said, "I found a side cavity in the vent. As I slowed the coach to study the hollow space, the nautilus began to buckle and shudder. So I woke you."

"What lies within this cavity?"

"Crumbled and blasted dwellings, Daughter. Ruins of structures unable to withstand the crushing weight of water this deep."

"A drow city caught in the backlash of Mystra's demise?" Nogah half smiled to think of a city of their old tormentors so overcome.

Curampah's silver-black eyes blinked rapidly. "No. It is illithid."

Nogah grabbed her staff and arrowed past Curampah.

The cavity was riddled with half-exposed, winding passages striated with the cryptic textures of illithid text carved in stone. The crust's split that created the vent a decade ago broke this deep dwelling mind flayer cyst wide open. The illithids likely hadn't even picked themselves up from where the quaking earth had thrown them before a weight of seawater had smashed through the breach, a quantity too great for even the wizened entity at the community's hub to deal with. The elder brain's basin was split asunder. All that remained of this illithid community's nascent proto-deity were fragments of flash-petrified cerebral tissue. Dried husks of larval illithids floated here and there throughout the ruin. Remnants of mind flayer garb, implements, and unidentifiable trash were everywhere, but of the adult illithids themselves, no sign remained.

"Did any survive?" wondered Curampah, as he stared over the side. Nogah had maneuvered the sea coach into the side cavity.

She replied, "The Spellplague's hunger did not spare those who derive their power from mind. Of course, it seems this community was destroyed as an indirect consequence of the catastrophe. We would have been attacked already, if any mind flayers remained in this drowned cyst."

Curampah inclined his head.

Despite her words, an irrational fear tightened her scales. She was a competent whip, but she couldn't hope to stand before a mind flayer's vicious brain blast. She didn't want to end up a meal, or worse, a mind-dead thrall. But she was being foolish, of course; how could that happen? The cyst was obviously long bereft of its former dwellers.

The senior whip urged the catfish deeper into the demolished community. It could be that which drew her into the depths below Faerûn would be found in this very space! The far wall of the hollow remained obscured in haze, and she wanted to be sure of the cavity's bounds.

The sea coach was drawn inward. It passed only feet over crumbling edges of unspecified structures without roofs, now only unmarked crypts where many monstrosities had met a sudden, moist end.

A new structure began to resolve from the swirling water. Its architectural style was different from the foregoing ruins. It retained most of its walls and many of its roofs. It was several stories high, unlike any of the other structures in the cyst, and it had no windows. Something about the new structure reminded Nogah of how the linchpin prayer had almost failed. Was it coincidence the divine ritual most vital to their foray would show instability just as they descended to the depths of the dead illithid community?

Perhaps the charm's collapse and the ruined cyst's proximity were no accident.

Nogah pulled back on the reins. "Curampah—"

The catfish screamed, a scale-shivering sound so intense Nogah dropped the reins. A region of free-floating detritus whirled in on itself, becoming a tight column of spinning water. Nogah scrambled for the reins. A moment later the whirling column expanded into a humanoid shape. Violet slime glistened over its rubbery skin. Its awful head riveted Nogah's attention. Four long tendrils writhed there, muscular tentacles with bloodstained tips. Its eyes were darkened hollows, empty save for seawater.

"It's undead!" croaked Curampah, bubbles escaping his mouth in two exclamatory clusters. His pincer staff quivered in his unsteady grasp. "Mind flayer undead!"

Nogah forgot the reins. She yelled, "Curampah! Think!" If Curampah would stop panicking, they could—

Malign influence burst upon Nogah's brain, trying to insinuate alien desires into her core awareness. The catfish's scream burbled away. Curampah gasped and let his pincer staff float free.

The vacant-eyed mind flayer drifted toward them, making no movement yet accelerating. It had gained a facility in the water in undeath that its kind did not possess in life. What hoary god empowered this husk? It should have rotted to nothing like all its compatriots.

The very fact she could still formulate questions meant she had avoided the brunt of the blast that had left Curampah drooling. But without her fellow whip, she couldn't co-generate an answering stroke strong enough to offer salvation.

She tried to think through the terror. Curampah wasn't dead. It should still be possible . . .

She slapped Curampah's limp shoulder with her empty palm. Instantly, the tingle that alerted fellow whips to each other's presence intensified into a full-fledged connection. An electric spark burned between them, an eel of chaotic, fluctuating light.

The contact literally jolted Curampah from his mind-numbed haze. The junior whip blinked witlessness from his eyes.

Thank the Sea Mother! In the Spellplague's wake, many whips had lost the ability to co-generate the storm's sword. But not her, and not Curampah. Its call to destruction burned away the aftereffects of the mind flayer's blast.

The illithid undead slowed its approach, its tentacles suddenly writhing in some new configuration.

Nogah drew back her hand, and the lightning bridged the two whips. The crackling arc widened, then began to curve, bowing out toward the approaching illithid. The creature's tentacles writhed so fast now, the water began to froth. The hollows of its empty eyes glimmered with red light.

The connecting spark widened, grew into a ravening bolt that seared the water, creating a shroud of twinkling bubbles. Jittering shadows danced madly across the cavity's walls.

Nogah released the bolt. The stroke discharged the full brunt of her and Curampah's redoubled strength into the mind flayer's necrotic flesh. Its left arm, half its torso, and its left leg flashed away into ash.

Another mental assault blossomed from the illithid, but its aim was off. Only the merest edge of the psionic cacophony brushed her awareness.

"Finish it," she commanded. But what could they do? They couldn't produce another lightning stroke immediately. They would have to call on ranged battle prayers—

Curampah tensed to launch himself from the sea coach's deck. Nogah snagged his harness with her free hand, restraining him. She hissed, "Fool! Don't stray from the coach or the sea's heavy foot will smash you!"

The illithid squealed something, a warning, Nogah thought, then melted into a column of spinning water. The column widened and dispersed, leaving nothing behind but drifting silt and sediment.

"That was more than a corpse reanimated by chance," breathed Curampah. "It was dead, yet could still call upon the mental abilities it possessed in life. I think it may have been partially vampiric. Yet we defeated it!"

"We chased it away—but we failed to destroy it," interrupted Nogah. "Because of your incompetence." She pointed at the junior whip with her staff. "If I were less merciful, I would slay you here and now and offer your unworthy hide as a sacrifice to the Sea Mother."

The junior whip froze, uncertain. He knew she didn't make threats lightly.

Nogah considered ramming the pincer tip through his throat, despite her talk about being merciful. No—but it wasn't mercy that stayed her hand. It was practicality. Despite nearly killing himself, and allowing the undead illithid to slip away, she still needed him. If Curampah hadn't been present, the illithid would likely even now be supping on the contents of her skull.

"Bah," she said. "We wounded the thing, nearly tore it apart. It won't seek us out again soon, at least until it has regained its strength and form. We have some time. Let's investigate what it guarded all alone down here in the depths."

The structure was nestled into the great cavity's rear wall. Though some of its outer rooms had crumbled, an inner core structure of greenish stone remained intact. A jade dome emerged from the rougher surrounding stone. Tools were scattered everywhere: shovels, picks, buckets, and a variety of more arcane equipment apparently useful for digging. Most had almost rusted away. Nogah also finally recognized the strange mounds arranged around the greenish outcrop. They were tailing piles, the refuse of a mining operation.

She saw no open mine tunnel. The mine mouth must be under the dome.

"The illithids thought they were digging up something

special here," she murmured. "Special enough to protect the mine mouth with this building. Not that it offered much protection when the water broke in."

"The dome reminds me of a temple, almost," volunteered Curampah. He gestured. "It even has a ceremonial entrance."

A six-sided extension protruded from the side of the smooth green rock like a tumor.

Nogah guided the sea coach to rest next to the extension and saw Curampah was correct. Within the protrusion was a dull black metal door, also six-sided. It was apparently still sealed against the surrounding water. She leaned over and touched the door's matte black iron. A familiar feeling thrilled up her arm and into her heart.

The strange influence of her dreams lived behind the door! The Sea Mother had guided her truly.

"We must enter," she directed.

"How, Daughter of the Sea? If we stray from the nautilus . . ." Curampah finished by squeezing his hands together.

"Do you think I am so ill-prepared?"

Curampah looked at her with half-lidded eyes, waiting.

"Bring me my chest. Be quick!"

The junior whip soon returned from the nautilus's interior with a delicate chest fashioned of polished mother-of-pearl plates and placed it at her feet. Nogah whispered the pass phrase that bypassed the magical trap, and popped the lid.

Amid the clutter of needful things lay several vials. She selected a few and closed the chest before Curampah was able to see and understand the nature of all her treasures.

"These," explained Nogah, "are magical draughts brewed in Sembia. I got them from Captain Thoster. You remember Thoster? His birth was an unlooked-for complication, but it has proved useful. In any event, if imbibed, this liquid allows humanoids to breathe water."

Curampah merely blinked, but Nogah recognized the confusion that tightened his scales.

"You wonder what use these are to us; after all, as a superior breed, we can already breathe air and water both. However, another effect of the elixir renders the imbiber immune to the crushing weight of extreme watery depths. It shall work for us as well as for any humanoid."

She handed the junior whip one of the vials. He carefully removed the wax-sealed stopper and sucked its contents down without mixing too much of it with the surrounding water. She did the same with her own elixir. It tasted of salt and kelp.

Curampah examined his hands and scaled forearms. He said, "I feel no different."

"We shall see," she replied.

Nogah gave a slight tug on the reins, enough that the nautilus shell moved several body lengths away from the green stone and the black six-sided door.

"Now, Curampah—open that metallic door. Let us discover what these mind flayers worked so feverishly to uncover." She gestured to the entrance with her staff.

The junior whip pushed away from the coach deck and swam toward the door embedded in the green mantle stone. To his credit, he merely hesitated, saying nothing, when he realized he swam alone while she remained behind, watching.

She judged the protective effect surrounding the coach ended somewhere half-way between the nautilus and the door.

When he made it all the way to the six-sided valve without ill effect, Nogah joined him.

Unsealing the valve was a lengthy process. Having no other way to force it, the two whips were finally reduced to directing co-generated strokes of lightning against the dull metal. Again. And again. They rested between each blast just long enough to rekindle their capacity to produce the next electrical discharge. Each subsequent blast showed some effect, just enough to hint that persistence would eventually sear the metal through. The only question was, how many bolts?

Nogah fretted. The effects of the elixir were temporary. Worse, the undead mind flayer was likely regenerating its own strength while they spent theirs against the stubborn entranceway.

Finally, the valve seared through.

Inrushing water snatched both her and Curampah, wrenching them through the irregular, red-hot puncture. Agonizing heat seared her flank. A mesh of madly spinning bubbles blinded her. The inrushing water dredged her forward, down an irregularly dug tunnel. She tumbled wildly, end over end. She flailed, trying to get a hold on something, anything. A muffled scream sounded somewhere within the roar of rushing water. Was it Curam—

A jutting rock smashed her temple, and she screamed too. She was hurtled along, her voice lost in the boil of crushing water. Nogah's mind whirled as she tried to gain her bearings.

She was able to do so only when the inrushing water finally filled the space beyond the door. Though remnants of turbulence still spiraled around the narrow tunnel, Nogah managed to halt her forward momentum.

Bruised and burnt, the whip praised the Sea Mother for her survival. She floated in cold darkness. A figure drifted past her, limp and slowly revolving. It was Curampah. His arms were broken, and his head bore a terrible puncture from which dark fluid thickly jetted into the water, spiraling around his drifting body.

She hissed, a loss assaulting her like a physical blow. Poor Curampah; his faith had proved too weak.

Then she saw what the illithids had delved so deeply to unearth. The merest edges of something. Something horrible. The mere act of trying to comprehend it was like scraping her naked brain with a trowel. Surely it was an abomination. She turned to swim free, flexing her legs for the first mighty escape stroke . . .

Nogah blinked, and in that instant, her perception shifted. Curiosity rekindled.

Instead of swimming away as if her sanity depended upon it, she drifted closer through the swirling blood and sediment, hardly realizing she did so. She still couldn't grasp the magnitude of the image. She tried to wrap some mote of comprehension around the object, partly chiseled from stone . . . from stone whose age dwarfed the mountains above. Which meant the enigma, the massive thing that refused to clearly reveal itself to her understanding, was older than continents.

Blinking, Nogah shuddered. Had the Sea Mother sent her to unbury this artifact, to finish what the mind flayers had started? A head-size stone lay near the greater object yet bound in its stone matrix. It seemed the illithids had broken away a sample from the far more gargantuan object still frozen in the wall, before their dig outside the seal had drowned.

She said a quick prayer to the Sea Mother, asking for guidance. Her inquiry fell into a void of silence.

Her hand moved to trace the spherical artifact. If she couldn't grasp the whole, perhaps the tiny piece would yield up clues.

She picked it up. What was it? A stone bauble? A tiny portion of a . . . what? A petrified remnant of some long-dead sea beast? Something like that, a strange certainty informed her, though even that notion was, somehow, a failure of imagination. If she grasped a piece of something far larger, that which was in turn only the merest tip of something . . . monstrous.

The elixir's duration was almost complete. Without giving herself time to weigh the decision, she retained her grip on the loose piece, rough from where the illithids had cut it away from its parent.

Her first impression had been correct—it was essentially round but already seemed lighter in her hands. Though the object was about the size of her head, she was able to carry it without difficulty.

As she kicked back toward the nautilus, past the drifting corpse of her junior whip, her fingers began to tingle, then her arms. Odd notions suggested themselves, like worms insinuating themselves through Nogah's consciousness. Odd, even disquieting.

But so fascinating . . .

CHAPTER THREE

Eleven Years After the Spellplague
The Year of the Secret (1396 DR)
New Sarshell, Impiltur

A thin man with a pocked face chalked a flat expanse of gray slate in quick, precise strokes. The sharp scent of limestone grew in the stuffy chamber with each mark.

The scratching chalk grated at Lady Anusha Marhana's ears. She glanced away from the lesson her tutor scribed to gaze out the open window. How she wished she were outside. She hated her lessons. She'd rather be down at the docks watching the ships come in, watching the men unload salvage from other lands.

More notably, she had planned to attend the revelry in the Marivaux mansion this evening. Anusha had bought a new gown, new shoes, had the servants do her hair, sent out a reply confirming her attendance, only to have her half brother dash her hopes. Behroun said Marivaux was of a social stratum lower than her own, and that it wouldn't do for her to mix with them. Rubbish! In fact—

"Lady Marhana." The reedy voice of her tutor pulled Anusha's attention back to the board.

"Yes?" she said, as if she'd been paying attention all along.

The man gave her an admonishing glare and said, "Lord Marhana pays me to advance your education. Would you waste his hard-earned coin?"

Anusha's first instinct was to shrug. Her half brother, Lord Behroun Marhana, cared only for appearances. He was all about the façade, and substance only for what it contributed to the image of courtly nobility. The man wanted to cement himself among the reforming aristocracy of scarred Impiltur. In an attempt to gain a seat on the nascent Grand Council forming after the failure of the royal line, Behroun required the family to appear to possess a polite education.

Despite her opinion, she restrained her instinctive, dismissive gesture. Anusha was twenty years old this month, and even without her recent course on high society manners, she recognized a shrug might be perceived as childish. Instead she merely looked her tutor in the eye, trying to appear interested.

The man sighed, shaking his head as he turned back to point at what he'd written on the board. "What does this say?"

Anusha read aloud, "I am old and battered and have left a heap of bloody, bitter mistakes behind me high enough to bury empires."

"Good diction," murmured her tutor. "Who said it, and when?"

"Elminster of Shadowdale, of course," replied Anusha. She had no idea if she was correct, but it sounded like something the old sage might have said. It was just one more quote among the hundreds he was known for. Who cared what year he'd uttered it?

Anyway, the old sage had dropped out of common knowledge after the Spellplague. He'd been affected like everyone else, and some whispered the old man's powers had been stripped in the disaster. She heard one story from a dockworker, who had it from a Cormyrean merchant, who heard from a Mulhorandi refugee, that Elminster was glimpsed wandering the Planes of Purple Dust, bald and tattooed with spellscars so outré that—

"Good," replied the tutor. He used the quote as a bridge into another historical fact about Faerûn, a story about how a black arrow was responsible for Imphras the Great's reunification of Impiltur. Three hundred years ago!

History lessons were hard. It was all so dry and . . . pointless! Everything before the blue fire was irrelevant to how things were today. Anusha had been ten or eleven years old when the Weave collapsed. In Sarshel, the event had come and gone with little to mark it in its first days.

She did recall one particularly lurid account of the event in a report circulated among the sea traders. When Behroun was out of his office, she had slipped in and penned a copy of the report for herself. She could remember it almost by heart: "Magic goes awry, and the world trembles. Magic, earth, and flesh too, burn beneath veils of azure fire that dance across the skies, day and night. The hardest hit are the mages, who lose their magic, their minds, and sometimes, their souls. Where the blue fire touched down, everything changes. Whole villages are gone, save for a few horribly altered former inhabitants, now monstrosities. It is some sort of spell plague, one that even the gods fear to catch!"

Anusha had several tendays of bad dreams after reading that. Nightmares, in fact, of blue fire burning her flesh away, leaving nothing but a substanceless image behind. Dreams that had returned to trouble her recently, in fact.

In Impiltur, no disasters fell from the sky. But stories of atrocities to the south and east continued to roll in from occasional crazed refugees, and the shoreline began to recede. Worst of all, spellcasters forgot their spells. Local officials were finally convinced beyond all doubt that something very bad was in the offing.

Certainly a sinking Sea of Fallen Stars had seemed disaster enough for a city reliant on the many docks and piers that serviced its sea trade. Then again, she had been too young to appreciate the slow fall of the water's level as something terrible enough to choke a city. Likewise, when magic began to go awry, she didn't personally witness it. Her family's shipping fortune shielded her from seeing wizards melting themselves in the street as they adjusted to magic's new regime. But she had heard all the gruesome stories.

It was during this period that her half brother learned of his inheritance. Marhana Shipping was all his. The same day, Anusha learned that her mother and father perished together on their flagship trading vessel with all hands in Sembia. Something to do with the Shadovar.

It was not something she wished to dwell upon. To Lady Anusha Marhana, the Spellplague was just one more event over and done with, no worse than her own personal history of sad remembrances. The Year of Blue Fire was best relegated to history's boring tomes of who said what and when.

". . . so Faerûn is splintered," continued her tutor, oblivious to Anusha's lapse of attention. "Communications and trade remain rare and may degrade further before things turn around. Whole nations are gone, never to return—"

Anusha's sigh was overloud, and the tutor heard it. He placed the chalk on the board ledge, turned, and flashed a tight smile. He said, "The lady is obviously overtired. The hour is late. I'll return again tomorrow, and we'll pick up where I left off. Please read the manuscript on the Heltharn dynasty.

Tomorrow I shall test your knowledge about Impiltur's royal line."

Anusha said, "I can tell you this without reading it—the Heltharn dynasty is broken, and the Grand Council is ascendant. So says Behroun."

The tutor's tight smile faltered. He looked suddenly tired. He said, "Perhaps. Perhaps it is so, and the king will not return." Without another word or his usual remonstration to study, the thin, pock-faced man walked out, letting the door to Anusha's suite hang ajar.

Anusha's brows furrowed. Had she said something in poor taste? Did the man have personal connections to the dead king and his family? Or was he merely a loyalist without a king to obey? Behroun said there were many like that around, interfering with the Grand Council's fledgling plans.

The girl pushed aside troubling thoughts and rose from her desk. Lassitude clutched at her. The tutor had suggested she get some sleep, and she was so very tired. Bad dreams of unending, heatless blue fire assailed her, making her dread the night. Not knowing how else to deal with the troubling images, she had fought sleep.

She entered her bedroom. Her canvases nearly crowded out the bureau, the nightstand, and her large bed. The coverlets, blue and pink, looked so soft, so tempting. She shuffled forward, knowing sleep would finally win out against her fear. She hoped the dreams would leave off tonight. Either way, slumber could no longer be denied.

Anusha opened her eyes. Had she dreamed? She couldn't remember anything since she'd flung herself onto her bed. Her bed right over there. Her bed where a girl still lay adrift in sleep's dark bonds.

The sleeping girl was herself. Her long skirts, ruffled

blouse, and long boots lay in a heap on the floor.

A moment's more confusion gave way to understanding. She was dreaming now! She was caught up in a tiny story being spun out by her mind, except she was atypically aware. She dreamed and knew it!

She tensed, but the terror she recalled fuzzily from her previous nights of nightmares was absent. All was quiet and restful. She'd heard that if one could learn to recognize when caught in slumber's nets, one could apply some conscious control over the dream. Instead of being caught up in the moment, as was usually the case, the whole thing could be more like attending theater. Like watching a play, written as it went along.

She liked that idea. I shall go with this as long as it lasts, she told herself. What will my mind conjure up?

She smiled to think of herself as separate from her mind— her tutor would tell her that was an illusion. But the fact that she could look down on her sleeping, slowly breathing body argued otherwise. No, wait—this was a dream, she reminded herself.

Anusha left her room, her suite, and the upper story of the manor. The front hall was empty but for a few servants polishing relics Behroun had staged around the space as if he were a real noble. Over the fireplace hung a slender long sword, which was scribed, right on the blade, with the Marhana crest. Anusha's father had, by all accounts, been an able swordsman in his youth.

The servants in the front hall couldn't see her. They didn't react to her presence. Why should they? It was her dream— her world! On impulse, she glided right through the front door as if it were nothing but smoke. A moment of darkness and disorientation, then she was through.

Laughing, she ran down the wide front steps. Anusha passed through the thick iron gates that separated the manor from the street, feeling only the slightest tug of resistance.

"How wondrous!" she exclaimed. A passerby started, glanced sharply around. Anusha studied the man in garish noble garb, but his gaze slid right past her. She covered her mouth to stifle a giggle. Small noises escaped anyway, emerging like a strangled wheeze. The man's eyes widened and he hurried off, pursued by a laugh she could no longer restrain.

Skipping, she set off down the street. She had to explore all the fun possibilities of this dream before she woke up!

First, she'd visit the docks. She loved the tall ships and handsome dockhands with stories of far places. Imagine seeing those same sail-topped silhouettes by night! She ran unseen through the street, straight on down toward the dock district. Despite Marhana's active role in shipping, they kept their mansion far from the piers. So she had to run quite a ways, over a mile. She didn't mind—it was her dream, and she decided not to feel tired by the exertion.

Just as she neared the first wharf, a strange pinch pulled a gasp from her. The sensation felt almost like the sudden jerk of an invisible cord. She slowed, but continued to move forward. The pinch came again—

Anusha opened her eyes in her bed. The saffron lengths of linen that swirled around her bedposts glowed in the candlelight from the single night-flame on her bureau.

"Oh!" she groaned, realizing she was awake, leaving her brilliant dream behind.

If she didn't think too much, maybe she could recall it. Sometimes good dreams could be picked up again, if she didn't clutter her mind with too many other thoughts. And she was still so tired from so many nights of too little rest.

She turned on her side, closed her eyes again, and tried to recall the dream.

She had wandered, conscious of herself in the dream, walking where she would, going where she wanted without others dictating restrictions, unseen by other dream dwellers . . .

Again Anusha found herself standing next to her apparently

sleeping body. She clapped her hands in triumph. She was back in the dream!

This time, she'd avoid the docks. She'd try someplace else.

How about . . . the Marivaux revelry! If she couldn't attend the Marivaux party in reality, perhaps she could dream about it.

She exited the Marhana manor, unseen as before, and ran down the street.

What must have been a full hour of wandering forced her to admit she didn't actually know where to find the Marivaux home. She had expected she would merely come upon the place, as such things happen in dreams.

But that hadn't happened. Just seedier and seedier storefronts, separated by larger and larger tracts of completely empty, broken structures—victims of the interregnum following the retreat of the wharf.

Was she lost? Anusha frowned. Was she not the author of her own slumbering fancy? Perhaps it was time to wake up, after all. She didn't like the direction in which this dream was headed.

Then she saw Japheth.

Anusha gave an involuntary gasp. Japheth walked the dark streets with his black cape drawn around him like a raven's wings, striding purposefully as if he, at least, knew where he was going.

Japheth was one of Behroun's agents. Anusha had seen the man around the manor and even exchanged a few words with him. His hair was black, as were his eyes—like wells reflecting a starry night sky. The last time he'd greeted her, just a few days prior, her cheeks colored, her arms felt too warm, and sensible words deserted her.

She fell in behind the cloaked shape, wondering where he was going. It was a ramshackle neighborhood. Did he know someone here? She didn't like to think of him being familiar with its stench-worn ways.

Japheth walked another block until he paused under the sign of a unicorn horn.

A single glass window provided a view into a bizarrely decorated interior display. Anusha shuffled closer and identified a shrunken head, heaped candies wrapped in colorful paper, playing cards depicting dragons, smoking accessories, fancifully decorated goblets and tankards, and oddities beyond her knowledge.

Japheth entered. She followed, passing through the closing door as if it were mist. Inside she spied a grandfatherly dwarf puffing away on an elaborately carved pipe.

The dwarf saw Japheth and launched his spiel, "Got some salvage? I'll give you a fair price. No? A gift, then, you seek? Or something for yourself. A keepsake! Look around; my inventory is second to none. Don't be afraid of the mess! Who knows what treasures you'll find hidden away in dark corners? Those willing to spend a little time come away with real gems."

Japheth raised a hand to silence the dwarf and asked, "Have you any traveler's dust?"

The dwarf's surprised breath covered Anusha's own. The dwarf darted a glance to the entrance. After a scan of the empty shop, the proprietor gave a slow nod. He said, "I might have a tin. It'll cost you. Supply has been tight lately."

"Yes, yes, I'm sure. I'll give you thirty pieces of gold right now. What say you?"

The dwarf's eyes narrowed. He replied, "How do I know I can trust you?"

"I am the very soul of discretion. Come—I've got gold in my pocket. You've got dust to unload. Let's deal."

When the strange transaction concluded, Japheth tucked a small, dull tin into a fold of his cape. Anusha fell in behind Japheth as he exited the shop.

But her mind whirled. Traveler's dust! Did Japheth walk the crimson road?

She hadn't noticed any of the telltale signs—trembling hands, sometimes slurred speech, and most telling, of course, eyes the color of blood. Anusha heard the substance appeared only a few years ago, but already it was banned in most civilized places because all who used it died, sooner rather than later. The crimson road led inevitably down to a final, bloody sunset.

Then again, Japheth was an adept—he was one of the new breed who'd learned the trick of calling upon magic in the Weave's absence. She'd heard Behroun refer to Japheth as a warlock. Perhaps he could mask the drug's effect, or hold off its eventual price.

Her childish crush on Japheth grew cold. If he walked the crimson road, he was not a man of honor.

Honor or not, Japheth led her directly back to Marhana Manor. So convenient; another reminder she dreamed. Which meant Japheth wasn't really a traveler—she'd merely invented it! Her thoughts were more cogent, more precise than any dream she'd previously experienced, and she kept forgetting what she saw now must all be pure fiction.

Her quarry entered by the main gate with his own key. He walked around to the South Wing of the manor, where Behroun conducted his shipping business. A lamp in the main office beckoned.

Japheth entered, and Anusha remained his shadow.

Her half brother, Behroun, was seated in his white leather chair behind a desk bestrewn with parchment, quills, and small devices useful for plotting nautical routes.

Behroun was surprised to see the cloaked man suddenly appear at the edge of his desk. "Japheth! You are quick! I sent a courier at dusk."

The warlock inclined his head. "I have eyes in many places, as you know. If you had merely placed my symbol on your manor door, as I instructed, I would have appeared even sooner."

Behroun shook his head as if in disgust, but said, "You're here, that's what matters. I've got something special lined up. Something vital to Marhana. I need my most potent and trusted agent to serve as my envoy."

"You'll turn my head with all your praise," responded Japheth, his tone indicating just the opposite. Anusha was familiar with Behroun's verbal tactics—flattery came first, followed by demands. When he set his mind to it, Behroun could charm the nose off a troll. But he only applied his charm to people he couldn't manipulate any other way.

The warlock said, "Tell me what you want."

"You're setting sail two days from now with Captain Thoster on the *Green Siren*. He—"

"No," interrupted Japheth. "He's a freebooter. And his bloodline is tainted. I'll have nothing to do with him."

"Your own bloodline is none too pure, warlock. Besides, you've dealt with Thoster all along."

"Incorrect."

"Don't delude yourself," sneered Behroun. "From where do you suppose all the Cormyrean coin I pay you in has come? Thoster."

"If you deal with pirates, that's hardly a concern of mine."

Lord Marhana snorted. "No one pays as well as I, you've said it yourself. Gold coin, pure and unalloyed. And you need all you can get, don't you? Otherwise, the crimson road will sweep you all the way to its final destination."

Japheth glanced sharply at the shipping magnate but didn't correct him.

"So, will you sail with Thoster as I've asked? I need you on board to keep me informed on a daily basis of his activities. He's apparently uncovered some vast opportunity. It could be the break Marhana needs. He says his alliance with a creature of the sea is about to pay fantastic dividends. Perhaps more than just gold: influence. Power. I need you on site to act as my proxy."

". . . I'll consider your offer."

All pretense of cordiality fled Behroun's eyes. He snapped, "Don't consider too long, or I'll break your pact stone. Then, no matter how far you flee down the crimson road, the wrath of your Lord of Bats will find you."

Anusha was already anxious, witnessing the conversation between her half brother and Japheth. A stress headache blossomed behind her eyes. When Behroun's cruel visage uttered his odd, incomprehensible threat, Anusha took an involuntary step backward, directly into an artfully stuffed osprey mounted on a slender rod.

The display toppled with a crash. Japheth and Behroun jerked around. The warlock's eyes focused past her, but they widened anyway. He exclaimed, "A phantasm!"

Japheth could see her! Lord Marhana was looking over the warlock's shoulder, but his eyes were not focused on her either, but at the wall behind her. Behroun yelled, "An assassin! Sent by a rival house—disperse it, Japheth!"

Anusha glanced back to see what Behroun and Japheth saw. Was there an assassin behind her?

They were looking at the silver-framed mirror Behroun purchased from a Calimshan trader. In the mirror's glossy pane stood a ghastly shape of shadow. She knew immediately it was a reflection of her dream shape! She raised a hand, and the image mimicked her action. She saw that her fingers, her arm, her entire body was like a shadow outlined in ethereal white and blue fire.

Japheth raised his arms, palms facing Anusha. His cloak flared of its own accord, revealing a void of absolute darkness within its folds. And from that darkness, a swarm of black motes winged forth.

Anusha wrenched herself backward, mentally demanding, *Wake up! Wake up! Wake—*

Her eyes snapped wide. A bedside candle revealed she lay twisted in her coverlets. In her bedroom. Her gaze wandered the serene, quiet expanse of her walls, the ceiling, the furnishings in her room. She raised her hand, saw it normally. The dream was concluded.

"What a nightmare!" she exclaimed, sitting up. She wondered how long she'd slept—darkness still reigned outside.

Standing, she shrugged into her nightrobe. She tied its belt securely around her waist before exiting her bedroom into the darkened hall. Water. Water was what she needed. Her headache, the one from her dream, persisted.

She wandered into the upper story of the manor, then down a curving flight of steps into the front hall. As she was about to pass into the back hall that led to the kitchens, Anusha saw a glint of light out the windows. She moved to the glass and saw that the lights in the south wing of the manor were lit.

Two men were illuminated in the glow of the strong lamps.

Anusha immediately recognized them. Her half brother, Behroun, and the warlock, Japheth, argued in Behroun's office.

Tiny wings seemed to pat and flutter in her stomach. The feeling accompanied a mad inkling. Could it be?

A chill swept from her brow down her spine, tingling as if with vertigo.

Her dream had come true.

CHAPTER FOUR

The Year of the Secret (1396 DR)
Near the Ruins of Starmantle

Darkness defined the length and breadth of the world, forever.

Timeless intervals passed. Ages and epochs, or days and tendays, no consciousness persisted to measure the void's period. Other worlds were born, matured, grew old, died, and passed away in that interlude. Or had the darkness lasted the duration of an eyeblink? Or somewhere in between . . .

The void's edges wavered, blurred, then peeled away. Behind was exposed a pale, misted light. The darkness contracted upon itself, becoming a dome, then a sphere, then a blot as it lifted up and away to nothing.

A cloud-shrouded sky of gray, lit with occasional flashes of distant lightning, was revealed.

Eyes slowly integrated elements, as if assembling pieces of a puzzle. Concepts of sky, time, and cloud leisurely assembled within a man's fragmented, subconscious mind.

The man's brow furrowed. A sudden disorientation collapsed his blank observation of the heavens.

Where was he? And . . .

Why couldn't he remember his own name?

The man turned his head. Or tried to. Some force resisted. His gaze rotated less than an inch. Scanning with only his eyes, he saw he was surrounded in some cold, unyielding substance. He was caught like a bug in some sort of greenish material.

Anger's flame woke. He tried to suck in a deep breath. He failed—he was completely isolated, apparently, even from air. A sliver of his mind wondered why he hadn't already suffocated. The greater portion of his attention focused on the crisis at hand. He must break free, or he would die. Whatever had kept him alive prior to this moment was failing. Already, lack of air made dark spots dance on the periphery of his vision.

A subconscious instruction surfaced: Shout! Scream a single syllable of concentrated desire with the last of your stale breath, and hope it is enough.

The man focused on his diaphragm, then expelled the final vestiges of air from his lungs with an explosive, guttural, "Kihop!"

The material surrounding his head shattered like dry adobe struck with a maul. Cool air suddenly caressed his face. He was still caught, but at least he could breathe.

He sucked in a long, deep breath, expanding his chest so much that the material surrounding him cracked.

He wrenched his body with a violent strength his limbs remembered, even if he did not. Pain knifed through his left shoulder, and the man loosed a surprised yell.

His left arm throbbed with a twinge so intense that blackness threatened to rob him of consciousness again. Was it broken? No way to tell while he remained trapped.

The man deliberately isolated his left arm while thrusting with his legs and remaining arm. It was difficult to accomplish, and agony spiked through his body once more.

What options did he have? He rested a moment, considering. The problem of his imperfect memory swam once more to front and center. It was maddening. He had to get free!

He wrenched his body again, sucking in his breath against the hurt. And again. Each time he tensed and thrust with his arms and legs, he gained a sliver of additional clearance. Each effort was accompanied with a sound not unlike splintering ice. With unflappable determination, the man struggled in the grip of the strange substance.

When his right arm broke through, extricating himself from the remaining brittle, honeycomb-like stuff suddenly seemed an actual possibility instead of a wild hope.

Finally, the man wrenched completely free. A powder of greenish material still clung to his body.

He examined his erstwhile prison, cradling his left arm in his right. He'd been encrusted in a cocoonlike material thrust from the earth. It wasn't mineral, or at least, if it was, it was particularly brittle. The portion from which he'd freed himself was a hollow space, still partly molded to the shape of his body.

The man looked around and saw he stood on a grassy plain. Here and there, other mineral encrustations broke to the surface, rising only a few feet in most cases. A few spires were larger, and reached dozens of feet into the morning light. Between the strange outcrops, prairie grass waved to the western horizon.

A forest, apparently partly dead of some blight, lay to the south. Skeletons of trees still remained mostly vertical, though newer growth was thick beneath the dead canopy. An ocean of saplings reached up through old, dry underbrush. The man was surprised a wildfire hadn't cleared out the detritus already. Rain and lightning seemed particularly thick in that direction. He wondered if he would witness a lightning strike touch off a blaze even as he watched.

He returned his gaze to the strange outcrops nearer at hand. At first the man thought the extrusions must be quite old. He saw dozens of instances where greenish spires had cracked and collapsed. Other outcrops, like the one he'd just emerged from, had weathered and broken into fragments.

Of course, as brittle as the mass he had emerged from had proved, perhaps the extrusions were not actually that old, in the geological sense.

He stood in place and slowly rotated, looking for something or someone recognizable. His own name seemed just on the tip of his tongue . . . but he couldn't dredge it up.

He looked east to the line of the horizon. Something in the texture of the landscape, the color of the sky, a scent in the air seemed familiar . . .

Bumps prickled across his arms and back as if with a chill. Something terrible had happened there. A monstrous calamity—

The man suddenly remembered.

Raidon Kane remembered.

His breath came harsh. His eyes tried to spin in his skull. Nausea threatened to bend him over.

Raidon clapped his hands to his brow, the pain in his left elbow nothing in that moment.

The world had ended. How could he have forgotten?

The fire. The pillar of blue fire had reached up over the horizon.

He saw again the pillar's fat crown of molten sapphire, tumbling and boiling upward. Closing his eyes merely brought the memory into sharper focus.

And the blast! That awful, land-erasing storm front that had swept out from the burning spire.

He remembered horrors: His horse, stumbling and

disappearing in the azure turbulence. The woman who'd grown wings of fire, only to be incinerated. The awful, twining hair pulling a goblin's head along the ground—

His amulet! It had burned away.

The wind tousled his hair, bringing scents of spring flowers and grass.

"By the Ten Tenants, have I gone insane?" bellowed Raidon, his voice hoarse.

He closed his eyes. He calmed his breathing. A monk of Xiang Temple did not comport himself thusly. Raidon searched for his mental regimen. He was a master of meditation. Images of a pillar of blue fire could not haunt him if he did not wish it.

He visualized his legs, his arms, his head, and that immaterial part of himself that recognized itself as his working mind. He visualized his thoughts as lines of energy. Normally serene arcs, now they were tangled and disordered. His confusion was a vibrating knot, a nest of snakes, preventing him from achieving clarity. He imagined an unseen force smoothing those lines, untying the knot, releasing the hissing snakes. Slowly, his higher will overcame his body's adrenal turmoil.

Tension leaked from his shoulders, and an incipient headache faded.

Such was the training of Xiang Temple. Like all who graduated from that monastery in Telflamm, Raidon was a master of his own body. His techniques for visualization allowed him to control natural processes within himself normally beyond conscious control.

He looked deeper, and saw where other lines, the lines representing his wholeness of body, were strained and even broken in the vicinity of his left elbow. He applied his focused clarity to the severed lines. The snapped cords of visualized energy merged, fused, and relaxed.

The pain in his shoulder faded.

He could see all the lines representing himself, vibrating with vitality, forming a shape in three directions: breadth, width, and height.

Furrowing his brow, the monk began tracing his identity lines in the fourth direction, in time. Perhaps he could discover some clue as to what had happened to him.

An oddity in the wire-frame model of his own body snatched his complete attention. A pulse of a color he couldn't describe slowly glimmered across his upper torso. Something blue, like the ember of some slumbering fire.

Raidon opened his eyes and looked down at his chest. His shirt, silk jacket, and overcoat were mere tatters, burned away, revealing a broad tattoo etched into his flesh. Overlapping inscriptions in a lost language, tiny and crabbed, radiated outward from the symbol, like stylized flames drawn around the image of a tree.

It was the Cerulean Sign from his destroyed amulet—now scribed on him!

How could that be? He ran a hand across the tattoo. The image possessed a palpable texture on his skin. It was real.

The vision of his amulet consumed in blue fire assaulted him. He recalled in those final moments how the symbol itself had persisted, as if liberated, while the substance on which it was inscribed dissolved. He had reached toward the crumbling amulet, ached for it . . . and the Sign had flashed into him. That was the very last thing he recalled, try as he might.

A tracery of the Cerulean Sign decorated his flesh. Had the reality-smearing blue fire transferred it from his amulet to his body? Why . . . how? And then, having so marked him, sealed him within a pillar of brittle mineral? It made no sense.

"Too many unknowns vex me," he verbalized, then he coughed. His throat was sandpaper, unused to speech. He swallowed, shook his head. Spinning unsupported scenarios based on guesswork would avail him nothing except the creation of unwarranted assumptions. To comprehend what had happened, how he had survived, and how much time had passed since the blue fire storm, he would have to investigate.

He turned east toward Starmantle and fell into a light run. Unless he was misplaced in space too, it shouldn't take him too long to reach the port city, or what remained of it in the aftermath of the blue fire. As a monk initiate of Xiang Temple, and exemplar of its code, few things could long eclipse his extravagant martial prowess and conditioning, even long miles of travel. A false comfort? Perhaps.

The brittle extrusions grew thicker the farther he traveled. Once, he saw a humanoid shape silhouetted in a large, green mineral outcrop. He stopped, thinking perhaps he'd discovered some other prisoner held timeless within, just as he had been.

It was a woman, but one whose flesh was half burned away. An expression of pure agony made her face a demonic mask. She was completely encased in the extruded, greenish sap.

If the woman in the amberlike stuff was still alive, but held in a strange stasis, it would be cruel beyond words to release her to suffer the pain of her burnt flesh.

Raidon turned away, his expression tight. He resumed his eastward run.

He didn't investigate any other half-glimpsed shapes preserved in green.

The monk reached the edge of Starmantle, or at least the hints of its foundations. The city itself was no more.

Starmantle was gone, replaced with a madman's fancy. The emerald outcrops, akin to the one he'd emerged from, were thicker than ever as he approached the ruins. Perhaps the blasted city was their locus and origin? No longer brittle like the one that had trapped him, these were gemstone hard. Worse, this close to the city, each hummed a single, flutelike note. In sum, thousands of spires produced atonal melodies that clawed at Raidon's ears.

Between the spires gaped fissures that harbored a flickering blue glow, the same blue he recalled from the original firestorm. Raidon backpedaled a dozen yards.

Obsidian masses slowly drifted on the open ground between spires and ravines. In shape they were like irregular chunks of black stone. A palpable animosity emanated from them. Whether merely animate or actually alive, Raidon couldn't tell with the distance. Not that he particularly wanted to know. His eyes ached as they scanned the insane vista.

He blinked and turned away. He would find no answers here.

But Starmantle's skyline tugged at his thoughts, unearthing a memory of his daughter, Ailyn.

"Oh," he gasped. The shock of his awakening had robbed him of why he'd set forth from Starmantle . . . how long ago? A mortal fear for Ailyn's safety squeezed all the breath out of his chest.

"I must go to Nathlekh," he whispered.

A screech snatched his attention back to the demolished city. A humanoid figure bounded up from the nearest blue-burning fissure. Three more gibbering figures appeared over the ravine's lip as the first saw Raidon. It gabbled something that almost sounded like, "I told you I smelled supper," and charged.

It was naked. Its flesh was drawn tightly over its bones. A carnivore's sharp teeth clacked in its mouth, and eyes like hot coals fixed on Raidon, communicating a ravenous appetite so pure it was nearly mystical.

A ghoul?

A seam on the charging creature's stomach opened, revealing

a gaping, toothed cavity. A tentacle-like tongue emerged from the abdominal mouth, flicking like a purple flame.

It was not a ghoul, or at least not completely. It was something aberrant.

As Raidon fell into the left guarding stance, unexpected coolness tickled his chest. A quick glance down revealed the symbol upon his chest flickering with empyreal flame.

Surprise ambushed him, nearly distracting him from heeding his attacker.

The creature was upon him. Melting from guarding stance to offensive stance, Raidon caught a clawing strike with his left hand, pulled the arm diagonally forward and down, and delivered a hammer blow to the back of the creature's elbow with his right fist. The ghoul-like monster screamed with both mouths. Its right arm now flexed loosely from the elbow, the joint shattered.

The monster's two compatriots rapidly approached. Their abdominal maws drooled and gibbered like the first's. Raidon retained his hold on his foe's broken arm. He twisted his body around, tripping the creature with a foot, and hurled its body into the oncoming attackers.

One of the two newcomers was slow to dodge Raidon's contrived missile. It stumbled and went down in a tangle of limbs. They began to writhe and thrash, clawing and biting each other.

The final creature paused. Its eyes gleamed as it studied the monk. Blood, not its own, darkened its cheeks and chin. Its lower, abdominal mouth chomped and writhed, and grinding noises issued from it. Raidon glimpsed something white and red inside being chewed.

"Hunger does not rule me as it does my brothers," the creature crooned in an awful, piping tenor. "I just ate."

It could speak! Could it explain what had occurred? His normal rule of avoiding all interaction with abominations was suborned by his need to learn.

Raidon clenched his fists and demanded, "What happened here?"

The creature cocked its head and blinked. It was obviously taken aback by its prey's lack of fear. It responded, "We have selected you to be our meal."

"No, no. Tell me, what happened to Starmantle? How much time has passed since the blue fire came? I woke encased in—"

The creature tittered, "You are soft in the brain? Scream and run, as food should. Trouble me not with memories of the Spellplague!"

"Spellplague? What is that?"

The creature growled, turned, and swept its arm past the grappling, biting forms of its "brothers" to Starmantle's skyline. "The Spellplague was the blue fire that came when the Weave failed. Pockets of it still live here. It is a fire that eats all things. Like a ghoul!" It wheezed in something like laughter.

"A blue fire that eats?" prompted Raidon. He remembered his compatriots and stones alike burning away in the fiery blast that preceded his long darkness.

"Some things the blue fire consumed, leaving nothing behind. Other things, it ate, then spat back, different than before . . . plaguechanged."

Raidon took in the warped landscape and the warped creature. He asked, "Is that what happened to you?" Raidon gestured at the creature's abdominal maw.

It tittered again. "Maybe . . . maybe not," it replied. It huffed with amusement as if recalling a funny story, but this one it refrained from sharing. Then the ghoul pointed at Raidon's bare chest. "But you! You are spellscarred, yes? You hold back some trick to surprise me?"

"What are you talking about?"

The image of the firestorm branding him with the Cerulean Sign swam before Raidon's inner eye. The coolness on his chest increased. It wasn't painful—it was more like the feeling when the sun moves behind a cloud . . . or like the coolness of his amulet when it detected enemies it was forged to destroy.

The creature tittered, then said, "Spellscarred or not, you are made of meat. It wouldn't do to let a sack of blood and meat wander off untasted."

The creature lunged. The monk reflexively extended one leg in a buffer-kick intended to keep his opponent at bay long enough for Raidon to follow up with a real attack.

He had only a moment to understand his mistake when his foot plunged directly into the gaping, abdominal mouth.

The mouth began to chew. Pain, the worst he'd ever experienced, exploded up his leg. He nearly cried out.

Raidon jerked savagely, trying to retract his foot. The abdominal maw's tentacle-tongue whipped up around his calf, holding him fast. The white teeth within the cavity mashed and clacked, and red fluid bubbled and spilled forth. Was that all his blood?

The ghoul's head snapped forward, its real mouth hardly any less horrid than the one trapping the monk's foot. It struck at Raidon's throat.

The monk's rising uppercut smashed teeth and jolted the creature's head away. Raidon wouldn't be overcome so easily.

The creature savagely jerked on his leg with its clutching tentacle, pulling his leg farther into its abdominal cavity. His foot, calf, knee, and lower thigh . . . how could it be? His whole lower leg was inside the thing, and the questing tentacle began to wrap around his thigh. More reddish fluid spilled forth in thin, steaming rivulets. How could his foot and calf fit inside the gaunt monster? Had it bitten off his lower leg? Queasiness clawed at Raidon's focus.

Agony poured up his nerves, making his arms quiver and his head ring. Would it hurt so abominably if his leg were already unattached? He desperately hoped the ghoul was bigger on the inside than its shape suggested.

The chill on Raidon's chest intensified. Without quite knowing why, he lay his left palm across the symbol blazoned there. A snap, and contact was made. Cerulean energy poured into him. It was the energy his amulet once lent him in the presence of aberrations.

A sky blue gleam shone from his body. It seemed the Cerulean Sign etched on his chest was more than a mere tattoo.

It was alive with the old power of his amulet.

His touch awakened it.

The symbol emanated the cleansing light he had once been able to invoke from his destroyed amulet. The Sign embodied the purity of the natural world. It was anathema to aberrations.

The ghoul's eyes widened as its horrible, abdominal tongue retracted. The cavity spat Raidon's leg out with such force that he fell to the ground.

His foot remained attached. "Thank Xiang," muttered Raidon. The thing's second mouth was bigger on the inside than the outside. But strips of skin were absent from his extremity, dissolved away as if by acid, revealing red and oozing muscle.

It was the most serious wound Raidon had ever received. But his mind passed over that particular realization to consider what he'd just invoked, unaided.

He had become his amulet. The energy pouring "into" him issued from him. Raidon grasped his focus, visualizing his mind and body again as lines of flashing energy. The glimmer of blue he had earlier observed blazed cerulean at its heart. At its edges, it burned the wilder, darker blue hue of the Spellplague. Had the firestorm he'd survived . . . had it infused him with his amulet's power? If so, why was its cerulean color contaminated—

The ghoul-thing smashed into him, bearing him to the ground. Raidon blinked away his untimely retrospection too late. The creature's claws and both mouths tore at his flesh. It panted, "I don't like your taste. Maybe you'll taste better dead."

A thumb to the creature's eye and a knee to its side did little to dislodge the ghoul. A crushing elbow directly to the creature's throat cut short its constant, maddening titter. That blow would have killed a mortal man outright.

The ghoul-thing was undead, and its nerves did not communicate messages of pain. Raidon struggled in its grasp, his breath coming quicker. The monk's deep knowledge of how to attack vital areas, like pressure points, joints, and organs, was almost useless against the walking dead.

He squirmed right, trying get out from under the crushing weight, then shucked left, hoping to fake out the creature. The ghoul's tongue-tentacle held the scrabbling monk fast.

Raidon was pinned on his back. The creature's disgusting, abdominal jaws gave it an unholy advantage, and the pain in his leg was slipping more and more into his consciousness, threatening to cripple his ability to seize the initiative. Even as he inched one hand toward the sign on his chest, the ghoul managed to grab his wrist. It quickly snatched his other wrist too. Its claws bit painfully into his palms.

It tittered, "No, you mustn't touch! Hold still, now, while I nibble the skin from your face."

Raidon's focus faltered. Concentrate! Hold onto your calm, or you are lost, he commanded his wavering discipline. But what chance did he have if he could not reach the symbol?

If I have the power of my amulet, what need have I to touch it to trigger it? Wasn't he always in contact with it, since it was part of himself?

He concentrated on the cool point above his heart. The symbol of a dead order. The Cerulean Sign. He imagined himself touching it with a tendril of thought. The Sign was a metaphor, an emblem that served as a door, a door Raidon visualized himself swinging wide, revealing wonders beyond . . .

The Sign on his chest pulsed. Shafts of cerulean light speared heavenward. Where the light touched the aberration, it howled. Pain was no longer beyond its ability to sense.

The ghoul's abdominal tongue retracted, and it writhed and fell away from Raidon. The light from the Sign faded.

The monk staggered to his feet, shaking and bleeding. *Zai zi,* he was sorely hurt! If he didn't tend to his raw foot and lower calf soon, he'd lose his leg, then soon enough his life.

The ghoul remained prone, writhing and drooling without regard to its environment. Its senses were overloaded, maybe burned out. He'd seen a similar response many times during his decade of abomination hunting. The Sign's mere manifestation affected weaker aberrations just so. The most powerful aberrations were less affected. Lucky these were not the most potent of their kind . . .

A flicker of movement brought Raidon's attention up and back. The ghoul-thing's two compatriots had ceased their rivalry. They stared at Raidon and the glowing symbol on his chest with calculating and fearful eyes.

Despite their trepidation, they advanced.

They saw the Sign and obviously recognized its potential to eradicate them, but they could also smell his blood. Raidon supposed that smell pierced their sense of self-preservation. For these ghoul-monstrosities, hunger was a drive purer and fiercer than fear.

They charged.

The monk cried, "Husks of abominable hunger, see the Cerulean Sign!" His chest blazed anew with sky blue light. Shafts of radiance flashed like blades from his body to lance the attackers.

One of the ghouls sidestepped the glow, but the other ran headlong into the brilliance. Its eyes shuttered in pain as the purifying radiance dazzled it. It tripped and fell, mewling.

The second ghoul, oblivious of its "brother's" fate, reached him. A claw slipped past Raidon's shielding forearm, slashing directly across the symbol tattooed on his chest.

The Sign's radiance instantly failed.

Raidon fell back, holding his focus. He released a flurry of fierce kicks to the ghoul's knees even as it clawed and tentacle-lashed him. While the creature couldn't feel physical pain, its body could be broken with sufficient force. Unfortunately, he couldn't kick with his ravaged leg.

Simultaneously, he shuffled left as he dodged, slipped, and blocked the ghoul's assaults. His adversary was too intent on sinking its teeth into Raidon to worry about the terrain. When the ghoul was in position, Raidon feinted, then pushed. It tripped backward over the ghoul who had nearly bitten off the monk's leg, who was just rising from its dazed fall.

Raidon took advantage of the reprieve to glance down at his chest. A bloody stripe bisected the symbol blazoned there. He closed his eyes and dragged forward his healing visualization yet again. There was no time to deal with his foot—but that was the lesser issue now. He concentrated on his upper body. He saw the partially severed lines of his symbol within the greater model of his own body.

In a manner no different from the method he used to heal other minor hurts, he imagined the severed lines growing closer, bridging the gap, and rediscovering the connection just severed. Coolness returned to his chest. Not as strongly as before, but enough.

Raidon's eyes opened. His opponents were already on their feet and advancing.

He pulsed with cerulean light once more.

Both creatures screamed when the light touched them. This last radiance proved too much for them. Shrieking and crying, they retreated backward toward the gates of Starmantle.

His reserves were exhausted. He turned his back on a chilling, rain-laden wind from the north. He looked south toward Gulthmere Forest. Black smoke furled into the sky, and he caught a whiff of burning pine. The already blasted forest was burning, again.

Without a word, Raidon hobbled west. He wondered which would be the agent of his death: his wound, pursuing Starmantle ghouls, fire, or freezing rain?

CHAPTER FIVE

The Year of the Secret (1396 DR)
Olleth, Sea of Fallen Stars

Nogah regarded the Dreamheart with unblinking eyes. She clutched the stone in both webbed hands. A year ago she'd pried it from the earth's nadir. Since then, she'd not allowed a day to go by that didn't include spending time with the orb.

The not-quite-spherical chunk of unfamiliar mineral was her all-encompassing passion. Though unimpressive to the eye, its presence was more than merely physical. It existed on the plane of mind too. There, the Dreamheart was a scintillating font of color, dreams, and possibilities. It was a beacon of power and a literal promise of knowledge and dominance to any kuo-toa with the temerity to take heed and listen.

Nogah listened. Oh, yes.

At first the influence was felt only when she slept. Images capered in time to unearthly sounds, nightmarish but also fascinating. But the stone had learned to reach her waking mind too. More and more lately, phantasms of glory visited her while she was fully conscious. Sometimes terrifying, sometimes eerie in their beauty, the visions always left her dazed. It frustrated Nogah that once the visions faded, she couldn't quite recall their full consequence.

Subconsciously, she retained more. Sometimes she would inadvertently refer, without the least forethought, to ancient events about which she couldn't possibly know anything. Only after the words escaped her throat did she pause in surprise, trying to pin down the origin of her own comment. Swirling images of a churning void and atonal vibrations were all she could consciously access.

Such gaps seemed an easy price to pay for the arcane secrets she slowly teased from the Dreamheart. From these abilities did her own aspirations spring. She imagined Faerûn shaped anew, under kuo-toa sway!

Of course, many of her too timid compatriots did not yet share her goals. They were too used to the old ways and reliance on old allies. Nogah smirked. Despite themselves, she convinced more and more to her way of thinking. They were beginning to accept the better place kuo-toa deserved in the world. In a world where Nogah would be transcendent. But first, she must bring all of Olleth to her side.

The city of Olleth was once a watery realm ruled by spell-savvy morkoth, who called their magocracy the Arcanum of Olleth. These cruel creatures ruled a city built on the labor of slaves. Morkoth slaves included captured individuals of several other aquatic races, including uncivilized locathah and even vicious sahuagin. In their arrogance, the morkoth ambushed a kuo-toa delegation that traveled beneath the Sea of Fallen Stars under a truce vouchsafed by the Sea Mother herself. Half the kuo-toa embassy was slain and eaten, and the survivors were brought to Olleth to serve morkoth masters forevermore.

The Arcanum erred when it failed to purge the surviving whips from their new contingent of kuo-toa slaves. Whips pledged to the Sea Mother make poor slaves, for their resources are only a prayer away. Within a decade, the Arcanum suffered so many setbacks, uprisings, and disasters, secretly orchestrated by kuo-toa whips both within Olleth and hidden outside the city, that it teetered on the edge of collapse.

Thus most believe that even in the absence of the Spellplague, when one in three morkoth mages dissolved in blue flashes and the remainder lost their grip on slave-taking spells, Olleth would have fallen to kuo-toa anyway. Regardless, in the aftermath of that day, the kuo-toa rose up and claimed the city for themselves.

Surviving morkoth of Olleth were purged, though a few escaped. Other creatures were allowed to remain, slaves still, beholden to new masters. The kuo-toa of Olleth called out to their kin, and so it was that kuo-toa came to the Sea of Fallen Stars in large numbers for the first time. Of the Arcanum, only bitter memories remained, as well as a few morkoth specimens preserved in pickling fluid to remind future kuo-toa generations of their past trials.

Nogah wondered how the old morkoth Arcanum would have reacted if they had found the Dreamheart?

They would have pursued the very stratagem Nogah had chosen, she supposed, and probably more successfully. They would not have had to put up with resistance among their fellows, who feared breaking tradition more than anything else. The Arcanum hadn't been tied to the dogma of a progenitor god like the kuo-toa were.

She blinked away fruitless comparisons and dead memories. The Sea Mother's creed would crumble soon enough, and she would usher in a new age of greatness.

Nogah rose from the lounging pool. She retained her hold

on the Dreamheart with both hands. For all her familiarity with the relic, it remained an awkward size.

Rivulets of clear water trailed on the tile behind her as she moved from her quarters to the outermost chamber of her hall.

There, under a great dome, her growing congregation would hear Nogah speak, as they had done for many previous tendays. Today, Nogah thought, I will show them something so extraordinary their souls will be mine forever.

An audience was already gathering in the chamber, some murmuring in anticipation, others looking timid and uncertain. Many she recognized, but as with most days, she saw several new faces too, who'd heard rumors of her sermons. There were even a few sullen locathah. Word of Nogah's creed was spreading. Soon enough, she'd have to find a larger place to conduct these gatherings. She'd already moved three times to accommodate the growing crowds. This spacious hall, half submerged under a mother-of-pearl dome, was located at the very periphery of Olleth.

Nogah's popularity grew despite her excommunication. The disruptions following the Year of Blue Fire were ongoing, and theocratic control over the city was still unsteady. On the other hand, things were much better than they had been a decade earlier, when random outbreaks of spellplague might suddenly ignite and burn away a kuo-toa or mutate him into a monster. Nogah's timing couldn't have been better.

When she began preaching her new creed, the church stripped Nogah of her status as a whip of the Sea Mother. Nogah's ability to utter prayers in the Sea Mother's name failed. They thought her helpless. They moved to strip her of life and limb too. But the Dreamheart trumped their power. Nogah's doctrine proved stronger that day. She had killed two whips with the power of the relic and sent the remaining priest fleeing from her hall.

The Sea Mother's influence was on the wane, while Nogah's strength was bolstered by a power more ancient! Her flukes warmed just to think of it. Her growing power emanated from the Dreamheart, or at least, was channeled by the stone from some strange, grim source.

The corpses of the three additional kuo-toa whips who'd returned later to slay her for blasphemy were proof enough that Nogah's claim of approaching transcendence was no idle boast.

These stories and other similar accounts of Nogah's defiance were galvanizing interest in her sermons. She couldn't have planned it better if she'd tried.

The ex-whip walked out onto a dimly lit dais beneath the humid dome, buffeted by hundreds of kuo-toa voices immersed in excited speculation. Only a few saw her.

"My children," Nogah said to the gathered crowd. They quieted instantly.

"My children, you have come to hear the truth. The truth! After a lifetime of lies, you deserve to know."

Whispers skirted the chamber's periphery. Illumination began to leak away, but around Nogah, the light intensified like approaching dawn.

Nogah continued, "I, like you, also believed the lies. I believed them so much, I entered the service of the Sea Mother. Like many of you, I was willing to sacrifice everything to her, regardless of the cost to myself. It was our way! How could I do otherwise?"

Eager murmurs rippled through the throng, reflecting off the knee-deep, clear water that filled the chamber. It was almost completely dark, even to kuo-toa senses. But Nogah shone like a star come to earth. Their attention was rapt upon her; she could feel their combined gazes like a caress.

Despite the sermons being declared taboo by the hierarchy of Olleth, the curious still found her. After all, what other kuo-toa had ever disregarded the commands of the combined opinion of the Sea Mother's whips with such impunity without being immediately expunged?

But she commanded their attention with more than spectacle; as Nogah spoke, she leached subtle dream magic from the relic she clutched like a talisman, and broadcast it into the receptive mind of every creature present.

"I, like you, accepted my lot. Even as a whip of the Sea Mother, I was below Her notice. To Her, I was as a slug—useful, barely, but worth not one bit of regard. I gave Her my undying attention and service. In return, She gave . . . what?"

A twitter of angry voices sparked in answer across the darkened audience.

Nogah interrupted, "Nothing! Nothing but more demands, still more commands for sacrifice. I obeyed, for what could I do? What could you do?"

Nogah raised the Dreamheart over her head. The light around her shone twice as bright from the relic. Twisting and twining strands of radiance burst out of the stone to extend up and over the heads of the audience.

"I have an answer for you."

A sound, low and rumbling, began to beat from the relic, like a dead heart shocked and stuttering back to life.

Nogah spoke, "You have a choice. Will you stay shackled to the Sea Mother and Her stagnant servitors, or leave Her behind? A new way beckons, right here, right now! I offer you a new vision to pursue. If you pledge yourself to me, your sacrifices and service will not go unrewarded."

She shouted over a murmur of protest, "Instead, you will be exalted! Come with me and find a new future. Even now, I can feel the current change. I am ascendant! I am the hand-maiden of an ancient strength that begins, even now, to turn its attention back to the world it so long forgot."

With a performer's flourish, Nogah released her grip on the Dreamheart. It did not fall. It was as steady in the air as a stone resting on solid earth. Then it began to ascend as the light emerging from it became elongated strands of swaying light. The relic reached a central position in the chamber and paused. The lashing tendrils of light grew ever longer and more elaborate, while the beat of its thunderous, repeating note thudded ever louder. The hearts of all those present began to synch to the overpowering, pelagic beat.

Nogah screamed, "Behold!" Her voice was amplified, not drowned, by the crashing noise.

"There lies a realm, beyond ours, of purity and power! A place where thought becomes action, and death is just another concept, mutable as a lie. The gods, jealous of their own power, have long blocked mortals from this land beyond all other places. But not all knowledge of it is lost. Here and there, portions of that outlying realm touch the world. Where such contact occurs, reality itself is blessed! When the touch persists, great wonders can be evoked!"

The self-styled handmaiden of the Dreamheart gestured and concentrated. The weaving strands of light swirled into a massive braid. A braid with a bulge at the center, where the Dreamheart was cupped in the tendrils of its own creation.

The braid rotated and pulsed in the air, like a gorged serpent slowly digesting a recent meal.

The bulge at the braid's center pulsed in time to the throbbing boom, expanding with each beat. The multicolored threads suddenly convulsed and unraveled, revealing the cavity it had grown within it. Of the Dreamheart, there was no sign. Instead there was a featureless expanse of pale radiance, like moonlight seen from behind a cloud, radiance so old that it should have failed long ago, but persevered.

"Look you well—the light falling into your eyes is older than all the light in the world, older than birth fires of the gods themselves. Isn't it beautiful? Isn't it glorious? Can't you feel your mind unravel in wonder in its—"

A great crash, louder still than the Dreamheart's pulsing

music, broke through Nogah's ritual of awe. The sound came from above, at the dome's rear.

Watery, afternoon light flooded across the startled, blinking audience. The moonlight radiance winked out. The Dreamheart was revealed as an unadorned stone. It dropped like a dead weight into the massed audience. A scream burbled away; the stone crushed the skull of a kuo-toa standing directly below it.

A strident voice called out from the newborn fissure, "Cease your blasphemy, in the name of the Sea Mother!"

Half blinded by the sudden glare, Nogah was still able to pick out the silhouettes of at least two senior whips bedecked in holy battle armor. With them stood the bulky forms of four kuo-toa monitors, warriors trained to fight with nothing but their own bodies since birth.

The audience screamed with one throat in terror of being found in the company of a blasphemer. Nogah tried to command them to turn on their attackers. But now the shouts of panic easily drowned out her directions. They hadn't stared into the enchantment she'd prepared long enough for them to fall under her sway. Her long-prepared ritual was undone.

A wild scramble in the bowl of the dome commenced as her audience sought to escape. Kuo-toa began to lose their lives as they were trampled by their fellows in blossoming panic.

She'd have to start anew, but she pushed all thoughts of preparations out of her head. All her attention was required to save her scaled hide from the attacking Sea Mother loyalists. Nogah leaped into the audience even as blasts of whip-directed lightning scoured the ground where she stood. The edge of the bolt caught her. She yelped but kept moving. Her natural resistance saved her from most of the bolt's fury. Still, Nogah knew she couldn't stand up to many more such blasts.

The stampeding congregation was like a storm-tossed sea. The attacking whips had closed off the exits! The trapped kuo-toa surged back and forth across the constricted space. Nogah fought through the press of thrashing bodies with Dreamheart-enhanced strength. She trod on more than a few mewling forms already brought low. Even out of contact with the relic, she was able to draw strength from it. Even now her lightning-burned skin healed.

She savored the thought that her abilities would redouble again when she renewed direct contact with the Dreamheart—

A flailing finger jabbed her left eye. An elbow clipped her right side. A big, sticky kuo-toa grabbed Nogah around her waist and tried to use her body to lever himself off the floor. His was a hysterical strength; she barely avoided being pulled down. She had to get clear . . . No. She'd joined the panic for a reason. Despite the dangers of the crush, she had to retrieve the relic. Just another few moments and she would have it.

The four monitors leaped from the fissure to land amid the screaming kuo-toa commoners. The monitors' finned hands, feet, knees, and elbows were weapons every bit as lethal as swords and spears. They began killing a path through the crowd toward Nogah, even as she continued to move toward them, or in truth toward what lay between them and herself. The relic cast a shadow on her mind, so that she knew exactly its distance from her.

What? The Dreamheart was moving! One of the panicked congregation had it. The kuo-toa was using it to batter his way to the left, toward some chimera of safety the idiot imagined he would find there . . .

The thief made surprising progress. Actually, not so surprising, Nogah realized. Even unconscious of its true nature, the fellow was energized by the stone. Soon enough, he would make it to the wall. And what then? Perhaps he would unconsciously borrow strength enough from the stone to create an exit.

The monitors continued to close on her, thinning the crowd with brutal efficiency. If the monitors cared so little about Olleth's citizens, then the whips still perched on the breach above were probably even now readying another bolt to blast her and any creature around her. They wouldn't hold back for fear of killing an innocent. And the idiot kuo-toa continued to draw away from Nogah, as if on purpose!

Nogah mentally reached for the stone, straining the thin connection that remained between them. Through that link she attempted to summon fire.

The Dreamheart roared with black flame. A piercing scream emerged from the thief an instant before his body flashed away to cinders. The stone fell back to the floor, already cooling.

The crowd shrank from the cremated residue, creating a buffer. Nogah rushed triumphantly into the space and snatched up the Dreamheart. Her link with the relic resurged. It made her a little giddy. The reunion wasn't a moment too soon.

A ray of brilliant green energy burst from the head whip's pincer staff. Wherever the ray reached, portions of the floor, clothing, and screaming kuo-toa disappeared in puffs of gray dust. The ray touched down some ten or so feet from Nogah, then tracked toward her.

She sucked energy from the relic, hardening her form against the ravening green ray. When the emerald light touched her, she couldn't help flinching. Then she smiled. The Dreamheart provided her more than enough strength to withstand the prayers of destruction granted by the Sea Mother. That was the point of her sermons, that she, Nogah, was ascendant. The green ray played over her form as if no more than colored light.

Nogah decided it was time to show all the kuo-toa of Olleth

that Nogah wasn't to be trifled with. Time to seize the reins of power. Time to call up the relic's untapped reservoir of energy, more than she had ever tried before.

The relic still hid most of itself from Nogah, despite her small successes in channeling some of its fringe energies. Every day she learned a little more. For instance, she discovered the relic could command the minds of certain kinds of creatures. Not a tenday ago she had urged the Dreamheart to extrude mental tendrils of influence across the Sea of Fallen Stars. Tendrils seeking creatures of the deep who might be convinced, with the relic's aid, to do Nogah's bidding.

More than one of those questing lines had grown taut since then. Like fishing lines, Nogah knew she had hooked some big ones.

Now comes the great gamble, she thought. Not knowing exactly what she summoned, Nogah mentally tugged on one of the Dreamheart's tendrils of influence. As she did so, a name resounded in her mind.

Gethshemeth.

The name was familiar . . .

Oh.

Nogah's recognition nearly severed the summoning tendril of connection. Gethshemeth was a great kraken, a monstrosity of the sea bottom. Truth be told, the kuo-toa of Olleth had hoped Gethshemeth was slain in the Spellplague. The great one had been an ally of the morkoth Arcanum and had no love for the whips for their part in wiping out the former residents of the city.

Could even the Dreamheart hold Gethshemeth to her wishes?

Too late for second thoughts. The great kraken was already close, as if anticipating being called. Or, as if the kraken had felt the Dreamheart's questing tendril days ago and had traveled over the last tenday to investigate the source of the strange flavor in the water . . .

"Nogah!" screamed one of the kuo-toa whips, "I see you! Though you struggle like a minnow in the net, we have you now! Give yourself up to the Sea Mother's just retribution for a blasphemer! Every moment you struggle is another eon your soul shall twine in the Sea Mother's grotto!"

Nogah shook her head in negation, almost sadly. She said, "It is your struggle that ends today. If you flee immediately or forswear the Sea Mother here and now, as I have done, perhaps I shall not take your life."

Incredulity widened both whips' already bulbous eyes. One of the monitors, having closed nearly to within striking distance, gave out an involuntary yelp of indignation.

Then a shadow fell across the whip's shoulders. It rose from behind them.

There was a sound like a bursting bladder, and one of the whips was gone.

Where the sky and light had been visible through the shattered ceiling was now a mountain of undulating, dun-colored flesh. Then came the stench of a thousand rotting fish, and the second whip screamed.

Gethshemeth had come.

A tentacle as tall as a tower squirmed into view. The remaining whip brought up his pincer staff and began to scream a prayer of dreadful power. Too late. The tentacle smashed down upon him. A spray of fluids rained down onto the kuo-toa below, whose own screams escalated in pitch.

Nogah concentrated on the Dreamheart and her connection to Gethshemeth. She sensed the kraken's powerful mind through the link. The squidlike brain was not suffused with hate, as Nogah would have supposed, for being forced to the will of another. No, the kraken felt only curiosity. And a gruesome sort of giddy greed.

A monitor punched her with a fist that felt more like an iron mace than flesh. Two more blows hammered her and she was down, screaming, protecting not her own body, but the

Dreamheart. Blood pooled in one of her eyes, blurring her vision.

Nogah directed a mental image of the two monitors who remained within the chamber into the relic, and out along the tendril connected to Gethshemeth.

Three more tentacles groped in through the fissure, crumbling the rent wider with the force of their entry.

Nogah screamed, her words mush with hurt, "Your flesh is forfeit for striking me, groveler!"

The monitor had time enough to glance back before one of the kraken tentacles snatched him up and retracted, bearing him instantly away. A faint scream and crunch followed.

The remaining monitor stood his ground, assuming a guarding stance. When the second tentacle lashed forward, he evaded, and in doing so, landed a kick. The kick's amazing strength sent an undulating wave up the tentacle. A mighty, monstrous voice roared in surprise.

The third barbed tentacle snapped forward, encircling the monitor around the neck. With a yank and snap, the kuo-toa warrior's head parted from its body.

Quiet descended on the ruined hall then, save for the raw-throated whimpering of the surviving congregation. They were too terrified to scream any longer.

A tentacle propelled itself along the broken ground and dead bodies. It quested toward Nogah like a side-winding serpent. It touched her on the leg, then reared up. The tip of the tentacle waved back and forth, as if waiting.

Nogah took short, painful breaths as she watched Gethshemeth's boneless limb gesticulate. Aches from the monitor's attack made her vision unsteady. It occurred to her that she needn't suffer so. With a thought, she drew wholeness from the Dreamheart. Well-being sparked out from her hands, up her scaled forearms, and vanquished the pain. Her facility with the stone was increasing.

Nogah rose, using the Dreamheart to push herself up

before finally lifting it to cradle it in her arms like a newly hatched child.

Scarlet light bathed the room. Nogah looked up at the widened fissure in the ceiling. A single, vast, red eye peered down through the rent. Her heart stuttered, and her breath caught.

Leave foolishness behind you, Nogah reprimanded herself. She was master, and this great leviathan of the deep was leashed to her will via the Dreamheart. Why else had it come?

Nogah spoke, "Great one of the depths, I thank you for your service."

The eye regarded her, unblinking. She felt curiosity through the light mental connection the Dreamheart provided.

Curiosity sidling toward yearning.

Nogah decided to send the great kraken away. She had proved she could summon the creature at need. She was growing uncomfortable under the creature's unwavering scrutiny.

She issued a mental command of dismissal through the relic.

The link jerked and parted, gone. Nogah took an involuntary step back.

The eye finally blinked. A basso scream blasted through the hall: Gethshemeth's voice.

"You misunderstand my role."

Each word was so loud it was like a separate assault.

Nogah sputtered. "I . . . you . . . you are here because I commanded your aid . . ."

"No."

The negation was like a gate crashing down, cutting off escape.

"I am here for what you retrieved for me from below."

"The stone is mine!" yelled Nogah in sudden understanding, clutching it and pulling back. "I summoned you, and I can dismiss you. Leave me!"

The tentacle tip swaying before Nogah lashed forward and struck her with the strength of ten monitors.

She blacked out. A moment later, consciousness blinked back. She was in the air, tumbling head over flippers. She didn't have the Dreamheart. "No—"

A wall arrested Nogah's trajectory. If not for her residual claim on the relic's power, she would have died in that instant.

As it was, she slid to the floor and crumpled into a heap. She could only blink as the kraken's tentacle tip encircled the Dreamheart. Tentacle and relic retreated up through the hole in the ceiling.

"That which was ancient before the world breathed is now mine."

Nogah tried to rise, collapsed.

"Divinity itself is now within my reach."

Nogah sobbed.

CHAPTER SIX

The Year of the Secret (1396 DR)
West of the Ruins of Starmantle

The rain sputtered a while longer, then stopped. It hadn't been enough to douse the wildfire that blazed to the south, burning a swath through the seedling pines of Gulthmere Forest. In some places, the fire flared so bright it cast orange highlights on the low clouds. Winding columns of smoke and soot twisted up toward those same clouds, merging into a single, ashen morass.

Raidon Kane coughed in the damp, sooty air. He wondered how far he had traveled. Not far, given his condition. Then how long had it been since he staggered west from Starmantle's crazed gates? Plaguechanged ghouls nearly ended him there. One tried to eat his leg. Raidon worried more about the creature's claim, that the monk was "spellscarred."

His exhaustion was a physical weight lying on his back. He was feverish, and his damaged foot had at last gone numb. His body's overwhelming fatigue tried to convince his mind that an immediate nap was the best possible choice.

Raidon struggled to crawl onto a large outcrop. He imagined it would be more defensible than the plain. He'd seen jackals sniffing around, and he worried other predators might be trailing him from Starmantle. Undead predators with too many mouths.

The rain made the outcrop slick. He kept losing his grip. Even when he found a good hold, the piece crumbled, sending him sliding back toward the ground.

Once a small ledge broke under his weight to reveal a cyst of red spiders, each the size of one of Raidon's hands. The wildfire gleamed ominously from their scarlet carapaces. The arachnids clacked oversized fangs at Raidon, then scurried away in a single line like a tendril of blood.

He was nearly to the top. Then a spasm in his acid-burned foot caused him to backslide. He slid down half the distance he had just so laboriously climbed.

"By Xiang's seven swords."

Raidon's concentration was absent. He couldn't summon the mental discipline necessary to heal his wounds. The skin from his foot and leg was peeling away, and blood constantly oozed from the raw wound. Dirt crusted everything. Infection had likely already set in.

Raidon tried to push aside concerns over his injury. He couldn't worry about that now. He needed sleep, and a safe place for it.

A new pain seared. The nerves in his lower leg were not quite dead. The sting sawed right through the shreds of his focus. Raidon slid all the way back down to the outcrop's base, scraping skin from his fingers and forearms.

He lay face down in the mud, coughing into the cruel earth that apparently had decided this day was to be his last.

Would that be so bad, he wondered?

"Try again, Raidon," came a voice from nowhere. "You have nothing more to lose."

The monk raised his head from the mud to glance weakly around. He was alone.

Of course. As his mind gave up its sovereignty over reason, he supposed chimeras would appear to bedevil him.

But the phantom voice had a point.

Unless he discovered the strength necessary . . . well, death would claim him. So why not try again? One more hard effort, he told himself. After that, he could rest, hopefully enough to lift the exhaustion that hung on his limbs and eyelids like ballast.

He endured another fit of coughing that threatened to scrape his lungs right out of his chest.

What was it the elders of Xiang Temple taught?

"The usefulness of a cup is its emptiness," he whispered.

Nothing could help him now but his own force of will. Anything was possible, or nothing.

He prepared for a final effort.

CHAPTER SEVEN

The Year of the Secret (1396 DR)
Leaving New Sarshel, Impiltur

Waves flashed past the prow. The water moved independently of the ship, giving the illusion the craft moved more swiftly than its true speed. The vessel was four days and four nights out of New Sarshel's port. The sky was cloudless, and stars in the millions studded the heavens, a plethora of riches hinting at distances and ages vast beyond comprehension.

An elaborate figurehead hung on the pirate ship's stem, below the bowsprit. The figurehead was a half painted, half sculpted woman with shimmering green scales in place of clothing. She leered into the night, her eyes unnaturally brilliant. The figurehead gave the ship her name, the *Green Siren*.

The *Green Siren* did not fly its true privateer colors; it still ran under the flag of Marhana Shipping.

A tall man cloaked in what seemed darkness stood at the ship's prow, above and slightly behind the figurehead. The edges of his cloak flapped in the wind, echoing the movements of the much larger sail luffing and snapping above.

The man withdrew a small, dull tin from his cloak. The tin contained death. A long, slow death, popularly conceptualized as a one-way trip down an imaginary road. A crimson road, red like the eyes of those who used what was inside the tin.

The man's eyes were not red, but he was most certainly a traveler. He owed his lack of symptoms to his pact with the Lord of Bats.

It had seemed like a good deal at the time, reflected Japheth.

He carefully removed the tin's lid. Inside lay nestled his supply of traveler's dust: tiny roseate crystals, each slightly larger than a grain of sea salt.

Shielding the contents from the wind with his forearm, he plucked forth a crystal.

Japheth tilted his head back and, with practiced grace, dropped the grain into his left eye. "Lord of Bats, protect me," he whispered.

Japheth learned of the entity called the Lord of Bats when he was an acolyte librarian working the back stacks of the many-towered library of Candlekeep. In the confusion and turmoil following the Spellplague, and later, the Keeper of Tome's mysterious disappearance, the magical wards that protected the sensitive and dangerous scrolls and tomes from casual perusal in Candlekeep failed for some time.

The aftermath of Mystra's murder also marked the period Japheth put his first tentative foot on the crimson road.

Back then, no one yet realized that, once addicted to traveler's dust, an early death was inescapable for the user, regardless of whether it was quick or prolonged.

The grain on his eye was dissolving. The flapping sail and the stars beyond began to blur and waver. Japheth blinked. Anticipation was part of the experience.

The essence of the liberated dust reached his blood and his mind, penetrating to his soul. The constraints of rules and preconceptions deserted his consciousness, leaving behind a red-hazed vista of breathtaking clarity.

Japheth felt transfigured, alive, and potent. Nothing else was like this feeling. It was bottled perfection, the crystallized blood of divinity itself, perhaps. While striding the crimson road, all sorrows sank beyond recall, while all joys were raised like blazing stars.

When Japheth began taking traveler's dust as an acolyte a decade earlier, his initial forays on the crimson road produced similar bliss.

At first.

It was under the compulsion of traveler's dust that Japheth dared the forbidden stacks, even while the rest of the staff defended the library-fortress from refugees swarming the Coast Way. In the wake of the Year of Blue Fire, chaos ruled Faerûn.

Not that Japheth had cared about consequences or chaos while in the grip of his newfound drug. The lucidity that accompanied a walk on the crimson road blinded him to things that customarily would have captured his entire interest.

Japheth recalled how, as a drugged acolyte, he had sauntered past wonders: a heavy book made of copper foil stamped with arcane sigils, bound between thin covers of beaten silver; a book bound between sheets of yellowish iron, whose indecipherable title alternately burned with fire and sparked with electricity; and a libram bound between two metallic angel wings, from which glorious voices issued.

No, under the influence of dust, he had passed by these glamorous wonders to the chamber's far corner, shadowed and dank. There he plucked a small, brownish tome from behind a larger book that pulsed with ominous power. To his dust-tuned senses, the small brown folio glimmered with a haunting, soon-to-be-realized significance.

The book's plain face was stamped in fading dye with the words, *Fey Pacts of Ancient Days*.

Young Japheth quickly retreated to his cell and closed himself away from his fellows. By then, the refugee surge had been beaten back, but the Keeper of Tomes needed finding. Japheth didn't care if he ever saw the Keeper of Tomes again. He wanted to be left alone with his traveler's dust and the tome he'd stolen from the forbidden stacks.

Within the book he found strange names and properties of primitive earth spirits, ancient and strong. Once, claimed the hoary tome, the beings attached to these names were worshiped as gods. Sadly, remonstrated the crumbling text, Faerûn had largely forgotten these ancient Powers.

The names in the pilfered tome called to him. And so he read, day in and day out. All would have been bliss, but for a change in his trips on the crimson road.

Japheth was approaching the "first bend," as the transition later came to be called, of his journey. In other words, the traveler's dust brought him less joy with each use, but his body's desire for the substance only increased.

It was around this time that traveler's dust was suddenly recognized as being a slow poison, not "distilled joy" as certain Amnan suppliers had successfully and lucratively marketed it. Amn had weathered the Spellplague better than most, and in its aftermath, Amn's merchants were already making a profit among refugee populations and untouched kingdoms alike.

Some cities banned the sale of dust, and its users, easily marked by their eyes, were shuffled off to secure cells where they could reach their journeys' end in peace, if allowed to keep their supply of dust. When their dust was confiscated, as usually happened out of misplaced morality, the resultant death was an awful thing to behold. Deprived walkers invariably became violent, first toward others, then to themselves.

All these things Japheth heard whispered beyond his door by the other acolytes. They knew the dust had him. They saw how his eyes slowly filled with crazed lines of blood. They witnessed how his hands shook so badly at times he could scarcely restack borrowed tomes. They remembered how he had boasted of being a traveler on the newly discovered crimson road.

Young Japheth despaired. He decided to end his life with what dignity he could muster. He decided to take all the traveler's dust he possessed in one gluttonous mass. He would dash to the end of the road with the speed of a racing hound.

The suicidal acolyte's vision burned as he poured twenty or more grains in each eye. He was catapulted out upon a scarlet plain and saw for the first time a literal road.

And he saw its awful terminus.

A shouted hail pulled Japheth from his reverie. A man approached along the unlit starboard side of the *Green Siren*.

Japheth didn't need light to recognize the swaggering figure of Captain Thoster. The captain sported a prodigious hat, a gold-trimmed coat that swept the ship's deck, and a slender, straight sword in a silver sheath.

With the sensitivity to magic lent him by the partial dose of dust still sparking through his blood, Japheth saw a translucent, greenish glimmer to the captain's skin, as if just below its surface, a scalelike contour yearned for release. The captain liked to joke about his "unclean parentage." Perhaps it was no joke.

Thoster closed the distance between them, apparently as

comfortable in the dark as Japheth. Another hallmark of the man's tainted blood, the warlock supposed.

"Any more sightings of your pretty little 'ghost girl'?" asked Thoster.

Japheth gave a curt shake of his head.

"Sure you ain't imagined her, bucko?"

"I am certain, Captain."

"Hmmph," snorted Thoster, pulling out a pipe and miniature coal urn from the pocket of his great coat. "I never saw her," he said, as if that was indictment enough of Japheth's claim.

"She manifested once in Behroun's office, and a second time a few days ago, as we boarded. She was standing where I stand now. I told you all this."

"Sure you ain't prone to imagining what just ain't there?"

"I have an . . . acquired sensitivity . . . to things seen and unseen. She is real."

The captain reserved comment as he skillfully lit his pipe with a cherry red ember.

"And she might be dangerous," added Japheth, though he had to admit he hadn't sensed any malevolence in the ghostly image. Mainly, he wanted to draw a reaction from the cocky pirate.

Thoster admonished, "Well, don't go spooking my hands. The tars stand up well enough to most anything the sea'll throw their way, be it a Cormyrean merchantman or sea devils. But they got an out'a proportion fear of ghosts and spirits of the dead." He shrugged and puffed. The glint in his eye belied his easy words. He was telling Japheth to keep quiet about the topic, or else.

The warlock replied, "I am on this ship as Behroun's agent. I don't much care what your crew thinks or fears. If I feel something endangers the mission, I will eliminate that threat. No matter its source."

"Easy, son. All I'm asking is you restrict ghost talk to me or my first mate, Nyrotha."

"I'm not a fool."

Another puff of smoke drifted into the night air, then, "Some say all who walk the crimson road are fools."

Japheth felt a flush warm his face. How had he come to this, that the words of a pirate could shame him? He said, "Behroun warned you would attempt to bait me, Thoster. For your own sake, hope you do not succeed in rousing my ire."

"Oh, ho!" laughed the captain. "Think I already have!"

Japheth turned away to look past the ship's prow and the open sea that reflected a million glittering stars. He could feel Thoster's amused regard on his back.

"Come, my friend, don't be so sour! We've both knocked around the dingy corners of this bad old world, haven't we? Who don't have their vices, eh? If you knew half what I pollute myself with, you'd wonder how I rise each day from my cot!" Thoster loosed a hearty laugh.

Japheth said to the night, "I have witnessed the wholesale reaping of thousands who walked, screaming, to the end of the crimson road. I beheld the terror of the gnashing teeth that rim that final abyss, the maw of a demonic god-beast. Those before me walked onward, shrieking in mortal terror for their immortal souls. They marched off the edge. They were sucked down into that awful darkness and were consumed. Snuffed out forever."

The warlock turned back to Thoster and asked, "Have you ever seen anything like that, Captain, in this 'bad old world'?"

The captain was silent for a moment. Japheth decided he'd managed to push the old salt back on his heel.

Thoster asked, "How's it you still live? Behroun told me you've walked the road for a decade or more. You should've perished years ago, ain't that right?"

It was Japheth's turn to laugh. "The fey spirits I commune with provide me with more than the words to curse the heart, still beating, from the chest of an enemy."

Thoster frowned, his easy manner finally dissipating. The captain recognized Japheth's veiled threat. He began, "Listen, if you—"

An ululating scream interrupted Thoster's response.

The yell of pain and terror resounded. Another cry followed. "Ghost! A ghost is killing Dorlan!"

CHAPTER EIGHT

The Year of the Secret (1396 DR)
Green Siren *on the Sea of Fallen Stars*

Heaps of black stone lay tumbled in plank silos in the moist confines of the ship's hold. A brownish fungus had a good start across the slick piles, an indication that the heavy ballast hadn't seen much rotation in recent months.

Begrimed barrels, filled with liquid barely more palatable than seawater, stood two high along the starboard wall under reams of white sailcloth folded on top. Along the hold's port wall, coils of thick hawser hung. Rope was like ship's blood. It could be used for hundreds of tasks, from lashing men and equipment to the deck during storm seas, to repairing sail lines during hot becalmed days when nothing else could be done. Also, rope was useful for punishment. Keelhauling wasn't unknown on the

Green Siren for crew members who defied the captain and his hulking first mate, Nyrotha.

Smaller kegs were stored under lock and key behind an iron portcullis, whose rusty expanse covered the port wall. Harsh fumes proclaimed their rum-filled contents to any who drew near.

A shelf next to the portcullis was stuffed with sheathed swords, spears, hanging crossbows, and a few well-polished shields.

The ceiling was composed of well-fitted planks, except for a wide, square opening directly above, which pierced the ship from the top deck, to mid deck, to hold, to the orlop deck. A rope ladder of rough hawser ran up the side of the opening, connecting all four decks.

Beneath the opening, a sailor lay on the stained, planked floor of the hold.

The sailor quivered and bucked as if possessed, and froth formed at the corners of his mouth. The veins that crisscrossed the exposed flesh of his face, arms, calves, and bare feet flamed scarlet with pain.

Anusha Marhana looked down at the thrashing, barefoot man, a hand to her mouth.

All she had done was touch him!

A dark-haired woman with a scar disfiguring the left side of her face perched half-way down the ladder leading into the hold. Terror robbed the woman of the strength to move up or down. Her ability to scream, however, was unhampered. The scarred woman's mouth was wide with a howl of dread, and her eyes seemed locked at something she saw near her writhing companion.

The scarred woman looked not at Anusha, but at one of the half-silvered shields that hung from the ship's weapon depot. Anusha followed the direction of the woman's terrified vision, into the face of the mirrorlike shield . . . and something looked back at Anusha. A humanoid silhouette of purest black, outlined in erratic white and blue flashes.

She recognized the silhouette as her own.

The first time Anusha had dream-stepped, she hadn't realized it.

She had awakened from what seemed merely an unusually detailed dream. During the dream she'd seen her half brother, Behroun, and the mysterious warlock plotting. True, upon "waking," her mind was almost ready to accept the first wild explanation that occurred to her, that she'd somehow stepped beyond her body and spied on events in the outside world as she slept . . . but she backed away from that explanation quickly enough. She managed to convince herself the experience was mere fancy, born of unsettled sleep.

She was able to hold on to that conviction for all of half a day.

The morning after her first dream, Behroun had summoned her to his office to warn her that enemies of Marhana were sending assassins into the manor. Shadow assassins that burned with a corona of azure fire.

Anusha realized Behroun was describing the very event she had dreamed! How was that possible—had she sleepwalked? No, she'd ghosted through solid objects without effort. It must have been a dream after all, but a dream dreamt beyond the confines of her own head!

Dazed with the insight, she sat dumbly as Behroun recounted his discovery of the assassin.

Nor did she contradict her half brother as he went on to explain how fortunate it was that his agent, Japheth, had been present to drive off the specter. Anusha remembered it was her terror of the darkness hiding under the warlock's cloak that proved impetus enough to awaken her physical body.

Behroun explained he had arranged for Anusha to summer beyond the walls of New Sarshel, where she would be safe from those who wished her ill. He described how getting her out of the city would allow him to concentrate fully on discovering which jealous noble house wished to destroy the soon-to-be-noble House of Marhana.

Anusha rushed back to her suite to pack, cold fear prickling across her body. But it wasn't the thought of assassins that scared her.

Behroun and Japheth had seen her! She had dreamed them, but they saw her, even though they had been awake.

Anusha was again convinced that the dream of the night before had been more than simple fancy. Something of it had been real.

A giddiness brought on by visceral fear stifled her wild packing. She stood frozen amidst a flurry of expensive clothes strewn on the floor and across her bed.

What was happening to her?

Behroun talked of assassins. Had some demonic creature lured her spirit beyond the confines of her body in order to steal it away? It had failed to find her this time, but would she be so lucky again? Would every foray into sleep be a cat-and-mouse game between her and some unseen soul stealer?

Then again, she had seen no evidence of such a creature. To fabricate the existence of a soul stealer to explain her too lucid dream based only on Behroun's talk of enemies of House Marhana was premature.

Especially because her half brother's belief in a potent rival stalking the family was based on his glimpse of her!

Anusha clenched her hands, then loosed them, one muscle at a time. She willed the muscles in her forearms to go slack, then the muscles in her shoulders and neck. She even imagined tiny muscles in her face and scalp drooping into utter relaxation. Her breathing slowed, as did her heart's frantic pace. She tried to push herself beyond the reach of a panic that could not answer her questions or explain what had happened.

When her body was her own again, she sighed and resumed packing.

If she wished to understand what had happened to her, she must think. What was the significance of her dream?

Perhaps it had been a one-time event brought on by some unknowable, arcane event beyond her ken. Or a glimpse provided by fate of a pivotal event that was somehow important to her future. Or, when all was said and done, a giant coincidence?

Anusha wondered if she was spinning fantasies no more likely than her first panicked invention of a soul-stealing stalker.

The only way to know what afflicted her was to experiment. As her tutor so often tried to instill in her, only repeated observation, study, and questions could uncover real knowledge. She needed to explore the experience again.

Her heart's pace quickened once more, but now in anticipation.

Could I, she wondered, walk purposely as a dream in the waking world?

Anusha dumped all the clothing, shoes, and purses she'd pulled from her closets into the great leather-padded travel chest Behroun had ordered delivered to her room. The chest was so large it reminded her of a coffin.

Once the bed was cleared, she settled herself on the soft, pink-hued coverlet and closed her eyes. Beneath the coverlet, her costly feather mattress pressed only lightly into her shoulders, calves, and ankles, but her skirts and blouse made her feel uncomfortably warm and confined. Sounds of distant horns, shouts, and braying animals in the market competed for her attention. The nearer clattering chime of servants working at their own tasks in other parts of the manor jangled at discordant intervals.

Sleep seemed far away.

She tried to evoke the sensation she'd felt when striding unseen down the streets of New Sarshel. She had been neither cold nor warm despite wearing only her sleeping gown. Not the least breath of wind had caressed her cheek, nor had the cobblestones pinched her bare feet. Yes, something like that.

This is not working!

She groaned and left the bed, feeling a sudden pinch as she rose.

"Oh," she exhaled quietly.

A girl still lay half swaddled in the quilt, fully dressed, eyes closed. It was herself.

She had dream-skipped out of her body again!

Anusha gazed down on the sleeping form. Her body breathed in a slow but regular pattern, very much like sleep.

She glanced away from the sleeping body and instead drew her dream hands up before her face. They looked completely normal, maybe a bit hazy if she squinted.

Anusha rubbed her hands together. The sensation was exactly what she expected.

She was further surprised to see her dream self dressed in the very same clothes worn by her sleeping body. Then again, why was she surprised? In a dream, anything was possible, wasn't it? Insofar as her consciousness existed beyond her mind, perhaps dream logic ruled what she could accomplish, just as in regular dreams.

Turning, she tentatively reached for the closed travel chest. She touched it. She could discern its leathery texture. It was cold, and slightly gritty with dust.

With a deep breath, she tried to reach *through* the closed lid.

She pushed her hand through the top of the travel chest as if it were mere smoke. The sensation was not unlike pushing her hand into a thin stream of falling water.

Inside the chest, her hand brushed the heel of one of the shoes she'd thrown into the great piece of luggage. She grasped it and pulled it out. Right through the still-fastened chest.

She could do more than observe the waking world; she could affect it!

The possibilities of what she might accomplish, why, they were endless!

What couldn't she do? She giggled as exhilaration burst up through her chest and throat. She dropped the lone shoe on the travel chest's top and strode to her door, just as it banged open.

Behroun stood there, scowling. Her irritated half brother stood only five feet from her. But he looked right past Anusha as if she weren't there at all. Instead, he fixed his glare on her real, sleeping body.

Behroun growled. "She sleeps when she should be preparing for her trip. If she weren't essential, I'd kill her myself."

Anusha gasped and took an inadvertent step backward. Her hand brushed her vanity mirror poised on a small stand. It shifted, wobbled, then fell to the tiled floor. It shattered with a violent, crystalline retort.

Behroun started. He swiveled his head back and forth, his eyes narrow and searching, his breathing accelerating. He took a half step toward the shattered mirror, then seemed to think better of it. Instead, he spun around to look back into the hallway.

"Who's there?" he demanded, his voice's normally basso rumble rising in pitch.

Getting no answer, Behroun returned his regard to the broken mirror, then to her sleeping form. His composure was as broken as the glass. He grimaced, then stalked off, rather too quickly for his dignity.

The scene would have been comical, Anusha thought, if Behroun hadn't just offhandedly revealed his desire to see her dead. He was talking figuratively, right?

She wondered.

She'd watched him utter those words, thinking himself unobserved and free to reveal his inner self. Anusha judged he'd meant them.

"You bastard," she breathed, as fear shivered her own composure.

She couldn't deny reality any longer. Her half brother was a perfect villain, as she'd always suspected but refused to ponder.

He was no fitting heir to Marhana.

"If I help him, am I any better?" Inaction on her part was as good as helping Behroun achieve his ends. His actions threatened to stain her parents' memory, with her as his unwitting accomplice.

Unless she took a stand.

A new surety of purpose enveloped Anusha.

She nodded her head, thinking yes, I will obey Behroun's command to leave the manor. But I'll choose my own destination!

He wouldn't be able to use her heritage to advance his claims of nobility. As little noble blood as she possessed, less flowed in his debauched veins.

And why shouldn't she depart on her own road? Although, her best bet would be to set herself actively against Behroun's schemes.

A smile curled across her lips. "You'll see, Brother. Or, actually, you won't!"

With her dreamer's ability to walk unseen, like a ghost even, dangers she would normally shrink from were transformed in her mind's eye.

Imagine, she thought, what sights I can witness, safe from all harm, only needing to awake to find myself safe back in bed!

She could go anywhere from the safety of her room!

Except that wasn't right. She recalled the very first time

she walked knowingly in a lucid dream. She had dream-stepped down toward the docks, a fair distance from her sleeping body. Only to be yanked up short before she quite made the distance.

Despite her inexperience with her ability, she thought it likely her dream form could reach only so far. What was the radius she could travel from her sleeping body before her dream self's connection became too attenuated? A mile or two, the dock experience suggested. She needed to experiment to discover her exact range, but it wasn't enough to allow her to stay safe at home.

If she desired to dream-step into danger, her real body would have to be somewhat close too.

Later that day, using her dream form, Anusha slipped unseen into Behroun's office and altered a bill of lading for the merchant ship *Green Siren* to include her travel chest. A travel chest to be delivered straightaway to the docks. A travel chest that would contain more than clothes—it would contain Anusha too! And a tidy sum of water, rations, and perhaps her journal. Once on the ship, safely packed away in the hold, she imagined she'd have the opportunity to physically emerge from her luggage to get occasional exercise and use the lavatory when no one was watching.

Her plan hadn't quite worked out as she'd hoped.

The barefoot sailor had proved a little too curious about Anusha's travel chest.

She'd seen him poking around a couple of days earlier. To distract him, she had created a ruckus in the aft hold by knocking over a crate half filled with belaying pins. The effort to push over the crate, something her physical body could have accomplished with relative ease, proved almost beyond her, but she'd managed it.

She theorized her dream body didn't have the strength of reality.

The interloper, startled at the sound, had relinquished his interest in the travel chest to investigate the spilled belaying pins. By his cussing response, it was obvious he thought they'd merely been poorly packed, not intentionally spilled. After picking up and stowing the crate, this time with ropes to hold the crates in place against accidental shifting, he'd left the hold. Anusha hoped never to see him again. She didn't know what he'd do if he found her sleeping body in the hold.

It was already disconcerting enough to discover one creature aboard the ship that could see her dream form whenever she drew near it.

The first time she'd tried to leave her cabin in dream form, via the short hallway that connected several staterooms to the upper deck, she'd come across a black dog. Tied with only enough slack to roam the hallway, the dog was obviously set to guard the approach to the captain's cabin at the end. When she'd dream-stepped toward it, the dog's ears had come up and its tail had gone down. It broke into a low, rumbling growl. It fixed her with its eyes and bared its teeth, warning her to keep her distance. The animal scared her for a moment, before she recalled she didn't possess a physical body the guard dog could bite.

Still, she felt sorry for the dog. She began feeding the guard dog bits of meat she stole from the constantly simmering stewpot in the galley. After only a day, she'd managed to calm the creature so much that her immaterial presence elicited a happy whine and wagging tail instead of vicious growls. Not knowing if it already had a name, Anusha called it Lucky.

Besides Lucky, she also suspected Japheth might be able to see her, as the *Green Siren* put out from port. The man's gaze seemed to meet hers. She'd stopped, appalled. But he took no action other than stare at her, his expression somewhat bemused. She immediately forced herself awake back in her travel chest, her breathing suddenly coming too swift for the enclosed space.

After a few days thinking about those dark, mysterious eyes, she worked up enough courage to seek out the warlock.

She'd entertained a little fantasy that she would reveal her stowaway status on the ship to the man. Despite knowing nothing of Japheth, she felt a slight twinge of . . . interest. But his lethal habit! How terrible. She wondered how he was able to control its symptoms. Perhaps she had mistaken what she'd seen in the curio shop in New Sarshel.

One thing was certain—loneliness weighed upon her like an anvil. After four days of speaking only to Lucky, she yearned for conversation and companionship more than food. Well, the fact that the rations she'd packed with her sleeping body in the travel chest were beginning to taste like chalk wasn't helping her mood.

She'd been dream-stepping across the upper decks by starlight, looking for Japheth, when dread tingled on her neck. Not knowing from whence it came, she descended to check on her body, only to find the inquisitive sailor had returned. He was hunched over her travel chest once more, this time inserting a pry bar under the travel chest's lid. With him was another sailor, a dark-haired woman with a terrible scar.

Anusha dashed forward and instinctively reached to grab the man's arm. Unlike all her recent practice with inert objects, her attempt to interact with a living creature failed. Her hand slipped right off the interloper.

Desperate, she reached for the man with both hands, thinking to grab the too curious investigator by his collar and haul him backward. Instead, her hands "slid" into his back, and she'd touched something slick and warm that had pulsed *thub-dub, thub-dub, thub-dub* . . .

The man screamed with a throaty, awful tone, fell backward onto the floor, and began convulsing.

The scarred woman looked at Anusha's image in the polished shield and screamed, "Ghost! A ghost is killing Dorlan!"

Anusha took another moment to gaze at her own terrifying image in the polished shield. A ghostlike image stared back, a burning silhouette in a girlish dress. If she didn't know better, she'd scream seeing herself too. Especially if one of Anusha's companions lay insensate upon the floor.

But Anusha was not a ghost, nor did she mean anyone harm. Normally, Anusha couldn't even bring herself to hurt spiders scuttling around the corners of her suite. Her grazing contact with the sailor's . . . insides . . . was an accident. He didn't deserve what she'd done to him, whatever that was.

Or did he?

The truth was, both the screaming woman and the convulsing man were pirates, not sailors. She'd overheard both Japheth and Behroun say it, and other evidence she'd found on the ship the last few days confirmed it.

The man and woman had probably done a lot of terrible things. Perhaps they deserved a little pain, if not something more drastic, in return. Perhaps she should reach up and quiet the woman too, before she drew a response. It wouldn't do to draw more people down here, wondering why one travel chest didn't show up on the hold manifest.

But she couldn't bring herself to follow through.

Besides, already voices echoed from the decks above, yelling questions. The ship was alerted that something strange was in the hold. Nothing she could do now would change that; she would only make things worse by attacking the woman.

A chill of foreboding touched the back of her neck. If her sleeping body was discovered, they'd forcefully wake her. Then what? Would they tie her behind the ship to drag through the cold, shark-filled water until she drowned or died of cold? Did pirates really do that?

Yes, of course they did.

Anusha moved until she stood just a few feet from the polished shields. With the new angle, she could no longer see the screaming woman's distorted image in any of the shields; hopefully, neither could the woman see her. Just to be safe, Anusha reached out and struck all three shields to the floor. They clattered loudly, and the pirate screamed the louder.

Bobbing shapes, visible around the edges of the hold opening, resolved as the heads of watchful, muttering pirates. They gazed down at their crewmates with varying degrees of surprise, humor, and real fear. None of them had seen Anusha's reflection.

A new voice blared down, "What's all this then, Brida? What's wrong with Dorlan? I wager you stuck him, but are trying to claim it's spirits that done it. Am I right?"

Anusha saw the speaker peering down from the top deck, the toes of his boots overhanging the square opening. The elaborate hat revealed the man as Captain Thoster.

The woman on the ladder, apparently named Brida, kept her eyes fixed on the fallen shield in which she'd glimpsed Anusha's dream image. Brida exclaimed in a fear-coarsened voice, "No, sir! It was a ghost! I saw it myself, right after it got Dorlan—right there!" She pointed. Her arm shook as she tried to indicate where she'd seen the "ghost."

Anusha took a few more steps away from the fallen shields, then paused. What would Captain Thoster make of the claim?

The captain turned his head and spoke to someone standing just back from the opening, his voice not loud enough for Anusha to hear his words. It sounded like a question.

Then a cloaked shape appeared at the edge of the hold access. Her breath caught slightly. It was Japheth!

Even from two decks below, Anusha could see Japheth's eyes gleamed red. His gaze locked with her own. Fear thrilled down her spine and her stomach tightened.

A third shape appeared next to Thoster, a woman dressed in a bone white sari wielding a scarlet-glyphed wand.

It was Seren, the *Green Siren's* mercenary wizard.

Thoster complained to Japheth and Seren, "I don't see anything."

Japheth looked up at the captain and the wizard, then back down into her eyes, still silent. Could he see her, or was she imagining it?

Seren traced symbols in the air with her free hand. Where her fingers passed, lines of magical energy persisted moments before fading. Syllables of pure arcane magic tumbled from Seren's lips. Her eyes flashed with a glint of citrine light.

"There!" said Seren, gesturing with her wand down at Anusha. "I see it now—an apparition! The spirit of a drowned woman, perhaps, lingers in your hold, Captain."

Anusha cursed. She nearly woke herself . . . but then thought, I've got to lead them away from my travel chest!

Instead of retreating, Anusha ran to the steps of the ladder and climbed. She slipped past the still petrified Brida on the broad rope rungs without touching her.

Seren cried, "It ascends; it attacks!"

Seren backed out of Anusha's view, as did Thoster, his features betraying bafflement and a hint of concern. Japheth merely cocked his head and observed. There was no doubt he saw her; his eyes didn't leave her as she climbed, and she ascended quickly. Without any real weight, rising required hardly any effort. She wondered, even as she clambered onto the top deck, apparently in full sight of Japheth, if she needed a ladder to ascend at all. She'd had dreams of flying when she was younger. Maybe if—

Seren hadn't run away; she'd merely retreated a few steps to cast another spell. The war wizard threw out her free hand,

and from her fingertips sprang a tremendous stroke of blinding purple-white lightning.

Anusha screamed as obliterating, mind-shattering pain coursed through her naked, unprotected soul.

CHAPTER NINE

The Year of the Secret (1396 DR)
City of Nathlekh

A remarkable bridge provided access to Nathlekh. Not long ago, no such bridge had been required.

A decade earlier, a slow but inexorable earth movement thrust a majority of the city's Shou ward several hundred feet higher than the rest of the city. Hundreds of structures along the edges of the fault were destroyed. By chance, the destroyed structures were mostly the homes of non-Shou, though the Shou faced their own share of loss. When the earth stopped moving, the survivors slowly forgot their fear, especially those whose homes, mansions, and businesses remained. As many pointed out too, the new city heights provided an unexpected but welcome defensive stance against a landscape suddenly more dangerous than ever before.

Thus, once the sky fires, earth movements, and attacks by plaguechanged monsters subsided, a collection of the city's Shou nobles poured a large portion of their considerable wealth into the creation of the bridge.

The Dragon Bridge supported a wide and thick stone span that sprang from the earth near the piers on Long Arm Lake to rise in a diagonal line all the way up to the Sky District. The Dragon Bridge was named for its supporting arches, each of which took the form of a sculpted, sinuous stone dragon. Each successively larger stone dragon bore the weight of its span section in a unique fashion—some on arched backs, others in wide maws, and even one, who stood closest to Nathlekh's stone column, in clawed hands raised high above its head as it reared on its hind legs.

A series of three massive, gated checkpoints along the bridge's span guarded against attacking ground forces, or, as happened on occasion even more than a decade after the Spellplague, groups of homeless refugees. Each gated wall contained barracks for a company of bridge guardians commanded by a gate captain.

Raidon Kane ascended the Dragon Bridge in the back of a cart drawn by two donkeys, driven by an old Shou farmer. Raidon silently wondered if he were, in truth, being brought to Nathlekh as the farmer claimed. Last time he'd been here, there'd been no Dragon Bridge.

It seemed impossible that such a dramatic change could overtake the city in little over a decade. Then again, the changes that occurred while the blue fire raged defied reason. In comparison to what he'd seen in Starmantle, Nathlekh's uplift hardly seemed worth mentioning.

His foot cramped suddenly, as if to rebuke him for recalling the awful image of Starmantle and the ghoul-like aberrations that inhabited it. He wondered if the wound would ever completely heal. Even now, wrapped in linens provided by the kindly farmer's wife, his foot seeped fluids.

Each new day, he concentrated all his healing ability on the limb, attempting to reknit more of the lost skin and sensitivity to touch. Each day, he convinced himself he made a little more progress.

In truth, the wound was much improved. Raidon might have walked this final distance into Nathlekh today, probably with just a minor limp. But the solicitous farmers, who'd found him crawling amid their turnip beds a tenday earlier, who'd nursed him back to health in their modest dwelling, wouldn't hear of him walking so soon. They offered to take him up to Nathlekh by donkey cart. In the end, he'd gratefully accepted.

The biggest mystery of all was his location. He was far closer to the city when the farmers found him than he should have been.

The last thing he recalled was falling asleep in the rain on top of a hard-won bluff near Starmantle. Even upon reaching the safety of the bluff's top, he half suspected he would never see another day.

But he survived. When he opened his eyes next, it was to a cool sunrise. There was no bluff, no burning forest, and no rain. He lay in a turnip field. He couldn't recall anything between falling asleep and waking along the edge of a farm. A turnip farm that turned out to be nearly two hundred miles west of his last location just outside Nathlekh!

Raidon wondered again if he were going insane. It could be he was losing his memory before his mind.

Or perhaps the Spellplague described to him by the ghouls had so altered the landscape that cities and other previously fixed points had become unstuck from their old foundations. He didn't have enough information to rightly judge.

A new thought struck him. Perhaps the Cerulean Sign had something to do with it. Had the symbol, now spellscarred into his flesh, somehow contrived to move him toward his unconscious goal while he lay at death's door?

Sometimes it seemed he could almost discern a voice speaking his name . . .

Raidon pushed these speculations from his head. Right now, all that mattered was finding Ailyn. He tried to imagine in what circumstance he'd find her. His anxiety over what had become of the girl was more painful than his throbbing foot.

They ascended the great dragon-supported bridge. As the cart approached the third and final gate, a gate guard signaled the farmer to stop his cart.

Words penetrated Raidon's apprehension. The gate guard was saying, ". . . only. Turn around and take your cargo with you, I said. Be glad I do not fine you."

"What is this nuisance?" Raidon spoke up. "Why are you holding us up? This man has no cargo today but me. He is due no merchant fees."

The guard sneered and returned, "In these dangerous times, non-Shou who wish to enter Nathlekh can only do so with an invitation."

"But this man . . ." The guard's implication struck home. The guard referred to Raidon, not the farmer.

Raidon began again, "My father is a son of the east, and he raised me in Telflamm, some thirty . . . nay, forty years ago. But disregard that; I am a resident of Nathlekh. I kept my residence here before the Spellplague. My daughter lives here even now. You cannot deny me entry to my home."

The guard tried to meet Raidon's gaze. And failed. Apparently he was unused to opposition from people in donkey carts. He scowled. "Stay here. I'll get the captain." The man stalked off.

Raidon usually passed as Shou, but sometimes strangers noticed his fey ancestry. His long-absent mother's blood manifest in him only faintly, but was visible to those sensitive to such differences. Raidon's ears were ever so slightly pointed, the shape of his skull was perhaps narrower than other Shou, and his bearing was straight, though no straighter than any other practitioner of Xiang Do. He thought of himself as Shou. Usually, his mother's blood didn't cause any problems . . . except sometimes among other Shou.

The farmer ventured, "The city folk have seen too many horrors during and after the Year of Blue Fire. They outlawed refugees and fey from entering the city five years ago. Xenophobia and nationalism grip even those who were once counted as wise."

Raidon grunted.

Normally when he suffered such slights, he imagined his mind a depthless pool of water in which insult, injury, and pain were feeble pebbles, easily swallowed.

Today his foot hurt, and he was worried about his daughter.

His focus was askew, and without its calming influence, he anticipated the possibility of the captain proving difficult. Raidon imagined what he might do in response. The teachings of Xiang Temple stirred, scolding him for holding himself beyond their guiding principles. Raidon clenched his fists, then allowed them to relax a finger at a time, exhaling as he did so.

The captain strode up with the hateful guard in tow. The captain was a tall Shou in laminated mail. He gave Raidon an extended look, then said, "Allow these through." He turned and stomped back to the commandery.

The original guard's frown deepened and he muttered, "You don't fool me. Don't think this is over." With that, he stepped aside and allowed them to proceed. The man's hate-filled stare followed them until the side of the gate blocked Raidon's view.

Once inside, the farmer let Raidon down from the cart. The farmer wished him luck in finding his child. Raidon nodded, thanking the man. He did not dishonor the man's generosity by offering payment. Sincerity was enough reward for those raised according to eastern traditions.

As the sound of the creaking cart diminished into the

distance, Raidon studied Nathlekh's vista. But his thoughts were on Ailyn. What had come of a child so young, left alone save for paid servants, in the face of the greatest calamity of the age without a parent's guidance?

Nothing good, his apprehension insisted.

His worry proved unbearably accurate.

Three days later, Raidon's search concluded at the foot of a four-foot-high, hardened clay structure resembling a beehive. All around him were similar structures. Clusters of clay markers of various dimension protruded from the ground, though the largest ones were central, and the smaller ones spiraled around them.

Raidon stood in Nathlekh's "city of the dead," where the deceased were interred.

He stood before one of the smallest clay markers, a desolate and broken man.

It was Ailyn's grave.

From an inner pocket of his jacket, he pulled with shaking hands a weathered, corroded bell.

He whispered, "I brought this for you, as I promised . . ."

He laid the gift before the marker. The tinkling, glad sound it made drew hot tears to his cheek.

Grief squeezed his heart. His chest was a hollow, gasping emptiness. He could barely draw in air, his throat was so tight.

Raidon had learned Ailyn perished in the first tremors preceding Nathlekh's sudden rise in altitude. She'd been dead more than ten years.

That knowledge did nothing to lessen Raidon's grief.

The staff he'd paid to watch over her in his absence had scattered to the four winds after her death, but Raidon had found one working in a scullery. This one described Ailyn's fate to

Raidon in shaking, terrified tones.

The monk wondered again what thoughts had flashed through her head, as the walls of their dwelling collapsed, and the servants had rushed from the domicile, leaving her alone. Had she cried out for him?

An anguished sob escaped Raidon, and he collapsed across the grave marker.

According to Shou tradition, if surviving relatives and descendants pay sufficient respect to their dead, the dead in their turn exercise a benevolent influence over the lives and prosperity of their family. Thus it was not uncommon for a Shou household to set aside a small area called a shrine, where small carved representations of one or more dead relatives were set. While a few shrines were populated with a plethora of figures with a one-to-one correspondence to dead ancestors, most Shou households kept only a single figure to represent all those loved and lost.

In his absence, Raidon hadn't been able to see to it that this simplest and oldest Shou tradition of mourning was followed.

Even after her death, he had disappointed his adopted daughter, Raidon thought, his head pressed against the cool clay of Ailyn's grave marker. He was despicable.

It was as if scales dropped from his eyes, revealing Raidon to himself with hideous new understanding. All his philosophy and mental disciplines, his Xiang Do and pride in his skill—were these anything more than crutches he used to hold up his own ego? No. They were but facades that hid his true, demonstrated deficits for the things that mattered most in the mortal world. He'd allowed his "monster hunting" and vapid search for his long-vanished mother to distract him from the one thing in his life with true meaning.

His daughter.

His dead daughter.

Raidon screamed, clutched at his queue and pulled, thinking he would rip it out.

"Raidon!"

The monk paused. Who'd spoken? His grief had broken his mind, and now he hallucinated. The idea of descending into the innocence that madness offered was sickening and appealing in equal measure.

"Raidon, look to the cemetery entrance," came a voice from nowhere. The voice had a familiar cadence.

His overmastering sorrow couldn't prevent his eyes' quick flick upward. He saw through the press of clay markers to the cemetery's granite entry arch.

A small mob of people poured through the graveyard gate, chanting a slogan over and over, though not in any particular harmony. The unruly group was led by none other than the guard who'd tried to refuse the monk entry into Nathlekh. The guard was not wearing his official tabard of the city—instead, a liquor-stained smock.

The slogan they chanted abruptly became intelligible to Raidon: "No fey in Nathlekh! No fey in Nathlekh!"

A distant part of himself was surprised how quickly his desolation ignited to red fury.

Before he quite realized it, Raidon was striding toward the mob. His hands itched to strike something, and these small-minded bigots had just volunteered to be his targets. That which remained of his training attempted to forestall his path. But Raidon's impulse would not be quelled.

Ailyn was dead because he'd failed her. What else mattered?

When thirty paces separated the mob from Raidon, the guard called for the chant to cease with an upraised fist. He began, "The new kingdom of Nathlan does not accept non-Shou! Especially not Shou with blood polluted by the half-breed elves! I told you before to stay out. Since you were too arrogant to listen, we . . ." The guard's shouted speech trailed off. The mob around him continued their inane chant.

The monk continued his steady advance, eyes fixed on the guard. The smoldering height of fury burning in Raidon's visage wasn't the reaction the guard expected. He tried to retreat, and failed. The press of his riled-up followers pinned the man in place.

Realizing his danger, the guard yelled, "He is about to attack—grab the outlander!" The man's voice squeaked with alarm.

The rabble's chant turned into a roar as they streamed forward. The guard stayed back, his fear ebbing as the mob blocked Raidon. The guard's brave face returned, and he called out something in a jeering voice, but his words were lost in the screaming mob's imprecations.

A red-faced, screaming Shou grabbed at Raidon's new silk jacket. Another in pleated corduroy tried to club the monk with a rusted mace. A boy scratched at his face with painted but chipped fingernails.

Raidon evaded the grab with a counterpunch that dropped the Shou, and a simultaneous kick sent the mace spiraling into the face of a third man, who crumpled. The boy laid two long welts down his cheek, but his attention was already shifting to more significant threats.

Two corpulent women rushed him, their hair unrestrained and harpy-wild, their meaty fists gripping sharp cooking implements. Simultaneously a hard-faced smith, still in his singed smithy apron, came up behind Raidon with a hammer. Raidon bobbed around one woman's flailing knife and arrested the smith's hammer swing with a palm-thrust to the smith's shoulder with his right hand. With his left arm, he caught the other woman at the elbow with his own, joint to joint as if preparing to do a jig, then swung her around by turning his own body. He flung her down into the path of two new attackers: dockmen with boat hooks. The woman tripped one of the men and distracted the other long enough for Raidon to leap to the top of a nearby clay marker. His damaged foot burned, but Raidon's anger flamed hotter.

Above the fray he saw the original guard, who still hadn't moved as the mob surged to do his bidding. The guard's gaze jerked up and fixed on his nemesis. Raidon pointed a finger at him and shook his head slowly back and forth. It was a promise that no matter the obstacles, Raidon would not be denied his target.

The man's face paled, but he waved back to the cemetery entrance. An actual force of Nathlekh guardsmen in uniform was assembling there, and the man seemed to take confidence from that sight. The guard yelled. Raidon made out his words above the mob's din by reading his lips. "If you hurt me, you'll face them!"

Raidon soundlessly mouthed back, "I don't care." Then he bounded over the heads of the reaching throng to another clay marker, closing a quarter of the distance between himself and his target.

"Raidon, this man is not responsible for Ailyn's death. If you kill him in your despair, your soul will be stained," came a new voice, somehow audible over the screaming rabble.

It was the same voice that had warned Raidon of the mob's appearance. Whoever or whatever it was, its reasonable advice inflamed his ire all the more. He replied, as he leaped again to a marker a mere ten paces from the guard, "Invisible spirit, mind your own affairs and leave me to mine!"

"Your affairs *are* my affairs, Raidon," came the instant response. "You have become my sole view into the world, and though I am pledged to obey a holder of the Sign, my pledge to the Sign itself is the greater duty. If you force me to it, I must protect its sanctity before your wishes. Past lapses must not be allowed to repeat themselves."

The words of the invisible demon intrigued that small

portion of Raidon's mind not overwhelmed with murderous grief. But he did not pause. The monk hurdled the last of the screaming Shou that surged between him and his target. He charged, leaping high off one last clay monument as if it were a ramp. A flying elbow to the guard's crown would—

An ozone scent and crackle of light appeared in Raidon's line of flight. He spasmed and twisted, violently attempting to alter his body's trajectory in midair. He failed. He passed through the discontinuity's dark orifice and was gone.

Raidon fell through a void littered with a million distant points that sparkled eternal white, ruby, emerald, and sapphire. Before he could gasp, he passed through another discontinuity.

He dropped sideways into weeds lurking around the base of a granite boulder. Disorientation and sunlight blinded him; he wasn't quite able to avoid knocking his head on the great stone.

The pain and unpleasantly loud crack of his skull meeting the rock produced a blaze of light and pain.

His anguish and anger spiraled away into a daze of dulled vision and distracted wit.

He lay where he'd fallen, flat on his back, blinking up at a blue sky streaked with high scudding clouds. Rotating his head to the right, he saw grassy foothills of some unfamiliar, though reassuringly terrestrial, mountain range. No multicolored stars.

He gradually rotated his head to the left, wincing at a muscle strain, and saw more far hills, more miles of empty prairie between. No roads, fields, lone homes, or walled cities lay their straight, artificial lines across his perspective. The uninhabited landscape, in its irregular and unexpected outlines, was a physical balm he absorbed across his entire body. Raidon lost himself for a time, watching the wind blow wave after wave through the green and yellow grass, while white clouds boiled in molasses-slow movements above.

An indeterminate time later, the call of a prairie hawk shook the monk from his inadvertent meditation.

"So I am losing my mind," he said as he sat up. He leaned back against the boulder on which he'd hit his head. From the new vantage, he gained a view of a distant feature he'd earlier missed, and gasped.

A great splinter of rock hung unsupported above the plain. Its lowest point narrowed to a ragged and splintered needle, but the unmoored rock's opposite, upper surface was broad and level. Even from where he sat, two or three miles away, Raidon observed trees, grass, a lake, and even a tiny waterfall feathering off the side of the gravity-defying, floating tract.

"To what realm have I come?" he whispered.

"Changes to Faerûn's landscape, such as the earthmote you see above the plain, are not uncommon since the Spellplague swept through," said a bodiless voice.

"You are still in Faerûn, in the southeastern foothills of the Giant's Run Mountains." It was the same voice as before.

Raidon jumped to his feet, swiveling to see if he could catch a faint gleam or wavering in the air that would betray the speaker's presence.

"I remember you!" yelled Raidon. "I heard you beyond the gates of demolished Starmantle! And again, in . . ." he trailed off. His head still resonated with the thump it received upon his arrival. He sensed some great dread hiding just beyond his attention, biding its time.

"Correct, Raidon. However, Starmantle was not the first time you and I conversed. We spoke at some length many years ago, when you traveled to where my physical body lies. My name is Cynosure."

"Cynosure?" The name was familiar, but he couldn't recall why.

"Yes. You visited me in Stardeep several years before the Year of Blue Fire. You accompanied Kiril Duskmourn on her return to the citadel dungeon where she once served as Keeper."

"Stardeep!" exclaimed Raidon. The threads of memory connected, and he remembered.

Cynosure was an artificial entity. A golem, but more than that.

He . . . it? It was an immense humanoid forged of crystal, stone, iron, and more exotic components, though when Raidon had met the golem, it was rusted, pitted, and stained by centuries of existence.

Cynosure was a golem whose sophistication eclipsed all other artificial constructs. It stared unblinking into the containment fires of Stardeep's inmost prison cell. Raidon had seen the golem descend into that cell and do battle with the thing housed there. A thing called the Traitor.

The monk remembered the design fused onto Cynosure's metallic chest—the Cerulean Sign. The placement was similar to the one Raidon himself now sported.

"How is it I hear your voice? Are you not restricted to Stardeep's buried corridors?"

"I remain so bound; however, I can act through any suitably prepared vessel, even far from Stardeep. Somehow, I can now also manifest my attention and some few surviving magical abilities of Stardeep through you."

"Through me? What abilities?"

"Speech, for one. Also, I teleported you from Starmantle to the edge of Nathlekh when you were hurt a few tendays ago, and again just now to pull you out of Nathlekh. Unlike speech, however, moving you such great distances saps my finite and failing reserves."

"You . . . pushed me through a portal? Without an actual portal gate? And without being physically nearby?"

"Yes. In a way, I am physically with you. Special circumstances allow you and me to interact, Raidon, though you and me only. I could not transport another, unless they were with you. My connection with you is possible because of the new fusion between you and your Cerulean Sign."

Memory painted an image of his amulet dissolving in ravening blue fire. He recalled the agony as the lingering symbol branded him. He dropped his gaze and opened the silk jacket he'd purchased in Nathlekh. The symbol of his amulet still marked him, its size scaled up to cover his entire upper chest, as if the Sign's power was sufficient to expand to whatever medium that contained it.

Cynosure's voice continued, "The Spellplague stitched your amulet's power into your mind and body. Raidon, you have become a breathing manifestation of the Sign."

The monk said, "In Starmantle, I was able to tap the Sign's power when aberrant ghouls attacked me. But I did so almost instinctively . . ."

The disembodied golem's voice said, "Your life energy has invigorated the symbol. Or else the Sign's potency was magnified by the Spellplague. Others touched by that changing flame, if they survived at all, were scarred with strange new abilities. In any case, your first use of the Sign drew my attention. As you know, I am also bound to the Cerulean Sign."

Raidon lifted his gaze again to the unsupported, earthen mass hovering above the horizon, though his mind traced images more fantastic. He suddenly remembered that Cynosure was more than a single golem. Stardeep's Keepers had told him Cynosure's sentience was housed simultaneously in several golem bodies distributed throughout the dungeon of Stardeep. The golem's arcane awareness stretched insubstantially between dozens of bodies scattered around the halls, tunnels, and galleries. Cynosure, a sentient construct with multiple vantages, was the perfect warden of the dungeon stronghold where a Traitor served his eternal sentence.

"You have many vantages on the world, then?"

"No longer. Raidon, you are my one remaining contact

beyond my trapped body. I can see and interact with the world in and around your physical location, as I once could with my other lesser selves in Stardeep, before it was destroyed."

Raidon said nothing for a moment as he wrestled with the implications of the golem's last words. Finally he replied, "Do you try to provoke me? What do you mean? Certainly Stardeep can't be destroyed, else the Traitor would be freed or dead. Either way, that would have ushered in a disaster."

"What other word would you use to describe the Year of Blue Fire?"

Raidon flinched and said, "You suggest that the prisoner of Stardeep, the Traitor they called him, the high priest for some forgotten group of aboleths, was released, and the Spellplague was the result? Not true. It was the goddess of magic's murder that collapsed the Weave and initiated the damned Spellplague. So I confirmed in Nathlekh while I searched for . . ." The monk trailed off, his concern over Stardeep eclipsed by the hollow recollection of his daughter's fate.

Raidon slid down the boulder's rough side until he sat once more, his ears filling with an inchoate roar.

Cynosure was talking. "Many threads were pulled when Mystra died. Most accept the goddess of magic's death touched off already unsteady zones of wild magic. But in the past, when the previous goddess of magic perished, no Spellplague resulted. I believe other factors contributed to the virulence of what finally occurred. I believe the Traitor's escape, timed uncannily close to Mystra's murder, was an additional constituent that co-generated the Spellplague."

Raidon heard the words, but their meanings did not distract him from an image of Ailyn playing in the courtyard with a passel of tame city cats.

The golem's voice droned on. "On the other hand, the disaster the Keepers of the Cerulean Sign most feared, the appearance of the Abolethic Sovereignty, never materialized. But perhaps our error was in assuming the Sovereignty would immediately return. Perhaps the Spellplague was a necessary ingredient, required to condition reality enough to permit the great old aboleths' return. Perhaps the Year of Blue Fire was so virulent that it reactivated previously dormant fossil dimensions . . ."

"Raidon, are you listening?" demanded Cynosure.

The monk followed Ailyn through several more happy memories, a path that concluded at a clay marker with his daughter's lonely name stenciled on it.

"Leave me, Cynosure," he murmured. "I grieve."

No further word emerged from the air. Raidon was alone with his loss.

CHAPTER TEN

The Year of the Secret (1396 DR)
Green Siren *on the Sea of Fallen Stars*

What infantile game is Behroun playing, wondered Japheth.

A porthole leaked watery daylight into the warlock's cramped cabin. A ratty travel duffel lay next to him on the cot. Japheth's things lay scattered from the duffel's open mouth. Empty vials, elixirs, crushed essences of this and that, and his other tools littered the rumpled blanket. A large travel chest sat opposite the cot and took up a majority of the cabin's floor space. He'd had it delivered from the hold to his room, claiming it was his own. The chest's side was stenciled with the Marhana crest.

No one had connected the "ghost attack" with the bulky piece of luggage open before him.

No one except Japheth. He had watched the

altercation of a few hours earlier unfold in a daze, but that was normal when walking the crimson road. It was just that detachment from reality that enhanced a walker's sensitivity to psychic and spiritual phenomena. Thus he'd seen the shadowy figure rise out of the hold. He'd observed when it was struck down by Captain Thoster's war wizard.

When the apparition shriveled beneath Seren's magical attack, his augmented vision noted a spark of blue fire zip away from where the shape disintegrated. Despite Seren's spell of seeing, she missed the fleeting movement. But Japheth saw the flame plunge into the side of a large chest in the hold.

Once the hubbub, inquiry, and heated recriminations by fearful crew died down, Japheth descended into the hold to see into which chest the spark had fled.

The chest turned out to be the property of Marhana Shipping.

Behroun hired Japheth to aid Captain Thoster, but also to gather intelligence about Thoster's privateer enterprise to make certain the pirate wasn't cheating Behroun out of more than could be overlooked. Lord Marhana had also apparently sent along a second spy, this one to keep tabs on Japheth himself.

Oddly, the spy Behroun had selected was Lord Marhana's own sister.

The warlock gazed into the open chest at a sleeping girl's features, loose and smooth as she lay nestled amid clothing and waterskins. Bits of food and other detritus lay in the chest with her—she'd obviously been living inside for several days.

Japheth would never have guessed the girl . . . what was her name? . . . Anusha! Japheth wouldn't have guessed Anusha had the proper mental mindset to become a spy. Impossible as it seemed, he couldn't deny the evidence of his eyes: Anusha possessed the same shape as the dark, burning silhouette he'd seen three times now, the last just hours ago when Seren had somehow discorporated the menacing image. If Anusha was its source, he supposed it was lucky she hadn't died in the psychic backlash. On the other hand, perhaps she was hurt in some mental fashion Japheth couldn't overtly observe; he hadn't been able to wake her by saying her name aloud or shaking her.

The warlock had vaguely noticed the girl around the Marhana estate over the last few years, without really paying her too much mind. Lately he noted she had started dressing more like a woman than a child. And why not? She had grown. She must be at least twenty years, come to think of it. An adult, despite how Behroun seemed to treat her. Looking back, he supposed she was held back from the rights and responsibilities of true adulthood, as the children of the privileged often were. If she had been born into the circumstances most faced across Faerûn, she would already be about her chosen trade in a journeyman's capacity, possibly even married and caring for children of her own.

Japheth said, "Anusha, wake up!" She stirred slightly, but did not open her eyes.

She wasn't unattractive. Now that he thought back, he remembered she had essayed a few awkward attempts to engage Japheth in conversation. He'd always cut those moments short. The warlock disliked Behroun so much that he'd instinctively backed away from any interaction with the man's younger sibling.

When he'd thought about her at all, he'd assumed she was a lonely girl to be pitied for her isolation, nothing more. He'd been proved wrong. Her apparent role at Marhana Manor must have been an elaborate ruse to fool anyone who had business with Behroun that Anusha was harmless.

Japheth continued to study her.

He never suspected Anusha might be spellscarred.

"Time to see what you have to say for yourself," he muttered as he snagged a blue vial from the litter of eccentric objects on his cot.

He popped the vial's stopper and poured its fizzing contents into the girl's mouth. The scent of honey and orange blossoms filled the restricted cabin. He was unconcerned she would choke on the fluid, despite her slumber. It was an elixir of healing; he could not harm her with the fluid even if he wanted to.

Anusha's eyes opened, bleary and wincing away from the light. She blinked a few times, then tracked around until she focused on Japheth. Her brows knit, as if someone had just posed her a riddle she couldn't quite solve.

Japheth said, "Hello in there. Anusha, isn't it?"

"Uh . . ." she said, her voice cracking with disuse.

"I must admit, you fooled me. I am in awe of your theatric skill. Still, the job Behroun set you in this ship to accomplish is done. Now that I know you're aboard, you'll not catch me unaware of your scrutiny again. Not that I had planned on double-crossing Behroun . . . though his mistrust wounds me."

"W-what?"

Japheth plunged forward. "What I find far more intriguing is how you pursue your spycraft. How long have you been spellscarred? I didn't think you were caught in the initial wave—of course, if you had been, you would be grossly disfigured, I suppose."

"Spellscarred?"

The girl continued to play her role, so well in fact that Japheth wondered if one or more of his assumptions were incorrect.

Despite himself, he reached out and said, "Let me help you out of there, eh? Then you can tell me your side of things. How your brother put you up to it and all that."

Anusha tried to sit up, groaned, and fell back.

"Take my hand," said Japheth, his palm still proffered.

Anusha took it, and he pulled her into a sitting position. Her fingers were cool and slightly clammy. She relinquished his grip, coughed, ran a hand through her tangled hair, and . . . blushed?

She said, "F-first, you're wrong. Behroun didn't send me. I came on my own; he doesn't know I'm here. This is probably the last place he'll think to look for me. He's a toad."

"A toad?"

"He doesn't care anything about me—only if I can help him get adopted into New Sarshel's lineage of noble Houses. Without me to back up his claim, there's no way they'll let him join their cozy club."

"I see," said Japheth, though he did not. "So why are you here, if he did not set you to spy on me?"

"I had to go somewhere!" She threw up her hands. "Behroun was trying to send me away to the country; he thinks assassins are after me." She snorted.

"Assassins that have a strange, ghostlike silhouette, perhaps?"

She looked down and said, "Yes."

Japheth waited a moment then asked, "A shape you call to do your bidding, am I right? Some sort of spirit of the air that answers and reports to you?"

"No, that shape *is* me," she blurted, looking directly into his eyes for a moment, then glancing down again. "The shape is . . . my dream self. I dream myself out into the world, leaving my sleeping body behind. Usually no one can see me. Except for you. And a guard dog on this ship. And . . . people can see my reflection."

"You're a wizard then, despite your tender years, able to cast spells of scrying."

"No, I—"

"Perhaps you have applied yourself to the mental arts and have learned psionic, remote viewing?"

"Nothing like that!" she protested. "No, it just happened one night. I was having a dream. One of those dreams where you know you are dreaming? And I saw you."

"Me?" He forgot his follow-up inquiry about how Behroun intended to communicate with her while she spied.

"Yes. I was lost in the city I thought a dreamscape. Then I saw you, and I followed you. I thought it was all inside my own head. You walked into an old curio shop, and, um . . ."

The warlock realized she had seen him purchase traveler's dust. Unexpectedly, a sliver of shame touched him. It was his turn to blush.

"Anyhow," said Anusha, "when you left the shop, I followed you back to Behroun's office. I saw you . . . agree to Lord Marhana's demand. I thought it was all a fantasy of sleep. Then I discovered everything I witnessed actually happened. I was seeing the waking world."

Japheth looked at the girl with narrowed eyes. He said, "I don't understand."

Anusha shook her head. "You think I do? It just happened to me. I took a nap, and next thing I knew, I was dreaming myself into the world!"

"Have you had any contact with spellplague?"

She shook her head, but her eyes grew thoughtful. Anusha said, "No, but I've been beset by dreams of burning blue. Isn't that how it looks?"

Japheth nodded. "I think my assessment is correct. You are spellscarred."

The girl shuddered. She said, "The one thing I know for certain is that I saw Behroun when he didn't know I was watching. He is an awful man."

"He has his peculiarities," offered Japheth diplomatically. The girl was a sibling of Lord Marhana, even if only by one parent. And she still could be spinning a great yarn and secretly working with her half brother.

"He is a killer, and I hate him," she declared, staring at Japheth as if challenging him to say differently.

The warlock changed tactics. "So you . . . 'woke' to strange new abilities and learned your brother was a bastard, who—"

"Literally a bastard," she interrupted.

"Yes, right," he sighed. "My question, then, is merely this: how is it that I find you stuffed, of your own accord apparently, into a travel chest on a ship of freebooters allied with your oh-so-hateful half brother?"

"I told you! He was trying to send me away, out of the city. I decided I would go, but somewhere of my own choosing. Somewhere he would never think to look for me. Somewhere I could see things I was never allowed to even imagine while I was kept safe in my suite. Since I can dreamwalk, I thought I could mingle even with pirates and stay safe."

"You sought adventure? I hate to break it to you, but the stories about the exploits of heroes leave out—"

"That's only half of it!" she snapped. "Mostly, I was worried. I wanted to see what Behroun is so excited about. I wanted to know what sort of deal he's going to make with pirates and who knows what else. I'm still loyal to my family name, you know, even if everyone treats me like I'm a child. If Behroun means to do something to drag the Marhana name through tar, I intend to stop him."

"Hmm," mused Japheth. He hadn't expected that sentiment. Perhaps she wasn't as emotionally shallow as he'd initially assumed.

Japheth said aloud, "If your words are not lies to blind me—"

He raised his hand to silence her protest.

"Why are you on board this ship physically at all? If you can dreamwalk, why didn't you just send your dream self to the ship? If we sink, you could have awakened safely on land. Now you'll go down with the rest of us."

"My dream form can stray only a little way from my body. Only about a mile, maybe two. I can't explore the whole world when I dreamwalk—only what's nearby."

Japheth rubbed his jaw, not certain if he believed the girl. He knew of a quick and dirty enchantment that could compel her to tell the truth . . . but if it turned out she hadn't been lying, the act of robbing her of her own volition, however briefly, would turn her against him. That was the problem with such inducements—one never really knew in the first place whether one had properly identified a reasonable target for harsh questions until afterward. That's why enlightened societies frowned on the use of involuntary, magical interrogations or even baser forms of physical torture.

Of course, in these post-Spellplague years, when things were only just coming under control, surviving institutions were not the sticklers for decorum they had been before the Year of Blue Fire.

More to the point, Japheth had worked long and hard on developing a persona that matched his circumstances. That façade he'd created for himself, friendless and cruel, hard to acquaintances and vicious to enemies, would force the truth from the girl in a moment, regardless of consequence.

Why didn't she show more fear? She even knew he walked the crimson road, yet she treated him in a strangely friendly manner, as if she didn't, in truth, fear him.

Japheth decided, for the moment, to act as if he believed Anusha.

"Very well, then, Lady Anusha," he said, surprising himself with the smile in his voice, "let's get you cleaned up and give you a little exercise, eh? You can move about here within my cabin unseen. No one has the key but me."

Japheth drew some fresh water from ship stores and filled a large hand basin for Anusha. He heated the water with a flourish of fire, smiled, and left her to her own devices.

It was tricky given the limited space in the cabin, but she managed a reasonably decent sponge bath. If nothing else, at least she had tendays of clean clothing in her travel case.

She found a hand mirror in the trunk and observed her image in its restricted oval. Presentable, she decided. Her hair was still damp, but she rather liked the look. She imagined it made her seem daring. Anusha wondered if Japheth thought so.

She struck a pose, then laughed. "How about that, warlock? You've found a stowaway who isn't afraid of your mysterious ways."

A voice outside the door silenced her.

"Captain? Can I help you?" It was Japheth's voice, faint as if from some distance away.

A much louder reply sounded right outside the door. "Japheth, ain't you a fair sight; just the man I was looking for. We have a problem."

Anusha stifled a gasp.

"What sort of problem?" Japheth's voice was closer now.

"Something's moving around your cabin. It may be our ghost still devils us."

Anusha began to stealthily gather her unpacked clothes, combs, and other oddments from the floor, cot, and tiny cabinet holding the hand basin. Her belongings were everywhere!

"Captain," came Japheth's voice, "you're right. Behroun sent along a secret spy to watch us. Seren flushed it out, but its presence remains."

She smothered a gasp of surprise.

"Damn me for a kobold!" came Thoster's reply.

"I'm afraid so. Fortunately I recognized the creature's purpose. It is a ghost in truth—the spirit of an executed murderer. Behroun suborned it with necromancy and set it to watch us."

"Beat me with a yardarm!"

"Indeed," returned Japheth. "Just in case the spirit survived Seren's attack, I set a trap for it in my cabin. Lucky I did! I caught it not more than an hour ago. It is held fast in a prism chiseled from a gorgon's heart."

"A gorgon's heart?"

"Dangerous to gaze upon, I know, but not to worry. Such things are extremely effective for holding ghosts and other immaterial wisps. Do you want to take a look? If you take just a quick peek, you should be all right, I suppose. I don't have to warn you what could happen if you stare too long at a prism carved from a gorgon's heart."

". . . no, no Japheth, I can imagine it well enough without taking a gander. Sounds as if you have the spirit well in hand. We can deal with Behroun when we return to Impiltur. Ain't no need to risk the *Green Siren's* captain, eh?"

Japheth laughed in agreement.

"Just see to it you don't let it loose again, eh? And don't speak of this to anyone, not even Nyrotha."

"Of course."

Anusha heard the captain's heavy footsteps recede.

A quiet knock sounded on the cabin door. Anusha unbolted the latch and stood back.

Japheth glided into the chamber and closed the door behind him. There was no place for both of them to stand except within half an arm's length from each other. The warlock smelled of musk and sandalwood.

"You look rested," he said, grinning. His eyes danced, and the brooding lines of his face melted.

"I thought you were giving me up!" she whispered, despite that she wanted to shout.

The warlock laughed, nodding. "I wondered if you could hear what I said. A shade of the truth to make the lie more believable, is all."

"What if the captain had decided to look?"

Japheth shook his head. "I knew he wouldn't. Thoster and his crew will do much to avoid the unquiet dead. Behroun told me the *Green Siren* had an encounter with a ghost ship last year. They lost a quarter of the crew. I suspected the captain would be happy to let me handle the 'ghost spy,' especially after I threw in that nonsense about a gorgon's heart."

"Still," she chided him. She grabbed his upper arm and squeezed.

Japheth looked down at her hand.

Anusha immediately released her hold and said, "Oh, I'm sorry! I didn't—"

"No, no, you can touch me. I don't mind. I mean . . ." Japheth cleared his throat and said, "We shouldn't be embarrassed of a little contact in a close space like this. It's bound to happen."

"Yes," she agreed, wondering what Japheth was really thinking. Her stomach fluttered as if butterfly wings trembled beneath her skin.

"In any event," continued the warlock, with perhaps just a touch of new color on his cheeks, "if you're concerned the captain will drop in unexpectedly, maybe you should slip out of here as a dream and look around the ship every so often, just as a precaution."

"I can't fall asleep on a moment's notice," Anusha replied. "I can only dreamwalk once I'm asleep, and I'm afraid I've been getting too much of that lately. The first time I dreamwalked, it was only after I stayed awake for nearly a tenday!"

Japheth looked thoughtful. He carefully pushed past her to his cot, his shoulder brushing against hers. He said, "See? Bound to happen," he said lightly, then turned his attention to his duffel and its contents.

"You know, Anusha, I could help you fall asleep whenever you wished, instead of waiting for tiredness to overcome you. Then you could dreamwalk at need."

"I could?"

He nodded, an excited smile turning up the corners of his mouth. His hands skimmed over the cluttered containers on his coverlet. He selected one glass bottle filled with a thick purple fluid. He popped the seal, gave a sniff, then recoiled. "This is too strong undiluted . . ." he said under his breath.

"Ah!" Japheth plucked a silver vial from the cot and uncorked it, looked in, and mumbled, "Empty, that's good." He allowed a single drop of the thick purple fluid to fall in.

The warlock grabbed the waterskin from his belt and filled the silver vial to the brim. A puff of white mist escaped the open vial like the exhalation of a panting beast. A smell like blackberries wafted through the cabin. Japheth capped the vial and held it out to Anusha.

She accepted the cold silver thing. She asked, "So what is this exactly?"

"It is an potion of somnolence," said Japheth, as if that explained everything.

"Is it a drug?" Anusha asked.

Japheth's gaze flicked down to the vial in her hand, then back to her eyes. He replied, "It will help you unleash your dream form when you're too provoked to sleep. Just a sip should be enough to send you off to dreamland in less time than it takes to count down from ten. But yes, I suppose you could call it a drug. Use it only when you have time to sleep for several hours. If you don't abuse its use, you'll be fine. But if you're worried, pour it out. I was only trying to help."

Anusha examined the vial, her mind turning over the warlock's gift. Because it was from him, she ultimately decided to keep it. She didn't want to hurt his feelings. And after all, the soporific fluid could prove indispensable in the right situation. It couldn't hurt to keep the elixir.

The morning dawned wet and windswept. Iron gray waves stretched away in all directions, save for the mist-shrouded line to the south. The line was the boundary between the sea and an island.

Foam-spotted wakes stretched away from the shoreline in both directions. Flashes of green fins, black gills, and long, muscular tails were visible even from the *Green Siren's* deck. Countless fish swam just below the surface. The swarm grazed some invisible nutrient, moving now in unison, now in erratic frenzy.

As the *Green Siren* drew closer, the shore resolved into a beach of acrid water, weeds, and brine pools. The polluted-looking sand was vacant but for gray rocks in heaps, oddly scoured rock formations, and a lone tower slick with dark fungus.

Captain Thoster had warned Japheth to expect the old tower, and indeed the small isle on which the tower was situated. He named isle and tower Hegruth. Both had been drowned beneath the surface of the Sea of Fallen Stars for millennia. The receding sea now revealed the forgotten ruin of unknown provenance. Its obscurity and appearance on no terrestrial map made it the perfect place for a clandestine meeting with . . . someone.

Thoster had been less forthcoming about the identity of she who was supposedly going to offer them the deal of the decade, a deal so fruitful it would make Marhana's fortune. Japheth knew their contact was a female by the pronoun Thoster used to describe her, but nothing more.

The warlock turned his gaze away from the tower to scan back along the *Green Siren's* deck. The crew not taking in sail or shipping oars openly stared at the approaching tower, apparently as unfamiliar with the beslimed spire as himself. Captain Thoster stood on the elevated poop deck at the pirate ship's stern. On the captain's left was the doughty helmsman, whose scarred hands gripped the wheel with casual skill. To Thoster's right stood Seren, the war wizard. The woman caught his eye and winked.

Japheth stared back without acknowledging the gesture. Seren was like him in some ways—she had learned, sooner than most others, to master anew the raw arcane energies that permeated the world after all spells went awry. Unlike him, she hadn't cheated by finding an easier route to reclaim arcane magic with drugs and pacts. By Seren's accoutrement, it seemed she had found her way back through study of magic with a vicious, unyielding determination.

He completed his scan of the deck. Nowhere did he detect a wavering, shadowy silhouette with the outline of an impetuous girl. That didn't mean Anusha wasn't present in her "dream form." With her sharing his cabin, he hadn't taken any traveler's dust in two days. Without the heightened sensitivity of the drug, he was blind to her direct presence.

His palms broke out with moist itch, even as his mouth dried. He recognized the signs; he'd gone too long since last he'd stepped foot on the road. He should take a pinch now. Just a single grain, that would be—

He squeezed his eyes shut, slightly disgusted at the sudden veering of his desire. He had resisted the urge to stride the road longer than normal, and now he was out of sorts. The itch on his palms grew more pronounced. Why did he resist the urge?

Anusha was the reason, he admitted.

Why was he suddenly so concerned with how she viewed him? It wasn't like him. Then his cloak fluttered of its own accord, as if something beneath its dark folds sought escape. Had he imagined it, or was his control over the portal stitched into the cloak's hem fraying with his lack of concentration? He couldn't restrain a worried groan.

A voice in his ear interrupted his internal dread. "Are you well, Japheth?"

The warlock blanched and spun around, recognizing the whisper a moment too late to quell his reaction. Anusha had apparently been standing next to him all along.

From the poop deck, Japheth saw Captain Thoster's large hat swivel toward him for a moment, then back to the approaching tower.

Barely moving his lips, Japheth said to thin air, "Do not startle me so. The captain notices my strange antics of late.

I think he's worried about the ghost in the gorgon heart."

He thought he heard a suppressed giggle, nothing else. The girl's physical remove from reality made her rash, he thought.

Then again . . . wasn't he being equally rash avoiding that which was required, if not now, then later? It wouldn't matter what she thought of him if his mind spun free of reason for failing to set spiritual feet on the crimson road.

His shaking hands produced a small, dull tin. From it, he produced a grain of traveler's dust.

"Japheth," came her instant whisper. He ignored the entreaty. He tilted his head toward the sky and dropped the miniscule crystal into his left eye.

The itch faded. His breathing steadied, and his hands ceased their shake. By the time the tin was restowed in the folds of his cloak, he saw the outline of Anusha's dream form fold itself into the scene. He smiled her way, then looked out again past the wooden railing.

The air was like crystal, the sky an open glass, and the water a translucent skin that his enhanced vision easily, joyfully pierced. The many wakes in the water were indeed, as earlier surmised, fish, though swimming among the crowd were several scaled humanoid forms, half hidden among the schools, keeping their heads just below the water's surface. Japheth wondered if those creatures were associated with the entity they were to meet. He mentally shrugged—it didn't matter that much to him at the moment, as the drug's euphoric effect blew through his mind like a gust of cool air.

Something emerged from the tower balcony. Some sort of humanoid, kin to those swimming beneath the surface in front of the tower. He'd made an astute guess.

Though still relatively far, Japheth's dust-enhanced vision saw the figure had a round face surmounted by wide, bulbous eyes that stared back at him, rarely blinking. Its lipless mouth was a long slit bisecting the lower face, closed, though he suspected rows of needle teeth within. The creature wore a gold crown on its head like an artificial crest. Its garments were singularly gold-hued, as was its pincer-headed staff. This must be the . . . female they had come so far to meet.

Captain Thoster's voice rang out across the waves, apparently magically augmented by Seren, "Hail, Nogah of Olleth! We have come, as you asked. Let us parley and see how we may serve each other, and in so doing, serve ourselves!"

The creature replied, her words also supernaturally loud, though blurred and lisped, as if being formed by a vocal apparatus never meant to choke out Common. She said, "Well met, Captain Thoster. Welcome to my abode, again."

The captain barked orders. The anchor was let out. The ship's launch was prepared for a landing party, then carefully lowered over the side. Those going ashore would include the captain, Seren, Japheth, and several nervous crew members.

Japheth just stared, absorbing all the frenzied activity but apart from it. Whorls and swirls of dazzling color intruded upon his vision, and just as reality seemed to waver in favor of a winding road of ruby, Thoster called him over to the side of the ship where they'd lowered the launch. Japheth forced his mind back from the imaginary trip it yearned to take. Instead, he climbed down a knotted rope ladder into the rocking launch.

Anusha's roiling, uncertain outline wavered at the prow. She gazed at the tower, though all aboard the ship but he failed to see her. The crew pulled on the launch's oars, not bothering with putting sail to the single, short mast. Quickly enough, the craft crossed the distance between the anchored *Green Siren* and the squalid shore.

Japheth disembarked. Seawater slopped over the top of his boots and soaked his feet. The odor of decaying fish burned his nostrils. Once the boat was pulled up onto the beach, the landing party made for the base of the tower, Thoster and Seren in the lead, followed by four pirates with their weapons drawn. Japheth brought up the rear. The girl, whose sleeping body still lay in the *Green Siren,* kept him company.

A gaping hole in the tower's base opened onto narrow basalt stairs that circled upward in shallow loops, tracing the tower's circular exterior. When they reached the first landing, the weapon-wielding pirates preceded Thoster and the others into the chamber where their host waited.

The room was moist, and the ceiling was so low the captain's hat threatened to scrape it. As before, Japheth's drug-heightened sensitivity revealed a translucent, greenish sparkle to the captain's skin in a regular, repeating pattern.

The warlock realized the pattern he saw below the captain's skin resembled the fishy scales of the creature standing before them, she who Thoster called Nogah.

Emboldened by his altered state, Japheth broke the mutual silence. "You are no sea elf, that's certain."

Nogah fixed the warlock with her dinner-plate eyes and blinked.

Captain Thoster laughed, then said, "Nay, sea elves ain't been seen much in the Fallen Stars since the Spellplague. Except for Myth Nantar, their cities mostly shook to rubble, and they're keeping beneath the waves—who knows when they'll be back, or if. Nogah here is kuo-toa. She's a 'whip,' which means something like a queen-in-waiting, maybe. Her folks have been gathering in the waters hereabouts ever since they seized Olleth—"

"Captain Thoster," lisped the kuo-toa whip, "your swift arrival is much appreciated. But who are these two?" The creature gestured with her staff toward Seren and Japheth. She didn't react to Anusha, who stood at the kuo-toa's elbow in immaterial guise.

"Nogah, these are the ones I promised who can help,"

said the captain. "Seren is a wizard, and Japheth says he's a warlock."

"They can access arcane magic?" she inquired, her eyes blinking rapidly.

"Yeah, quick studies, they are. I seen 'em both hurl spells, which is better than most the old mages can claim, except for all the liars."

"Good," she crooned.

Seren stepped forward. "Yes, *I* am here to help; I don't know about him." The wizard waved toward Japheth. "Thing is, I don't know with what. The good captain wouldn't tell me. He just kept repeating that meeting you would be worth my while."

The kuo-toa gazed a few more heartbeats at Seren, then swiveled to stare at the warlock.

Japheth's buzzing thoughts finally lined up enough for him to say, "I have the proxy of the shipping magnate, Behroun Marhana of New Sarshel. While I have many talents of my own, I can also call upon my patron's material and financial resources, if I judge what I hear today to be in Marhana's interests."

Nogah rasped something in a tongue Japheth didn't know, then added, "Listen, then, and see."

The kuo-toa gestured toward the balcony opening. "What do you see?" she asked.

Beyond the balcony's stone railing rolled the wide sea. The *Green Siren* rode the swells, and the numberless marine creatures along the shore continued to fulfill ancient drives to eat and propagate. Japheth also saw the other kuo-toa below the surface, much closer now than they had been before. They must be moving closer in case their mistress needed help in dealing with her visitors.

Captain Thoster said, "A whole lot of nothing. So?"

"I see a world ready to be plucked," replied Nogah. Japheth tried to ignore her squishy, lisping inflection to Common, like she was trying to suck the marrow out of a bloody bone with each word. His state of mind made it difficult to concentrate.

She continued, "I see a world crying out for new direction. A world where those who align themselves properly will be rewarded with riches beyond their wildest dreams. What do you say to that?"

"I see that every time I pull alongside a merchant ship and demand the contents of their hold," boasted Thoster.

"Baubles compared to what I offer." Nogah sniffed.

"What exactly *do* you offer?" asked Seren.

"I offer you a measure of protection and even control when I summon up old lords and old races. When I call upon antique powers that dwarf any our world has heretofore known, everything changes. I'm offering you the chance to survive that change, and what's more, profit from it. Perhaps even exercise some measure of control over the events that fate might otherwise dictate."

Neither Thoster nor Seren had an immediate reply. They seemed a little taken aback. Japheth said, "A very kind offer, to be sure. Especially since most of us have just met. You must want something from us, if you're willing to give so much?"

The kuo-toa whip nodded, her eyes blinking rapidly. She said, "Of course."

"If you have the strength to call up these 'old lords and old races,'" queried Japheth, "beings that can reorder the world in the manner you describe, what help from us could you possibly require?"

"Ah, that is the tangle, drylander. I have lost the talisman required to begin. It was stolen from me, and I need help to retrieve it."

"Sure," said Thoster. "Why's it you can't get aid from Olleth itself, a city filled with kuo-toa? Come, Nogah, what need have you for me and folks I can gather?"

"You are perceptive, Captain Thoster. One of the reasons I

enjoy our dealings so much. But your assumption is incorrect; Olleth will not help me. In fact, they want me dead."

"You're a whip. They can't strip you o' that."

"They can. They have. I have been named race traitor, blasphemer, and I've been excommunicated from the Sea Mother's church. No kuo-toa will have anything to do with me, other than try to skin my hide as a trophy."

Japheth held his tongue, even though he could see kuo-toa below the water line with his crimson gaze. Obviously Nogah exaggerated the degree to which her own race reviled her. The kuo-toa he could see there were drawing closer still. Many had moved so close to the tower's base that the warlock could no longer see them below the balcony's floor. The kuo-toa had a strangely feral look to them—their eyes were smaller than Nogah's, more bestial. Strange.

Also, the day's light was waning. A sea mist was rolling in across the waves. Already the *Green Siren* was enveloped and lost to sight. The fog's leading face churned onward, sending streamers of mist snaking toward the shore and tower. Japheth had never seen anything like it. Then again, he rarely traveled by sea. For all he knew, the phenomenon was natural. The kuo-toa he saw converging through the wave-tossed shallows were not alarmed by the advancing mist. In fact, by their sudden unnerving grins, it seemed they welcomed its arrival.

Thoster was saying, "For the sake of argument, let's say you ain't lying to me. You really do need my help and that of these others. Who stole this talisman from you, and where can we find the thief?"

The warlock wanted to know more about these "old lords and old races." Japheth had some experience with ancient beings who promised great power. Nothing was ever simple when it came to such extraordinary guarantees. The single "old lord" he had discovered and entered into a pact with had ultimately proved an alarming force in Japheth's life.

Certainly, if not for the Lord of Bats, the crimson road would have claimed the warlock long before now. Being alive, no matter the situation, had to be preferable to being dead. Right? It was a question he often asked himself. And despite his ties, he did delight in the various arcane tricks and amazing curses he was now able to call upon. And what about the impressive space hidden within the folds of his cloak? Other men would give far more than he to be able to wear such a thing as an article of clothing.

On the other hand, if not for the pact he'd sworn to the Lord of Bats, he wouldn't have to daily attend to the bidding of Behroun Marhana, a fouler and pettier man Japheth had yet to meet. What a convoluted series of events had put him in such thrall, he mused. If only—

"You're insane!" Seren's sudden accusation brought Japheth back to the present. While he had been touring, for the hundred thousandth time, his past indiscretions and failures, the others had continued their discussion. Something had riled up the war wizard, and even Thoster's eyes were wide with unexpected surprise. What had he missed?

Nogah raised a conciliatory, webbed hand. "I grant that on its face, the task we must accomplish . . ."

A rivulet of mist edged across the tower and into the balcony. It seemed a live thing, a fog tentacle seeking something.

"How peculiar," said the warlock. He wondered if the opaque cold front was natural weather after all. For one thing, his dust-enhanced vision was having difficulty piercing it.

Alerted by his comment, the kuo-toa glanced at the advancing mist streamer. She shrieked, then lisped, "Gethshemeth knows!"

She backed away from the advancing streamer. She rasped, "The mist is merely a cloak—it hides whatever force the great kraken has thrown at us!"

Great kraken? Japheth repeated mentally. What folderol is this?

The war wizard spat out a flurry of loose syllables and waved her red-runed wand. A gentle breeze issued from nowhere to blow toward the balcony opening. The mist's ominous advance slowed, hesitated, then began to retreat in the face of the mild but unrelenting draft. But how long would the woman's casting keep it at bay?

A ululation of feral anticipation soared up from somewhere below the tower, hollow yet somehow more threatening because of the muffling, mysterious mist.

"The kuo-toa . . ." began Japheth, his voice a dry croak. He tried to shake off the lethargy the traveler's dust sometimes produced when he didn't succumb to its vision of the burning road. "The kuo-toa outside that are converging on us—are they with you, Nogah?"

She hissed, blinked rapidly. She said, "Fool! I told you I am anathema in Olleth. The Sea Mother has demanded my head for my affront. But worse, all those I subverted with the Dreamheart now follow Gethshemeth, the great kraken. It sends them against me now, lest I contrive a plan to take back what it stole!"

Seren broke in. "Fool? You're asking us to go against a great kraken and call *us* fools?"

The moist patter of many squishy feet sounded loud on the open stair.

Captain Thoster drew his slender straight-sword from its silver sheath. Metallic disks inset flush in the blade's side whirred and spun with golemlike precision. A greenish fluid pulsed within straight, hair-thin conduits that ran from hilt to tip, whetting the fine edge of the blade with an emerald sheen. Thoster called it his Blade of Venom, an antique but deadly weapon found among Lantan's watery remains. A product of vanished gnome craftsmen, who infused knowledge of golems and gears into their works.

Seren began the opening phrases of a spell.

Anusha . . . Japheth couldn't see her. Was she gone, or had the sensitivity granted by his traveler's dust passed?

"Are we facing the great kraken itself?" asked Thoster. The captain stared into the wide, fog-obscured opening on the balcony. "It could reach this high, I think."

Japheth replied, his voice growing surer, "I saw only kuotoa converging, no kraken small or great."

"Well . . . maybe we ain't all dead!" exclaimed Thoster. A small grin chased away worry lines with deeper grooves. "Fish-men I can handle. No offense, Nogah." The captain turned to face the stairs, his blade whirring and clicking like a hungry insect.

Unless the kraken has come in the meantime, thought the warlock. Better be sure.

Japheth projected an arcane summons into the space hidden within his cloak, to his hidden fortress, shadow-drenched Darroch Castle. The call roused those he sought from their lightless roosts. Crying and chirping their eagerness in registers higher than men could hear, they emerged as a dark swarm from Japheth's billowing cloak.

Seren and Nogah both exclaimed in tones surprisingly similar for such disparate family trees. Thoster, familiar with the warlock's many abilities, grinned wider.

The cloud of flapping black motes arced straight into the wall of mist, immediately lost to sight.

But bats did not rely on eyes alone, and now, neither did Japheth. Nay, he *was* the bat swarm. Closing his eyes on the tower interior, he opened his perceptions to the audibly sculpted, texture-defined world the bats inhabited.

His fingers, grown long and composed only of sound, caressed the tower as its rounded sides fell away behind. The wet, uncertain boundary of the sea lapped up from below. Bipeds with large, noise-muffling eyes and hard scales scampered from the water's edges up the beach of sound-scattering sand, to join their brethren already snorting and giggling at the tower's base.

Japheth directed the darting swarm out over the water. His touch-sight stretched down to pat the sea's inconstant surface. The water was impenetrable, but its fluid, ever-changing nature betrayed the shapes of what lay beneath. Mostly, that was bulging swells of water that rolled endlessly to the shore, there to break and froth on the sand. But the swarm also discerned schools of fish as small mounds sliding along the surface, the edges of a half-formed coral reef, and what might even be a drowned shipwreck.

Nowhere could he perceive what he most feared to discover: great, sinuous bulges in the water hinting at tentacles hundreds or more feet in length, or a great bulblike central body with a brain more ancient than the founding of Impiltur. Japheth had seen pictures of kraken in the Candlekeep stacks.

He found no evidence of such a shape, but something else was fast approaching.

A handful of ballista-like shapes arrowed through the water. They left **V**-shaped wakes behind each one's single high fin that pierced the boundary into air. Sharks, and big ones. Worryisomely, the contours of reflected sound revealed each bore a rider, but the swirling seawater foiled him from teasing out real shape from fancy.

The swarm veered closer, darting down to intersect the line of the onrushing fins.

Japheth saw a warty arm rise from the water and point. He had just a heartbeat to study it, to recognize that its oozing, sound-absorbing flesh wasn't the scaled arm of a kuo-toa, before pain cut his connection to the swarm.

He opened his eyes, his mouth dry.

"What?" said Captain Thoster.

"Kuo-toa, maybe twenty. Well, maybe they're not exactly kuo-toa; they looked warped somehow. And, I think . . . a covey of water witches."

CHAPTER ELEVEN

The Year of the Secret (1396 DR)
Green Siren *on the Sea of Fallen Stars*

The slushy, damp patter of kuo-toa feet on the stairs knifed terror through Anusha. She instinctively tried to get away—

The girl woke in her flesh body as if from a nightmare, breathing hard and struggling to sit up.

Pain smote her forehead. Dazed, she fell back, blinking in darkness broken only by a ruler-straight thread of light that ran from near her left temple down past her left foot. It was the seam of the travel chest's lid, in which her body slept away her dream travels. Not for the first time, she imagined it was like this inside a sarcophagus. Unlike most sarcophagus residents, though, she could leave whenever she wanted.

She slid open the custom-installed bolt that unlatched the lid from inside. With only a little effort, she pushed away the covering. Brightness brought tears to her eyes. Even though the light from the cabin's porthole was dimmed by mist, she had to squint.

The roiling fog beyond the porthole was the same mist she'd seen rushing across the water to blockade Hegruth Island. The same mist that cloaked the scaled, fishy kuo-toa as they converged on the tower.

Her cheeks warmed. They couldn't have hurt her, or probably even seen her. Yet she had done the equivalent of scream and run. Had Japheth seen her depart in fear? She hoped not. He probably had.

"Am I such an infant, to flee at the first hint of danger?" she wondered aloud. "You can do better."

A gurgle of hunger diverted her self-rebuke.

With one hand, she grabbed a piece of unwrapped hardtack from the clutter on the adjoining cot. Her other hand sought the wineskin Japheth had also provided. She bit and chewed the stale, unsalted biscuitlike texture, moistening it with the watered-down wine. She had incorrectly supposed that spending most of her time lying still and dreaming would cut her appetite by half or more. Instead, the yawning chasm in her stomach told her she must eat, if she was going to launch yet another dream walk. The activity seemed to suck far more out of her than a natural dream. Already her clothing was becoming loose and baggy. If she didn't increase her food intake, she would waste away to a dream in truth.

Anusha choked down the last of the biscuit, took another pull on the skin, then pulled the lid closed as she reclined back into the travel chest.

After several rafts of empty moments floated past, she recognized the hard truth her body already knew.

She wasn't the least bit sleepy.

"Oh, please!" she whispered fiercely, frustration making her voice shrill.

She spent a few more moments attempting to control her breathing and calm her thoughts. It simply wasn't working. Her heart still pounded with the memory of kuo-toa on the tower stairs.

Her hand moved almost of its own accord, feeling through the things she kept with her in the chest. She found the cold silver vial Japheth had provided two days earlier. The "elixir of somnolence," he'd called it.

A drug, she knew it to be in truth. One she was on the cusp of taking, despite her disdain for Japheth's habit.

"No time for prissiness," she remonstrated. She twisted off the lid and brought the cold vial to her lips. The taste of blackberries bloomed across her tongue, and her lips tingled as if she'd bitten into a mint leaf. Recalling Japheth's words about counting down from ten, Anusha quickly restoppered the vial.

She didn't feel any different. Had he given her colored water? Perhaps the warlock—

Everything blurred away.

She stood outside the travel chest, intangible as a hallucination.

Japheth's potion wasn't colored water, that was certain.

Anusha rushed from the cabin, *slap* through the door without pausing. The guard dog, Lucky, still standing vigil in the narrow hallway, yipped and wagged his tail. She took a moment to pat his head, saying, "I'll bring you a treat later, I promise!"

She emerged from below the stern deck onto the main deck. The crew stood in disorderly groups, weapons in hand, glancing nervously into the impenetrable vapor that pressed in on all sides. The high masts poked up into a ceiling of white, fluffy film. It was as if the entire ship was cocooned in a great down pillow.

Now what? Could she swim in her condition? Walk along the bottom? Her dream form didn't need to breathe. She supposed she could pass through water as easily as solid walls.

A crewman at the starboard railing suddenly gasped out a surprised oath. He pointed over the deck. He yelled, "Something's coming out'a the soup!"

Anusha and several pirates joined the man at the railing.

A woman emerged from the fog. She balanced on some sort of low raft, narrow and long, adorned with a protruding fin like a shark's. A shape stroked alongside the woman on her strange raft, just beneath the surface, but lingering fog made the swimming thing impossible to identify.

The woman was *old!* Her flesh was sickly and yellow, covered with warts and oozing sores. Her hair was filthy and appeared to be composed of rotting seaweed.

The woman's gruesome appearance pulled a groan of horror from the crew. Several crumpled, as if all the strength fled their limbs, like water pouring from a cup.

The newcomer gurgled like a creature on the edge of drowning; it was a titter of delight. The crone locked her gaze on the pirate who'd first identified the old woman's approach. A red pulse lit her eyes from within, flashing so brightly the scarlet glow illuminated the fog a dozen paces in all directions.

The crewman gasped, then fell to the deck, his limbs and head suddenly as loose as a rag doll. He was dead.

The remaining crew screamed and bellowed in a decidedly non-pirate fashion. They scrambled away from the railing, knocking into their fellows and, in some cases, trampling them. Anusha was right in among the retreating crew, voicing her own shock and fear, though her voice was lost among the others' cries. Those who couldn't run pulled themselves from the ship's edge. In moments, the only one still by the railing was the one whose heart had been silenced with an evil look. All eyes stared at the railing, silhouetted against the roiling mist, dread thundering in their chests.

Anusha listened for more gurgling laughter, or worse, the sound of something attempting to climb the ship's side, but she discerned only harsh breathing, mumbled prayers, and water lapping against the side of the *Green Siren*.

"Damn me for looking, I told the captain we'd signed scairt children instead of freebooters at our last stop. Looks to me I was right!" came a mocking voice.

Anusha turned and saw the hulking first mate, Nyrotha. He stood by the great cavity that connected the lower decks, hands on his hips.

"Nyrotha," pleaded a woman to Anusha's left. "A . . . a water witch is in the fog! She snuffed Roger with nothing but a *look!*"

The first mate roared, "Damn Roger, he was a fool anyhow! Now, pay attention, I'm saying this just once: you ain't paid to whimper and squeal when the *Green Siren's* attacked! Get off your butts and repel boarders, you bastard children of diseased mudflats! Draw your weapons and defend this ship, or by Bane's black nails, I'll see all of you dance the hempen jig!"

Several of the crew, apparently as frightened of Nyrotha as of the creature in the mist, drew their weapons. A few even took a few tentative steps toward the railing.

A crunch sounded from below the water line, and the entire ship canted slightly. Pirates shrieked. Nyrotha cursed and strode forward, a great black scimitar clutched in his corded hands.

Hands three times as large as the first mate's appeared on the railing, followed by a hulking body of dark green scales and ropy hair. An overpowering odor emanated from the creature, like a barrel of unpreserved fish left rotting in the dark for three days. It roared, revealing a swath of blackened teeth in which the half-masticated remains of previous meals lingered.

The crone Anusha had seen below rode the beast's shoulders, clutching its ropy hair for balance.

"To me!" shouted Nyrotha. The mate engaged the creature. Nyrotha no longer seemed hulking compared to that awful aquatic humanoid menacing the *Green Siren*. Half the pirates stumbled to help the first mate. Another quarter stood rooted in place, numb with fear. The remainder fled the deck, nearly weeping in their terror.

And what shall I do? Anusha wondered. She glanced down on her unreal body, saw she was clad in the noble's gown she unconsciously seemed to prefer while in a dream. Hardly the outfit of a warrior.

She recalled then the panoply of Imphras Heltharn. Imphras was the great war captain who had rid the Easting Reach of hobgoblin marauders three centuries ago, ending the Kingless Years. The old king's fantastic, golden armor was on display in New Sarshel in the Atrium of the Grand Council. She had looked on it many times. The armor's significance was one of the bits of historical knowledge that had taken up residence in her memory. Her tutor would be proud.

Could she effect a change in wardrobe merely by wishing for it, after the manner of regular dreams? Anusha concentrated. Her gown shimmered and flowed.

A tall helm enfolded her head, a slender gorget spread across her throat, wide pauldrons defended and magnified her shoulders, cunningly articulated couters grew from her elbows, fluted vambraces enshrouded her forearms, and a golden cuirass of breathtaking strength and beauty hugged her torso.

She flexed her gauntleted hands, articulated with flawless dream joints, and realized she required a weapon.

Into her upraised hand flashed a long sword on whose slender blade burned the Marhana family crest. It was the same blade that hung over the fireplace in the great room of the family estate. In life, it was too heavy for her to wield. In dream, it was as light as a switch of hazelwood.

She breathed deeply, exulting in the vision in which she'd clothed herself.

Enough, she scolded herself. You changed your clothes, that's all.

Accoutered for a fight instead of a noble ball, Anusha advanced on the already raging skirmish.

The smelly monster towered over the press of pirates, though several lay broken on the deck. Nyrotha still stood, wielding his scimitar with precision, managing to keep the great beast at bay with defensive slashes and sidesteps. The creature's scaled arms streamed red from a dozen wounds.

The sea hag had dismounted and remained with her back to the railing. The hag gestured with her water-wrinkled hands, chanting in her gurgling voice. The fog above her head stirred. Neither Nyrotha nor the crew noticed; their attention remained riveted on the monstrous, troll-like thing trying to eat them.

Anusha traced the fight's periphery until she reached the railing. Neither pirate nor attackers noticed her new dream form. She halfway wished they could see her fabulous new likeness. Her fear of discovery was vanquished by the elation of her successful transformation.

The witch still chanted, and the writhing fog above her head was fast becoming a rotating whirlpool, growing wider and wider. At its center, a red light glimmered. The light reminded Anusha of the illumination that had twinkled in the hag's eye, only to leap out and steal Roger's life. This scarlet whirlpool looked big enough to encompass all the ship . . .

Fear found Anusha again despite her armor. The urge to race away or wake up returned.

What a mistake waking up would be, she thought. If the ship is holed and sunk, I'll drown in my own body! Anusha strode forward and raised her dream sword high.

Doubt ambushed her, blade still in the air, even as the alarming aerial vortex swirled wider and quicker. The "sword" she held wasn't even real.

She'd pushed things and touched things with her unreal

hands. Why not her unreal blade? Why not do more than move them; why not cut them? She had to try to use her sword to affect the waking world. Should she try to imagine the dream blade steel hard and capable of cutting more than phantasms? Would that even work? She didn't know.

No, she decided, I'll imagine the sword as ethereal as my hand and body, an extension of it. Her dream form could pass through anything, including living creatures, but as she'd learned down in the hold, she also adversely affected anything living through which she passed. Dream flesh and real obviously did not get on too well.

Anusha advanced a final few steps and brought the sword down in an awkward slash. At the last instant, the sea witch's eyes flickered, somehow sensing Anusha's presence. The hag jerked to the side, but not enough to completely avoid the blow.

Anusha's dream blade grazed the hag's forehead. A burst of dark blue flame briefly illuminated both witch and armored girl. The hag loosed a surprised howl of agony. The red swirl growing overhead instantly collapsed into so much disturbed cloud-stuff.

When Anusha had touched the pirate down in the hold, he immediately collapsed into a quivering, unconscious heap.

The witch quivered, yes, and was obviously hurt, but she did not fall. Instead she screeched, "Protect your mother!"

The hulking sea monster glanced back, the gnawed boot of an unlucky privateer protruding from its mouth, the battered body of the coxswain in one hand. The monster had been using the screaming coxswain as an improvised club.

Nyrotha took instant advantage of the creature's distraction, making a deep cut across the creature's stomach. The monster staggered and ichor spurted. It dropped the coxswain. It returned its full attention to the first mate, forgetting its "mother's" command. For the first time, Anusha thought the pirates might just defeat the creature from the sea. If the sea witch was dealt with, anyhow.

The water witch continued to back away from Anusha, her haggard eyes darting this way and that, squinting. She held her hands out in a warding gesture. She screamed out into the fog, "Sisters, I am assailed by a ghost! Gather near, that we may banish it to the Shadowfell from which it strays!"

It wasn't the first time Anusha had been mistaken for an empty spirit. Too bad the witch couldn't see her new armored splendor. Then she'd know she faced more than a wandering apparition. Then again, when the hag looked at Roger, he'd flopped dead.

"Sisters! Return! I am beset!"

Anusha followed the retreating witch step for step. Yet she continued to hold her swing. She just couldn't bring herself to strike down the hag. Anusha intellectually knew the woman was a monster, something that would kill and eat her . . . but now that she was at the cusp, she couldn't follow through. If she struck down the hag, would it be an assassination? Would the hag scream and die, kicking? She lowered her sword, indecision growing into anguish.

Instead of striking, Anusha said, "If you promise to leave the ship and depart forever, I won't hurt you?" Irresolution made her ultimatum a question.

The wandering eye of the water witch tracked Anusha's words. The witch muttered, "Gethshemeth can do worse than kill me. Look into my eyes, and I'll show you!"

Anusha's gaze unthinkingly darted to the witch's.

The hag's red eyes flashed the color of fresh-spilled blood. Anusha recognized death itself in that bloody gaze. It grasped her.

A wave of nausea visually distorted her dream form, sending cracks and shivers through her. Hopes, memories, and hates dropped from her like dead leaves from a tree in winter.

Wake! she commanded herself. Wake up, wake up!

She did not wake up. The sea hag's blazing eye held her rooted in place . . . or was it Japheth's drug? He'd told her only to use it when she had a long time to sleep. She wouldn't escape this peril so easily. Her choice was to kill or die.

With dream armor unraveling like funerary linens, Anusha raised her shivering, splintering dream blade and plunged it into the sea hag's stomach. Real blood spurted from the wound.

The witch's scream possessed a keening, yearning quality that nearly made Anusha pull back. But she persevered. She held her wavering sword so it transfixed the creature from the sea, willing it real and as sharp as a razor for this moment. She plunged the blade deeper, concentrating on its keen solidity.

The witch's final, sorrowful plea for her sisters' aid trilled out into the fog. Then the hag collapsed and lay without movement or breath. In death she had the guise of a sleeping grandmother, placid and hardly a threat to anyone. Blood trickled from her wound, red as any human's.

The only response the sea hag's entreaty elicited was the appearance of a swarm of darting bats, which rotated and swirled across the *Green Siren* from stem to stern. Even as the mist around the ship began to break up, the investigating bats twirled back out over the sea, toward the tower island.

"The *Green Siren* weathered the fog," reported Japheth, his breath still coming in gasps between his sentences in the fight's aftermath. "I knew I saw three hags! The one that didn't attack us tried to scuttle the ship."

"What? What about my ship?"

The warlock continued, "Your crew beat the hag." His eyes remained closed as his servitor bats relayed the image of the wrinkled form crumpled along the ship's railing, and something dark and large stroking away from the ship toward open water. "A . . . sea troll? Nyrotha drove some sort of sea monster back into the water. Good thing you left him aboard."

"An accident," mused Captain Thoster. "The lout was so drunk on grog I couldn't wake him."

Japheth's winged servants swarmed through the open balcony window and into his bottomless cloak.

Seren, her voice ragged from too many spells, commented, "Nice shawl you got there, Japheth."

He simply nodded. The woman didn't need to know his cloak's provenance.

Seren stood near Thoster. Not far away, Nogah leaned against a wall, and the two surviving crew members watched the entrance. The unmoving forms of defeated kuo-toa littered the floor and choked the stairs beyond. Among them lay the charred and still smoldering sea witches who were finally downed with Seren's last impressive spell volley.

"We persevered," said Nogah in her gurgling way.

Seren whirled, pointed an accusing finger. "Because of you, we've gained the enmity of a great kraken! We did *not* agree to your ludicrous scheme, but already it sends servitors to eliminate us. I say we kill you now, and show this Gethshemeth we're not its foes." The woman looked to the pirate captain for support.

Thoster put a hand on the war wizard's shoulder, "Seren, mayhap we'll do exactly that, but let's talk a bit first, eh?" Japheth noticed that, despite the man's solicitous air, the hand not on Seren's shoulder rested on the pommel of his venemous sword.

Seren huffed, visibly battling her desire to launch a particularly nasty attack on the whip from her armamentarium of spells. Finally, she spat, "So talk."

Captain Thoster nodded and said, "First, I want to know what sub-breed of kuo-toa we just faced? I've never seen their like before now."

The whip gave a slow nod, her eyes large compared to those of the many dead creatures lying around them. She said, "Gethshemeth's doing, using the Dreamheart. It has corrupted their forms. It is a potential I sensed in the Dreamheart, but not one I ever called upon."

The captain frowned, seemed about to ask something else, then thought better of it. Instead he grinned and said, "Consider, all of you. This unprovoked attack is a message. Gethshemeth revealed its hand, so to speak. The great kraken's afraid! It tried to scare us off, make us let fear drive us the direction Seren suggests we take. It hopes we'll run with sails at full mast from Nogah. Well, here's how I see it: the great beast must think we have some chance of succeeding to go to such trouble!"

"Rubbish," replied Seren. "You're seriously suggesting we engage something so powerful, so prescient, that it knew when and where to attack us even before we agreed to oppose it?"

Nogah intruded, "Gethshemeth knew we gathered against it, likely through its study of the Dreamheart. But Thoster is correct. The great kraken knows I held the stone far longer than itself. It knows I have the greater mastery of its power. The closer I draw to it, the more influence I can exert over it and Gethshemeth too. Get me close enough, soon enough, and I can snatch it back! I've prepared for nothing else these last several months."

"If you're so proficient with this rock, how'd the kraken steal it from you in the first place?" Seren countered.

"It caught me by surprise. The possibility that something might attempt to take the artifact from me had not entered my calculations. But, as I explained, I've been making preparations. Next time I'm close enough, Gethshemeth will rue the moment it stole my birthright!" Greenish spittle flecked the kuo-toa's wide lips.

"Mmmm, yes," mused Thoster, his zeal of a moment earlier fading somewhat. He looked at Japheth. "What do you think?"

Japheth thought it possible Nogah was slightly insane. But he suspected insanity was a common condition among kuo-toa, something they had learned to deal with. The warlock answered, "Both of you are correct. Gethshemeth rightly worries about anything that would oppose it. But how much does it need to worry, really? Its abilities can't be discounted; a great kraken could easily destroy us."

"Right!" said Seren.

"However, despite its already considerable power," continued Japheth, "Nogah explained the relic Gethshemeth stole could amplify its strength, magnify it so much it could threaten more than the denizens of the Sea of Fallen Stars. I would not like that to happen, if I could stop it."

Thoster smiled. The warlock knew the man didn't care a whit about the safety of creatures below, on, or beyond the sea, but he was satisfied with the direction Japheth leaned. For his own part, Japheth was nonplussed as he vocalized his concern for others. Must be some remnant of the traveler's dust talking.

On the other hand, if the Dreamheart was as powerful a relic as Nogah claimed, it really wouldn't do for a kraken to have it. Or, come to think of it, a mad kuo-toa whip. Then again, Lord Marhana wasn't really a good choice of caretaker, either. No good choices were possible when it came to evil artifacts.

Seren realized Thoster, Nogah, and even Japheth were on the same page. She reiterated loudly, "I refuse to be part of this. I will not—"

"Then do not!" exploded Thoster. "We three will continue. Go your own way. We'll find another to round out our number. But you are marked, Seren. The great kraken knows you now. If we fail, Gethshemeth will eventually find you, alone and without friends, and take its vengeance."

The war wizard sputtered, her face red as she searched for a retort.

Thoster didn't give her a chance to respond; he regarded Nogah and asked in a voice returned to placidity, "So where is Gethshemeth?"

Nogah shook her staff, perhaps connoting anticipation. She licked her lips with a sinuous tongue, and declared, "Thoster, you spoke more truth than you know. You said the great kraken gave us a message with this attack. I agree. It revealed to us that it fears it can be beaten. More than that, it also told us where to begin seeking it."

"Did it?"

"The kuo-toa it used to attack us—they are not from Olleth, as I first thought. They bear the tribal markings of the only other kuo-toa colony in the Sea of Fallen Stars."

"Ah, clever of you to notice." The captain nodded. "Where is this colony?"

"These kuo-toa bear the markings of those who went to dwell in Taunissik."

The captain raised his eyebrows and waved his hand for Nogah to explain further.

Nogah said, "For all your sea lore, it would surprise me had you heard of Taunissik, Thoster. It is a failed colony, of little consequence. A few hundred dispossessed kuo-toa left Olleth six years back. They were part of a sub-sect whose charter demands its adherents always seek to expand kuo-toa territory. So they departed Olleth to set up an outpost on a deep atoll. Taunissik, as old morkoth records called it, boasts a massive coral growth on a submerged mountain. Time passed, and no word of the colony's progress ever came. In Olleth, we thought the colony dead. Apparently, we were wrong to assume Taunissik failed; Gethshemeth found the colony. The colonists were enslaved to the great kraken's will."

The captain clapped his hands. "Aye! We have another voyage ahead of us! Back to the ship. We set course for Taunissik! Nogah will be our guide."

Seren scowled, but didn't gainsay the captain.

Japheth offered, "I am not a strong swimmer. How much of this colony is under water?"

"Worry not, human," said Nogah. "I have an elixir that will preserve you and the woman, should it be necessary to descend beneath the waves."

"What about him?" asked Japheth, pointing to the captain, whose back was turned as he stooped to retrieve his hat, which had been knocked off in the fight.

Nogah shrugged. "Thoster needs no elixir."

CHAPTER TWELVE

The Year of the Secret (1396 DR)
West of Nathlan

No food passed Raidon Kane's lips. Every so often he sipped from his waterskin. His eyes were open, but he looked inward. Memory became theater, disgorging his past. He retrieved and relived every event that contained Ailyn. A master of his own mind, Raidon's recollection was extensive.

On the second day, tears brimmed, then broke from his eyes. Raidon tasted salt.

On the third day, he sighed. He reached into his pouch and produced a ration composed of dried dates, almonds, and apples. He nibbled. Later, he ate the entire close-packed morsel, and then another.

On the fourth day, Raidon levered himself to his feet with the aid of the great, dirt-grimed boulder. Pain knifed through his stiff joints. Physical pain was something to which he was becoming accustomed. Others might have taken the agony as an omen of their own inadequacy. Raidon decided to perceive the new barbs and the lingering aches as evidence of his continued existence. His hurts were a connection to his past he couldn't gainsay. Pain grounded him and held him sane when images of Ailyn bringing him a daffodil during Spring Feast, Ailyn receiving a gold Cormyrean coin from his hand, Ailyn looking for him in a game of sneak-and-hide . . . these and other poignant memories threatened to crack him wide open, again.

The mountain on the horizon remained steadfastly in the sky, defying nature and perhaps even Silvanus . . . assuming that one had survived into the present. According to the golem that spoke from nowhere, even the gods were in disarray these days, as their lofty realms buckled and crumbled toward a new balance.

Raidon rubbed his chin, wondering why the sentient effigy had not attempted to renew their conversation. If it lay buried in an extraplanar dungeon, the golem must be lonely. Then again, it wasn't alive—it was a magical construct. Perhaps concepts like loneliness held no meaning for it.

His voice rough from disuse, Raidon addressed the air. "Cynosure, are you near?"

"Of course, Raidon," came the instant reply.

The monk said, "I am glad. The world has moved on without me, it seems. All save for you."

"I was never part of the world, Raidon, at least until you woke. I resigned myself to decades more darkness. Then light broke from the void when you first called on the power of your Sign, and I knew I was not forsaken. Of the two of us, I would hazard that I am the one who feels most glad."

Raidon nodded. Perhaps the construct could feel something like loneliness after all. But could it feel loss? When it recalled past acquaintances now gone, did a hollow cavity in its chest emanate a hopeless tide that threatened mental desolation? He didn't trust himself to reply, fearing his voice would shake.

After a few moments, Cynosure asked, "What do you propose to do, Raidon?"

"I know one thing, golem; I hunger. I need food."

"And after you find sustenance? What will you do?"

The monk shook his head in negation. "Nothing. I propose to exist. That is all. My deeds and past struggles have all yielded nothing. My greatest act of kindness concluded with the death of a child all alone. I'll not make such an error again. Misguided efforts to improve the world only deepen its imperfections. My masters had the right of it: be in the moment; do not shape it."

A high, white cloud edged a limb over the sun, throwing a cooling shadow across the hillside.

Cynosure spoke again, "You have the Cerulean Sign—"

"I would cast it away, for all that it was a gift from my mother, if I could. It has brought nothing but trouble. And the Traitor of Stardeep is released, you tell me. The Sign scars my flesh only to remind me it is a worthless symbol of a failed cause."

"The cause has not yet failed."

"No?"

"The threats the Keepers of the Cerulean Sign formed to fight remain active, perhaps closer to the surface than ever before. In the Dawn Age, monstrosities slipped into the world from sanity-shredding realms. These creatures, great and small, instinctively work toward the day when Faerûn itself is consumed and made anew in their own mad image. As a Keeper, it is your duty to oppose this."

"I am not a Keeper."

"Raidon, though I may be wrong, it is possible you remain the sole, mobile Keeper in all Toril."

"I did not choose that role. I am not a Keeper."

"You fought aberrations whenever you came upon them.

Though you took no oath, you acted as one sworn to the cause. For ten years you did so, nearly without respite, prior to the Spellplague."

Raidon frowned, then he ventured, "What of the other Keepers—Kiril and Delphe? And what about yourself? You are of the Sign, and a potent defender of it, as I remember it."

"Delphe ventured into Sildëyuir fifteen years ago and never returned. With that realm's fall, I do not know her fate or the fate of any of her kind."

Raidon queried, "And the swordswoman?"

"Kiril and the sword Angul left Stardeep. They re-entered Faerûn, and continued on much as they had before. Kiril sold her sword arm to anyone with sufficient coin to keep her in drink and lodging. Eventually, she met up with a previous employer, a dwarf named Thormud. I lost track of her in the change-ravaged Vilhon Wilds. She survived the Year of Blue Fire, but afterward plunged into the heart of an active pocket of spellplague, from which she never returned."

The monk grunted. Though not definitive, the construct implied the only two pledged Keepers were missing and likely dead.

Raidon persisted, "You survive."

"At this time, I am cut off from the world. I can only interact with Faerûn through you and your Sign. I can provide you support, advice, and even transportation on occasion, but I cannot personally enter the war."

"A war, you say."

"The conflict has begun. Only skirmishes now, but soon, a wholesale slaughter, when the ancient buried city of Xxiphu emerges."

The monk walked the perimeter of the boulder's weedy edge, one hand trailing along the rough stone. He was not being impolite, walking away from the golem; its attention was always centered on him. He wondered if he could sever the link. But the name Xxiphu sparked alarm somewhere in his memory.

"Cynosure, I recall that name, but neither you, Kiril, Delphe, or anyone else properly described the nature of Xxiphu and this 'Abolethic Sovereignty' to me. Aboleths have long slunk below the world. What, really, is more terrible about Xxiphu?"

"Two things. First and least, regular aboleth colonies are safely ensconced below the earth, immovable. Xxiphu is different. It is mobile. It may indeed breach to Faerûn's surface, as previous divination revealed."

The monk nodded. That was certainly a worry. "And second?"

"Second, Xxiphu contains the *original* aboleths. These are the progenitors of the race who personally squirmed into the world before it cooled from its creation fires. These aboleths were old when the sun was still young. Xxiphu is the seat of the Abolethic Sovereignty, possessed of a malignancy inconceivable, and ruled by the Eldest, an aboleth of such size its age is incalculable. Certainly it is older than when Abeir-Toril split asunder. If Xxiphu rises and the Eldest wakes, then Faerûn will face yet another catastrophe, this one directed by alien, unfeeling minds that do not perceive the world as you do, or even I."

The monk didn't respond. Instead, he looked to the southern horizon, his pose noncommittal.

"If that occurs, Raidon," Cynosure continued, "many more children than Ailyn will perish in fear."

The monk sucked in his breath as if a mighty kick had caught him in the stomach. His eyes darkened, and his fists clenched. With no target other than the boulder, the monk balled his hand and assailed it with a thundering strike. The stone cracked, and splinters of rock winged away. His knuckles stung, then went numb.

Raidon hissed, took a lung-filling breath, then dropped

both hands back to his sides, outwardly back in control. The pity he earlier felt for the construct was gone. Cynosure was a manipulator first and last, he saw. It said only what it calculated would be most likely to induce the actions it desired. Very well, he would treat it as it deserved.

"You seek to shame me into action, Cynosure?"

"I merely speak the truth."

"Indeed. I wonder. But, for the sake of argument, let us imagine that I do take up this challenge. What can I do to prevent the rise of the Abolethic Sovereignty?"

"You must meditate upon the Sign that is now part of you. You are not trained in its use, but I can guide you. It can show you that which transpires across the land, what threats now gather, and what you can best do to counter them."

"You claim much authority."

Cynosure was silent.

Finally Raidon asked, "Is the Sign I carry up to this task?" The monk dropped into a lotus position, one suited for meditation.

"The Sign is only as potent as its holder."

"Then let us hope my training does not desert me."

The monk supposed the construct attempted a new stratagem with its last statement. As if he were shallow enough to respond heatedly to such an obvious ploy. But Raidon wondered. Regardless of Cynosure's tactics, if anything the sentient effigy said was true, wouldn't it behoove him to help? Unless Raidon chose death rather than continued existence, didn't his honor demand he do as the construct requested? Perhaps he required more information, if only to make a more informed decision.

"Cynosure, I would know more. Tell me how to proceed."

The golem of Stardeep didn't hesitate in its response. "Meditate on the Sign. Wake it with your will. Ask it to show you the danger that gathers."

No novice to meditation, Raidon called upon his focus. He

stifled his surprise on discovering his inability to immediately find it. Much had occurred since he'd lost himself in the harmony of a single thought. So he sat awhile, remembering the sensation. A tickle in his brain, becoming smoothness. Distractions dropping away, one by one . . .

His focus returned. He imagined it as a crystalline lens. He directed its attention upon the unwanted design that blazoned his chest.

He could just discern the symbol's treelike outline, blurry like half-recalled faces of friends long absent. With single-minded deliberation, he compelled it to reveal its secrets.

It revealed nothing.

He was not impatient; he had nothing but time. He continued to observe the image. As they used to say in Xiang Temple, Raidon could stare the paint off the walls, if given the time.

Gradually he noticed discolorations within the lines, smears of gray on black. The blurs became colors; then the colors became shapes. The lines of the symbol pulled away on all sides to become a window onto another place.

Raidon saw a fog-shrouded tower on a small island. Dozens of scaled, fishlike humanoids burst from the water's edge and stormed the tower. Behind them strode two watery crones who chanted obscenities.

The creatures had an aberrant taint. Raidon wasn't sure how he knew that, but he assumed the knowledge was communicated to him by the Sign. Though the creatures were not aberrations themselves, a portion of their spirit was pledged to something abominable.

The fishfolk sought to overpower several defenders who held the tower. The tower denizens included a sea captain in ostentatious dress, accompanied by four humans in ship-scrounged finery; a woman in a body wrap the color of snow; a man with eyes like blood and a cloak so black it seemed more an aura than clothing; a striking young woman as hazy as a dream; and oddly enough, another scaled humanoid touched with the taint of aberration, who stood with the humans instead of its attacking kin.

The young woman with the hazy outline gasped and disappeared before the attackers landed their first blow.

The assault was fierce.

The captain lost his hat in the initial offensive, but his clicking, whirring sword dispensed death each time its damp tip pierced an attacker's scales. Two of the humans in ragged ship's attire fell in the initial blitz.

The cloaked man uttered what seemed more like a plea than a spell. A massive iron crown coalesced upon the head of one of the crones. The prongs atop writhed in metallic agony, and as if stricken mad, the afflicted hag began slaying her own allies. Fishfolk fell dead as her killing eyes raked them.

The woman in white discharged fire and lightning into the invaders' ranks. Her eyes danced, and she yelled with grim jubilation with every enemy she laid low. She destroyed the remaining crone with a blast of fire.

To Raidon's practiced eye, the attackers had woefully underestimated the depth and strength of the tower defenders. The fight was over.

Yet it wasn't over, not really. For Raidon perceived through the Sign-enabled scrying window that the attackers were pawns of something else, something that had not entered the fight. Lines of association ran like fishing lines away into the sea. The fishfolk and sea hags were mere fingers for an entity greater and more terrible. Something perhaps even aberrant, or at least something infected with madness most foul.

What was it? He concentrated on the immaterial lines of connection, trying to follow them from the attackers back to their source. He was aware of Cynosure's attention, sharing his conjured view through the Sign. He understood the construct silently aided him, allowing him to use the Sign in such an extraordinary fashion despite his lack of training in its multifarious functions. With the Sign now part of him, he needed to learn to use it consciously and without aid. But for now, he allowed the golem to guide his disembodied travel along the wispy tendrils across the water, flashing west over miles uncounted.

In ten measured heartbeats, the Sign-generated scrying window framed a seamount surrounded by coral protruding from the sea. The small island appeared in the shape of a fat sickle moon from Raidon's aerial vantage. A salt lagoon filled the open central portion of the island, and rounded, jumbled structures sprawled between dry land and soggy marsh.

Even as the monk tried to identify the strange architecture, his viewpoint flashed into the murky depths. The sun's yellow light turned green, and then, as the descent continued, blue. More of the strange, rounded structures he'd noted on top of the island were jumbled around a yawning cave at the seamount's base. Humanoid figures swam among the drowned structures.

"More fishfolk," Raidon murmured.

Cynosure's voice replied, "They are named kuo-toa."

The viewpoint slowed as it approached the dark cave mouth. Disturbed silt hung in the water, making the cave's already dim interior even more difficult to discern.

Inside, something rested back from the opening on the rocky floor, its shape long and cigar-shaped for the most part, though it was thicker at one end. Striations ran in parallel lines along the thinner portion of the shape, but the bulblike thickening at the other end was smooth.

The silt and lack of reflected light robbed the scene of meaning. Was the shape on the cave floor a natural jumble of drowned rocks? The lines of association the Sign followed terminated with the unmoving, contoured outcrop. The shape itself was not aberrant, but it contained something whose taint was like a bottomless pit.

Suddenly, the great shape shifted.

Raidon's assumptions flipped. He readjusted his sense of scale and nearly lost his focus in surprise. The shape was no jumble of rocks; it was a colossal squid, one of incredible bulk!

Two spots on each side of the bulk opened, revealing shield-sized eyes gleaming with awareness. It knew it was being observed. Its tapered end suddenly separated into a forest of suckered arms. It writhed, and a blanket of silt billowed to obscure all. But not before Raidon saw the true obscenity, clutched firmly in one tentacle.

It was a black stone, roughly the size of a man's head. To his Sign-enhanced sight, it seemed the stone was a vortex of aberration, sucking and drawing down all of the natural world to a nether space where utter abomination lurked.

Pain seared Raidon's temples, and he jerked his eyes wide.

A breeze pushed the grass across the plain in soothing waves of green. Scents of growing things and clean earth were a welcome balm from the vision that still burned in Raidon's memory: whipping tentacles, boring eyes, and a relic whose wrongness was so acute, it constantly tore at the world. And for all that, Raidon had the sense, perhaps imparted by the Sign on his chest, that the relic was perhaps only the tip of a much more horrific truth.

"What did we just see?" Raidon asked the air.

"A kraken. A great kraken named Gethshemeth. It holds an artifact somehow tied to Xxiphu itself. The stone it clutched, did you see it?"

"Yes. Who were those people who fought the kraken's puppets?"

"A good question. Something for us to discover, but their identity is not vital to our interests."

Raidon said, "Very well. How is it the kraken came to possess such a relic?"

"I do not know how such an object has been raised to the surface," mused Cynosure. "Perhaps in the earth movements that followed the Spellplague . . . But that is mere speculation. Regardless of how it happened, a great kraken possesses a sliver of connection to Xxiphu."

"What does a sea squid, intelligent or not, want with such a thing? Power, I suppose, as all creatures seem to desire, as if control over others will somehow bring them greater satisfaction."

"You are likely correct," said Cynosure with a note of appreciation in its voice. "The kraken's mind surpasses even my own cognizance. But with an artifact of Xxiphu under its control, it will learn to channel more and more strength, and become a force not easily withstood. Its reach might swell past all the bounds of reason."

"Cynosure, you need not be coy. You want me to slay it before it attains its peak of power."

"That is advisable."

Raidon nodded, thinking back on the worst creatures he had eradicated in the name of the Sign in the years before the Spellplague. "Illithids are bad enough. Faerûn should not also have to face aberrant-infused kraken."

"You should know that another outcome is also possible, one even worse than an empowered kraken. If we do not take this relic from the kraken soon, the connection it has to Xxiphu will grow broader and more certain. In a short time, the connection could be sufficient to raise the city whole. Then Toril shall really have something over which to weep."

Raidon repressed a shudder. He was suddenly and simultaneously cognizant that, with the scope of the situation before him, he hadn't thought about Ailyn for a great span of daylight . . .

The monk sighed, clenched his fists, and lost his focus. Of what real purpose was his life? He'd failed the one person who needed him. He'd outlived his own time and survived now only through a fluke of magic and circumstance. He didn't deserve or much care if his own existence continued. He yearned for an end to his struggles, an end to his shame. On the heels of that insight, an idea followed.

He said, "Once your capacity to move me is rejuvenated, transfer me directly into the kraken's presence. It will be caught off guard. I will strike with all the art of Xiang Temple in my fist, and kill the kraken before it knows it is threatened. Its death convulsion will kill me, and if not, I will drown before I reach the surface. I do not fear such an outcome. I would welcome it."

Silence was Raidon's response.

"Did you hear, Cynosure?" demanded the man of the air, his voice infused with uncharacteristic volume. "Send me along now. Let me slay this kraken and be done with it all."

The sun was sinking into the west, and a coolness grew on the plain. Raidon spied a wolf in the valley below, sniffing along the track of some hoped-for twilight meal.

Finally the voice replied, "I appreciate your fervor, Raidon Kane. Were I able to transfer you thus, assuming I could place you so close to the great kraken within its wards, which I cannot, perhaps you could kill Gethshemeth. But in killing it, and yourself, you would alert Xxiphu."

"Surely, I can slay Gethshemeth quickly enough," returned the monk, though with less certitude. "I would have a few moments to catch it by surprise—"

"It has held the relic too long. Even if I could put you in the right place at the right time, which I have just explained I cannot, killing the great kraken is not enough. We need to kill Gethshemeth and simultaneously sever its connection with the relic, and therefore, its connection to the Abolethic Sovereignty. Your Sign alone is insufficient to that task."

Raidon pulled his fingers across his close-cropped black hair, massaging away a germ of annoyance. The construct was becoming more long-winded and circumspect by the moment.

"Then what, Cynosure? What can I do?"

"You must discover the fate of the sentient sword, Angul. It alone, in your hands, can accomplish what must be done."

"Angul. Yes, a powerful blade. But was it not an item infused with its power by the Weave? With Mystra's fall, how could it still function?"

"You ask a penetrating question. A complex answer exists; the simple answer is that it simply does. Will that satisfy?"

Raidon frowned. His emotions were as out of control as they'd ever been. If Cynosure were standing next to him just then, he would have struck the golem.

Cynosure must have sensed something of the monk's mood. It said, "I apologize. Listen, then. Many magical items such as swords, cloaks, boots, and especially relics and artifacts survived the Spellplague and still operate, though sometimes with altered abilities. A magical item's abilities were scribed into these devices when they were created, so even though the Weave was used in their making, the Weave no longer plays any part in their continuing operation. Likewise, though a forge flame is used in the making of a sword, if that forge flame later goes out for good, the sword is no less sharp. Does that answer you fairly?"

Raidon thought on Cynosure's words. He recalled the effects of the Spellplague on a person. The caravan chief, who'd died in its hungry grip, for instance.

The monk grunted. He asked, "Why not tell Kiril all this? She's Angul's wielder. And a swordswoman. While I am proficient with blades, I prefer not to rely on them. You would be better enlisting her than me."

Cynosure replied, "As I said before, I lost track of Kiril after the Year of Blue Fire. She bears no Sign, yet in a dim way I was able to discern her condition. After she left the ruins of Ormpetarr, she and her dwarf employer plunged into something local survivors call the Plaguewrought Land. I have not detected her or Angul's presence since. And, moreover, you are the only person with whom I can converse."

"How do you know Angul lies within the Plaguewrought Land?"

"I do not. But it is the only lead we have. Perhaps you will learn more when you visit. A small settlement lies on its outskirts—you could get yourself a meal when you arrive."

Raidon's stomach spoke up of its own accord. He was still ravenous. His grief-inspired fast had sapped his strength. A sit-down meal . . . perhaps that was what he needed. With a pot of steaming tea on the side.

"Then send me on to Ormpetarr, when your strength is recovered. I will eat. After that, perhaps I will discover Kiril's fate, and if I decide you are not dealing with me falsely, take up the sword, Angul, as my own."

CHAPTER THIRTEEN

The Year of the Secret (1396 DR)
Green Siren *on the Sea of Fallen Stars*

Y ou can't stop yourself, can you?"

Japheth looked up, his hand half out of a fold of his cloak, his fingers clutching a dull tin.

He frowned at Anusha. The girl perched on the edge of her travel case, nearly knee to knee with him as he sat on his cot. The porthole illuminated the cabin's cramped expanse, though poorly. Her face was half shadowed, but he could read her expression well enough. She was concerned. Constant proximity to her over the last days had worn away much of the distance he preferred to maintain between himself and others.

He had been lulled into a growing camaraderie. At first, she had done all the talking, relating to him the vivid details of her fight on deck against the sea hag. Japheth enjoyed her enthusiastic rendition of the events. In another person, he might have judged the story overlong, but somehow he hadn't minded as the account poured from her lips. She'd never successfully stood off a determined attack by foes eager for her blood before—why shouldn't she be flushed with success? More than that, he was interested to hear more of her peculiar sleepwalking ability.

Her question about his traveler's dust made him wish he'd maintained his customary reserve. The girl was becoming too familiar. Who was she to question his habits? Annoyance flared as a biting reply rose like acid in his throat. But he didn't voice it. Why?

Why did he not speak his mind with her? Why did he treat her so . . . delicately? Perhaps it was the fine cut of her jaw, her smooth-faced youthfulness. Her presence, in some way, recalled to him when he'd related to the world as she did, when he was still unscarred and saw limitless potential in everything. He had been like her not so long ago. Listening to her, watching her, he realized just how many dark events had got behind him. She radiated youth's naivety and energy, unconsciously and without regard to its scarcity.

If he allowed his guard to crumble further, he might make the mistake of dwelling overlong on her feminine attributes. It was better to think of her as a child, as when he'd first met her, rather than what she really was.

He imagined cradling Anusha's head in his hands and kissing her until they were both out of breath.

Lord of Bats forefend! Where had that come from? He shook his head, attempting to dislodge his thoughts from that track. He didn't need the complication of a relationship, however fleeting or innocent.

He tried to think of something else, anything else. An image of his tin filled with roseate crystals popped into his head. His palms itched in immediate response. His concentration shivered, and he growled.

"Are you all right?" Anusha asked, leaning toward him.

"My business is my own," he finally replied. He tried to make his voice cold, but it came out cracked.

Wait! He remembered what his mind kept trying to forget. Despite her protestations to the contrary, she could still be an agent of Behroun.

But once all was said and done, his hand seemed to spasm open of its own accord. The tin dropped back into his cloak.

Anusha watched him a moment more, then asked, "Do you suffer? I don't understand. You said your Lord of Bats keeps you from succumbing to the effects of traveler's dust."

"True, but the craving never leaves me."

"Maybe you're not getting the full benefit of your arrangement."

Japheth considered, then said, "I have taken more than the Lord of Bats was willing to offer. I may not negotiate further without risking all I have already gained."

Anusha digested that, then she asked, "What is a 'pact stone'? In my half brother's office, Behroun said he'd break your pact stone if you didn't do as he said, and something about how that would make the Lord of Bats so mad he'd come for you."

The girl looked at him, waiting for a reply. Confident she'd get one. Was this unearned confidence a product of her youth or her privileged upbringing? Or, it dawned on him, perhaps it was merely her personality.

"It is a complicated story."

Anusha stretched back. "We have days before we get to the atoll, you said. Tell me."

Japheth rubbed together the thumb and forefinger of the hand that had so recently held the dust tin. Why shouldn't he tell her?

The warlock said, "All right. This is the story. Before it became widely recognized that traveler's dust was ultimately lethal, I traveled too far down the crimson road. I knew I was to die, so I decided to perish in dramatic fashion, at a time of my own choosing. I took all the dust I had at one time. A lethal dose."

Anusha put a hand to her mouth.

"The crimson road leads directly into what may be the literal Abyss. Demons wait, hunger chasing across their glassy eyes. Victims of the dust walk, screaming, into demonic embrace. The road ends in a precipice, and in its tooth-lined gullet the drug-addled are consumed, mind and soul."

The girl's eyes were wide. The high color in her cheeks drained to parchment white. She believed him.

"Terrified, I regretted my decision and called out for succor, promising anything, if someone would save me from my self-inflicted fate. And thus, when a great bat sailed down from the burning sky, I thought it was my savior. It grasped me up before I could plunge to the road's terminus. Its claws held me tight, but they also cut me."

Japheth's words quickened. "It winged up through a tempest of fire, ice, and lightning, until we emerged into an enchanted reflection of the world. I saw streams of crystal water, vivid forests of living green, and mountains so high their beauty and majesty stopped my breath. I recognized it as the same landscape described in a tome I had been reading, *Fey Pacts of Ancient Days*. I realized the great winged creature was an entity also named in that tome, and I knew fear again. For the creature that held me could be none other than the Lord of Bats."

Into the silence that followed, Anusha asked, "Who is the Lord of Bats? A god?"

Japheth shook his head. "No god, but a powerful and potent creature, if called up in just the proper fashion. More by luck than wit, I had done so in dabbling with the ancient tome that named him, and my subsequent promise to enter into a bargain with any that saved me. The Lord of Bats had the strength to find me, save me, and seal a pact between us."

"A mutually beneficial pact?"

"It might have been, but in the urgency of my need, I promised everything and all; I pledged my soul, though I needn't have done so, had I known better. The Lord of Bats took advantage of my desperation. He sealed my pledge to him in a physical object—a small emerald pendant. The pact stone. It is the pact stone Behroun threatened to break, if I didn't do as I was told."

Anusha's brows tightened with incomprehension.

"My pact stone is, for all its small size, laden with consequence. Because it exists, I can call upon fell powers and feats of magic that are known to the Lord of Bats. Moreover, I can command the Lord of Bats's lesser minions, use his implements of power as my own, and even travel to his shadowed fortress. The stone is a potent tool, and it binds me to him, and him to me."

"Why would he cede you so much of his power? That seems like a mistake."

"The pact stone has one more function. The Lord of Bats pledged to take back my pact-born powers, then to drink my blood and eat my body, should the stone ever be destroyed. He invested the stone with such consequence so he could hold it to ensure my good behavior. If the pact stone is broken, I lose my powers and the Lord of Bats comes for me to collect his due."

"Oh!" Anusha gripped his shoulder as if to comfort him. He didn't shrink from the contact.

"The Lord of Bats showed me the pact stone. He told me he would destroy it if I did not do as he commanded in all things. He said I would be his puppet in the world that had banned his entry. He said that through me, the Lord of Bats would hunt the world again, as he had done in the days when humans were still 'beasts without language' and Faerie hadn't receded from the world."

The warlock clenched both fists and said in a louder voice, "Snatched so recently from the crimson road, I had little to lose. Without pondering the danger, I called swiftly and without full understanding on the power the Lord of Bats bequeathed me. I wrested the pact stone from him even as he brandished it!"

"He let the stone go?"

"His ego was his undoing, I suppose. He couldn't conceive I'd have the effrontery or wit to immediately act. Perhaps he was used to dealing with primeval men of duller wit. Perhaps his fey nature prevented him from recognizing my mortal desperation. After he realized his error, it was too late. With stone in hand, I commanded a portion of his power, and I held the implement through which he'd planned to leash me. We fought, but I imprisoned him in the highest spire of his own fortress. I claimed the castle as my own and returned to the world. I was my own agent, and the world seemed alight with possibility and promise. Until your half brother stole the stone."

"Behroun is a criminal and a bastard," agreed the girl. "I can't believe I share even half his blood. But he is no wizard or sage. How did he discover the significance of the stone?"

"That question has long troubled me. I suspect the Lord of Bats sent out messages on bat wings far and wide. The Lord of shadow-mantled Darroch Castle schemes always to break the stone, whereupon he would free himself and find me. He must have made contact with Behroun and showed Lord Marhana the significance of the stone. Not long after, I received a cordial invitation to visit New Sarshel."

The girl sniffed. "He has a way with words, when he tries."

"Yes, and my guard was down. I had no reason to suspect a trap. Moreover, I didn't expect anyone in the world to recognize the pact stone's significance, and I was lax in its safekeeping. Once I arrived in New Sarshel, your half brother employed master thieves to bring him the stone. His instruction from the Lord of Bats was to smash it. But upon gaining my pact stone, Behroun was too savvy to break it. Instead, he uses it to compel my service even as the Lord of Bats meant to."

"I am so sorry, Japheth."

He made no reply. He merely looked into her eyes. They were dark pools of mystery hinting at unplumbed depths.

She leaned forward, her lips slightly parted. It would be so easy to bend to meet her halfway and touch his lips to hers.

His heart tried to escape his chest, beating with two coequal emotions: confusion and desire.

The warlock stood abruptly and said the first thing that came into his head. "Would you like to see Darroch Castle? I can show you. We can use my cloak as a bridge."

The moment was broken, as he'd intended. And now half regretted.

The girl sighed. Then she cocked her head and smiled. She nodded up at him. "I'm on a ship bound for who knows where because I wanted to see wonders beyond Sarshel. Now you say you want to show me the castle you keep in your cloak? Of course . . . but is it safe?"

Japheth already wished he'd come up with some other way to derail the moment. He didn't want to rescind his offer, though. He replied, "Safe enough, as long as you stay close to me."

"Now?" The girl rose from the edge of her travel case. He smelled her warm scent.

Exhilaration made him incautious. He knew it, but didn't give himself more time to think it through. "Why not?"

Japheth swirled his cloak off his shoulders. He turned toward the cabin's door and held the fabric with his arms outstretched before him and slightly raised, so that the hem just touched the floor. He took one quick pace to the door and pressed the narrow rectangle of darkness he held into the door frame. When he released his grip and stepped back, the cloak remained in place, obscuring the wooden door behind it.

"It looks like a door of darkness," Anusha breathed.

He nodded. "It is. It leads to my castle."

They stepped forward. Anusha flinched as if expecting to bump her head, but instead, shadows grabbed them. Cold hands pulled them along a tunnel whose floor, walls, and ceiling were composed of leathery, undulating wings. With a flurry of flapping and a whiff of ammonia, the darkness released them.

They stood in a subterranean vault whose dimensions were lost to cobwebbed corners. Behind them along a rocky wall wavered a door-shaped opening. Japheth's cabin was blurrily visible within the rectangle.

Piercing gold and silver light from their right made them both squint. The light poured inward from an irregular, natural-looking cave mouth. Through it Japheth saw a verdant mountain meadow whose vivid colors stole his breath, as always, and whose piercing scents brought tears to his eyes. He'd never ventured in that direction, for Darroch Castle was the other way.

The gold and silver light from the cave mouth slowly fell to purples, blues, and shadow black. Over the span of a few hundred feet, the dim illumination was transformed to a dreary radiance of hopelessness. The last glimmers of light were enough to reveal a vast castle, one whose mortar was black and whose bricks were immense blocks of void. A central spire rose above the walls, so high it brushed the vault's stalactite-toothed ceiling. Immense wings stretched out from each side of the spire, rapacious and dragonlike in their span, like hunger itself made manifest.

Anusha stifled an involuntary cry and shrank back.

The noise set the ceiling to churning and chittering. It was thick with roosting bats of every variety. Many had never flown the skies of Toril.

"Shh, it is all right, Anusha." He reached for her hand, and she clutched back tight.

"The bats on the ceiling will not harm you while I am near. The vast wings you see on the castle are immobile. They possess no life, not now, anyway. The Lord of Bats is safely bound and cannot enter his shape of old while he remains imprisoned. And I don't intend to release him."

In the wan light, he saw her slowly nod, though her eyes didn't leave the unmoving shape that crouched atop the structure.

"Perhaps we should return to the *Green Siren*," suggested Japheth.

Anusha gazed around with rapt eyes.

"No . . . no. It is just . . . amazing. To know where I now stand, someplace so far from the . . . world itself? I've never traveled by magic in such fashion. It is like the stories of the spells wizards commanded before the Spellplague."

"Those abilities are returning to many across Faerûn," said the warlock.

"Yes, and not too soon. But even the most powerful of the old wizards would have been hard pressed to travel so far in a single step. We are not even in the world any longer." Her wide eyes met his. Even in the dim light of the cave, it was a connection he couldn't long hold, if he didn't want to be drawn into a rash act.

He blinked to escape her gaze. He was glad she couldn't see him well in the darkness. Why had he brought her here? To impress her? His base instincts worked against his reason, perhaps.

No, a small cynical part of him remonstrated. You know exactly what you are doing.

He said, more to defend himself from his own accusing thoughts than in answer to Anusha, "I merely make use of what I've stolen from the Lord of Bats."

"I am sure it is all beyond me, whatever the source."

Japheth coughed and suggested, "We should enter soon, if we are to do it at all. I can only successfully travel here once out of every four or five times I try. Access depends on a lunar schedule I haven't quite worked out yet. And I am more vulnerable without my cloak. So time is of the essence."

She nodded.

They walked forward, past a growth of dark purple mushroom caps, each the size of a dinner plate. Japheth pointed and said, "I should gather a couple more of those caps. When distilled, their taste can cause any creature to fall asleep. It is what I made your potion from, now that I think of it!"

Anusha didn't respond, and Japheth remembered she was still suspicious of his gift. A twinge of guilt touched him. In truth, when they'd returned to the boat after the attack of the sea hags, it had taken several hours before he was able to rouse Anusha from her somnolence.

He led the girl through the gates of Castle Darroch and down a long entry gauntlet. He ordered the creeping, wrinkled, guardian homunculi back to their holes in the side walls before Anusha could see their horrific features. The castle was defended by the Lord of Bats's many "children," who answered now to Japheth as if he were their creator.

They reached the foyer, which was lit by countless candelabra burning with green flames. A wide but shallow pool of dark water half flooded the space, and long, pale forms darted beneath its surface.

Japheth guided Anusha past the pool up four flights of stairs. They passed busts of enigmatic, slender humanoids on each landing. Lords of the Feywild, Japheth had always assumed. Anusha lingered, but he urged her onward, explaining again that they should not dally.

Finally, they entered the Grand Study. There, paintings of surreal landscapes, sculptures of fantastic beings, and objects too strange for mortal classification were displayed behind glass. The collection spanned centuries and worlds.

"This is all yours?" asked Anusha, finally relinquishing his hand. "It must be worth a king's ransom!"

"These belong to the Lord of Bats. The collection could well be priceless, but I've never removed even a single item."

Anusha moved to gaze upon a painting of a spray of orange and yellow: a desertscape in the grip of a storm. The hint of some vast tower was visible behind the haze of blowing sand.

"Why not?" she asked.

He shrugged, said, "It is just a feeling I have. I fear too many changes could upset some balance I'm not consciously aware of. Like the game where children remove twigs, one at a time, from a pile, until one twig too many causes the pile to topple. I fear to disturb things too much lest I accidentally release the Lord of Bats from his confines."

The warlock's eyes unconsciously sought a balcony overlooking the Grand Study. The balcony was accessible via a narrow stair on the wall. The high space was bare but for an iron door.

Anusha's eyes followed his. "He's up there?"

Japheth nodded.

She studied the door with wide eyes, then said, "I hear talking."

Japheth cocked his head. Sure enough, the slight buzz of voices, at least two, sounded from the balcony.

Vertigo clawed his abdomen. With eyes tight, he sprang up the narrow stairs, two at a time. He felt off-balance without his cloak streaming behind.

The steel door to the balcony was open a crack, and yellow light flickered beyond. He shoved open the door and gasped.

A great oaken table dominated the chamber beyond the door. A feast of rare sumptuousness was laid out on silver platters, heaped in golden urns, and sloshed in crystal decanters. Chairs lined the sides of the table, each one unique in design and workmanship, as if every piece was imported from a completely different kingdom or culture. A few were so oddly shaped that a regular person would find it difficult to sit.

A thin man, bald and pale, with narrow squinting eyes, pointed ears, and drab black clothes sat at the head of the table on a chair as grand as any throne.

It was the Lord of Bats in his least form. He sat as he always sat, where Japheth had bound him in a feast never-ending.

The warlock sucked in his breath as if struck because of the two people sitting to each side of the Lord of Bats. They shouldn't be there; they couldn't be!

But they were.

One was a woman. Her slender limbs and graceful poise transcended mere humanity. Her white skin literally glowed like moonlight, and her eyes were utterly black. Her hair was dark blue-black, and her ears were pointed. She might have been a moon or sun elf, but he'd never known a moon or sun elf to glow before.

The other was a man in unremarkable clothing. A man whose features were rough and uncouth in comparison to the woman's. A man who was terribly familiar.

"Behroun Marhana?" gasped Japheth.

The man to the Lord of Bats's left turned midsentence. He stopped speaking, and his eyes widened on seeing the warlock.

"Japheth?" asked the man. "Why, it is! Our host never informed me you could visit here in his home-turned-prison."

Japheth's mouth remained open, but he had no words. As unlikely as it was, the man was indeed Behroun. But how? Disorientation made him dizzy. He couldn't connect the threads.

The pale man spoke, "This one stole my skin; he uses it as a cloak. With it, he can travel between the world and my domain." His white hand plucked a cherry tomato the color of blood from a silver platter. He tossed it into his mouth and chewed with gusto.

"What is the meaning of this?" Japheth demanded of the Lord of Bats, attempting to assert some control over events that careened beyond his comprehension.

"I have guests. It has taken me some years, but my invitations finally went out and were answered in person."

The woman merely gazed upon Japheth with emotionless, ageless eyes, as if nothing he could do or say could ever surprise her or break her from centuries-long ennui.

Behroun chuckled, said, "Neifion promised me extraordinary things, but only if I shatter a certain emerald he revealed to me. I think you know the one."

The Lord of Bats glared at Behroun, saying, "You have yet to destroy it."

"Neifion?" wondered Japheth.

"The Lord of Bats has a name, same as you and me," Behroun explained. "But that's hardly important."

"Ah . . ." temporized the warlock, well beyond his depth. Then, "The Lord of Bats, uh, Neifion, he was the one who told you about my pact stone? I knew it."

"*My* pact stone," interrupted the pale lord. "Which you stole from *me*. I sent my last loyal children into the world to find an ally, and found Lord Marhana. He agreed to retrieve my property. But he failed to complete the task I set him."

"Your grace, as I said from the beginning, be patient. When Japheth has finished his current task, I shall give you the emerald as I promised."

"That is what you have been telling me for some time now."

As the Lord of Bats spoke, Behroun absent-mindedly picked up a succulent pear from the table, one of several heaped in a crystal bowl.

The woman to Neifion's right reached her slender arm across the table and slapped the fruit from Behroun's hand before he could take a bite. The fruit spun across the room and landed in shadow.

The woman said, "I told you. Do not eat from this table. If you do, you shall never leave it."

Behroun blanched. "I know that, Malyanna, but damn the old king if this food doesn't look enticing!"

The elflike woman replied, "It is a lethal enchantment given a pleasant guise."

Japheth knew that the woman, whatever her otherworldly origin, spoke the truth regarding the great feast—it was one of the Lord of Bats's own tricks. Japheth had commandeered it and used it against its creator when he'd assumed control. The warlock wondered again if she was native to the bright, fey lands beyond the cave. Perhaps she was a moon elf "noble," an elder native of the Feywild, inscrutable and dangerous. What was her place in all this? Was Malyanna her name or a title?

The woman speared Behroun like a fish with her glinting stare. Behroun wriggled and gasped until she turned back to regard Japheth. She said, "You look confused, poor human. For all your stolen power, you're only a plaything here. All of you are, Behroun too, though he thinks himself the ringleader." She sighed and looked to the ceiling as if bored beyond the capacity for words.

The Lord of Bats sucked down another bloody red tomato and announced, matter-of-factly, "I shall murder each of you in a manner so grisly that veteran warriors shall shudder and weep when they hear of it."

The woman continued to inspect the ceiling, her face managing to convey weariness for all its otherworldly perfection.

Behroun spluttered, his features draining of color, "But once I break the pact stone, you will have all you desire, Neifion! You'll have your powers returned, with Japheth here to punish—"

"The longer you delay your side of our agreement, the greater latitude I'll have in interpreting our deal," declared the Lord of Bats, his dead-white lips smacking in anticipation.

Behroun glanced at Malyanna, then he snapped his attention around to Japheth. "Warlock! How goes the mission? How close are you to retrieving this object, what did the captain call it, the Dreamheart?"

With a dull voice, Japheth replied, "We sail to the lair of the creature that holds it even now."

"You hear?" asked the shipping magnate in too loud a voice. "Once I get the Dreamheart, Japheth'll be yours. I'll have all I need to press my claim on Impiltur. With a relic as potent as Captain Thoster claims this one is in my hand, I won't have to be satisfied with a mere seat on the nascent Grand Council. No, with an eladrin queen of the Feywild at my side—"

Malyanna's voice drowned out Behroun with a simple, "Please, don't you ever cease your mortal prattle?"

Behroun's face crumpled. Trying to recover, he snapped his fingers at Japheth. "Shouldn't you get back to your ship?"

Japheth looked at the man. A small man with grand ambitions was Lord Marhana. He had no power of his own, only a knack for being in the right place at the right time. Though he possessed no moral sense, he had a mean, ratlike cleverness.

The warlock once confronted Behroun, asking the merchant why he should do Behroun's bidding. After all, if Japheth did not, Behroun promised to smash the pact stone. On the other hand, Behroun had implied that at some future date he would return the pact stone to the Lord of Bats, who would promptly smash it.

Either way, the stone would be smashed and Japheth would wind up dead. So why, the warlock had yelled, should he do what Behroun wanted when his choice was to die now or die later? Behroun had winked and replied that he didn't actually intend to ever give the pact stone back to the Lord of Bats. *If* Japheth did his bidding, promised Lord Marhana, Japheth could live out his life without fear of being slain by a vicious Feywild spirit bent on brutal revenge.

The memory evaporated in a haze of reignited hate. Emotion burned the warlock's throat as he stepped forward a pace. He was only about ten feet from Lord Marhana's chair.

Japheth asked in a casual tone that belied his anger, "Do you have the pact stone with you now, Behroun?"

Both the woman and the Lord of Bats simultaneously swung their heads around to regard Behroun, real interest animating Malyanna's face for the first time.

"What does that matter?" snapped Behroun.

Japheth advanced another pace. As he did so, he saw the image of someone behind him reflected in a silver decanter. A figure in full, articulated plate armor that shone like gold. The figure held a long sword as if it were weightless. Surprised, he glanced back. Nobody was there. But when he looked in the decanter once more, he saw again the figure. This time, he also noted the armored warrior was limned in small blue and black flames. The cuirass was molded to a figure with a distinctively feminine cast.

Anusha? If so, she didn't look anything like the meek dream image he'd glimpsed before. Was she, as he had half suspected, really working for Behroun? Would she attack him if he threatened her half-witted half brother, who might very well have left the pact stone back in the world? If he struck suddenly enough to kill Behroun, then he could return to the world and retrieve his pact stone from wherever Behroun had secreted it. He'd be free!

Indecision cost him. Malyanna rose from her chair, pushing it back so hard it slammed into the wall and splintered. She did not stand—no, she hovered in the air with no support, her hair whipping dramatically in a wind as cold as the Hammer's worst blizzard. She pointed a finger at Japheth and said, "Think not to harm this fool. Behroun is under my protection . . . for now."

Japheth realized he was flanked by enemies. A dream

assassin at his back, maybe, and an eladrin noble before him, whose abilities he couldn't gauge, though he suspected she was formidable.

And he didn't have his cloak.

Japheth smiled at the floating woman, at the still seated Lord of Bats who watched the proceedings with great interest even as he nibbled on an apple, and finally at Behroun, whose struggle to stand up ended with both him and his chair sprawled on the floor.

He said, "I'm done with fear, Behroun. You should have brought the pact stone with you."

Japheth uttered his most potent curse, aimed it at Behroun, and loosed it as if it were a hunting kestrel.

A blaze of fire swept down upon Behroun, who already sprawled behind his fallen chair. When the flames settled over the man, he began to scream.

The hovering eladrin noble sang out a single syllable. The motes of flame bedeviling Behroun instantly died in puffs of white smoke. A backwash of cold air touched Japheth's cheeks.

The Lord of Bats began to laugh, even as he reached for a platter of sugar-crusted toast.

The warlock reflexively moved to step back into his cloak, to retreat into shadow. He failed. Of course he failed; his cloak still served as a bridge between Darroch Castle and the *Green Siren* back in the outer cavern! He cursed anew, this time with words devoid of arcane power; they were merely fragments of frustration and renewed fear.

Malyanna looked down her nose at him. A hint of interest, passion even, animated her eyes. She said something in a tongue Japheth didn't know, a language that would have been beautiful in nearly any other creature's mouth. In her mouth, it seemed sinister. Suddenly she switched to Common and said, "I will kill you now."

A skirling blast of winter began to chase around her

upraised hand and arm. She flung it at Japheth. It raked him as if an ice-clawed beast.

The warlock uttered a counter chant, sending eldritch rays of red light to nip and bite at the eladrin's flesh. She flinched with each impact, but her eyes only grew wider and more excited, even as the miniature storm of ice she'd summoned continued to enfold Japheth.

He began to bleed, but his blood froze before it could drip on the floor.

This woman was powerful. Too powerful to be a moon elf native to Faerûn who'd spent her life wondering about stories of a fey realm nearly unreachable, until now. No, this was an eladrin who'd lived always within the Feywild. She had never suffered a separation from her homeland as so many of her kin had. Now that the Spellplague had reunited the world and Fairie, moon and sun elves of Faerûn could seek their ancestral homeland. For the first time, it occurred to Japheth that eladrin might have an interest in Faerûn equal to what the moon and sun elves of Faerûn had in the Feywild.

The woman's strength was, he recognized, too much for him. Its chilling cold communicated an old and deadly determination. Ice crystals accumulated and began to encase his skin. He sent another red bolt Malyanna's way, which she caught on a shield of ice and deflected. He wondered if he had met his end. Without his cloak, it could be. His cloak, which indeed was once the Lord of Bats's, contained half his power.

"No!" yelled Behroun, trying to shout over the Lord of Bats's insane mirth. "Malyanna, we need him! If you kill him, all our plans will be for nothing!"

Malyanna sniffed. "Another will serve. That pirate captain of yours will get the relic. Thoster? This one is mine. My blood's up, and I mean to finish." She drifted forward, her hand still outstretched, her fingers subtly whirling with the icy winds that thieved away Japheth's life. Her eyes were rapacious, as unlike a moon elf's as any he'd ever witnessed.

Japheth drew a breath to utter his last true curse, but the air was like sandpaper granulated with ice crystals. Instead, he fell into a coughing fit. His cloak! He needed it! Could he summon it to him? Try, damn it, he pleaded with himself. But he was so cold . . .

A crystal goblet of sloshing wine rose from the table without any visible means of support.

"Now the crockery is haunted?" murmured the eladrin.

Only Japheth had the proper angle to see a distorted reflection in a bowl of pomegranates. The goblet was in the hands of the armored figure Japheth had seen reflected moments earlier.

"Anusha?" whispered Japheth. His voice was too faint for anyone to hear.

"What trick is this, Neifion?" inquired the eladrin, glancing to the Lord of Bats. When her eyes left Japheth, the cold immediately lessened. "Stop playing games."

Neifion, still laughing, merely shrugged and shook his head.

The goblet suddenly rushed at the eladrin noble, its enchanted, red contents sloshing uncontrollably from its lip.

Behroun and Malyanna simultaneously uttered, "No!"

A moment before the liquid could strike the eladrin, she faded in a flurry of blowing snow.

The goblet continued its lazy arc and smashed messily on the flagged floor.

If it had struck the eladrin in the eyes or mouth, she would have been bound to the table with the Lord of Bats, there to eat away eternity, until released by Japheth.

The warlock started breathing easily again. The ice coating his flesh was already melting. But his strength was uncertain.

He felt a hand upon his arm but saw no limb. A whisper

in his ear urged, "We must flee before she returns!"

"Wait—" he began, turning toward Behroun. But the man was already gone. He must have disappeared with the eladrin. Which made sense. Lord Marhana did not possess the craft to reach this realm under his own power. The man would survive this day, it seemed. He might already be back in his home, looking for the pact stone. Japheth had missed his chance to end his bondage.

Seeing where Japheth looked, the Lord of Bats ceased laughing. In a voice containing not the least hint of hilarity, he said, "Let us hope he is breaking that stone even now. I find this feast has whetted my appetite. Perhaps I will quench it by dining on your liver before the day is done."

Japheth shuddered. He allowed Anusha's unseen pressure on his arm guide to him through the exit.

He slammed the iron door and slid home the bolt. Not that he had any confidence left in its ability to keep intruders out of Neifion's prison.

He turned and took the steps into the Great Hall two at a time. At the bottom of the stair lay Anusha's sleeping form, curled on her side like a child. He tried to wake her. She didn't stir.

A tiny silver vial rolled away from her right hand.

"Oh, Anusha!" He picked up the girl. Her head lolled on his shoulder.

"Japheth, I can't wake up!" The voice came from a few paces to his left.

"Yes, yes, don't worry. It's the potion. It'll take a few hours to clear out of your blood. Plus, you last used it only a few days ago."

"Oh, sure, of course," she replied, relief evident. "It's a strange feeling, not being able to release my dream form . . ."

To distract her, he said, "Quick thinking, that was, throwing the wine at the eladrin."

"Too bad I missed. Something was not right about her. She was too old for her skin, or something."

Japheth nodded soberly. "Indeed."

They walked quickly from Darroch Castle, a ghost at his side, and her warm flesh cradled in his arms.

CHAPTER FOURTEEN

The Year of the Secret (1396 DR)
Ormpetarr, Vilhon Wilds

The Year of Blue Fire and its consequences wrought calamity on Chondath, Sespech, and other nearby lands. The great body of water called the Vilhon Reach splintered into several smaller lakes. The black-walled mesas punched out of the ground, destroying roads, farms, and whole cities. Crazed pockets of gleaming light and sound, where madness and reality still churned, visibly writhed and coiled across the landscape even years after the Spellplague was thought concluded. Most of the people in the region who survived the initial onslaught fled as best they could. Many died in their exodus, and the rest found themselves unwanted refugees in far kingdoms that had their own disasters to deal with.

According to Cynosure, only the hardiest

explorers dared the great frontier these days. Hideous, plaguechanged monsters haunted dark ravines. Ruins of cities devastated and deserted lay broken along old trade roads, near drained lake and river basins, and scattered in broken bits and pieces along the sides of newly birthed landforms.

The sentient golem noted that Ormpetarr had arguably weathered the transition better than any other in the region.

Raidon stood north of Ormpetarr's battered, leaning gates, taking in the view from a rise in the rutted, weedy path once called the Golden Road. A moment earlier, he had been west of Nathlan, but the sentient golem of Stardeep "transferred" Raidon through a starry medium in the space of a heartbeat. His ears rang—the trip had been much rougher than the previous time the golem transported him.

Many of Ormpetarr's ancient brass spires, famed for their ability to reflect the setting sun like flame, now lay broken and strewn down the rocky side of a steep precipice. The precipice separated the surviving neighborhoods of the city from a permanent, eye-watering cloud of color that churned south away from the city like the old Nagawater used to. This was the Plaguewrought Land, a pocket where active spellplague still cavorted and contorted land, law, magic, and the flesh of any creature that entered.

"You are certain people remain in this ruin?" Raidon inquired of the air, his gaze caught by the nausea-inducing area beyond the city.

No reply.

"Cynosure?"

The effigy had warned the monk that moving him so far across Faerûn would exhaust its energies for a time. Apparently, the golem was so drained it could no longer maintain simple communication.

"I pray you did not overextend yourself," Raidon murmured, on the chance Cynosure could still hear him.

The construct had provided some background on the area, but he was on his own to learn what mattered most. Raidon walked south, down the road to the gates.

A one-armed dwarf appeared in the gap between the two leaning gateposts. The dwarf wore chain mail half gone to rust. He cradled a stout crossbow on one shoulder with his single limb, sighting down its length at Raidon. Apparently the dwarf was well practiced making do with one hand.

The dwarf called out, "Beg your pardon, traveler! Sorry to bother ye this fine spring day, but please stand still a moment, eh?"

Raidon paused. He stood some twenty feet from the gate.

The dwarf grinned through a beard whose tangles competed in size and intricacy with its braids. He said, "That's a good fellow, eh? We don't get many visitors, and those we do get are not always polite, if ye know what I mean."

Raidon replied, "I am no outlaw ruffian. Will you let me pass? I have business in Ormpetarr."

"What remains of Ormpetarr, you mean," chuckled the dwarf. "I can see ye are no ravening beast, and better still, ye can speak, which argues all the more for what ye claim. Well then, I suppose I should ask after what brings ye here, and charge the customary fee?"

Raidon silently hoped the dwarf wasn't courteously trying to rob him. He said, "An old companion of mine came here not long after the Spellplague. I seek to find what trace I can of her."

"Mmm, hmmm," grunted the gate warden, his curly eyebrows raised to a skeptical height. "Why'd she come here?"

"I hope to discover that."

"Scar pilgrimage, as sure as water runs downhill."

Raidon asked, "What do you mean?"

The dwarf dropped the point of the crossbow and used the entire weapon to motion Raidon forward. "Ye'll find out within. And, since I'm feeling friendly today, a single gold crown will see ye through Ormpetarr's gates, such as they are." The dwarf nodded toward a great wooden chest chained to a granite slab. Raidon guessed the wide slit in the top served as a coin slot.

Raidon walked through the gates, dropped a coin in the opening, and continued into the city.

The dwarf wished him a good day, but Raidon didn't waste more breath on the fellow. He was already past, his eyes crawling over the landscape of half-collapsed and abandoned buildings. Then he smelled charred meat on the wind. He stopped moving. His mouth watered.

The odor was ambrosial. His empty stomach commandeered his feet and turned him toward a rambling edifice just inside the gate. Like the other surviving structures he'd glimpsed, this building was cracked and worse for wear, having seen little if any upkeep. However, light, voices, and the smell of cooking food issued from it. No sign or exterior glyph indicated the name or nature of the place.

Raidon pushed through the open door into a wide, low chamber. It resembled the common rooms of travelers' inns he'd seen all across Faerûn, complete with some four-footed beast sizzling on a spit in the fireplace. Raidon took a deep breath, savoring the odor.

About a dozen people were present, gathered into three distinct groups, save for a lone grandfather near the door snoring into a spilled tankard of ale, a woman in a barkeep's apron bustling around the chamber, and a boy manning the spit.

A man muttered from his drink, "Look 'ee, a half-elf." All eyes swiveled to regard Raidon.

The monk raised a hand, said, "Greetings. I seek a meal, and information."

The barkeep yelled, "Grab a table, traveler, and I'll bring you ale and stew. The boar'll be done enough to cut up later, if you're having any?"

"I am," affirmed Raidon. He walked forward, past the inquisitive locals, and sat himself down at the bar. He could feel the weight of curious eyes on his back, and hear the beginning buzz of speculation.

The barkeep pulled his drink and set it before him in a wooden tankard. Raidon eyed the frothy liquid but decided against asking for tea. He doubted the establishment carried such niceties of civilization.

The woman yelled, "Merl, stop idling over there, and get this fellow a bowl of stew!" The boy at the spit started from his daydream daze and darted into a back room.

"My thanks," Raidon told the barkeep.

She nodded without a hint of cordiality. She said, "If you're here to join these fools on their 'Scar Pilgrimage,' then I doubt I'll ever see you again. Might as well spend your gold now, because once you're dead, it'll do you no good."

Uncertain of her meaning and as yet unwilling to reveal his ignorance, Raidon merely returned her look without reply.

The boy reappeared from the back room with a fired clay bowl filled with cold stew. The boy set it before the monk, then returned to his position by the fire to give the spit another turn.

Raidon fell to. He couldn't later recall the flavors, he consumed the dish so quickly.

The barkeep cocked her head, asked, "Nothing to say? Hungry enough, though. I can see by your clothing you're no brigand come to spend ill-gotten loot. You'd be dressed more elaborately and would have ordered hard spirits. What kind of scar do you think you'll find in the Plaguewrought Land?"

"I do not seek more scars," Raidon said, wiping his mouth on a piece of linen.

The barkeep laughed, shaking her head.

"You ain't here for a pilgrimage?" came a voice behind Raidon.

The grandfather was awake. His brown eyes twinkled, and laugh lines crinkled around them. His beard was streaked white and black, and so was his long hair tied back in a single braid. His clothing was damp from the spilled ale he'd been dozing in.

"I am not seeking a scar in the Plaguewrought Land. Why would I?"

"People don't come here for any old blemish," said the old man. "They come to be scarred by the Plaguewrought Land."

"To be scarred by . . ." Raidon trailed off, recalling what one of the ghouls outside Starmantle had said, before it tried to eat him. It babbled something about spellscars. About how spellplague didn't killed everyone it touched, but changed some instead. Sometimes monstrously.

Raidon inquired, "Are there those insane enough to subject themselves to active spellplague?"

A few of the people gathered in the bar shifted to expressions of self-conscious doubt or embarrassment; other faces hardened into looks of defiance. Raidon realized he'd erred.

"My apologies," he said. "I did not mean to offend. Pardon me for my ignorance of your ways. Suffice it to say, I am not here to undertake a scar pilgrimage, nor do I possess sufficient experience to comment on what you seek."

The eyes of the tavern's occupants remained on him. A few seemed mollified, though not all. Regardless, he might have no better chance to ask his questions.

He continued, "No, I am here for another reason. I am looking for an old friend who came here a few years after the Spellplague. A woman, a . . . a star elf actually, attired as a warrior. She was named Kiril Duskmourn, and she bore a sword called Angul. Were any of you here then? Did any of you see Kiril?"

The barkeep shook her head. "A lot of people come through here, and most never return once they leave. Those who go on the scar pilgrimage usually stay a few tendays or months building up their nerve, then I never see them again. A few do come back, ecstatic or horrified, depending. Anyway, I don't remember this woman."

"I remember her," declared the old man.

Raidon swiveled back, his pulse responding but his face betraying no hint of his eagerness to know. "What do you remember?"

The grandfather put a finger to his lips, shook his head. "It weren't too long after the Spellplague picked up Ormpetarr and tossed it down again, like a child throwing a tantrum. Ormpetarr was reduced to its present sad state in moments. Many were killed. I remember the screams and cries of the survivors, I do."

The grandfather took a pull on his tankard. The barkeep must have refilled it during the old man's doze.

"But some of us survived. And a few of us stayed. That's right, I stayed!" The man's tone verged on belligerence. "Where else could we go? Plus, we had our own special souvenir of the Spellplague: a pocket that didn't fade away like most of the rest in Faerûn. It lingered, just beyond the city. Ormpetarr's claim to fame in the wider world, eh? These ruins aren't home merely to crazies, ne'er-do-wells, and criminals. No. Well, we got them, but we also got pilgrims."

Another sip, then he continued, "People began to trickle in, just one or two every month. The swordswoman you're describing was one. She wanted to enter the Plaguewrought Land."

"Why?" demanded Raidon.

"Probably heard the story of Madruen Morganoug and wanted to try for herself, same as the rest of the pilgrims that came later."

That name drew smiles and nods of happy assent from many others present.

Raidon cocked his head to signal his unfamiliarity with the name.

"You don't know much, do you?"

A thread of heat urged Raidon to grasp the man's head and bang it hard against the table. Slightly shocked to even entertain such a thought, the monk outwardly revealed his discomposure by narrowing his lips. He requested, "Explain."

The grandfather laughed. "Well, Madruen entered the Plaguewrought Land, and unlike everyone before him, Madruen returned. 'Course, it was an accident he'd fallen in at all, and the rest of us figured he was dead. A day later he walked back into town, his skin aglow with blue fire and a smile plastered across his face. He was touched by the spellplague. He was the first spellscarred anyone ever heard about."

More nods from the clientele and even a couple of cheers.

Raidon said, "Why did Madruen smile? Why did his skin glow?"

"He smiled because he wasn't dead. His skin glowed because he soaked up the wild magic of the Plaguewrought Land, and it remade him. His skin was like iron—almost impossible to cut through. He could withstand daggers, swords, even ballista! Madruen was a walking palisade!"

Raidon took a deep breath and found his focus again. The image of the Cerulean Sign tattooed on his chest flashed before him, and he supposed, indeed, he was spellscarred like Madruen, but with a different outcome.

"When his story spread, others started coming here, hoping to share in Madruen's good luck."

"How many who enter the Plaguewrought Land return?"

"Well, at first the survival rate wasn't too good. We're a few years in now, though. Pilgrims got a chance to get in and get out without dissolving into slime or blowing away in a puff of wind."

"And how many come back spellscarred?" pressed the monk.

"One out of every ten who survive in the first place," pronounced the grandfather as solemnly as if he were relaying news of a new king in Cormyr.

"And how many survive?" prompted Raidon.

"Not always the same. Sometimes it's one out of five, other times one out o' twenty."

Nearby patrons blanched.

"So Kiril Duskmourn entered the Plaguewrought Land," said Raidon, "and never returned." He uttered the last as a statement, not a question.

The old man nodded. "Yes. She was with a dwarf; his name I don't recall. He said he was a geomancer who wanted to study the Plaguewrought Land from the inside."

"His name was Thormud. But a geomancer? What's that?"

The old man shrugged. "Who knows? He said he was seeking something. A . . . a 'chalk horse,' I think. The dwarf and Kiril went in, and . . ." The old man shrugged again, then called loudly for another drink.

The barkeep complied. As she passed Raidon with another sloshing tankard, she said, "I sell safe routes into the Plaguewrought Land. How much you willing to pay?"

Raidon examined the map penned on rough parchment. A trail called the "Pilgrim's Path" was crudely marked. It snaked past Ormpetarr's gates and on into the hazy edge of the Plaguewrought Land. The path meandered relatively straight for a few miles until it rounded a landmark labeled "Granite Vortex." The route zigged and zagged between several more unlikely sounding locations, slowly wending toward the heart of the discontinuity. The last portions of the map contained several alternate routes, all marked with a symbol indicating ignorance of what lay beyond it.

The barkeep had assured the monk that if he stayed on the path, there was a better than even chance he'd survive. At least until he got closer to the center, at which point it was anyone's guess. But only those who pressed forward at the last were rewarded with a spellscar. Well, the handful who were not caught up and consumed. It seemed a mad gamble to Raidon. He hoped his own previous contact with the spellplague would offer him some protection now.

The pack burro to Raidon's left issued a complaining bleat. A gray-haired woman was hanging another waterskin to its already prodigious load. The woman's name was Finara, and she was a mage, or had been, before the Spellplague. She'd lost her way since then. She had not been able to learn the new weft of the Weave, and thus could no longer perform magic. Upon losing her spellcasting ability, followed soon by her wizard tower and livelihood, hard times found her. Finara explained she was a pilgrim now because it was the only option remaining. If she couldn't find a new understanding of magic in the Plaguewrought Land, she was happy to accept death in its stead.

To the monk's right stood a young man in simple leathers. An old long sword in a battered sheath hung on his belt. The man said his name was Hadyn. He'd traveled far to become a pilgrim. All the way from Waterdeep, he had earnestly explained. Even after the rest of his party had fell to gnoll marauders in the Greenfields, Hadyn had pressed onward. He said his journey took him the better part of a year. He said a dream sustained him. A dream of wielding a piece of the Weave, like a god of old.

When Raidon bought the map from the barkeep, she'd explained that a small party of pilgrims was readying for a trip into the Plaguewrought Land the very next morning and that he was welcome to join them. The barkeep explained groups had a better success rate for bare survival than lone explorers. Raidon thanked her and agreed to join the foolhardy band.

"Are you ready?" inquired the monk of his chance-met companions.

Hadyn smiled and gave a firm nod.

Finara looked worried but said, "Of course."

Behind them stood a small crowd, mostly would-be pilgrims who had yet to gather the courage for their own try at a spellscar. When Raidon, Hadyn, Finara, and the burro started forward, they loosed a ragged cheer.

Before them was the steep precipice that divided the surviving half of Ormpetarr from the cloud of churning color that consumed the southern portion of the city. An enterprising carpenter had rigged a wooden ramp down the least steep portion of the slope, held in place by rope and iron pitons. The ramp descended into the mist. The rickety platform marked the beginning of the Pilgrim's Path.

They descended the wooden ramp, its boards creaking with each step. The burro complained loudly, but Finara managed to yank it along.

They paused at the interface's edge. From a distance, it looked like bluish fog. This close, it was more like gazing down into a rippled, partly murky pool. Everything outside was sharp-edged and clear, and everything within was blurred and wavering. Shapes and colors writhed beyond the boundary, but from this side, it was impossible to determine what they were.

Raidon concentrated on the Cerulean Sign blazoned on his chest. Despite his fears, it was quiescent. It detected nothing blatantly aberrant in the Plaguewrought Land, at least here.

Taking a deep breath, Raidon plunged through.

A cold, tingling wave prickled across his skin, tugged at his clothes, and pulled his hair out straight. Hues he'd never seen or imagined danced across his vision. He blinked, trying to clear his eyes, and finally succeeded. Before him lay the Plaguewrought Land.

A warped, quivering vista spread away south. Land slid and mixed like slowly boiling mud. Not only land, but rivulets of blue fire, ruins, trees and foliage, and even the sky itself dipped down here and there to touch the ground. It all flowed together as if contained in a cream churner whose edges were the horizon. The earth, streamers of blue fire, air, and half-glimpsed items of incomprehensible aspect mixed, melded, then separated, emerging from the morass as some new, more bizarre feature of the landscape.

To the ramp's left, an object, half stone, part color, and perhaps partly living—slowly heaved up out of the undulating earth below. It was the size of a city building, and it blazed like an azure bonfire. It groaned and shrieked, reached a handlike appendage for the pilgrims. It dissolved into a cacophony of screams, gleams, and flowing liquid before it could reach them.

"Gods!" Hadyn burst out. He backpedaled but was blocked by the burro.

Finara grabbed Hadyn's shoulder and yelled loud enough to be heard above the roar of the subsiding object, "Wait! Stay with us!"

The young man struggled in her grasp. Finara spun Hadyn around and said, "We knew we'd find something like this! We knew the spellplague still cavorted here! We can't turn back now!"

Finara's eyes sought Raidon's. Despite her words, her tone and glance seemed to be asking Raidon: or can we turn back after all?

Raidon studied the wooden bridge, which stretched forward across and through the tumult. Somehow, the wooden construction remained inviolate. At least as far as he could see, though a bend in the path took it behind a glimmering indigo mound and out of sight.

The monk said, "I intend to press onward."

Finara let go of the young man. He released a shuddering

breath, then he said, "Sorry about that. I—I was caught off guard. I want to keep going too. I want a spellscar."

They started again. Raidon tried to keep his eyes on the wooden planks before him, but flashes of light, roars of outrageous sound, and sudden winds kept flicking his attention up to one side or the other. Each time he did so, his focus trembled.

A hundred paces farther on, Hadyn stopped, bent over the side of the wooden bridge's railing, and was noisily sick.

They waited, saying nothing, eyes averted. Raidon suspected the wavering perspective was confusing the young man's senses as much as it tried to disrupt his own. Raidon's martial focus provided protection, and by the smell of Finara's breath, spirits apparently provided her some insulation from the mad panorama. The young man had to rely on willpower alone to keep shuffling forward.

"What keeps this bridge safe from the spellplague?" Hadyn gasped, wiping his mouth.

Finara squinted at the wooden struts, then shook her head. "I've lost my sensitivity to magic. Perhaps it is enchanted? I can't tell."

Raidon had wondered the same. Hopefully it wasn't some quality they needed to know about to survive.

Hadyn signaled he was feeling better by taking the lead. Raidon allowed it. Finara and her burro brought up the rear.

They rounded the great mound, and Hadyn pulled up short. The monk looked up and saw the object of Hadyn's fear. The wooden bridge extended out over a great pit, without apparent support. A grinding, splintering sound emanated from the hole, and rock dust blew into the air. The bridge vibrated with a terrible rending sound. Raidon edged forward, past the still motionless Hadyn, until he too paused when the trembling planks beneath him grew worrisome, as if they intended to fly apart, leaving behind their former unity as a bridge.

Even from where he stood, Raidon could see some distance into the pit. Great slabs of stone, all in motion, swirled around a central column of sapphire flame. Each slab stretched a hundred feet or more in length. When the slabs slammed into each other, a booming crash rang out. From above, the sound was so loud it threatened to collapse the monk's eardrums.

A hand touched his shoulder. It was Finara. She yelled into his ear, "This is the Granite Vortex. This is the first landmark on the Pilgrim's Path!"

Raidon produced the map and studied it. Yes, that must be what this was. Unfortunately, the vortex had apparently shifted somewhat since the map had been drawn—the path wasn't supposed to pass right over it.

"We should consider leaving the bridge here," Raidon yelled back. "It looks like the burro will be able to just make it down too—"

"But then we'll be off the path!" protested Hadyn. "We'll be vulnerable!"

Raidon shrugged and returned, "Whether here or five miles farther on, we were destined to leave the marked path. I mislike the look of this vortex. You must choose."

CHAPTER FIFTEEN

The Year of the Secret (1396 DR)
Taunissik, Sea of Fallen Stars

Captain Thoster studied the distant mote on the horizon through a tube of black iron. He stood at the *Green Siren's* bow with the kuo-toa priestess, Nogah, at his side. Her skin was mottled with saltwater droplets.

Japheth watched the two, wrapped in his cloak against the direct light of the sun. He was trying to figure out what Behroun was up to, how and why he had allied with an eladrin noble out of the Feywild, and just what was in it for a creature of her power to throw in with a mortal.

Nogah croaked, breaking the warlock's reverie, "Do you see it? Can you see Taunissik?"

"Aye, I see it, your fishy greatness," replied Thoster. "Don't get your scales in a twist."

Japeth shaded his eyes with a hand and squinted into the glare. A smudge was still several miles off, just above the horizon. But even so far, and without a spyglass, he could just make out regular planes and angles that bespoke a city of some sort.

Seren lightly elbowed Japheth in the side, murmured, "What do you think of our chances, really? I am not without power, and my foes would not call me a coward. But a great kraken! Are you not concerned?" Seren was companionably close, even though he'd edged away twice. Each time he'd done so, she'd bridged the distance again. Was she needling him purposefully?

Japheth rewarded the woman's persistence with a nod. He said, "Our task will not be easy. But I have no choice. I must see this through to the end."

Seren smiled suddenly and said, "You are a noble one, aren't you? You come off all hard and nasty, but it turns out you have a soft spot running through you a mile wide."

The warlock frowned, uncomfortable in the woman's overly wide smile and eyes that kept trying to meet and hold his own.

He looked away, only to feel the wizard's hand on his shoulder. She said, "It's an endearing trait, you know. Thoster, here, he cares for nothing but himself. But you! You have a heart large enough to care for others. That is something I could come to admire."

Seren's hand remained on Japheth's shoulder and squeezed lightly. Even through his thick, batskin cloak, he could feel the warmth of her palm.

Japheth took a step away, so that her hand fell loose. He said, "If you think I am softhearted or noble, you have woefully misjudged me."

Seren gestured so that both palms lay open and empty, a gesture of entreaty. Her wrists were thin and shapely, her hands well formed. Japheth looked up to her face. She asked,

"Why do you constantly pull away from me, Japheth? I like you. Are you so wrapped up in your gloomy thoughts that you haven't noticed that?"

"Yes, I have been preoccupied," allowed the warlock. He recalled Anusha's sleeping body in his arms as he'd carried her from his fey castle.

"Well, there's no more excuse to ignore me, now that all our cards are on the table, so to speak." Seren grinned with a certain ferocity.

"I . . . I am flattered, Seren. But now is not the time. We go into the lair of the beast. Best we do not even begin down that road."

"Are you lonely?" she inquired, her voice soft. "I know I am, by myself in my cabin each and every long night."

An image of Anusha on his bunk eating trail rations briefly obscured Seren's form. She was wearing a shift that left her neck and shoulders bare. His cheeks warmed, though he doubted the wizard could see him blush under the shadow of his hood. If she could, she'd likely misinterpret it. He and Anusha were working toward something, it was clear, something more than friendship. His heart beat faster.

What Seren wanted was something like that, but without the friendship. He kept his face hard.

"Well?" asked the wizard, her own face also beginning to redden, not from embarrassment, but from the anger of incipient rejection.

"Hoy!" Thoster's call cut through the line of tension running between them. "Japheth! Seren! What're you two squabbling about? Step up here! We have little time to devise our strategy!"

The wizard studied him a moment longer. Then, instead of letting her face break into a scowl, she chuckled. She winked and said, "This trip isn't over yet. If we defeat the great kraken, perhaps you'll be in a more celebratory mood."

She joined Thoster and Nogah at the railing, leaving

Japeth shaking his head. The white-clad wizard was not used to being denied, that was clear.

He approached the group, putting the kuo-toa between himself and Seren. Nogah was responding to some biting question the wizard had just asked. "It isn't as hopeless as you suppose, human. I can safely guide us through the city and down to where the kraken rests. I can sense the Dreamheart even now. I'm close enough to obscure our approach, and the closer I get, the stronger I'll become!"

Japeth and Thoster exchanged a quick glance. The captain flicked his eyes to the kuo-toa, then back at him, then gave a slight negative shake of his head. Was he saying Nogah shouldn't long be allowed to keep the Dreamheart, if they successfully retrieved it? Perhaps. Or perhaps the warlock was merely projecting what he wanted to read in the captain's signal. Regardless, Japeth would have to take it for Behroun, whatever Nogah thought or Thoster wanted. The warlock decided he wouldn't volunteer his intention just yet. It was possible Thoster no longer considered himself in Behroun's employ, with such a great prize at hand.

"May I see?" Japeth asked Thoster, gesturing for the spy tube.

Thoster passed over the viewing glass. Japeth raised the cylinder to his eye and squinted. The distant mote leaped into focus. He saw an island on which oddly canted structures sprawled between dry land and a sickle-moon-shaped lagoon. A noticeable dimness suffused the air over the island, as if the day's sunlight was reluctant to illuminate the kuo-toa community.

"There is a quality to the light I mistrust," the warlock noted. He wondered if he shouldn't take a grain of traveler's dust, just to make certain nothing slipped past his perception. With that thought, he perceived tiny ants crawling across his palm. He didn't look—he knew the sensation was in his mind.

Nogah interjected, "We should go now. Prepare a small craft for those of you who can't swim."

"Which would be all of us," Seren replied.

Nogah glanced at Thoster but only nodded.

"If you can protect us from being detected, shouldn't we take the whole ship closer?" the wizard pressed.

"I can obscure a small craft but not something as large as the *Green Siren.*"

Thoster bawled out orders for the small launch to be readied. When it was lowered over the side, the captain, Seren, Japheth, six crew members assigned to row, and even the first mate, Nyrotha, climbed down into the rocking craft. Though he couldn't see her, Japheth supposed Anusha accompanied the landing party. Again, more powerfully this time, the urge to withdraw a speck of dust from his hidden tin made his throat feel swollen. The ants now felt like they were crawling up his forearms too. He gripped the gunwale to keep his hands occupied.

Nogah simply dived off the side of the *Green Siren.* She arrowed into the chop with barely a splash. A moment later, the kuo-toa's scaled head reappeared near the launch, her wide eyes blinking through the bluish gray waves.

Thoster loosed the knots, and the rowers began their backbreaking sculls. Slowly, the launch began to close the distance to the isle. Nogah swam alongside, gurgling a half-audible chant. Japheth at first thought she was praying, then remembered she was outcast from her goddess. She must be drawing power from the Dreamheart in some ritualized fashion. Presumably the chant provided protection against the observers on the island, though he couldn't perceive any obvious effect. The warlock was impressed she could call upon the stone's power from so far. He hoped Gethshemeth didn't notice.

Tiny spots became visible in the gloom above the island. He pointed them out to Captain Thoster. The captain trained his glass on them. He swore.

"What is it?" demanded Seren.

Thoster wordlessly passed the glass to the wizard. She looked, and her pale skin turned even whiter. "How can that be?"

Japheth took the spyglass from the woman's nearly limp hands.

The glass revealed five flitting sentinels circling the island's periphery in lazy loops. The sentinels were kuo-toa, their forms predatory like the ones earlier encountered. The strange kuo-toa rode steeds that appeared to be great masses of seaweed. Each mass trailed a writhing nest of suckered arms that undulated in wavelike synchrony as they glided across the sky. Streamers of inky blackness marked each rider's wake, slowly dispersing in the wind, but accounting for the general gloom that cloaked the island. Each kuo-toa clutched a lancelike spear under one arm.

"It is the power of the Dreamheart!" called Nogah's voice from the water.

"How? Why?" demanded Thoster.

"The stone taps some greater font of energy that liberates creatures formerly consigned to life below the waves. To the few selected, the boundary between sky and sea is erased, and movement and breath in both are as if one vast realm! See? Those creatures flitting about are enslaved morkoth! Gethshemeth has repurposed them as flying mounts!"

The ex-whip's words came fast and furious, becoming almost indecipherable as the kuo-toa began to thrash in the water.

"Easy, Nogah," cautioned Thoster. "Are you all right?"

"Let us hope," interrupted Seren, "Gethshemeth does not give itself this ability to glide through the air like a bird."

"Actually," Japheth found himself saying, even as his eyes stayed locked on the spiraling sentinels inking the air, "that would make it far more convenient for us. I don't look forward to swimming down to meet the great beast."

Nogah huffed and wheezed, but began to calm. Finally, she continued, "I foresee Gethshemeth will meet us halfway."

Japheth wondered what that meant, but Nogah silenced his query unasked with a quick shake of her head. She said, "Now, quiet your tongues. I must redouble my efforts. I didn't expect such sentinels."

The launch resumed its journey. The isle drew ever closer. Japheth kept his eyes on the unfettered squid things and their riders, waiting for the least hint of alarm. When the bottom of the boat suddenly scraped up on the rocky coast of the isle, he started.

The dripping form of Nogah rose from the rolling breakers. She still hummed some atonal tune under her breath, and merely pointed.

All but the rowers disembarked. A high wave poured shockingly cold water down Japheth's boot, and he hissed.

To the right and left, a thick tangle of mangrove roots and branches prevented easy access to the shore. Nogah had cleverly selected a site of their landfall not visible to the rest of the island. Small fish, shrimp, crabs, and mollusks played in the clear seawater washing between the reaching mangrove roots.

The ex-whip took the lead, pressing into the dense tangle on something that wasn't so much a path as a small, salty estuary. The kuo-toa had yet to cease her rhythmic humming. Japheth looked up. He couldn't immediately spy sentinels, but he didn't doubt they still flew.

He wondered if he should chance a little magic of his own, but decided against it.

What he really needed was the extra perception granted by a grain of dust.

It was foolish, he told himself, not to call on all his resources now that things were becoming so desperate. He'd take only a half grain. That would be enough to enhance his perception without dulling his reactions too much. Or worse, pull his mind out onto the road.

The tin was already in his hand. He popped it open and plucked out a crumb. It was one of the smaller ones. Proud of his restraint, he dropped the ruby red particle into his left eye.

"Oh! Japheth, why now?" came Anusha's voice from nowhere.

Captain Thoster glanced back. "Eh, what's that?" His eyes squinted with vague puzzlement.

Japheth asked, "What was what?"

"Thought I heard someone say your name. Not happy with you, neither."

Japheth shrugged. "You're hearing things, Captain."

Thoster frowned, but turned back to sloshing along the trail after Seren.

Japheth cocked his head slightly to regard Anusha's armored form, which was blurring into his perception. He gave the phantom a half smile and winked. "I'll be all right," he whispered. The armored head gave a small shake, then faded. Either he hadn't taken enough dust to perfectly resolve her presence, or she'd decided to leave. Because she was disappointed in him? The thought concerned him. But it was a pale sort of concern, attenuated by the euphoria that accompanied the first moments after partaking of traveler's dust.

Japheth melted into the moment.

The mangroves thinned ahead, revealing the first of several greenish gray structures. Like coral in texture and in their seamless solidity, the structures were not rough jumbles of growth, but rather stood in coarse parody of more mundane buildings. Walls, doors, windows, towers, and spires were visible, separated by plazas and courtyards, and many clear pools. Structural lines sometimes seemed to converge too sharply, or diverge where they should have stayed parallel.

Or perhaps the lines were perfectly straight, mused Japheth. Maybe it was just the dust.

The kuo-toa settlement lay in murky dimness under the debris of sentinel wakes. The smoky veil overhead gave the illusion the village lay within a subterranean cavern. Bestial kuo-toa moved purposefully between the structures, but a few played in the pools, cavorting and splashing as if human children. These kuo-toa were not goggle-eyed and sticky-skinned, like Nogah and her kin, though they were just as awkward when moving on land. But the creatures gained something like grace when they darted through the surface pools. Watching them move, an undercurrent of something Japheth couldn't quite name brushed him. Some churning dread, squirming just below the surface, like worms hidden in an apple.

That last feeling was certainly the dust, he thought. Or, then again, perhaps it was a true perception—perhaps his enhanced senses were picking up the traces of Gethshemeth's control over these hapless and partly metamorphosed creatures.

Nogah sidled up to a particularly large building. Glyphs, disturbing in their sinuosity, were carved in a frieze all over the edifice. The ex-whip motioned the rest of them to follow her, then slipped into a small side entrance.

Not a single kuo-toa noticed their passage. Their guide was proving as good as her word. She'd said her previous ownership of the Dreamheart would empower her, and she hadn't lied.

Nogah waited for them in a low-ceilinged vestibule. Three basins were carved into the walls, each resembling an open-mouthed, upward-facing fish. Clear liquid spilled onto the floor from each gaping mouth. Beyond the basins, two arched corridors provided deeper access into the structure, both lit by a wan yellow radiance.

"What do the scaled ones get up to in here?" asked Thoster.

Nogah merely pointed to the right-hand archway and grunted, "This way leads, past many windings and disputed ways, to Gethshemeth's audience chamber."

"You don't say?" blurted Japheth.

"The Dreamheart. It tells me much. Now do not distract me with prattle, either of you. We are close! I must fully concentrate on hiding my connection to the relic from the great kraken. If he discovers my presence too soon, before I actually stand in his presence, Gethshemeth will slay us all easily, or command his minions to do so."

Japheth looked at her, squinting. He could almost see the merest hint of something, a thread of energy spiraling out from the kuo-toa's forehead. The thread plunged across the chamber and into the passageway she indicated. However, overlaying that, Japheth's dust-enhanced eyes noted a glimmering haze, something superimposed that was less like a thread and more like a long, sucker-covered appendage . . .

"Are you certain he doesn't already know we're here?" Japheth asked.

"Of course," huffed Nogah. "I spent far longer with the relic than this upstart creature."

Thoster laid a hand on Japheth's shoulder. "She's our only hope, mate. If she's right, we've got a shot. If she's wrong, we're all dead already. We just ain't figured it out yet."

The warlock frowned, but he was having a difficult time working up enough concern to argue. It could be, in truth, the dust was feeding him untrue visions, and he was drawing unwarranted conclusions. That was its downside, he philosophized. Well, one of its downsides.

Nogah advanced, following her thread. The more Japheth looked at the sensory impression, the more it appeared as a wriggling tentacle. He tried to blink the association away.

The hall quickly became a narrow staircase leading downward. Relief-carved kuo-toa heads emerged from each wall at intervals, their eyes gleaming yellow.

"We've just descended below the water level," Nogah commented. "If we were outside, we'd be swimming now." She said this last bit somewhat wistfully.

"And I'd have turned back," replied Seren.

The stairs continued their descent, mercifully clear of water.

Past a switchback, the stairs leveled into another straight passage. The passage was slightly narrower than the stairs, and the lights were less frequent.

The sound of falling water slowly grew, as did Seren's frown.

The tunnel opened into a wide space lit by a trio of sculpted kuo-toa busts some thirty or forty feet above. The area was dominated by a central pool, around which several shrublike plants grew. An aroma that mingled honey and blueberry hinted at flowers, though Japheth spied no blooms. A dry platform rose marginally above the water's surface at the pool's center. Bones lay scattered upon the platform, along with bits of cloth, spilled coins, and other objects. On the far side of the pool, Japheth discerned an archway leading into a completely lightless passage.

Ripples dappled the pool. Thoster advanced alone and gazed down. "Albino fish, everywhere," he reported, "and a spiral staircase, drowned beneath the pool. It descends a long way . . ."

"It is not a pool, it is our path," intoned the ex-whip.

"What!" exclaimed Seren. "I told you I cannot and will not swim!"

"Don't you have a spell to give yourself gills?" asked the first mate, Nyrotha, his voice hoarse from disuse.

The wizard replied, "Not since the Spellplague, damn it all! I'm heading back to the ship. I'm done with this foolish expedition!"

The ex-whip strode to stand next to Thoster, then looked back to regard the rest of them. She said, "Fear not. You may descend these stairs without drowning. The pale fish, see them? They are rune-charged creatures. In their presence, you could walk the depths of the seafloor as if strolling through a green meadow."

"Really?" Seren's interest in magical lore battled with her anger at the thought of drowning. Anger that cloaked healthy fear, Japheth figured.

Seren and the warlock both eased up to the pool's edge. Japheth saw eyeless slivers darting about, each pulsing with pale radiance. Seren extended a hand, her brow furrowed with concentration. Then she smiled. She reported, "How extraordinary! I'll have to take a few of these with me after—"

A twinkle of greenish light wrenched Japheth's attention up. Concern struggled to pierce his dust daze. He should probably warn the others. When they approached the pool, he had vaguely noticed several figures on the garden's periphery, hiding in the shadows. Perhaps the figures were not mere statuary as he'd first assumed. Perhaps . . .

Crossbows snapped. Twin bolts appeared in Nogah's body, one in her chest, the other protruding crazily from one eye. An acrid odor curled Japheth's nose even as the whip began to scream. Poison!

Nyrotha and Thoster dropped as quarrels buzzed the space formerly occupied by their heads. A third struck Thoster in the shoulder, but he made no sound. Seren stood unmoving, shock momentarily freezing her limbs, but no quarrels found her.

Japheth felt a faint tug as two or three bolts struck his cloak. Without conscious direction from the warlock, the black folds of his garment deflected the bolts onto a trajectory beyond the world, one that ended in the darkness of a bat-filled cavern.

His pulse quickened, and the lackadaisical demeanor lent him by the dust shattered. Japheth gasped, "Ambush!" Too late.

Someone grabbed him, pulled him clear. A line of coruscating acid just missed him. "Thank you," he mumbled, assuming his rescuer was Anusha's dream.

The ex-whip yelled, her voice shaking with pain, "Geth-shemeth knew!"

A granite block boomed down from the ceiling, neatly filling the passage they'd used to enter the strange garden hollow. The light fell by half.

More figures scurried around the periphery of the chamber. All kuo-toa except for one—a giant quadruped with too many limbs and skin darker than coal. Were those wings unfurling, and a serpent's tail? It was hard to make out through the odd growths surrounding the pool. It loosed a primal hunting scream that tried to root them all in place with fear alone.

"The pool! Into the pool," gurgled Nogah.

As if on cue, the rippled water disgorged a blob of bluish green slime. The amorphous mass poured forward, extruding long pseudopods ending in starfishlike appendages of goo.

"Nogah," said Thoster, rising, "what . . ."

The ex-whip fell to her knees, staring dumbly down with one good eye at the blood-soaked bolt buried in her chest. "My species . . . will become as these? How could I have been so blind? The Dreamheart poisoned my mind! Sea Mother, forgive—"

She coughed a spray of vicious fluid, shivered as if devil-possessed, then collapsed. Nogah lay without breath on the beslimed flagstone.

Thoster tore the quarrel from his shoulder with hardly a flinch. The air around him seemed to burn, and he drew his clicking, whirring blade.

Nyrotha stumbled upright and began to hack at the tentacle-like streamers of slime. His eyes bulged, and spittle flecked his lips. A pseudopod lanced forward. The flayed grasping pad struck the man's face full on, sealing his voice behind a gag of putrescent ooze.

Flesh and blood began to boil under the grasp. In moments, there was only bone and cartilage where Nyrotha's face had been.

Disgust and stomach-churning terror dispersed the last of Japheth's dust haze. He grabbed for Seren's and Thoster's shoulders, one in each hand, and tried to propel them around the pool toward the arched passage he'd spied upon entering. "This way, or we all die!" he yelled. Seren was weakly accommodating in his grip, but Thoster shrugged away.

Savage, small-eyed kuo-toa converged from all sides. Japheth grabbed the captain again, mouthing a spell as he did so. They all fell into his cloak.

And immediately appeared on the opposite side of the pool, as if having made a single step. A warlock's transposition—the spell had only strength enough to move him, and him alone, hardly more than ten paces. But with the Lord of Bats's own skin wrapping his body, he was able to bring others along.

"Now follow me!"

Japheth ran into the darkness, Thoster and Seren at his heels. Behind, a great roar of fury drowned out the gurgling of slime-digesting flesh.

The tunnel punched downward into stone-lined darkness.

Behind him came the swish of the wizard's slippers, and Captain Thoster's iron boot tips ringing on the stone floor. Following them, monsters scrabbled and shrieked.

Japheth uttered three fell words, and his vision returned, though distant objects remained cloaked in black haze. He said, "I can find—"

The tunnel beneath their feet fractured. They plunged into ice-cold saltwater.

CHAPTER SIXTEEN

The Year of the Secret (1396 DR)
Plaguewrought Land, Vilhon Wilds

City-sized blocks of granite churned within the crater, forming a vortex that sucked air and anything unfortunate enough to fall within its grinding grasp. The clamor of stone on stone was a physical thing. The sound threatened to dislodge Raidon Kane from the wooden span that somehow, even without visible supports, bridged the ravenous gap.

Streamers of blue fire scudded across the sky, like rivulets of water finding their way down a cliff side. Or, Raidon thought, like blue veins pulsing close under the skin of a giant's fleshy back.

The monk blinked away the unwelcome image and fixed his attention on his companions.

"Well? What have you decided? Leave the bridge

here or continue across the vortex?"

Finara, the gray-haired former mage, shook her head with exaggerated care. "Both choices could prove fatal. I cannot decide."

"I can!" broke in the youth. "The bridge, we stay on the bridge! The path is safe, up to its terminus—we all know this to be true!"

"The Granite Vortex has moved. That is a change. Other things may be different too," explained Finara. "Nothing is certain here."

"We stay on the bridge," Hadyn repeated, defiance hardening his face.

Raidon considered. He couldn't predict which route was safer. If the bridge spanned the horrendous gap, they should be able to do the same by staying on it. Perhaps leaving the bridge sooner than necessary was the worst choice. He said, "Hold tight to the handrails as we cross. The vibration will try to shake you to a long fall."

They passed over the vast empty gulf, ringed by swirling stones whose fluid mobility and resounding impacts attempted to knock them physically from their footing and mentally from their belief in the world's comprehensibility.

Though he owed his traveling companions nothing, the monk found himself periodically glancing back to monitor their progress. They were nearly across when Raidon saw a portion of the old wood railing give way beneath Hadyn's desperate clutch.

Hadyn pitched out over the chasm, his face convulsing in terror. The ringing granite crashes blotted out his scream.

Raidon lunged for the man's hand. His fingers found the flailing youth's wrist. The weight yanked the monk down to his chest against the bridge's wooden slats. Pain jangled up his arm. Raidon gritted his teeth and retained his hold.

Hadyn dangled over the churning maw, his eyes fixed on Raidon's, pleading. *Save me,* they said.

The monk began to haul Hadyn up. From the periphery of his vision, Raidon noticed a single streamer of blue fire. Its flow dipped uncomfortably close to the bridge. The streamer bucked, became erratic, and dispersed into disconnected globules of blue fire.

A second streamer twisted out of the sky and speared the youth in the chest.

Regardless of its flickering, flamelike guise, it wasn't fire. The radiance spreading across the youth's suddenly convulsing body was naked, potent, active spellplague. It was a germ that infected earth and stone, flesh and blood, magic, and even space itself.

Raidon overrode his first instinct to let go.

The youth's convulsions redoubled. His skin began to glow blue. Hadyn's eyes gleamed like those in the grip of a divine vision. His hair whipped and sawed as though underwater. Unaccountably, he grew heavier.

Muscle suddenly rippled on Hadyn's forearms, shoulders, and chest. The youth's frame lengthened, as if to accommodate even more strength, and yet more muscle rolled onto him. The pressure of Hadyn's grip on Raidon's hand doubled, then redoubled. Raidon heard the bones in his hand grind together.

"I feel . . . strong!" yelled Hadyn.

Then the youth screamed.

Already Hadyn's boots were a blaze of fire, and Raidon could see naked bones in his lower legs. White sticks burning. His upper legs were like translucent wax melting inside a stone oven. Or like Hadyn was a candle, and spellplague, the flame.

In three more heartbeats, Hadyn was consumed. Burning ash dispersed in the wind.

Raidon rose, looked into Finara's terrified eyes. He didn't really see her.

His mind remained fixed on Hadyn's death. Or, more accurately, the manner of his death. A vision of the dissolving caravan chief who died so long ago assaulted him for the hundredth time. As always, he couldn't help wondering if Ailyn had perished similarly. Had she screamed like Hadyn? Had she called his name? Or cursed it?

The monk's gritted teeth couldn't restrain the groan at the image of Ailyn's death clawing its way into his mind.

If he wanted to end that personal misery, now would be an easy time to do it. Just a step or two . . .

No. The weakling's way was not his, no matter the provocation, even his own failure to follow through on his promise to protect Ailyn. He let the images flow away from him like a river until his mind was empty. Let focus be his only emotion.

The sound of the Granite Vortex returned. The past faded, for the moment.

Ahead, the bridge terminated in a meadow of tall, scarlet grass strewn with boulders. The boulders didn't actually rest in the grass; each hovered a foot or two off the ground. Some were stationary, but several drifted in random directions. By the scars each bore, it seemed likely they'd all survived impacts.

Raidon checked the map. Some previous traveler called the meadow Cyric's Table. According to the legend, their route required they leave the bridge and pass through it until they reached the roots of something labeled Grandmother Ash. Glancing up, the monk spied a fantastically tall tree in the misty distance. Its topmost branches bore a canopy of blue fire.

He motioned with his head to the bridge terminus.

Finara stood rooted in place, morose and muddy-eyed. She clutched her own copy of the map in one hand; the other held tight to the burro's reins.

"I can't do it, Raidon. I can't step off the bridge. Hadyn was . . . The odds are against me."

He nodded.

She looked at him, her eyes beseeching him for words of encouragement. He had none. He replied, "Perhaps this is not your day."

Tears broke from her left eye, but she nodded as relief struggled with anguish and fear.

"Gods willing, I will see you back in Ormpetarr in three days," she said. "If you return with a spellscar, then I know it is possible and not merely a tale told to bilk the incredulous."

Raidon clasped her shoulder, then turned to regard his path. He excised concern for her safe trip back from his consciousness.

A drifting cube obscured the distant tree for a moment. Above, a jagged trail of blue lightning split the sky, sending a flash across the plain. Blinking away the after-image, Raidon left the bridge and entered the plain of red grass. He did not look back.

The long-bladed, crimson grass crunched beneath his feet. The boulders drifted like tiny versions of the earthmote he'd seen west of Nathlekh. Unlike that massive air island, these moved and left wakes of bluish radiance. He wondered if the masses were solidified spellplague. He avoided the darting masses with the diligence they deserved.

He left the unmoored rocks behind and reached the edges of the exposed, tangled root mass. The field of burrowing roots stretched perhaps a mile, maybe more, surrounding the tree in the distance. He'd misjudged the tree's size. It was larger than he'd thought. At least no grass grew between the great, fingerlike roots that clutched at the earth so fiercely. He studied the roots for a time. It seemed they slowly twined and churned the earth, moving, but only as quickly as earthworms through soil.

He moved out across the root field. They offered solid footing and did not react to his weight. He quickly reached that which the roots all supported.

The bole of the tree was more like a cliff face than an ash trunk. No limbs offered access for several hundred feet, but those above were as thick as roads. The sound of the wind in the rooflike leaves high above was like the roar of a distant cataract. Each leaf gleamed like a tongue of sapphire flame.

Raidon scratched his chin, then drew out his map. The Pilgrim's Path led to the Grandmother Ash's base. A dotted arrow led away from the tree into the heart of the discontinuity, as if the cartographer had lost confidence in the route in this final leg.

He decided to scale the tree, if he could, to get a lay of the land from on high.

He placed one hand against the tree's grayish, deeply grooved bark. It was sun warm and pleasant beneath his fingers. Raidon mused, "You've survived this Plaguewrought Land well, it seems."

Intense gladness washed across Raidon. It came without warning and smashed through his focus as if it were nothing more than rice paper.

The monk snatched his hand from the tree, and the sensation was gone.

Raidon studied the tree several long moments, considering.

He ventured, "Are you conscious?"

No voice answered, nor unwarranted feeling. He laid his palm again across the tree.

Acknowledgment suffused the monk from his crown to his toes.

"I greet you, Grandmother Ash. I am Raidon Kane. I am sorry to disturb your solitude, but if you please, I have a question, if you will hear it?"

Curiosity prickled up Raidon's arm.

"Thank you. I seek an old friend, an elf woman, who may have ventured past you some years back. She would have carried with her a powerful sword and had a dwarf as a traveling companion. Does that sound familiar?"

A "green" feeling of assent settled upon him, then . . . fear.

"What makes you afraid, great one?"

The tree shuddered. A blue flame ignited beneath Raidon's hand. The monk snatched his hand away, leaving a trail of fading flame. He anxiously regarded his palm for several heartbeats, then let out his breath in relief.

The point of flame on the bark remained, grew into a line that quickly traced the outline of a humanoid figure. The shape bulged, and then stepped from two dimensions to three. It was a woman, perhaps, but she was bark and leaves, stem and bough, with hands of knotted root. Thick strands of moss made up her hair and her eyes were twin forest pools limned in blue flame. Her bare skin was the ridged, grayish bark of an ash tree.

"Who says I am afraid?" the woman asked him, her voice vibrant with the music of a major chord. She wasn't much taller than Raidon, though he had the feeling she wasn't fully unfurled.

He resisted the urge to retreat a step. He replied simply, as if women emerging from trees was nothing less than what he expected, "Perhaps I misspoke, madam."

The woman examined her digits, wriggling them as if checking to see that they all functioned. Satisfied, she glanced back at Raidon. She asked, "Why do you seek those three in particular? Many more pilgrims have traveled the Plaguewrought Land since them."

"The elf's sword, Angul, has duties to perform in defense of Faerûn."

"You do not seem a swordsman," the woman said, somewhat critically.

"I am trained in their use: fist, foot, sword, sling, and more I have studied. Regardless,"—Raidon waved away the topic, surprised to find himself extolling his own virtues—"Angul is required. Have you seen him, or his wielder, Kiril the elf, or her companion, Thormud the dwarf?"

"I saw those you describe. I manifested a form much like this one so that we could converse. I attempted to dissuade them from their goal. They sought the Chalk Destrier, a fiend of white stone who was empowered the same time I was awakened."

"In the Year of Blue Fire? You are a spellscarred . . . tree?"

"The few creatures that survived full contact with the most virulent wave of spellplague are more than merely scarred, but utterly transformed. Plaguechanged. They are monstrous entities of rage and destruction. The world is lucky most of these creatures are bound to one location. Of course, I am an exception. I am prone more to philosophy."

Raidon suppressed the urge to explain that he too had been touched and changed by the initial wave of spellplague. Did that mean the Cerulean Symbol bound to his soul was more than "merely" a spellscar, as well? He looked down at the massive root field surrounding the ash tree, then back into the woman's burning eyes.

"I am bound, yes. But unlike the Chalk Destrier and others, my mind remains uncorrupted. Perhaps it is because I had no mind before I was awakened by the touch of unleashed, wild magic."

"Yet you have a shape like mine." Raidon pointed at the woman. He flirted with the idea of asking if she were a dryad. Some instinct made him refrain.

"I am an avatar only, a seedling," she replied. "In this form, I can move within the bounds of this changeland, but not beyond. Not yet."

Raidon frowned but chose to ignore the last.

"Can you direct me to this Chalk Destrier?"

"It will prove your death, as it did your friends."

"They have perished, then? You know that?"

"In time, I can taste all that occurs on the surface of the Plaguewrought Land. That which rots is absorbed into the earth, even soil as unstable as that found in this region. My roots spread even farther below ground than is visible above. I tasted their essence diffused into the loam some years ago. True, my subterranean tendrils cannot reach all the way into that creature's lair. Perhaps they were only wounded. But my knowledge of the Chalk Destrier leads me to believe otherwise."

Raidon nodded. "We suspect the same, but we think the sword remains."

"We?" inquired Grandmother Ash's avatar.

"My advisor, Cynosure. He is not with me now." Raidon looked around wondering if a voice out of thin air would prove him wrong. But a few more moments proved that hope false.

"Ah," said the avatar, her head cocked in a human fashion, indicating her uncertainty.

"I must retrieve the sword Angul. Events outside the borders of your land require him. Angul is a relic of vanished Sildëyuir. He has the power to oppose the Abolethic Sovereignty."

The woman brushed her hair back with a delicate, bark-skinned hand. She said, "I am unfamiliar with this Sovereignty."

"It is a group of creatures who are like the plaguechanged you described—fiends from the deep earth that must be opposed."

"And it is given to you to oppose them."

"The task has fallen to me, yes."

The woman clapped her hands, making a sound like two planks slamming together. "A hero! The pilgrims' tales sometimes described such. You're my first."

The avatar smiled.

Silence stretched.

"Will you help me?" Raidon was suddenly weary.

"Usually pilgrims must give me a story in return for my aid. But for you, a hero brave and true, I require only that you allow me to accompany you. When you meet the Chalk Destrier, my old foe, perhaps I can distract him long enough for you to look for your lost sword, if it's there."

Raidon bowed his head slightly. "Thank you, Grandmother Ash."

"This way, hero." The avatar touched his elbow and turned him to face a new direction. South. Southeast, perhaps. The strength in her root fingers was incredible, and the gnarled wood abraded his skin.

Releasing him, she pointed. "We must pass into a maelstrom of greater activity to reach the heart."

So saying, all the individual tendrils composing her form were sucked into the ground, like a plant growing in reverse, until she was gone.

Confused, he looked back to the great tree. Hadn't the woman just indicated she'd accompany him? The vast shape provided no answers.

Raidon glanced in the direction the avatar pointed. A stormy cloudscape hovered on the horizon, somehow half familiar. Blue lightning played within it.

A hundred paces from where he stood, a stem burst from the earth, followed instantly by dozens more. They twined and condensed. An eyeblink later, Raidon recognized the avatar.

She called, "Come along, hero. This way!"

CHAPTER SEVENTEEN

The Year of the Secret (1396 DR)
Taunissik, Sea of Fallen Stars

Anusha screamed the worst profanity she could ever recall hearing, something her half brother once said to a servant. The darkened cabin aboard the *Green Siren* absorbed her outburst, and quiet returned.

Japheth had moved too far for her dream to follow. Just when he needed her most! With Nogah killed, how would he ever find what he looked for? How would he ever find his way back out again? He could retreat to his castle—but there he risked dying at the hand of a Feywild witch with murder in her heart. If he didn't kill himself first with his tin of traveler's dust.

Think, she commanded herself. Panic won't help, girl.

Easy enough said, hard to follow through. But

she attempted to calm her breathing. She concentrated on the sound of her too fast heart. She willed it quieter, until she could no longer hear it beating in her ears.

Her body was too far from the island's center. How could she get it closer without risking detection? Did it matter anymore? With Nogah dead, perhaps the great kraken already knew the ship lay at anchor off the seamount's coast. Slimy kuo-toa swimmers and the ink-trailing aerial sentinels could be turning their attention this way even as she imagined the possibility.

She pushed those thoughts away. They made her heart race. She wouldn't be able to fall asleep again.

That thought alone signaled it was already too late, she knew. When one is most desperate to fall into slumber, sleep is furthest away. Awake or tired, she knew she was in for a long period before she could relax enough even for a nap. Worse, it seemed the more she used Japheth's potion, the less she was able to fall asleep naturally. Concern puckered her brows at the thought.

She was becoming just as addicted to that silver vial as Japheth was to his damned dust tin.

"No," she mumbled.

Maybe, she thought. It didn't matter. She could leave Japheth to his fate or try to help him. Simple as that. She pulled the stopper from the silver vial and drank.

Even as she lay back and closed her eyes, her dream pair opened. Anusha stepped from her slumping physical body clad in the plate armor of dream.

She stowed the silver vial carefully back within a pocket in her sleeping body's skirt. She vowed she wouldn't use the vial again. As she had told herself last time.

"Stop it! You've got more pressing issues, now."

She took what seemed like a real breath. "A dream I am, and so I perceive the world about me," she affirmed, trying to convince herself.

Anusha closed the lid on the traveling case, her body still snug within. She reached into the interior, and slid home the latch from the inside.

"Now the hard part. Maybe."

She bent, arms wide, and grasped the brass handles on each side of the carrying case. She heaved. The chest moved slightly, no more.

Anusha frowned.

"In my dream, I am as strong as I need to be," she asserted.

She heaved again. Another inch of movement.

She relinquished her grip and said the profanity again, but this time it was only half-hearted. She plucked a crumb-laden trencher from the sideboard. This she could lift easily as her waking form could. Why should limitations of the waking world shackle her dream?

Because, deep down, she expected the rules to be the same. Despite the fact they manifestly were not the same—she could walk through walls and move invisibly. Why should her ability to affect the world remain the same when everything else was different?

Anusha grabbed the handles again, new certainty firing her. This time, she did not heave. She concentrated. Then she merely picked up the entire travel chest by the two grips. Part of her knew its full weight, but in her determination she tried to imagine it as heavy as a trencher, at least in this dream.

Her sleeping self snored within. Hearing it, she realized again how much she carried and nearly dropped herself. One edge rapped hard against the floor. She let down the chest, not quite dropping it. Her drugged body didn't respond to the rough handling.

She realized she was probably at her limit. It would be hard to focus enough to lift more than this. Why pick it up, she realized, when she could drag it?

Anusha kicked open the door to the cabin and stepped out, the chest in tow behind her. Lucky snorted his pleasure on seeing her.

"Want to help me out, boy?" she whispered to the mongrel.

The dog's ears cupped forward, and its tail wagged.

If she managed to convey her body to the island, a sentinel would be required to stand watch over her sleeping self.

Rushing water sucked Japheth into an all-encompassing embrace. He tried for a last breath and instead inhaled a smothering gulp of sea. The rough water twirled him around and knocked his head against stone.

After that, he wasn't quite sure what happened. Perhaps someone grabbed his ankle and towed him. His cloak flared around him in the water. An object slipped from the hem. He saw his tin of traveler's dust spin out into the turbid water. He reached for it, but it tumbled down, down, until darkness claimed it. He cried out as if struck, finally forcing the water from his lungs. Coughs wracked him.

He found himself on a damp expanse of stone, just beyond a torrent surging by on both sides. Seren lay near him, looking as battered and half drowned as he felt. On the other hand, Captain Thoster appeared unharmed, if hatless. His long hair was swept back, and his skin glistened with beaded water. A slight smile dimpled his expression as he turned to regard Japheth.

"You going to live, bucko?"

Japheth nodded, tried to reply, but instead released another body-convulsing cough.

Seren said, "You swim like a seal, Thoster."

The slight smile became a grin. "Something like that, wizard."

"Why so lighthearted?" Seren snapped. "We lost our guide

and main protector. Now we're lost below the seamount. How long before the great kraken comes by and collects us?"

"We ain't dead yet," the captain replied.

"I can't swim," Seren replied, her tone robbed of its usual vindictiveness. She glanced at the rapids. The turbulent flow foamed along the narrow track just a few feet beyond their perch, then fell away onto a steep slope, becoming a cataract falling who knew how far.

"You're addled, lass. Look there." Thoster pointed to his left. Across the breadth of water, Japheth could barely make out the edges of what appeared to be a stairwell, leading up. "No need for us to swim just yet."

The torrent was narrow enough even the wizard had no difficulty leaping it. They took to the steps. The stair was a spiraling tube leading upward. Fifty paces saw them into a new cavity.

Seren exclaimed, "How interesting."

Tiny points of gold-green light flitted over domes and obelisks of shaped coral. The drifting points illuminated a subterranean vault whose size seemed, at least by the fey light of the drifting star points, equal to the breadth of the isle above.

They stood in silence, looking for kuo-toa or any other sign of malign attention. Silence lay over the space like a swaddling blanket.

"What's this place for?"

"Nogah would have known," replied Thoster.

The wizard sniffed. "She's dead, Thoster. I'm asking you." He shrugged. "For us, let us hope it provides an exit."

Seren actually smiled. "Now you're talking. Let's get out of here and leave the Dreamheart to its new owner."

Thoster paused. "Nay, lass. Despite this setback, we need to try for it. I wouldn't leave without it, now that we're so close. Which way do you suppose we should go to find the big squid, Japheth?"

"I don't know." He was so bedraggled he wondered if Seren didn't have the right of it. Events had obviously proved too much for Anusha.

The captain grunted. "Well, we should look for a way out too. It wouldn't do for Captain Thoster to be marooned! I expect the kraken will find us soon enough. That'll be our chance to try for the bauble. You think the poxed thing will prove easier to deal with than the servants it sent to ambush us?"

Japheth said, "Seems unlikely—"

"Because we didn't give a very good account of ourselves."

Protestations rose to the warlock's lips: he had been taken by surprise, he hadn't unleashed his full arsenal of curses, he had been concerned with the welfare of the others. But he remained quiet. Their guide had been slain, and the rest of them had barely escaped with their lives. And perhaps it was his own fault.

How had he allowed it? The bald truth wouldn't creep away and be ignored. He'd been in the dazed grip of traveler's dust. If he'd been in his right mind—

The memory of a metallic container tumbling down through dark water assailed the warlock. His breath caught. He slapped his cloak where the tin was kept safe. He couldn't detect the comforting bulge. His eyes dilated as he frantically searched through the folds of his cape. Empty.

Japheth's supply of dust was lost.

The captain watched Japheth through this anxious display, his expression quizzical.

"I have to go back," Japheth explained. "I lost something in the water."

"Go back, then!" exclaimed the wizard. "We're going forward."

Japheth glanced at her. Seren was wringing out her hair. She looked up, saw the warlock's desperate expression, and said, "You're cute, but I'm not going back down there."

An image of a road composed of ground bone on a crimson plain flashed before him, then faded. Japheth took another few gulps of air, crazy impulses flashing across his mind. Images of diving, alone, into the cataract . . .

Too crazy to consider for more than heartbeats. He'd have to do without, despite the risk to his sanity.

"Never mind."

Thoster skewered Japheth with a look. "You certain you're still in the game?" the captain asked.

"I have no other choice, it seems," breathed the warlock. "Let's see what's in here, shall we?"

Japheth pushed to the fore and stepped into the vast space lit by glittering witchlights.

The rounded sphere tops and protruding obelisks mimicked the buildings on the surface. They were built, or perhaps grown, of something similar to coral. However, the structures in the dark seemed older, centuries older. None possessed any obvious entranceways or windows, either. Several had script upon them, but in a language none of the explorers knew.

Japheth began to see a pattern to the drifting points of light. Sometimes they clustered around one particular dome or obelisk, only to languidly redistribute themselves in different densities around other features. The lights never paused in the empty air between the monument-like structures. A small enough pattern, but possibly significant.

The warlock considered his own paucity of power in the arena of gleaning information. Though he knew curses that could unleash feral, hungry forces upon his enemies, making mute stone speak wasn't in his repertoire.

He glanced at Seren, wondering. She was a wizard—didn't she have spell or ritual capable of providing deeper insight?

"Seren," Japheth said.

The wizard paused. "What?"

"Do you—"

"Listen. If you're asking me to consult my spellbook for a handy solution to this mess, don't bother. It is a stroke of luck I've relearned as many spells and rituals as I have in the last eleven years. A damn sight better than most. In time, the rest will return, I'm certain. Until then, stop bothering me with insipid requests!"

Thoster grinned and shook his head.

A spire ahead enjoyed a particularly large number of slowly circling lights. Japheth headed toward it across the damp, uneven ground. It worried him that little pools of seawater pocketed the stone here and there. How long had it been since this entire area was drowned? More important, would the water return? They were already far below sea level, but that didn't mean tides didn't have a role to play beneath Taunissik.

He reached the base of the pedestal. Japheth realized the stone wasn't exactly like the others. It was no simple obelisk; it was some sort of statue—a twelve-foot-tall effigy, roughly like a kuo-toa, carved of purplish stone, though its lobster clawlike hands were black as pitch. Runes, like those written across the other structures, were inscribed on the figure. But unlike the script on the other formations, the runes on the statue seemed to trace ancient lines of power across its limbs. Worse yet, in place of its head, a single glyph was scribed, from which a thin streamlet of seawater dribbled.

Thoster said, "Japheth, stop. This is a kuo-toa holy place. We tread on sacred ground, at our peril."

The smell of seawater intensified, and a dozen more witch-lights flocked to the figure. Their combined radiance wavered between purple and green.

"This is a likeness of the kuo-toa god?" asked Japheth.

"Goddess," replied Thoster, his normally confident voice slightly wavering. "Come away!"

A crack of rending stone saw the statue shudder into movement. With two steps, the figure jerkily cleared its low pedestal. A heavy claw reached for Japheth.

He jerked back and the claw scraped across the ground.

A screech of what seemed like pain issued from the animate beast.

"What is it?" yelled Seren, her wand suddenly in hand.

"An eidolon of the sea!" replied Thoster, even as he backed away. "A kind of construct kuo-toa create as half living altars. They're animated by a shard of power from the Sea Mother herself!"

The creature lunged at Japheth once more. Again the warlock evaded the relatively slow-moving bulk.

"Why does it attack us? We have not suborned its followers—the kraken has."

"It ain't received a sacrifice since Gethshemeth commandeered this colony," returned Captain Thoster. "It's blinkin' insane with hunger!"

"Sea Mother!" Japheth called out. "We are enemies of your enemy—the great kraken, Gethshemeth, has overpowered your people! We seek to destroy Gethshemeth. Grant us your aid, and perhaps your people may come back to you!"

The effigy paused, as if considering.

Seren muttered, "Quick thinking, Japheth. Let's hope it works!"

Thoster shook his head. "This ain't the Sea Mother—it's merely a focus for devotion meant for her. In fact, I do not ever recall seeing this particular image. It ain't quite right. Regardless, this eidolon has been untended so long it may have gone rogue!"

"Rogue?" asked Japheth. Then he had his answer.

The rune that served as the statue's face suddenly spewed blood red seawater in all directions.

Japheth's cloak intervened, shunting the brunt of the liquid aside, but some still spattered his face and forearms. Pain blossomed across his skin where the seawater touched it. The warlock cried, "The water is caustic!"

Seren pointed her wand. A line of flickering lightning

briefly connected its end with the animate statue. It sparked and staggered, and the sharp order of ozone blurred Japheth's vision. He blinked and thought better of rubbing his eyes with the back of his seawater-spattered and burning hand.

A shape suddenly materialized from the blur his vision had become.

"Look out!" yelled Thoster. Japheth tried to duck away, but his senses were too confused. Instead of slipping out of the way, he darted directly into the grasp of the stony lobster claw.

Pressure crushed his chest and back, and his feet were pulled free of the ground. His legs worked foolishly in the air. His right arm was pinned to his side, and his hand went numb with the pressure.

The eidolon had him. Japheth blinked away the tears and saw the thing had raised him high above its head. Preparatory to smashing him down, most likely. He heaved against the stone pincer holding him in place. He succeeded merely in goading it to squeeze all the harder. He couldn't draw in a new breath.

Japheth called on his cloak to transfer him back to the ground. It whipped and strained, but failed. He was caught in a grip more than merely physical.

Below his flailing feet, Thoster darted in with his golem-work blade. The clang of metal on stone reverberated up the effigy's form. Farther off, Japheth saw Seren ready her wand for another strike, then pause, a frown of indecision on her face. He wondered if she considered striking the statue with another bolt of lighting even though he remained in its grasp. It surprised him she even paused to deliberate.

Japheth finally managed to get his free hand on the animate statue. With the last breath that remained in his contracted lungs, he uttered the Blight of Writhing Shadow.

The swarming witchlights dimmed as tissue-thin streamers of black fog issued from the ground. The darkness wrapped the effigy's legs in semisolid bands of sinuous force.

The creature tried to step out of the shadow that clutched

at it, but found itself caught in slicing, cold darkness. Shuddering, it redoubled its effort to escape. Simultaneously, the pressure the thing exerted on him noticeably eased. Japheth gasped, drawing new air into his aching lungs. In another few moments he would have blacked out.

Thoster yelled, "Can you wriggle free, warlock? I don't want to strike again what might be an idol to she to whom I pray for calm seas!"

At the sound of his voice, the eidolon stopped struggling. Its empty rune face seemed to ascertain Thoster's position despite its lack of eyes, ears, and nose. Simultaneously, Japheth smelled a rank odor of rotting fish and something far worse, like the smell of shadows decaying.

Thoster blanched but shook his head. He said, "Begad! That ain't the Sea Mother!"

The rune on the idol's face sprayed red water. The fluid arced through the air, curving up and over the captain's retreating form. Even as the wave's leading edge was about to strike the damp ground, it solidified. The captain was gone. What remained was a compact coral dome, on which runes were scribed. Japheth could read these runes, for they were in Common. The words read, "Captain Aulruick Thoster. Preserved for sacrifice 1396."

The captain's shocking entombment jolted the warlock into a frenzy. He writhed without regard to how he might hurt himself against the hard stone—

Before he quite realized he was free, he struck the ground, turning his ankle. He didn't pause to examine it; as soon as he hit the floor he called on his cloak to transfer him as far as it could . . .

Japheth was spit from the discontinuity of his cloak some fifteen paces behind the animate statue. For the moment, it couldn't see him.

Its non-gaze swept to the left, stopping at Seren. She screamed, "You'll not have me, stoneborn!" and released a torrent of electricity. The jagged white gout carved great smoking craters in the idol's rock carapace.

The light of the wizard's electrical attack was brighter than the floating witchlights. So bright that Japheth glimpsed something moving up and behind them. Something vast. In the shadows of the great cavern, many sinuous arms fluttered and coiled, each longer than the *Green Siren's* deck. One clutched a head-sized orb of stone. The long arms all emerged from a fleshy cylindrical mantle, from which two white eyes burned with hate. Each time the great arms moved, the animate statue rocked and shifted.

Nausea roiled Japheth's guts and his breath caught. Gethshemeth.

"Seren! The eidolon is not the true threat! The great kraken is in here with us! The statue is its puppet!"

The wizard glanced away from the idol, and saw in the fading light of her final blast what Japheth described.

Even as her mouth opened, in dawning surprise, the eidolon sprayed another gout of seawater. Seren tried to evade and failed. Where the wizard had stood was a small obelisk labeled, "Seren Juramot. Preserved for sacrifice 1396."

Japheth mentally reviewed his options, even as he sidled away from the idol and from the darkness behind it that hid Gethshemeth.

He could channel arcane might wrested from primeval entities. He could commune with infernal intelligences and fey spirits, scour enemies with potent blasts of eldritch power, and bedevil them with compelling curses. While he wore the Lord of Bats's cloak, all his abilities were redoubled, at least. But even with all his advantages, he knew he could not defeat a great kraken and its eidolon ally alone. Especially a great kraken whose own power was magnified in some unholy way by the enigmatic relic the ex-whip had called the Dreamheart.

On the other hand, he would certainly die if he put his back to the threat. He stopped. Japheth squared his shoulders and turned to fully face the idol, and yes, the hints of swift movement just visible behind and above the animate statue. His hands came up, and from his lips leaped words that were transformed into a golden mist. A great cloud of shining, yellow haze billowed forward, bypassing the unthinking eidolon, expanding in size even as its interior light began to more fully illuminate the great kraken beyond. For the first time, Japheth realized how strange it was that the creature seemed completely at ease in open air. Was that ability to transcend water an effect of the Dreamheart, as Nogah had suggested?

The haze enveloped the massive squid. Japheth continued uttering the syllables that fed the spell, giving it the power to plunge Gethshemeth into a waking dream of eldritch beauty and illusion.

The haze was having an effect! Or, was it? Wait—

The idol's rune flashed like a star. Water sprayed through air toward the warlock. Drops of the transformative moisture speckled Japheth's upturned face and unprotected hands.

His spell was ripped from him. A cold tide overtook him, and his body was locked in a vault of stone.

CHAPTER EIGHTEEN

The Year of the Secret (1396 DR)
Plaguewrought Land, Vilhon Wilds

Blue, green, and gold streaked the ground beneath Raidon's feet, as if some god had knocked over creation's easel, spilling change over the world. The paint still ran, congealing and mixing to form ever stranger colors and textures.

The air was a haze of wavering orange and sapphire, thick with the scent of jasmine and licorice. He could hardly make out his hand before his face. It was as though he walked through the base of a heatless, if pleasant-smelling, flame. Raidon wondered if the dancing color was the spellplague itself, or merely a telltale by-product of the infection that writhed below the earth. Thankfully, he showed no signs of illness or dissolution . . . unlike Hadyn.

The avatar of Grandmother Ash guided him

forward through the brilliant murk by song. Her voice was a wind whistling through a forest of pines, leading him. His feet found solid ground with each step. The womanlike being of bark, leaves, and root disdained walking. Instead, she grew into each new point on the landscape she desired to visit.

Her latest incarnation came clear from the burning haze as he approached. With each new manifestation, her precise configuration of flowers, thorns, roots, and bark differed slightly.

As her eyes found his, she ceased her guiding song. This time, her eyes appeared as two blooming irises.

Raidon asked, "Do you send rootlets burrowing ahead each time you rise up?"

The avatar craned her head to one side. She said, "Why send new shoots if my root system already lies beneath all in the Plaguewrought Land?"

"Ah." Raidon wondered if Grandmother Ash was being truthful about the extent of her growth. If so, her real size, including all the woody growth below the earth, was something he couldn't quite imagine.

The avatar continued to stare at him. She said, "That is strange."

"What?" Had he become infected and didn't realize it? He quickly checked his hands, arms, and legs.

"I sense two entities inhabiting your fleshy form, where before I detected only one. I am concerned."

"Well met," came a voice. Cynosure's voice. Raidon breathed easier.

"Worry not, avatar," explained Raidon. "You sense the presence of my friend, Cynosure. I mentioned him when we first met. Cynosure, where have you been?"

The voice came again, "Recuperating from my last effort that saw you to Ormpetarr's gates."

"Are you well?"

"Yes, Raidon. For now. I used more strength than I

expected, but I have a last bit to give. Which is lucky, because once you retrieve Angul, I can send you on to destroy the Dreamheart directly."

The leafy form of the avatar rustled as if to draw attention to itself. It said, "Cynosure . . . I've heard that name before. An extraplanar meeting ground for the gods."

"A coincidence of names, nothing more," came the sentient golem's voice, amusement clear in his tone. "But what are you? I detect you are far more extensive than the humanoid shape Raidon sees with his eyes."

"I am an avatar of Grandmother Ash," explained the woman, as if that were sufficient.

"Ah," returned Cynosure.

Raidon said into a growing silence, "She guides me to the Chalk Destrier, a creature Kiril and her dwarf companion sought when they entered this changeland. The avatar believes Kiril and Thormud were slain."

"Sad news," mused Cynosure. Then, "Lead on. Now that I have renewed contact with Raidon, I'll provide no further distraction until my services are next required."

Grandmother Ash's form dissolved. A few moments later, her voice came from ahead, raised once again in a song of guidance.

The monk continued his trek through the burning miasma, following the temporary, living guideposts the avatar provided.

Some large fraction of a day passed in such manner. The sameness of the surrounding bluish fog made it difficult to estimate time. Finally, Raidon broke through the haze into a new region.

He stood near the opening cut of a mighty canyon, steep-sided and long. The canyon sides revealed hundreds of varicolored bands in the stone, as if an account of some vast track of time. The sedimentary layers alternated between dozens of shades of brown, though a few layers seemed more crystalline than rocky. One exposed layer looked suspiciously like flesh. The canyon walls rose hundreds of feet on both sides.

The avatar retained her position at the very edge of the haze, declining to fully step forth. She pointed down the canyon. "Continue down this ravine, bearing neither right nor left down lesser clefts, and you'll find the Chalk Destrier at its end."

"You will go no farther?" asked Raidon. He was surprised to find himself wistful at the prospect of losing his one companion who was more than a mere voice.

"I told you my roots extended below all the Plaguewrought Land. That is true, save for this mass in the Plaguewrought Land's heart. I sense it is a misplaced fragment of another world, though its nature was obviously affected just as thoroughly by the Spellplague as Toril. I am not able to send my roots farther than its edges."

Raidon wondered if he should remind the avatar of her promise to distract the destrier long enough for him to find the sword. He decided against it. If she was having second thoughts, well, his words wouldn't sway her.

"Thank you for guiding me as far as you have, Grandmother Ash."

The woman gave a fair imitation of a bow. "As I said, you are my first hero. Perhaps, if the Chalk Destrier does not slay you, you will return and tell me of your exploits and what drives you with such determination."

"I look forward to it," responded Raidon, returning the gesture.

With a rustle of shifting earth, the avatar's many branches, vines, and stems blurred out of a female shape, then pulled into the earth.

"Cynosure?"

"I am here, Raidon."

The monk frowned, nodded, and strode into the ravine.

The walls leaped up on both sides, but the way widened

so that he walked along a flat expanse a hundred yards from either wall. A track meandered back and forth along the floor of the canyon. Murky liquid sluggishly flowed through the track. It might have been muddy water, though Raidon half expected it to burst into blue burning fire at any moment. The canyon seemed far too mundane to lie at the heart of the Plaguewrought Land.

The farther he walked, the higher the cliff walls grew on each side. Soon he was walking in deep shadow, and he had to carefully watch his footing amid the muddy track. He wondered how high the walls must be. They towered into the gloom, each cliff like a mighty sea wall built by giants.

Now and then, dry tributaries split from the main canyon, but Raidon followed the avatar's advice and continued straight along the way.

At one such juncture, a trio of great beasts grazed, as large as dragons but slightly less fierce in demeanor. They went on four feet and sported long, serpentine necks, but their eyes were dull like cattle, and they had no wings. Raidon slipped past the great creatures without drawing attention. The monk privately thanked providence that Cynosure hadn't taken it upon itself to make some observation, although perhaps he was being unfair to the sentient effigy.

The canyon found its conclusion ahead. A great white cliff filled the vast cleft from wall to wall. Was it snow? It didn't shine and twinkle in the setting sun like snow or ice would. Limestone? No, of course not.

It was probably chalk.

Raidon continued forward.

He walked another couple of miles toward the white wall, during which time full darkness grew. Stars came out above, brighter and more colorful than Raidon had ever noticed. He wasn't a sage of the skies, however, and didn't know enough to hazard a guess on whether they were familiar constellations, here in the heart of the Plaguewrought

Land. He didn't ask Cynosure.

One other light source offered itself besides the stars. As twilight deepened, the great white cliff ahead glimmered, taking on a glow not unlike moonlight. As its glow brightened, indeed it seemed that the far cliff face was a full phase of Selune herself, brought to earth and captured between the two canyon walls. Or perhaps not captured, but merely resting, waiting to spring up once more into the heavens.

Finally, Raidon asked the air, "Is that the Chalk Destrier? A moon fallen to earth?"

"If a moon, not one native to Toril."

"How close should I approach?"

"My senses are blunted here. I can barely retain my connection with you. Something interferes."

The monk nodded. He was on his own, despite the construct's voice and predilection to instruct Raidon. He found he was happy to find the construct's limits. On the whole, he'd had enough of all-knowing entities who surpassed his own knowledge. Then again, it could well be he was about to face something more potent than Cynosure at his most powerful.

Raidon walked until he stood some hundred or so paces from the pocked cliff face that glowed with its own celestial light. He put his hands to each side of his mouth and yelled, "Hail! I am seeking the Chalk Destrier! Let us parley and find mutual benefit in so doing!"

The stars above seemed to darken as the great white cliff face slowly waxed, becoming brighter, then brighter still, until Raidon was forced to squint into the glare.

A sound as of a massive river rushing over stones resounded down the canyon, so loud the earth shook. Within that overwhelming noise, Raidon detected patterns. Words. He missed the first few, but finally understood, " . . . come to ask a question, I demand a gift. What gift do you offer, pilgrim?"

Raidon cocked his head, unsure. He asked, "Are you the Chalk Destrier?"

"What else?" came the breathtaking voice. "If you have come to ask a question, you must first provide your gift. Do you offer your life or the life of another in payment? A relic? A secret?"

He wasn't here to tap whatever oracular power the entity implied it possessed, but he did have a question about Kiril, and her sword. He said, "I do not seek hidden knowledge, sage advice, or visions of the future. I seek only to know the whereabouts of one of your previous visitors, a swordswoman named Kiril and her dwarf companion."

"What gift do you pledge to secure my aid?" replied the earthshaking voice.

The monk stopped short of indicating he had no gift. Instead, he began to run through his store of lore, trying to think of something interesting that might satisfy the inanimate cliff's desire.

Cynosure suddenly said, "I know several secrets. Here is one: The elf realm of Sildëyuir, hidden behind the forest of Yuirwood, is not destroyed, as most assume. Many parts of it were pulled into Faerie, called the Feywild. Many star elves are now reunited with their kin, the eladrin."

The monk started, recalling his earlier conversation with the construct about Sildëyuir. Cynosure had then implied the starry realm was "fallen," not partially transferred to a fey dimension. If it was true that some of that realm yet lived, why had the construct allowed the monk to think otherwise?

He shook his head, realizing now wasn't the time to quiz the construct. Instead, he waited for the Chalk Destrier's response.

The cliff's brightness dimmed over many heartbeats, then waxed once more. The voice came, "You have given me a gift of knowledge previously unknown. I respond in kind: When the swordswoman Kiril, the geomancer Thormud, and the dragonet Xet came before me, a passage to the new lands fused to the world that lie across the western seas was requested of me. I provided that portal. They left this continent years ago for Returned Abeir."

The monk's stomach lurched. He had no idea what or where Returned Abeir was, whether a land across the sea or another plane entirely. Regardless, it seemed clear the quarry he'd thought he was on the brink of discovering was gone. Kiril and her blade could be anywhere by now. A black feeling of defeat and anger threatened to shred his calm focus.

Cynosure said, "A mighty gift must have been given for you to open such a far-reaching portal."

"Indeed. A soul shard, naked in a shaft of sharp steel."

Raidon exclaimed, "Angul? They left the sword with you?"

"Yes. A grand gift I treasure still."

"May we see it?" requested Cynosure, interrupting Raidon before he could demand the blade. "We've heard much of this storied sword and would look upon your great treasure."

"Treasures such as Angul should be displayed to admiring eyes," agreed the Chalk Destrier.

A grating vibration tried to knock the monk from his feet as the cliff face simply rotated upward. White dust plumed. The screech of stone on stone was like daggers in Raidon's ears. When the face stopped its movement, a hollow was revealed. The gap opened onto a passage leading back into the cliff face. The white walls of the tunnel glimmered with the same moonlike radiance as the exterior.

Raidon darted into the opening and down the smooth corridor beyond to get away from the dust. The air within was thankfully clear. The passage was slightly curved, so that even after only twenty paces, the entrance was obscured behind him.

The passage deposited the monk into a great arched hall decorated like a mad king's treasure vault. Giant shields, glowing swords, gem-crusted staves, sculptures of all shapes and materials, and panoplies of magical garb were displayed on both walls and suspended from the ceiling. A clear space ran down the center of the hall, some thirty feet wide. Raidon started down it.

As he walked, he noted many of the shapes he had first thought to be sculptures were actually trophies of the hunt, stuffed or otherwise bodily preserved. He saw a tiger, an ettin, an amulet-wearing mummy, and other vanquished threats. He also saw a man in wizard's robes, a woman garbed in formfitting leather wielding a glowing punch dagger, and other humanoids similarly preserved.

The monk came to a wider space, circular, and fronted by several alabaster pillars. A creature claimed the opening's center. It glowed with the familiar radiance of the cliff face. The creature's shape was like a centaur, but sleeker. He had expected its skin to be stone, not flesh . . . though its surface was eerily milk white and fluid. Perhaps it was chalk of some enchanted variety after all.

"Welcome to my fortress," said the centaur-thing. "Would you look upon the soul shard?"

"Yes," replied Raidon, "but are you the Chalk Destrier? I at first thought the cliff we addressed answered to that name."

The centaur said, "What an impressive girth I could claim were that true, but no. I am as you see me." It leaned in and confided, "I tell you that without expectation of a gift."

"You are most kind," spoke the monk, though he wondered what kind of creature this Chalk Destrier was to expect payment for every exchange of words.

"Now then, look upon the Blade Cerulean, Angul, which shelters a splinter of a human soul. Afterward, I shall claim my last gift from you."

"What do you mean?" asked Raidon. He glanced at the stuffed trophies.

The Chalk Destrier did not answer—it gestured with one milky palm. Light blazed like the rising sun, washing away Raidon's visual perception of the chamber.

Raidon blinked against the brilliance. Tears rolled down his cheeks. He wiped them away and saw a boulder, nearly five feet in diameter, now lying on the floor in the space between the monk and the pearly hued centaur. A long sword was plunged tip first into the boulder. The weapon was unblemished, the lines utilitarian, but the hilt was set with a cerulean-hued stone. The faintest of glimmers sparkled in the stone's depths.

"Is the soul extinguished?" asked Raidon. The last time he'd seen the blade, in its owner's hands some twenty years earlier, it had blazed with cerulean light and pulsed with righteous potency.

"It sleeps, that is all," replied the Chalk Destrier. It continued, "You have looked upon my treasure. Now I can claim my gift in return."

Even as the centaur spoke, the floor trembled. A sound identical to that which had accompanied the opening of the tunnel into the outer cliff face echoed in the chamber.

"You are sealing the entrance?" Raidon asked. He doubted it was opening wider.

"You are the gift," the Chalk Destrier announced, moving forward. "I wouldn't want you to scamper off." The creature raised one of its hands. The digits melted and flowed, becoming a long, thin blade, a skinning blade. "Please stand still; I do not like to reconstruct my trophies."

The monk loosed his concerns, reached for his focus that allowed his body and mind to become one. He hurdled the boulder pinning Angul, spinning so he only touched the stone with his palms. His time perception slowed. As he topped the rock, he pushed off with all his strength and training, feet toward his foe. He hammered the Chalk Destrier high on its humanlike chest with his feet.

The crack of contact jolted through Raidon's soles, calves, and knees. A network of fine cracks bloomed at the point of impact. He kicked himself away from his foe in a spray of rock chips, somersaulting back through the air. He landed, out of reach of the oversized creature's long arms, even the one that had become a blade.

The creature's milky pallor warmed until the Chalk Destrier was the color of freshly spilled blood. It leaped.

Raidon dived, avoiding the flashing ruby hooves and at the same time ducking beneath the centaur's slashing blade. As he dodged, he unleashed a punch of his own, striking the creature along its right flank. The impact punished his knuckles, and worse, seared him. The creature's red color was not mere show—it was red hot!

"Raidon, take the sword," Cynosure's voice urged.

"Angul can't help me against the Chalk Destrier," Raidon breathed as he avoided another charge. "As odd and amoral as this creature seems, I detect no aberrant hint. My own Sign remains quiescent."

"You must take the sword soon, or I'll not be able to extract you. The edifice in which you fight is receding, whether in space or time I can't discern. My connection with you is stretching. In another few heartbeats, it will snap. You'll be sealed in with the Chalk Destrier, perhaps forever, as one of its trophies."

The centaur reared, then fell forward, its front legs kicking. The monk sidestepped, but the handblade sliced across Raidon's forearm. The creature was impossibly fast, hard as stone, and as hot as a forge fire. The monk flipped backward as if to flee, but it was a feint; while still standing on his hands, he heel-kicked, catching the creature in one flaring red eye as it leaned forward and down. A crunch like breaking crystal was music to Raidon's ears.

But the creature didn't react like a living thing would. It bore down with one hand and one blade, and very nearly skewered the monk. He reversed the back flip he'd initiated to draw the creature in, and flashed past the creature, trying to get behind it. Back on his feet and another five feet behind Destrier—

The centaur mule-kicked him. Years of rote training alone saved him then, so instead of staving in his head, the blow merely knocked stars into his vision and banging cymbals into his ears.

He dropped to the ground, just avoiding a second rear-leg kick from the centaur. The floor was cold and gritty beneath his fingers.

"The sword!" Cynosure urged again, his voice noticeably weaker, as if he were shouting from a great distance.

Raidon didn't waste breath explaining he'd been trying to follow the construct's advice all along.

"Now or never," came the construct's warning, half as loud.

Raidon threw himself sideways, rolling toward the boulder, knowing he was opening himself up to an attack. The Chalk Destrier did not disappoint. It stomped him once before he stood, pulling himself up the side of the rock.

As the cold pommel of Angul fell into Raidon's grip, the centaur reared up again, kicking him in the shoulder and stomach with its front hooves. He curled and rolled backward. The weight of his falling body wrenched Angul from the stone.

"Got you!" he heard Cynosure exclaim.

A parabola of blue light spun out of nothing, engulfing him.

CHAPTER NINETEEN

The Year of the Secret (1396 DR)
Taunissik, Sea of Fallen Stars

Anusha wondered what was happening back on the island. Anxiety prickled through her dream form.

She pulled her travel chest out of the hallway onto the main deck. The *Green Siren's* launch was gone, but two much smaller lifeboats remained. Lucky followed her, the dog's chain severed by a single stroke of her dream sword. To the eyes of any watching pirate, it would seem as if the chest slid along the oiled planks of the deck of its own accord.

"The ghost!"

A dark-haired, scarred woman stood between her and the closest lifeboat, her eyes wide. It was the same pirate responsible for nearly revealing Anusha's presence several days ago. The woman wasn't looking at her, but at Anusha's reflection in the dirty glass of a signal mirror mounted not three feet from the travel chest.

Annoyance briefly eclipsed her worry about Japheth. How many reflective surfaces were there on this blasted ship?

Anusha released the chest and summoned her dream sword. She smashed the signal mirror with the blade's tip. From now on, she decided, she would smash every mirror she came upon.

The pirate screamed, "Ghost attack!" and ran, diving into the open hold. Questioning cries and answering yells sprung up around the ship.

"Brilliant," commented Anusha as she relinquished her sword. It faded like a dream. She grabbed her travel chest and pulled in earnest, quickly towing it to the railing. The seamount of Taunissik, ringed in streamers of darkness, remained just visible as the day's light began to fall to twilight.

Anusha studied the mechanism securing the lifeboat. Some sort of pulley connected to a lot of thick ropes and knots. She briefly considered having at it with her sword. No, she should lower the boat first . . .

Pirate calls of alarm went up across the craft, in response to the incessant screams of "Ghost!" down in the hold. Anusha found the latch securing the pulley. She got a good hold on the chest, then heaved her travel chest into the lifeboat. She couldn't have accomplished that feat in the flesh, but even so, she nearly lost her concentration and dropped herself into the chop.

Anusha jumped into the swaying launch and called Lucky to join her. The dog barked excitedly and bounded aboard. She released the latch controlling the pulley. The handle spun out, and the lifeboat dropped into the waves alongside the slimy bulk of the *Green Siren*. Safely down in the water, she severed the overhanging ropes with a couple of swipes of her shimmering dream blade, then grabbed the oars.

Her plan nearly failed then. It was far easier to push, pull, slash, and heave things in her dream form than to hold and manipulate a discrete object over long periods, let alone two simultaneously. The oars kept slipping from her hands even as she tried to fit them to the oarlocks on each gunwale.

Several heads poked over the railing above her, some pointing, all yelling. One man was yelling, "The ghost is stealing the captain's dog!"

Someone else yelled, "By Umberlee's rusted trident, what're you fools jabbering about! That's not a ghost—we got us a thief with an invisibility spell!"

Cries of disagreement, revelation, and surprise came back. A discussion broke out over whether wizards had relearned the art of magically tricking the eye.

Anusha continued to struggle with the oars. Desperation was not helping her concentration. She recalled suddenly the effort it had taken her to learn cursive writing under the stern eye of her tutor. With a similar effort, she blocked out the pirate talk above and slowly, methodically, placed one oar in its lock, then the other. Once so placed, she discovered it was far easier to row.

With swift strokes, the lifeboat nosed toward Taunissik. She left the pirate babble behind. Lucky positioned himself on the lifeboat's prow, and for a short time, served as its figurehead.

Halfway to the isle, the small dots trailing misty streamers of darkness resolved as squid-riding kuo-toa. Anusha suddenly recalled Nogah's role the first time a landing party from the *Green Siren* came ashore. The ex-whip had chanted the entire time, to keep the attention of the sentinels and Gethshemeth elsewhere. Anusha ceased rowing and looked hard at the distant flyers. Their patterns didn't seem any different. They hadn't noticed her yet, down here on the darkening sea. Had Nogah been wrong? Considering the ambush the others had walked into, it seemed possible the ex-whip had accomplished exactly the opposite of her stated aim. Anusha resumed rowing.

Her pace quickened, until she sawed at the oars like a madwoman. Why not? She didn't need to pause for rest or breath. It wasn't heavy work, just tedious. She sped across the water. In short order, she beached the lifeboat next to the first launch, in a thick tangle of mangrove roots. Nothing had found or disturbed the site, as far as she could determine.

She wondered what had become of the rowers left by the first sortie. Nothing pleasant, she guessed.

Anusha debated whether she should pull the travel chest completely ashore or leave it in the boat for a quick getaway later. She decided to leave it in the boat.

She addressed the guard dog. "Lucky! Good boy! Good boy! Stay here, Lucky. Guard! Stay until I return, all right?" Lucky tried to lick her proffered hand and settled himself directly on top of the travel chest. What had she done to deserve the trust of such a loyal, innocent little creature? She patted him on the head, then turned toward the isle's interior.

Raidon hurtled through a gap between nothing and everything, through a space where people were not meant to go. Light speared his eyes and burned his face. His teeth rattled in his jaw. All the bones in his body tried to burrow out of their fleshy cocoon. His chest ached as he gasped over and over, trying to draw in another breath of air. But there was no air. A gray haze narrowed his vision smaller and smaller . . .

A guttering blue parabola snatched him out of the no-space where he trespassed. Raidon and Angul fell ten feet onto a flagstone floor.

He couldn't suppress a long, hacking cough, even though his ribs seared with each contraction. He lay on his side in a half fetal position, riding out his body's mutiny. When the coughing subsided, he rested.

Where had Cynosure dropped him this time?

The chamber was a great stone vault filled with hulking, dimly glowing rectangular objects. Most protruded from the floor, but some stuck out from the walls and several hung from the ceiling. Ancient, magical script glimmered on the blocks; the source of each object's glow was this script-born light. Two walls were collapsed beneath rubble, and many of the blocks were sundered, their runes darkened.

Slender tubes of dully pulsing light protruded from the stone blocks, one or two from each. The corralled light was gathered in thick bundles, suspended from the high ceiling by fancifully carved stone gargoyles. Many of the cords were frayed and snapped, their light dead, and others lay in snake-like disarray on the rubble-strewn floor.

It was cold too. Raidon's breath steamed, and his face and hands were already chilled.

Other than the cold, nothing immediately threatened him except the wounds the Chalk Destrier had given him as their fight concluded.

He closed his eyes, reaching for his focus. He visualized his chest and the bones that gave his torso shape as lines of energy. They were cracked and misshapen—a few were broken. Pulses of pain spiked out from them through the rest of his body. He imagined the spikes as real objects, then imagined their pointy ends eroding away. These sorts of visualization tricks aided his concentration. When the piercing pain receded enough for him to continue, he mentally grasped each broken and damaged bone, one after another, and straightened it. New spikes of agony shot through his body, ones he couldn't dampen. But he did not stop until every bone was mended.

Raidon finally released his focus. Stabbing pain had been replaced by a body-wide dull ache. He lay awhile longer in the winter-cold chamber of rubble and strange objects. Stray thoughts of his long-dead life intruded. He saw Ailyn playing in the courtyard of their home in Nathlekh. She wore a yellow dress, and her face was grubby. She clutched a great mass of wild daffodils from the garden. He could smell them.

The monk smiled. Ailyn returned the impish grin he knew so well. His heart clenched. "Hey, little girl," he murmured to the phantom. His throat was tight. Ailyn laughed and skipped away.

A new pain pulled him from waking reverie. Something hard and painful lay below his prostate form. He shifted and saw the object was Angul. He looked at its dull length for a few moments. His vision was blurred with unwept tears born of his daydream.

The monk rubbed at his eyes until they were clear.

He grabbed Angul's cold hilt and stood. From this new vantage, he could see farther into the chamber. The lines of light that were not burned out seemed to lead to a nexus at the chamber's heart. He walked toward that gathering point, favoring one foot slightly.

At the center lay a crumpled, half buried shape, like the husk of some fantastically large spider's recent meal. The shape was a humanoid figure forged of crystal, stone, iron, and more exotic components, but it had fallen over. Its surface was rusted, pitted, and cracked, and half of it was buried beneath a section of collapsed ceiling. A partially visible design winked from its dented metallic chest—the Cerulean Sign.

"Cynosure?"

The figure did not respond. Despite that, Raidon was certain he was in the presence of the artificial entity who once served as Stardeep's warden.

"Are you awake?"

He bent, tapped the golem's forehead. Was that a slight glimmer of light deep in the idol's stony eyes? He couldn't be sure.

"Did you exhaust yourself pulling me from the Chalk Destrier's domain?" he asked. "If so, thank you. I hope it does not prove your last act. I'm not worthy of such sacrifice."

He frowned. "You sacrificed yourself to save me, someone you hardly know."

His thoughts turned backward. He murmured, "Me, I left the heart of my life to die alone while I slept in safety."

Even as he spoke aloud, he recognized he half consciously reflected the golem's noble act back upon himself. A pathetic show of self-pity, and for whom?

He was far more human, with all the failings that implied, than he'd ever admitted to himself. He was only a fool with an outsize ego, like every other fool who pranced and paraded through life, deluded they were somehow finer and better trained than most others, until shown the truth.

He turned, disgusted. His hip brushed a stone block, closer to the golem than all the rest. The glyphs on the stone flared into life. Their shapes fluttered and morphed, until the monk saw they spelled out words in Common. He read:

Raidon,

If you can read this, I have consumed my last remaining store of animating elan. Fear not, I did not trap you. With your Sign, you can access Stardeep's functions and propel yourself across the face of Faerûn one last time. You must go to the seamount we earlier scried, where Gethshemeth lairs. You have the Cerulean Sign. Worry not about your lack of training. Concentrate on Stardeep's spellmantle, and you will be able to access it as I have. Go to Gethshemeth. Subdue the great kraken. Destroy the relic of Xxiphu it wields. Much depends on you, Raidon. Though I have no spirit or life that will persist beyond my physical death, I wish you well with all the fiber of my faltering existence.

Your friend,
Cynosure

"I am doubly unworthy of your trust," Raidon murmured.

He gazed long at the stone block. The runes he'd read were changing, forming a great ring. The ring lifted off the stone until it hung vertically before Raidon. Within it, an image resolved.

Raidon saw the isle where kuo-toa cavorted above, and a tentacled monstrosity lurked in the watery hollows beneath.

The view through the scrying circle showed him the island's surface. It was night, but noisome glows and glimmers gave outline to the sentinels that continued their circuit above the island.

"Angul, are you ready?" The monk raised the sword, gripping it. The cerulean light in the blade's pommel continued to glimmer, no softer, but no stronger.

He recalled one of the last times he'd seen the sword. It had been more than ten years ago, more like twenty, he supposed.

Kiril had stood before Angul, considering relinquishing the blade that had cursed her with its overzealous nature. Cynosure's words came back to him: "Angul's life is only a half-life. Without a living wielder, the soul-forged blade will fail, releasing the soul to its final peace. All that will remain is a dead length of sword-shaped steel."

The memory faded, but concern tightened Raidon's eyes.

If his memory reported true, then when Kiril had given up the blade to the Chalk Destrier, Angul lost his living wielder. He hadn't had a living wielder for years . . .

"By Xiang's serene teachings, you had better not be broken!" exclaimed Raidon.

The sword remained as quiescent as when he'd first drawn it from the stone.

Warmth flushed the monk's cheeks. He resisted smashing the sword on the stone obelisk before him, even though it was what he wanted to do more than anything in that hot moment.

No, he commanded himself. I am an heir of Xiang. Focus. Calm yourself, or your pledge to defeat Gethshemeth in Ailyn's name will fail.

Raidon unclenched his chest and shoulders, standing taller. "Angul," he said, his voice calm but commanding, "I beseech you, wake! A foe you were forged to destroy threatens Faerûn with a relic of elder days. If it and its foul artifact are not obliterated, you will fail your own purpose."

Had the dim pulse of blue in the hilt grown slightly brighter at his words?

No. They hadn't changed at all.

Raidon tried a few more appeals to the sword before concluding the soul-shard in the blade was too far gone to be conscious of such petitions.

He regarded the Blade Cerulean. It was a tool of the Keepers of the Cerulean Sign. A sign of which he himself had become a living manifestation.

He loosened his jacket, revealing the ruddy Sign on his chest. He placed the blade's hilt directly upon it and willed his Sign to pulse.

Something tickled the back of Raidon's mind. A query, so faint he thought he might have imagined it.

Raidon pulsed his Sign again. This time, he clearly heard a forlorn question, a question asked without sound.

Kiril, is it you? Has my Bright Star returned?

The monk said, "Angul?"

No response. He frowned and infused the blade a third time with his Sign.

The voice, no stronger than before, spoke anew into Raidon's mind.

I am so tired. So tired. Why won't you speak, Kiril? I thought you shut of me, finally sworn off this shattered soul that can never know peace. I don't blame you. I have no restraint, none whatever, as you know so well . . .

Raidon addressed the blade again. "Kiril has moved on."

My Bright Star . . . She was my all, and I was her bane.

"Angul, listen to me—"

Angul? Is that my name? No, it was something else . . .

"You are called Angul. I speak true."

. . . I remember. I am Angul. I was Kiril's companion and righteous tool. But I have fulfilled my oath. My task is complete, and peace beckons. Why do you disturb me?

"A new wielder has need of your strength. A blight threatens the world, a menace you were specifically fashioned to vanquish. You are needed!"

So tired . . .

"Aboleths from ancient days, Angul, are poised to poison the surface world," pleaded Raidon. It seemed the blade was actively resisting him, actively trying to descend once more into complete, unknowing somnolence.

Leave me be. Perhaps this time I can be reunited with Kiril as a whole and complete—

Raidon pulsed the blade a fourth time.

Like a candle begets a wildfire, his Sign finally ignited Angul. The paper-thin personality he'd been interacting with, ghostlike in its tentative, fleeting nature, charred and burned to nothing. Beneath lay the true Angul, hard and bright and unforgiving.

Aberrations shall be purged, a voice pronounced in a tone completely shorn of the pain and loss of the earlier persona. This voice was keen for what awaited it, eager to strip the world of all who were unfit to walk its face.

His hand disappeared in a nimbus of burning, searing fire, a fire that burned away his own self-pity, his doubt, his focus, and his half-realized desire to walk away from the entire escapade. Something more than aspiration took hold of the monk—it was moral certainty, simple and absolute. Some things could not, could never be suffered. Angul was the first, best, and only tool to accomplish that end. Gethshemeth, and its stone of corruption, would be eradicated. He knew it—he and Angul would be the instrument that accomplished that righteous deed.

Afterward, Raidon decided he would turn his hand to the multitude of lesser moral failings still plaguing Toril.

CHAPTER TWENTY

The Year of the Secret (1396 DR)
Taunissik, Sea of Fallen Stars

Anusha retraced the path she'd taken a few hours earlier. She didn't need to squeeze between gnarled roots and under reaching limbs; she passed like a ghost without regard to the difficult terrain. Unlike the previous time she passed, her dreaming, physical self was miles closer. She didn't have to concentrate nearly all her attention on holding herself in place.

On the other hand, with her body so close and vulnerable, she was reluctant to move too far from it. Twice she paused in her tracks, listened intently after some imagined noise, then raced back to the lifeboat to check on the sanctity of her travel chest. Both times Lucky had been happy to see her return. Both times were false alarms.

Full night had arrived, and she was no closer to finding Japheth.

"I'm not scared," she said. Was it true, she wondered? Why was she still lingering here, outside the city, when she knew where she had to go?

"I'm not!" she iterated.

Despite her resolve, she still shrieked in surprise when a blaze of cerulean blue dropped from the sky to land somewhere off in the mangroves. She waited for an explosion, as she supposed would accompany the impact of a falling star, but heard nothing.

Should she ignore it? What if the firefall was some sort of warlock signal sent by Japheth? Anusha turned and made directly toward the point of impact.

Instead of a chunk of burnt skystone, she found a man. A half-elf, actually, though one whose human parent obviously hailed from Thesk or elsewhere eastward.

He was dressed in sandals, loose trousers, and an elaborate silk jacket open to the belt. A flaming sword in one hand and a tattoo on the man's chest burned with the same sky blue fire. The flame's color didn't quite suggest spellplague to Anusha. The hue was clearer, somehow purer than what she associated with her nightmares.

The man stood in a burned area but was physically unharmed by what Anusha guessed had been a rough arrival. On the other hand, she judged by his expression that his mind could well be broken; his open mouth and blank eyes implied he might be crazed.

Hunting screams resounded from above. The sentinels had noticed the newcomer's dramatic appearance too.

One of the sentinels dropped from the sky, its wriggling shape limned in green lambency. The kuo-toa rider gripped a long, slender lance of coral aimed right at the man's heart. A black trail roiled in the wake of the creature's dive.

The half-elf's empty eyes darted upward and narrowed. As

the flyer stooped upon him, the man brought his sword into a high guard position. Just as it seemed the man would be pierced by the rider's cruel lance, he slipped ever so gracefully sideways. With one hand, he ran his blazing sword through the body of the morkoth as it flashed by. The sword tip tore through the creature as if it were no more than tissue paper. With his free hand, he plucked the kuo-toa rider from the saddle. The limp, blood-spurting corpse of the morkoth piled into a mass of trees on the other side of the clearing.

Anusha watched the man, her mouth wide in amazement. His display outshone anything she had earlier witnessed, even that icy eladrin in Japheth's castle. The half-elf must be a hero of old, she thought. But she didn't recognize him from any of the stories her tutor had taught.

The man held the struggling kuo-toa high by the throat. He said, "Tell me where I can find the abomination Gethshemeth."

The kuo-toa redoubled its efforts to free itself from the newcomer's vicelike grip.

A hint of movement above caught Anusha's attention.

"Watch out!" she yelled. Two morkoth-mounted sentinels flying in side-by-side formation dropped like hawks on a rabbit, intending to bracket him between two arrow-swift lance tips.

The swordwielder released his captive even as he jumped straight up. The half-elf cleared ten feet easily. The sentinels flashed beneath him. One accidentally skewered the kuo-toa rider the man released as he leaped. The other attempted to raise its lance at the last moment, but the man, even as he spun head over heels in the air, shattered the lance with a single strike of his sword.

The sentinels mounted back into the sky. The man landed lightly upon his feet, moving with the grace and economy of action she didn't normally associate with a sword fighter.

He scanned the area near where Anusha had called her

warning, failed to see her, then picked up the kuo-toa he'd earlier snatched from its saddle. It was already unmoving from the wound its compatriot had delivered. He said, "Aberrations shall not be suffered." He hewed the unmoving form with the sword, splitting it asunder.

Anusha gasped.

The man's head jerked around, his eyes blazing. Did he see her?

Apparently not. He continued to scan the area, then he said, "I must find Gethshemeth. I must . . ."

The man's expression twisted, as if he struggled to remember something vital.

Then he grunted and tossed the sword away, as if it burned his hand. The sword fell point first into the earth.

The weapon continued to burn, but the half-elf's tattoo immediately dimmed. Human expression returned to the man's face, and he wiped his suddenly sweaty brow with the back of his hand.

A scream of alarm mounted off to Anusha's left, where the city was located.

"Angul," the man said, apparently addressing the sword, "if you wish to destroy Gethshemeth, you must swear on the Cerulean Sign we both serve never to overpower my mind again."

The sword continued to pulse with sky blue flames.

"Can it talk?" Anusha blurted before she could stop herself.

The man looked up, his face remarkably serene. He said, "No, invisible one, at least not to anyone not holding it. Who are you?"

"Anusha," she replied. "I, uh, I am here to destroy Gethshemeth, too. My friends and I. We were separated, but I'm returning to them now."

The man cocked his head, glanced up at the sentinels that circled above. They seemed to be keeping their distance for the moment. Anusha didn't blame them, after seeing the man in action.

"Will you help us?" she asked. "My friends were attacked; that's when I lost them. I don't know what's happened since then. But I know they need help!"

"Who are your friends? Unseen sprites like yourself?"

"No! And I'm no sprite. I'm just, uh, not quite all here, which makes me hard to see. My friends are Japheth—he's learned spells and curses from some creature bound in the Feywild—and Seren—she says she's a wizard and she casts spells too. And Captain Thoster. He's a privateer. Actually, Seren and the captain are not my friends, just Japheth."

The man rubbed his chin, then he asked, "How old are you, Anusha?"

Her cheeks colored. She was glad the man couldn't see her. She had been nearly babbling, she had to admit it. She shot back, "And what is your name, man who falls from the sky?"

He executed a sudden and sharp bow. "Raidon Kane, disciple of Xiang Temple."

"You're a monk?"

The man nodded, said, "And a Keeper of the Cerulean Sign, and reluctant wielder of Angul, whose moral sense is suspect despite his zeal for destroying evil. I have suffered much and traveled far to arrive here, all that I might destroy Gethshemeth and the relic he holds."

"Oh! Well, then you will help me?"

"I detect no taint of aberration about you, so I shall put my trust in you until you prove unworthy of it. I already know I cannot trust this blade."

So saying, he grasped the sword. His expression hardened. His hand shook. But composure settled back into his features. He said, "We don't have time for more elaborate introductions, Anusha. Please lead the way. I can follow your verbal directions."

Anusha plucked a loose stone from the ground and explained, "Just follow this."

She dashed toward the city. Fear and anxiety loosed its overwhelming grip on her. Now that she breathed easier, she wondered whether she would ever have built up enough courage, if the half-elf monk hadn't turned up.

She dispersed the thought—it didn't matter what might have been. With Raidon Kane at her side, she allowed herself to hope. She just might see Japheth again.

Anusha led Raidon into Taunissik. Even in the middle of the night, the coral-like, jumbled structures and clear pools glowed with a pale, algal light. The kuo-toa who'd earlier lounged in the pools were absent, but sinister shapes looked out every window of the city, their vacant faces shadowed by dim glows behind them. The sentinels continued to circle overhead, keeping Raidon at the center of the circuit.

"At least they are keeping their distance," Anusha said, trying to break the tension with something more helpful than a scream or whimper.

"They will allow us to enter, then block our exit—what else but cowardly tactics can one expect of aberration-touched creatures?" The half-elf's voice rang with a righteous zeal. Was the sword affecting the man's mind again?

She ran toward the large structure. Raidon easily matched her tireless pace.

The sinuous glyphs carved on every surface of the building flickered between green and wan red light. She plunged into the entrance, the disciple of Xiang Temple a breath behind. They passed through a low-ceilinged vestibule where three basins collected effluvia from fish-faced busts. Anusha took the right-hand path from a choice of two arched corridors and plunged down a narrow staircase. Relief-carved kuo-toa heads emerged from either wall at intervals, their eyes spilling yellow radiance.

After one switchback, the stairs emptied into a straight

tunnel Anusha flew through, the stone she held to guide Raidon in one hand, her dream blade in the other.

They passed into a chamber lit by a trio of sculpted, ten-foot-diameter kuo-toa busts on high walls. A granite block stood loose, just inside the room—Anusha remembered it had crashed down and sealed the exit. Something had pushed it aside since then.

Where the central pool had been was a drained, slime-coated cavity in the floor. Dead albino fish lay within it like so many withered leaves. A hole in the cavity's basin was a spiral staircase, now open to air, leading downward.

"Raidon, this is where we were separated," she exclaimed. "I don't know what happened when I was . . . pulled away, but the basin in the floor was filled with water last time I was here."

"How long . . ." Raidon's query trailed off as his gaze tracked higher.

Anusha followed his eyes. A dragon perched atop one of the kuo-toa busts above them like a lazing savanna cat. Humanoid remains lay between its outstretched legs, but from her vantage, she couldn't identify them. Her stomach, despite being immaterial, convulsed.

The dragon, seeing it had the monk's attention, stretched. Its wings unfolded like a webbed, thin-fingered hand opening to reach up and scratch the ceiling. It yawned, revealing bloody fangs as long as Anusha's forearm. The dragon's deep-socketed eyes and hollow nasal openings were almost skull-like. Large spikes extended from its jaw, and two rows of small horns lined its brows.

"You bear the taint I cannot abide," Raidon accused the dragon, his voice cold as iron.

"You trespass and have found your death," replied the dragon, its voice a scratchy rumble. It tensed, preparing to spring.

Anusha cried, "Where are the other trespassers, those who entered this room a few hours ago?"

The dragon froze at the sound of her voice. Its eyes scanned the room, and its nostrils flared. Its wings retracted backward to lie low along its back.

"They have gone below to offer obeisance to Gethshemeth," hissed the dragon, its eyes flickering with the intensity of its search.

"Liar!" screamed Anusha.

The dragon's brow creased, as if in consternation at not being able to locate its prey. Its body language now screamed caution—it was no longer on the verge of dropping on Raidon.

"Liar you name me? You are wrong, hidden one. My name is Scathrys," said the dragon. "I'll leave you and your Shou friend to discover who in this chamber is a liar. Mayhap it's you? Gethshemeth and your friends lie below." The dragon extended a massive claw and pointed to the stairs at the bottom of the slimed floor cavity.

Rage bit Anusha. She cocked her arm and threw her dream blade as if it were a spear. Indeed, to her eye, it lengthened in midflight, becoming a spear in truth. At the last moment, Scathrys, somehow sensing something of the intangible dream, dodged. The spear struck the dragon through one wing.

It roared in anger and confusion, releasing a stream of green fluid that scored the walls. The spear held the dragon in place for a moment, even as the creature exploded into frantic efforts to free itself from what pinned it.

Pain smote Anusha, right between the eyes. Even as she gasped at its onslaught, the spear faded to nothing. The head-ache eased too, but a dull pain persisted as if to remind her that reality could be bent only so far by her dream wiles.

The dragon, free of the invisible thorn that had stung it, did not flee. Instead, it hunkered down on its perch, relying on the bulk of the stone head to shield itself from further unseen attacks. It hissed, "Your friends are even now swearing their eternal souls to the void that lies between the stars. Yet you dally here." It guffawed, its mirth mocking and harsh.

Raidon scrutinized Scathrys, the Blade Cerulean naked in his hand. Tongues of blue flame rippled its length.

"Raidon, let's go! Japheth needs us!"

The monk scowled. Sweat beaded on his lip. He looked murderously at the dragon but said, "The greater abomination lies below, Angul."

The half-elf wrenched himself away and stepped into the open cavity. With uncanny grace, he skied down the slimy, nearly vertical wall and into the bowl, easily avoiding the shaft containing the stairs.

Anusha leaped after, with far less refinement. Not that it mattered, since no one could see her and she couldn't be hurt by a mere fall. She wondered if she should try to dream her blade forth once more? She decided to wait. Her head still smarted fiercely. It seemed clear she had overtaxed her ability to affect the waking world by lancing the dragon at a distance.

The monk raced down the spiral stair, narrow and slick with recently evacuated water. He didn't stumble once. Anusha followed, his unseen shadow.

CHAPTER TWENTY-ONE

The Year of the Secret (1396 DR)
Taunissik, Sea of Fallen Stars

A coppery taste filled his mouth. Blood? He twisted, eyes nearly spinning in their sockets as they sought something familiar. Where was he?

A dull red glow stretched above and to each side of him. A fire? Emberlike points of light flared, brighter and brighter, until they fused to become a red-hazed vista.

He walked out upon a scarlet plain beneath a bleeding sky on a road of ground bones.

He continued walking, because he knew he had to do something very important. Something that lay in the direction he traveled, perhaps. Something quite vital, he was certain. Urgency burned just below his awareness, on the brink of shattering the glass between anxious unknowing and terrified understanding. But he couldn't quite recall precisely what he was supposed to do . . .

He paused. The road seemed familiar somehow, like something he'd glimpsed once in a dream. Or a nightmare, truth be told.

Perhaps he dreamed even now. That would explain the gap in his understanding. And why he wore no clothing.

Why, he couldn't even recall his own name!

Was that normal for a dream?

He started forward again. Perhaps if he reached the end of the road, the dream would end, and he would wake up. That sounded good. It might even be true. He quickened his pace.

After a time, he realized the faint roar he heard might be a waterfall. The sound rose and fell from somewhere ahead. His choice had been the correct one! At least, it seemed he was heading toward something interesting. He doubled his speed.

The road dipped beneath the level of the surrounding plain. Shadowed walls of veined stone grew up on each side. The roar echoed strangely through the canyonlike aisle, sounding almost like . . . screaming?

The sound, unnerving enough by itself, touched another memory. He'd heard it before. He wondered again if he were having a nightmare. The fact he couldn't recall his own identity took on an ominous edge as the screams coalesced.

He stumbled to a halt at the edge of a precipice. He stared down into an endless abyss that reached beyond his eyes' ability to discern details, seemingly limitless in its depth. It seemed to him the gap descended through the world and out the other side, still a void, one that reached forever . . .

The next beat of his heart brought with it his identity.

"I am Japheth! By the fey-cursed pacts I swore, I am Japheth!"

With his name came the realization that he'd misplaced his cloak. On the heels of that insight, he recognized where he was.

He stood at the end of the crimson road, where demons hunt those who give their souls over to traveler's dust. It was where everyone who took the arcane poison eventually ended, sooner or later. Japheth had avoided that fate years longer than any other, thanks to his pact.

The fact he stood here once more suggested his period of grace had concluded.

This time, there was no Lord of Bats to wing down through the bleeding sky and pluck him from certain dissolution. How could the Lord of Bats do so? He was prisoner in his own castle, thanks to Japheth's scheme. Or perhaps the Lord of Bats had freed himself, and that freedom had ended Japheth's immunity from consequence. Either way, he had reached the end of the line.

Japheth stared, goggle-eyed and dry-mouthed. He tried to shuffle back from the edge. Agony seared his legs, as if his bones locked into place by suddenly extruding spurs into his muscles. He swayed, his toes overhanging the unending abyss. His internal struggle dislodged a portion of the earthy lip, which rained dust and pebbles out and then down. Gone.

Raw, terrified throats loosed drawn out screams. He jerked his head around and saw his wasn't the only road that emptied onto the great pit. Hundreds of other gaps poked through the abyssal wall, some higher than the one he stood in, others lower, all endpoints for roads composed of ground bone. And upon them, other victims walked. Walked screaming, protesting, and begging as they hurled themselves, still screaming, into the abyss.

He wanted to avert his gaze. But horror locked his eyes on each new victim who fell past. Some, the yawning chasm of infinite darkness swallowed. But many more did not reach that boundary, or at least they did not reach it in one piece. For in that space between an infinite fall and the false hope for salvation, demonic creatures laired and hunted. They skimmed through the air on scaled wings, spearing windmilling figures out of the air with claws, spiked tails, retractable tongues, and other appendages too horrible to comprehend.

When a demon stooped on a falling screamer, that victim's voice redoubled in godsforsaken frenzy, then abruptly ceased. The remains of each feast were finally relinquished, to fall wet and silent into darkness.

Japheth couldn't help screaming himself when, without willing it, he stepped off into the void. He fell. He windmilled his arms, just like all the others, no matter that it did nothing but fuel his terror. He told himself to stop, but it was impossible to do anything else.

A shape sailed down from the burning sky. It closed on him with vicious certitude. It snatched him from the air.

Why wasn't it tearing into him? Comprehension touched him—this was no demon.

It was Anusha. Anusha in her golden armor of dream, though without her helm. Golden wings of whimsy sprouted from her back. They beat with a strong, steady cadence, bearing both of them higher.

She held him, and he her. She bore him up, higher and higher. He stared into her dark eyes and was lost. He was as disoriented as when he'd stared into the abyss, but fear left him.

He said, "You saved me, Anusha. I owe you my life. I . . ."

She only smiled. He leaned closer into her embrace. His lips touched hers, and her smile melted into eager warmth.

Japheth opened his eyes with a start. A great dark blur, punctuated here and there by tiny, moving blurs of light, surrounded him. He lay on something hard, damp, and painfully unyielding.

"Where—?" he began, then he coughed. His throat was raw as if from screaming. Or as if coated with rock dust. His eyes too were gritty with sand, and his whole body was bruised, as if he'd been squeezed too hard on every extremity. And a pain stabbed the left side of his chest with each breath.

He rubbed at his eyes to get some tears flowing to wash away the grit. When his vision cleared, he saw the unpleasant object on which he lay was a small coral dome. Words scribed on it read, "Japheth Donard. Preserved for sacrifice 1396."

A man's voice, smooth and mellow but with a strange accent, said, "You are free of the stone. Anusha pulled you forth a moment ago. You were entombed in that coral mound."

Japheth coughed again and saw the dark-haired speaker. He wore a silk jacket open at the chest to show off a great tattoo that glowed with cerulean brilliance. The man's lithe shape hinted at a touch of elf blood. A sword burning with the same sky blue fire stood point first in the rock before the man, as if, lacking a sheath, he had plunged it into the stone.

"Where is Anusha?" Japheth asked.

"Perhaps she stands next to us unseen, though her silence argues she is attempting to retrieve the others from these nearby biers."

Japheth rose, his bruised and battered limbs protesting, but he breathed a sigh of relief when he felt the folds of his cloak move around him. He had only dreamed he'd lost it! And it must have been a dream too, that he had nearly succumbed to the terminal stages of traveler's dust abuse.

Or had it been a dream? The man said Anusha retrieved him from the coral dome. Had her dream form pulled him free of more than a stone cocoon?

A flare of blue fire on the dome closest to Japheth's revealed two figures—a woman in armor, and another woman limp in her arms. "Anusha!" Her name escaped Japheth's mouth without his volition.

Anusha pulled the other woman, Seren, from the stone and

laid her across its coarse surface, just as Japheth had found himself arranged. She waved, even as the blue fire outlining her began to fade. Her voice rang out, "Only one more?" She pointed to the dome printed with Thoster's name.

"Yes," replied the warlock, beaming. Just as in his dream, she wore no helm.

"One moment," she returned, and was gone.

Seren began to cough, her throat sounding as encrusted as Japheth's had been. Pale dust covered her, lending her an unhealthy pallor. He supposed he sported the same layer.

Anusha appeared from the last dome in another burst of azure flame, carrying Captain Thoster. She bore the man's considerable weight without too much effort, Japheth noted. Her ability was strengthening.

Thoster opened his eyes the barest sliver and whispered, "Water."

The warlock cupped his hands and dunked them into the tidepool at his feet. He transferred the water three steps and dribbled over the man's white, ash-streaked face and into his open mouth, which pulsed, open and closed, in a weirdly fishlike manner. Thoster gasped when the water touched him, and some color returned to his skin. Seren was already standing on her own power, muttering.

Japheth turned to look at Anusha, whose identifying flames were already nearly absent. He said, suddenly clumsy with his words, "I'm glad to see you."

"Japheth! I'm so sorry I left you! It was too far—"

"We ain't safe," Thoster's throaty rasp cut her off. "Where's the beast?"

Japheth guiltily jerked his gaze from where Anusha's image faded, and scanned the great space. He looked for hints of sinuous arms moving in the shadows. Glints of gold-green light flitted over the domes, obelisks of shaped coral, and tidepools of seawater that dotted the great subterranean vault. Nothing else.

The stranger spoke up then. "We have not seen the great kraken since we arrived, though we faced down a few of Gethshemeth's servitors." He pointed behind him at a pile of rubble. Japheth recognized a few of the glyphs on the broken rock—it was the eidolon Gethshemeth had commandeered to hold him in stone!

"You destroyed the walking statue?" asked Thoster.

The man nodded and grimaced, looking at the sword punched into the stone before him. "I did, with Angul's aid." He looked up then and said, "I am Raidon Kane, a monk initiate of Xiang Temple. I am here to destroy Gethshemeth and its aberrant relic."

"Your aid is sorely needed!" enthused Captain Thoster. "We ain't got the tools, I think we proved."

Seren frowned. Japheth did too, but not because he was upset Thoster demeaned their abilities. It was because of Raidon's stated desire to destroy the Dreamheart. That second goal wouldn't serve the warlock.

Japheth ventured, "If we destroy Gethshemeth, its relic will be powerless, surely." Maybe the monk wouldn't know any better. Thoster winked at Japheth, his eyes twinkling. The captain didn't want the Dreamheart destroyed any more than Japheth did.

The monk's brow creased ever so slightly as if in surprise; then he gave a curt shake of his head. He said, "The relic is the source of the problem. Its destruction is required, lest some other creature claim it for malicious ends, or worse, call up from the earth those to whom it truly belongs."

The sword emitted a sudden cerulean flare as if to highlight the monk's words.

Japheth nodded as if in agreement but inwardly wondered what he would do.

Thoster said, his tone light as if he were relating a joke, "Well, let's not count our coins before we open the chest, eh? The beast is still around, and the beast is what we must deal with first. After that, we can talk about who's going to destroy what, aye?"

Japheth nodded again. Perhaps then he could convince the half-elf Shou to give up his desire to destroy the relic.

Raidon met the captain's gaze steadily, saying nothing.

"Are all of you cracked?" demanded Seren. "We were roundly and easily defeated by Gethshemeth. I am not going to fight it again! We need to get out of here! I'm leaving." She shot a desperate glance Japheth's way, as if pleading for his support.

The warlock said, "Seren, we can't escape without facing Gethshemeth. If we divide our strength, it'll merely kill us one by one, alone. Together, with Raidon's aid this time, and Anusha's, perhaps we can overcome the kraken."

"Who's Anusha?" Seren demanded. "Let me guess—the 'ghost,' right? Anyhow, you must know you're lying to yourself." The woman's voice rose, echoing through the chamber. "We came in here five strong, remember? I doubt Nogah and the first mate would agree with your assessment about how well we operate as a team. I'd ask them, but, oh yes, I recall now, they're already dead!" Seren's last word was a piercing screech.

"Seren, shush," came Anusha's urgent suggestion from somewhere to the woman's left.

The wizard whirled, her eyes searching for the speaker.

"And you!" Seren accused. "I should have dealt with you permanently the first time around, ghost girl. I'm sure your ability to hide will prove ever so useful against a kraken!"

Thoster chuckled.

"Seren, she saved your life," Japheth protested despite his desire not to get drawn into the wizard's childish rant. Angry blood pounded in his temples.

"No time for squabbles," Raidon Kane interjected. "Something approaches."

A distant gurgle grew louder. Japheth had been aware of the noise for a while but had discounted it as just one more strange background noise. He did so no longer. It was the sound of water flowing. A lot of water.

A bolus of liquid blasted the top off a coral dome not ten paces from Japheth. The coral cap was propelled so swiftly upward by the water jet that it crashed into the vault's ceiling, exploding into rubble. The geyser of water remained, a column of flowing sea connecting floor and ceiling, cold and dire, threatening to fill the entire vault if its flow was not dammed.

Rock detritus and water rained down, pelting everyone.

A piece of shrapnel drew a bloody line down Thoster's left cheek. He swore an oath in a language Japheth didn't know.

Seren uttered an arcane word, and a mundane-looking wooden shield materialized. It began to whirl around its mistress, too late to shield her from a stone that had clipped her head.

Fed from the inrushing water, the pools dotting the vault's floor began to reach toward each other. The darting witchlights were blurred with the haze of water vapor in the air. The farthest domes and obelisks became difficult to pick out. But moving shapes on the periphery snatched Japheth's attention.

A phalanx of perhaps twenty shuffling, spear-carrying kuo-toa emerged from the mist, no more than thirty or forty feet away. Their skin glistened with moisture from the roaring water jet. They didn't seem hindered by the rising water, which lapped at the creatures' calves.

Seren hurled a narrow stream of fire, crisping the lead combatant instantly. Japheth matched her with a sizzling eldritch blast of his own, disemboweling a kuo-toa. It stopped and pitched over face first in the water. Their fellows didn't flinch—they trampled their former compatriots' bodies without shifting their vicious, predatory gaze.

"Your sword!" yelled Seren, pointing at the burning blade.

"Angul is not yet required," the monk replied.

The kuo-toa's forward progress paused a moment as they launched a flight of spears. Japheth's cloak wrapped about one that tried to enter his skull through his eye, diverting it elsewhere. Another spear struck Seren's whirling shield, splintering it.

"If your weapon is as powerful as it looks, we need it now!" the wizard returned, her voice cracking.

Raidon retrieved the spear that had shattered Seren's shield. He hurtled it back into the advancing mob, skewering a kuo-toa in the throat. He replied, "The sword's ego is overwhelming. I prefer not to subject myself to him until absolutely necessary."

The pirate captain's eyes narrowed, his eyes suddenly avaricious. "Him?" asked Thoster. Raidon didn't respond or seem to notice the pirate's expression. Instead, he charged the phalanx, his feet slapping small craters in the water with each step. The monk's sword blazed brighter as if petulant at being ignored. For all its light, it burned impotently, point first in coral.

Captain Thoster glanced once at Angul, then lit out after Raidon, unsheathing his golemwork blade. Water beaded up and ran off Thoster's sword as if the weapon were forged of mallard feathers instead of iron.

The kuo-toa phalanx, down three from the dozen or more that first appeared, tensed against the monk's charge, drawing new spears from those strapped to their backs. They extended them, intent on skewering the man.

Raidon leaped, and his trajectory became an arc. He rose neatly over the highest spear tip. He landed in the midst of the phalanx. Their formation broke apart, as all instantly attempted to turn inward. The monk's hands were like water wheel pistons, a blur of motion Japheth could barely discern. The cerulean tattoo on his chest seemed to gleam brighter with each creature he slew.

Thoster crashed into the outer circle of distracted kuo-toa. He struck down two instantly with his envenomed mechanical blade, opening a hole in the already crumbling formation.

"This is too easy," muttered Japheth. He scanned the periphery of the vault and glimpsed movement.

"Over there!" he yelled, pointing. At least three more groups of kuo-toa spearwielders materialized through the mist. With them came other creatures, some recognizable as squidlike beasts the size of hounds, a few so misshapen he couldn't immediately classify them.

The warlock uttered a series of arcane words and directed a beam of dire radiance into one of the groups, dazzling their eyes and disrupting their forward progress.

"And above us, Japheth!" Anusha's voice yelled in his ear. He looked up.

The kraken was back.

CHAPTER TWENTY-TWO

The Year of the Secret (1396 DR)
Taunissik, Sea of Fallen Stars

Icy warnings blared from the Cerulean Sign on Raidon's chest, a new pulse with each heartbeat. As if he didn't already know all these fish-men were touched by corruption.

Still in a guarding stance, Raidon palmed a slashing spear haft with his left hand. He jerked, pulling the kuo-toa forward, directly into a rising right knee. The kuo-toa's head crunched, and the creature fell away. The monk retained his grip on the spear, spinning it like a staff. He spun it around one-handed, landing a resounding blow along another kuo-toa's head. He leaned into the rebound to clip a second foe, then put his other hand on the shaft so he could thrust the butt end of the spear into a third foe's throat. The kuo-toa tried to scream but choked instead. The staff lengthened Raidon's reach, but the blows it delivered were not as powerful as his Sign-enhanced fists.

The choking kuo-toa cried out, tried to turn, but fell into a bloody heap instead. The ship captain stood behind the corpse, his strangely clicking sword beaded with water and blood, a manic expression making his face a strange mask. Something in that expression and the shape of the man's head reminded Raidon of the kuo-toa themselves.

"More's coming, my Shou friend," panted the captain. He pointed the tip of his blade at the scurrying fish-men drawing nearer through the artificial rain. The captain's grin expanded. "More for us to kill."

Raidon's symbol suddenly turned as cold as a blizzard. He looked up. Just visible through the water streaming down from the ceiling he glimpsed . . . a great flock of bats? No. A single creature, one with vast arms of squalid black muscle. It was the very beast Cynosure had revealed to him. Gethshemeth.

The great kraken clutched a head-sized orb in one tentacle, and in another, a humanoid figure carved of stone, a mere doll in Gethshemeth's tentacles. It hunched over the tableau, its arms flickering and weaving overhead as if it cast a spell requiring all its gesturing arms.

As if being waved forward, a half dozen more kuo-toa formations rushed across the flooding vault. Before they reached Raidon, Gethshemeth reached down and set its doll down not far from the monk. He saw it was actually about twice his height. Another stone behemoth, like the one he'd dispatched on first arriving in the chamber.

The statue shuddered forward, its arms rising.

Raidon charged it. From his focus of concentration he projected stone-shattering force into the heel of his right hand. Threads of coolness reached from his chest, down his arm, and interlaced themselves with his focus. His spellscar, its shape that of the Cerulean Sign, aided him all on its own.

The lobster-clawed humanoid sprayed him with crimson fluid.

"Raidon, no!" he heard someone shout, perhaps the invisible girl, or maybe the panicked wizard. Then silence claimed him.

When a coral dome sealed the monk away, Anusha's fear returned like a thick gag threatening to choke off her breath. She'd expected Raidon Kane would rise to this final challenge, as she'd seen him do against the threats they'd faced on the surface. Instead, the kraken neutralized him with its first move.

Close by, the wizard Seren seemed to be crying, even as she launched a wave of lightning at the closest kuo-toa phalanx. A crack of thunder knocked six or seven fish-men backward, head over flippers, to land in a heap, dazed and hurt. But more kuo-toa continued to pour into the area. Seren's lament grew louder even as she prepared another blast. She sobbed, "We're all going to die!"

Anusha stood near Japheth. His eyes were locked on the kraken, or perhaps the orb the kraken wielded. Her fear crystallized. "Wait!" she counseled him, thinking he was about to engage Gethshemeth himself. "Wait for Raidon's help! I can free the half-elf as I did you!"

Without a backward glance she dashed through the press of scaly bodies. She called up her dream blade and lay around her with it as she passed. She imagined her blade's edges as real and sharp as Angul's steely edge.

Anusha's passage was a bloody furrow through the kraken's advancing minions. Composed as it was of dream matter, no blood stained her armor or even her sword. That's how she dreamed it should be, and that's how it was. The creatures only sensed her by her bloody deeds. Kuo-toa squealed and died.

She reached the lobster-clawed statue where Raidon was entombed. Captain Thoster had so far avoided a similar fate, but what was he doing? Thoster was on his knees in the pooling water facing the eidolon, his sword sheathed and his arms outstretched as if in entreaty or worship. The man chanted something in a singsong tone, perhaps a prayer.

His strangely liquid vowels were having some sort of effect. The statue wavered, tried to step, paused, vibrated, then shuffled sideways.

"Whatever you're doing, keep it up," she murmured, and plunged into the stone that imprisoned Raidon. She had just trawled three similar stone shrouds, so she knew what to look for. Almost immediately she located Raidon's form. She grabbed the rigid monk beneath his arms and heaved, but her hands slipped free. She tried again, remembering to will his flesh to be as her dream body, like smoke flowing through air. She heaved once more, and a moment later the man was free of the clutching stone.

Raidon resumed his charge as if nothing had detoured him. Even as Thoster retained the eidolon's attention, the monk jumped at the end of his trajectory and smashed the statue in the chest with the heel of his palm.

The crack of rending stone echoed through the chamber. Fine lines burning with cerulean fire suddenly spidered the statue, thickest at the point of impact.

Anusha came up behind Raidon and brought down her dream blade. Jarring impact surprised her.

"No!" said Thoster suddenly "Don't attack her!"

Her? Anusha wondered why the pirate would suddenly refer to the animated statue as a "she," and wish to protect it. Had his mind been suborned by Gethshemeth?

Raidon spared a puzzled glance at the captain's insane plea but didn't cease his assault on the stone figure. Even as stone claws snapped toward the monk, he evaded them by slipping to one side and around the statue. From there, the monk launched into a fury of stinging blows. The sound of crunching stone, like Anusha imagined might issue from a mine shaft, accompanied Raidon's unstoppable onslaught. The half-elf's hands and feet had somehow become harder than stone.

The kuo-toa swarming into the cavern paused to watch, their eyes fixed on Raidon. Moments later, the statue's swift demolition was complete. Raidon stood on a pile of slick, wet rubble above the rising water line. His hair was molded to his head in the constant drizzle and his clothes sopped, but in that moment he seemed unstoppable. The monk's eyes lifted and focused on the kraken itself as if in challenge.

The immense, slime-slick monstrosity didn't fall upon the man with its tree-thick arms, as Anusha had guessed it would. Instead Gethshemeth writhed its tentacles over them like baleful clouds. As if in response, every single kuo-toa in the vault screamed with a single voice. It was the sound of unquenchable madness. A madness that threatened to infect Anusha's mind with its awful atonal volume.

The screaming kuo-toa charged, forgetting formation, forgetting discipline, and forgetting their fear of death.

The wizard cried with such anguish, Anusha heard her over the roar of the kuo-toa. Her shoulders shaking, Seren managed to call up a perimeter of burning fire, as if to mark the site of her last stand.

Raidon leaped from the pile of stone, grabbed Captain Thoster by the lapels of his flapping coat, and dashed back toward Japheth, Seren, and Angul. The pirate allowed himself to be pulled, but his eyes remained fixed on the rubble pile. He had already slipped into insanity, Anusha judged. Or perhaps not. Despite his limp posture, Thoster retained his grip on his blade.

The monk used his free hand to bat away the swarming kuo-toa between him and his goal. Their screams hardly changed pitch even after a solid blow knocked them prone.

Anusha moved with them, helping Raidon ward off stray claws, spear thrusts, and bites.

A fish-man, bigger than the others, appeared suddenly in Raidon's path. The large kuo-toa brandished a harpoon with cord attached to it. It carried a wide, slime-slick shield. Several additional harpoons were lashed to its back.

The monk instantly transferred all his forward momentum into his arms. Even as he stopped dead, he released Thoster in a high arc that cleared the harpooner's reach by a couple of feet. The pirate captain crashed down with a great splash within the protective circle of fire that burned despite the cold seawater still pouring down from above.

Watching the captain's flight distracted Anusha, and perhaps the same was true of Raidon. Even as Thoster came down hard, the harpooner loosed its broad-bladed spear. It caught Raidon in his left leg. Blood sprayed from the wound, black in the witchlight-illuminated cavern.

Raidon jerked away, too late. The point broke off in the wound with the cord still attached. The harpooner gave a terrific yank. The slick, water-covered ground betrayed the monk, and he went down. The swarming, screaming kuo-toa were on him in an instant.

Japheth was entranced by the sinuous movements of the great kraken that, unaccountably, failed to help its slaves kill them. A single slap of one of its ten-foot-thick tentacles would crush two or three of them at once. Why did it hold back?

The warlock guessed it was playing with them, like a cat toying with a mouse. How often did such sport offer itself to the beast?

Not that its thronging, screaming servitors required any help. Out of the corner of his eye, Japheth saw the Shou fall beneath on onslaught of writhing, scaled bodies.

I'll be next, he predicted.

Three kuo-toa near the perimeter fire hissed, sounding more like snakes than Japheth imagined fish could, then leaped over the barrier into the ring. The fire blazed up, crisping each one instantly.

Seren whispered, "I can only keep out four or five more—if more than that rush us, the perimeter will collapse." Her eyes were red with grief, and she looked at Japheth as if for answers.

He felt as drained and exhausted as she looked. He had no hope to offer the wizard. The kraken's mere proximity was sufficient to extinguish heroism and squash the aspirations of the boldest.

Japheth glanced around, hoping to glimpse Anusha. She was nowhere to be seen, of course. She might even have retreated to her physical body once more. He wouldn't blame her if she had. In fact, he hoped she had fled.

He didn't want her to see him die.

The mass of writhing kuo-toa where Raidon had fallen continued to shake and writhe. The monk was still fighting under the shroud of scaled flesh. Amazing.

Japheth forced himself to look up again at the nightmare hovering over them.

The Dreamheart was so close! He could see it, clutched at the tapering end of one of Gethshemeth's many arms. The stone seemed to glow with an anti-light all its own. It was too close for Japheth to ignore any longer.

He glanced at Angul. Should he take up the weapon Raidon said was forged to kill aberrations? He released a short grunt of derision. No, he'd never so much as held a sword before, not even in play as a child.

He'd have to rely on the Lord of Bats's gifts.

Claws raked Raidon's back, face, and exposed forearms. Teeth bit at his calves, exposed chest, and even his ears. A hundred mouths screamed their unending, insane paean, even as they strove to smother Raidon under the press of their bodies and drown him by holding his head beneath the rising water.

The sheer number of wrestling forms was the only reason Raidon hadn't already succumbed to the onslaught. Far more claw rakes and bites scored bleeding gashes and gaping wounds on other kuo-toa than were visited on the monk.

But he couldn't take much more. He was dribbling blood from the wound given him by the harpooner, and his thinking was growing fuzzier by the moment, thanks to the incessant scream. He managed to get his head above water long enough to suck in another desperate breath. One of his foes pulled the harpoon head out of his thigh. More blood flowed.

His vision narrowed, and the screams around him deepened, as if he entered a tunnel mouth. He knew his perceptions were skewing, not reality.

A sweet, curious voice out of time asked, "Papa? Are you hurt?"

"No, Ailyn," he responded automatically. "Just taking a little rest."

"Can we play, Papa?"

"No, Papa has something he must finish first . . ."

Raidon blinked away the waking vision. He didn't want to be seen a liar, even if it was a lie told to his daughter's trusting memory.

The spellscar fire on his chest guttered, as if in danger of failing. He'd forgotten it. He was growing addled indeed. He put Ailyn from his mind and concentrated his focus through the Sign, and it blazed bright and cold once more, illuminating the cavities of the dark, living heap he struggled beneath.

Wide kuo-toa eyes shuttered in pain as the sudden purifying radiance dazzled them. Raidon took his opportunity and struggled upward through the press like a man swimming upstream through rapids. Rapids composed of cold, scaled, wet fish-men. He couldn't seem to draw the same vigor from his Sign he'd used moments earlier to render the statue to a pile of broken rock. He sensed he hadn't given the spellscar time to recuperate. It was tired, just as he was. The jolt of vigor he'd managed to pull from the Sign was already running its course, and his limbs burned again with overexertion.

A clawed hand clamped down on his left bicep. Hampered by his position, Raidon couldn't simply tear it away. It held Raidon fast and began to squeeze.

Then a kuo-toa below him bit his foot, the same foot the plaguechanged ghoul in Starmantle had nearly bitten off.

A shriek of pain burst from him as a stream of bubbles. That old ghoul-bite had never healed right, and all the pain it had given him returned threefold.

The monk thrust his free hand straight up past wriggling bodies, a desperate gesture, his hand working spasmodically, looking for purchase.

Someone took his hand and pulled. The hand was small, but it was strong. Strong enough to lift him up and pull him out of the scrabbling kuo-toa. It pulled him higher still, until he was ten feet above water. It had to be Anusha who'd saved him. Again. With the help of his savior, he kicked free of the tumult, save for two fish-men that retained their grips.

One dangled from his bicep, the other continued to bite down on his foot.

Raidon breathed freely in great heaving gasps. With his body finally unimpeded by dozens of clawing foes, he was able to torque his free leg upward to deliver a vicious knee to the crown of the kuo-toa holding his arm. A crunch of bone and it stopped its scream and limply fell away.

The one on his other leg was scrabbling for a better hold, but its mouth remained clamped tight on his foot.

The big kuo-toa with the harpoons chose that moment to loose another spear. Raidon saw him this time. He pulled up both legs and twisted, interposing the kuo-toa on his leg between himself and the harpooner. The spear buried itself in the creature's back. It gurgled and dropped.

The hand holding his began to shake. The girl was tiring, Raidon guessed. He couldn't imagine how she was holding him up in the first place. Before she could drop him, he swung his legs back, then forward in a violent jerk, releasing Anusha's invisible hand as he did so.

Raidon somersaulted through the air and landed just inside the wizard's fiery, water-defying perimeter.

His wounded leg and bad foot buckled, as he'd suspected they would. He managed to save himself from falling face first into the cold water by dropping into a seated posture. The jolt on his tailbone traveled up his spine and rattled his teeth.

The jet of water forming a solid column of water suddenly ceased, stoppered as if by Gethshemeth's mere wish. And it was likely so.

The raw-throated screaming of the kuo-toa fell to nothing, as did the background roar of jetting water. The deluge of cold water splashing and dripping off the ceiling diminished to a sprinkle. The mist encompassing the vault began to clear. The thousands of ripples across the surface of the water filling the vault to a depth of a foot or more died away.

Without the constant pattering rain, the surface of the water calmed to become a perfectly reflective surface. Raidon saw reflected the monoliths, domes, kuo-toa, and the shadowed, menacing shape of the great kraken over all.

He saw his own weary reflection in the surrounding water, and that of his compatriots, including an image of a woman in golden armor standing midway between where he sat and Japheth. She stood on the water's surface as if it were solid ground.

Japheth's gaze followed Raidon's, and his eyes widened. "Anusha, flee!"

"Flee?" responded the girl, incredulous. "I'm not running again! I—"

A voice pealed from a chitinous beak that protruded from an orifice beneath Gethshemeth's enormous bulk. "I see you, ghost. Enough of your interference."

Seren clapped her hands over her ears and squeezed her eyes shut.

The warlock yelled a desperate garble of arcane syllables and pointed a finger at the behemoth. A shimmering emerald coil of eldritch power projected from Japheth's finger, higher and higher. When it reached the soft, sinful flesh of the great kraken, it began to coil around the creature, round and round, as if to restrain the great beast. Where the green energy touched the kraken, its skin blistered and grew scorched. An odor akin to fried meat and dog excrement blew wetly through the vault.

Gethshemeth shrugged its colossal tentacles. The green coils shattered into so many disconnected links in an eyeblink, and faded to nothing.

A lone tentacle extruded from Gethshemeth's mass, the one enwrapping the round stone. It dropped down toward Anusha's reflection.

Raidon's heart froze. He lunged for Angul's hilt and felt a tearing pop in his leg.

His fingers grazed the cool, smooth metal of Angul's hilt. Even that brief contact was enough to erase the harpoon pain in his leg and lessen the burning fire in his foot. He dragged himself another few inches closer and grasped the hilt in both hands.

A portion of his anxiety melted. A hint of new strength rippled through his muscles, starting in his hands and spreading quickly through his body. When the energy reached his chest, his Sign responded with a pulse of illumination nearly equal to the blade's pure fire. With the energy of his own Sign, he was able to shield his thoughts from the sword's overweening ego.

Raidon freed the blade from the stone with a jerk and turned, raising the sword over his head.

The Dreamheart in Gethshemeth's too large tentacle hovered only about ten feet over Anusha's reflection in the water. Raidon heard her yelling to herself, "Wake up! Wake up!"

But she didn't wake up. She looked at Japheth and said, "I . . . I took the potion of sleep!"

Anusha's image warped, stretched, and elongated upward. Her words became a scream of horrified agony. Like water spiraling down a drain, her taffy-stretched image corkscrewed once around the black stone before being viciously sucked in.

The image of the chamber reflected in the water no longer showed the least trace of Anusha.

Japheth's anguished cry was drowned in the explosive renewal of the raw-throated screams of the mad kuo-toa. The mass began to press closer to the ring of Seren's protective fire.

A hint of grief at Anusha's fate tugged at Raidon. But he and Angul were agreed; nothing else mattered other than plunging the burning blade into Gethshemeth's corrupt bulk.

Apparently Gethshemeth decided the same. The monster, a hundred feet of squirming monstrosity, simultaneously lashed forward with all its arms save the one holding the Dreamheart high.

One tentacle snapped through the moist air like a ballista. It flicked Thoster's body full on, accelerating the pirate captain in an instant to the same speed. The man's body whirled through the air, arcing out of sight on the vault's far side.

Another ten-foot-wide tentacle punched down like a falling redwood, smashing on the spot where the warlock Japheth stood. An instant before impact, Raidon glimpsed Japheth step sidewise into his cloak and disappear.

The horde of kuo-toa chose that moment to break the perimeter, sacrificing a few of their number to the guarding flame. The insane creatures were beyond caring. The survivors' scaly hands grabbed Seren.

The wizard shouted out a spell that electrified two creatures that touched her. Four more took their place and bore the wizard out of the snuffed perimeter circle. Seren's terrified cries were inaudible over the victorious kuo-toa's endless shriek.

Three of Gethshemeth's tentacles converged on Raidon. His training lent him grace to sideslip two. The third clipped him, so hard that he was knocked out of his guarding stance, and indeed, so hard he nearly dropped Angul.

Use me, Angul's silent plea echoed in the monk's consciousness, *before you are slain.*

"I shall," pledged Raidon. He managed to clamp both hands back around the hilt.

He dissolved the mental blockade he'd devised, opening himself fully to the blade's influence. The pain, even in his foot, dissolved, and concern for Anusha and the others was forgotten. A single thought seared into his mind: death to Gethshemeth. The Blade Cerulean flamed triumphantly in his suddenly glad grip, its star blue fire burning and boiling the stagnant, moist air of the vault.

Then a tentacle had him around the waist. He was lofted into the air and shaken like a terrier shakes a rat to break its neck. But Angul was like an anchor, and Raidon drew equilibrium from the sword even as blood surged back and forth between his feet and head. He brought the sword down on the tentacle.

A pulse of loathsome energy from the tentacle holding the Dreamheart preceded his slash by the barest moment, briefly limning Gethshemeth in a greenish black radiance.

Instead of cutting, Angul bounced off the slick flesh as if it were adamantine. For the second time he almost dropped the sword.

Angul raged. Raidon felt the blade reach into itself, and perhaps into the monk's Sign too, for extra strength. Raidon allowed the blade every iota of energy it demanded.

He raised Angul and the sword's blue-white light redoubled, a blue-tinged sunrise dawning in the vault for the first and last time. Together he and Angul said, "All abominations will be vanquished."

He cut, and the tentacle holding him fell free. He and it fell.

Raidon dropped fifty feet and rolled into the impact, requiring none of the Cerulean Blade's aid. He rolled out of the path of the severed tentacle, lest it crush him as it hammered down. In an eyeblink he was moving again, charging the suddenly frenzied blot of flesh, jumping the one that spewed purple-black blood.

He somersaulted one lashing limb and severed another. He was determined to shove Angul's length directly into Geth-shemeth's brain.

The creature coughed out three arcane syllables. Raidon's perceptions wavered—no, it wasn't his perceptions—the great kraken's outline turned fuzzy and uncertain. Raidon had suffered through enough instantaneous travel recently to recognize the effect. Gethshemeth was on the verge of escape!

The only thing that mattered more than killing the great kraken was destroying its artifact. It was why he'd suffered so much to retrieve Angul.

Raidon crouched, coiling his muscles, infusing them with Cerulean fire from his Sign and Angul. He leaped.

The monk raced upward as if invisible wings bore him, leaving a sky blue trail. The tentacle holding the Dreamheart was fuzzing into nothingness with the rest of the cowardly great kraken.

Raidon rose to meet it. Even as the limb blurred to nothing, Angul lopped it off. The severed tentacle and what it held snapped back into focus.

Gethshemeth flashed away. With the full fury of a thunderclap, air rushed in to fill the space the creature's great bulk had filled.

The wave of sound brushed the monk's serene arc through the air, sending him tumbling. The expanding wave blew through the vault, knocking every single kuo-toa flat into the water, ending their screaming fit.

Raidon fell, rolling in the air to regain control over his descent. The severed tentacle fell next to him. Unlike the previous one he'd cut, this one whipped and spasmed like an enraged python. Indeed, the Dreamheart it still clutched at one end was like a tiny head. Unable to evade, the monk received a smashing, full-body blow that hammered him into the flooded vault floor.

Pain seized him when he lost his hold on Angul. His foot, the same damn one, felt like it had a spike driven all the way through it. He gulped a lungful of water.

His body betrayed him in a sudden series of desperate coughs. Raidon managed to lever his head out of the water, but he couldn't see anything through his body's frenzied attempts to clear fluid from its lungs.

Zai zi, get a hold on yourself, Raidon thought. Xiang taught you better—you don't need a magic sword to heal your hurts!

Finding his focus, he stopped coughing and looked around.

The masses of kuo-toa that had flooded into the vault with the water lay mostly unmoving, like puppets with cut strings. He saw Angul's sputtering glow beneath the water, some ten feet from him. Even from this distance, he could discern the blade's fury at being dropped.

Neither the pirate captain nor the wizard was anywhere to be seen, at least from his current vantage. But he saw

Japheth, standing over the tentacle that had clutched the Dreamheart.

Raidon stood, took a limping step toward the warlock. "Be careful," he advised. "Don't touch the . . ."

The monk trailed off as Japheth slowly turned. The warlock held the dark, circular object in both hands.

"Drop it, now!" Raidon commanded, his voice shocked. "We must destroy it!"

"No," came Japheth's voice, drenched in sorrow. "No, not yet. It has Anusha's dream. I must wake her. It is my fault she can't wake up!"

"If you don't release the stone, it will claim you too," replied Raidon. He sidled toward Angul's flickering length.

Japheth ignored the monk. All his attention was on the stone. He gazed into it as if it were a scrying ball. He began to chant words slippery with magic.

"What are you doing? Stop, lest you disturb it further," Raidon urged.

Japheth ignored him. The warlock yelled into the stone with a voice augmented with magical tremolo, "Wake up! Wake up! Anusha, if you're in there, wake up! Ignore the thrice-damned elixir!"

The Sign on Raidon's chest fell in temperature so precipitously the monk's breath began to steam.

"Wake up!" Japheth yelled again with all the force of an invocation.

The Dreamheart bucked in the warlock's hand.

It woke up.

A seam on the stone parted, an eyelid shuttering open. Raidon met the eye's primordial stare.

It was like looking down on the clouds of some distant, storm-tossed world, clouds that ringed a pupil empty as death.

Japheth gasped.

Raidon took two more steps, plunged his arm into the water, and came up with the Blade Cerulean. It was the only tool capable of destroying the relic. He whirled, charged, yelling, "Release it!"

"No," replied Japheth. "I'll not abandon Anusha so easily."

The great eye blinked. The darkness in the pupil's center rushed out, seemed to billow and inflate the warlock's cloak with a malign influence all its own.

Japheth stepped backward into the darkness and was gone.

This ends Book I of the
Abolethic Sovereignty.
The story continues in
Book II, *City of Torment*.

DRAMATIS PERSONAE

Anusha Marhana (a-NOO-shah mar-HAN-a)
The spoiled daughter of the Marhana merchant
family. Anusha is haunted by dreams that sometimes prove a little too real. Anusha is the younger
half sister of Behroun Marhana. She does not share
her older half brother's designs on nobility.

Japheth (JA-feth)
A pact-sworn warlock with abilities that defy
common wizardry. He "walks the crimson road,"
and thus his soul is foresworn. He manages to avoid
his ultimate destiny through abilities derived from
his pact.

Nogah (NO-guh)
A kuo-toa priestess ("whip") of the Sea Mother whose prophetic dreams of personal transfiguration drive her to unthinkable acts.

Raidon Kane (RAY-dun KAYN)
A Xiang Temple-trained warrior with an unwanted "knack" for finding and killing monsters not born of the natural world.

Other Characters

Ailyn (AYE-lyn)
The adopted daughter of Raidon Kane.

Behroun Marhana (Bh-ROON mar-HAN-a)
The Lord of the Marhana merchant family with schemes on nobility, troubled by few qualms in his efforts to achieve such status. Behroun is the older half brother of Anusha Marhana.

Captain Thoster (THAWH-stir)
The captain of the pirate ship *Green Siren*. Thoster is generally considered to be without conscience but not without his own peculiar sense of honor. He often boasts his blood is "unclean," though what he means by such claims remains unclear.

Chalt Destrier
The odd proprietor of a fallen moon fragment, possibly once native to Abeir.

Curampah (KUR-am-pa)
A junior priest ("whip") of the Sea Mother, companion to Nogah. His faith in Nogah is greater than that of most kuo-toa.

Cynosure (SIN-oh-shur)
A sentient golem-construct physically buried in the fragmented plane of lost Sildëyuir.

Grandmother Ash
A sentient treelike creature rooted in the Plaguewrought Land.

Gethshemeth (geth-SHEH-meth)
A greater kraken that abides in the misty depths of the Sea of Fallen Stars.

Kiril Duskmourn (KI-ryl DUSK-mourn)
A "star" elf brigand whose blade drove her to unspeakable acts of righteousness before she disappeared.

Seren (SEER-en)
A wizard who relearned the knack of casting spells in the wake of the shattered Weave more quickly than many others.

Lucky
The ship dog aboard the *Green Siren* privateer vessel.

Malyanna (mal-YAN-na)
A noble eladrin of the Feywild whose past hides deeds that belie her race's reputation of genteel civility.

Neifion (NEH-fee-on)
An enigmatic elder creature native to the Feywild. Usually referred to as the Lord of Bats.

LISA SMEDMAN

The New York Times best-selling author of *Extinction* follows up
on the War of the Spider Queen with a new trilogy that brings
the Chosen of Lolth out of the Demonweb Pits and on a bloody
rampage across Faerûn.

THE LADY PENITENT

BOOK I
SACRIFICE OF THE WIDOW
Halisstra Melarn has been a priestess of Lolth, a repentant follower of Eilistraee, and
a would-be killer of gods, but now she's been transformed into the monstrous Lady
Penitent, and those she once called friends will feel the sting of her venom.

BOOK II
STORM OF THE DEAD
As the followers of Eilistraee fall one by one to Halisstra's wrath, Lolth turns her
attention to the other gods.

BOOK III
ASCENDANCY OF THE LAST
The dark elves of Faerûn must finally choose between a goddess that offers
redemption and peace, or a goddess that demands sacrifice and blood. We know
what a human would choose, but what about a drow?

June 2008

FORGOTTEN REALMS®

They were built to display might.
They were built to hold secrets.
They will still stand while their builders fall.

THE CITADELS

NEVERSFALL
ED GENTRY
It was supposed to be Estagund's stronghold in monster-ridden Veldorn, an unassailable citadel to protect the southern lands . . . until the regiment holding Neversfall disappeared, leaving no hint of what took them.

OBSIDIAN RIDGE
JESS LEBOW
Looming like a storm cloud, the Obsidian Ridge appears silently and without warning over the kingdom of Erlkazar, prepared to destroy everything in its reach, unless its master gets what he wants.

THE SHIELD OF WEEPING GHOSTS
JAMES P. DAVIS
Frozen Shandaular fell to invaders over two thousand years ago, its ruins protected by the ghosts and undead that haunt the ancient citadel. But to anyone who can evade the weeping dead, the northwest tower holds a deadly secret.

SENTINELSPIRE
MARK SEHESTEDT
The ancient fortress of Sentinelspire draws strength from the portals that feed its fires and pools, as well as the assassins that call it home. Both promise great power to those dangerous enough to seize them.

Stand-alone novels that can be read in any order!

TRACY HICKMAN

PRESENTS

THE ANVIL OF TIME

With the power of the Anvil of Time, the Journeyman can travel
the river of time as simply as walking upstream, visiting the
ancient past of Krynn with ease.

VOLUME ONE
THE SELLSWORD
Cam Banks

Vanderjack, a mercenary with a price on his head, agrees out of
desperation to retrieve a priceless treasure for a displaced noble. The
treasure is deep within enemy territory, and he must survive an army of
old foes, a chorus of unhappy ghosts, and the questionable assistance of
a mad gnome to find it.

VOLUME TWO
THE SURVIVORS
Dan Willis

A goodhearted dwarf is warned of an apocalyptic flood by the god
Reorx, and he and his motley followers must decide whether the
warning is real—and then survive the disaster that sweeps
through their part of Krynn.

November 2008

RICHARD A. KNAAK

THE OGRE TITANS

The Grand Lord Golgren has been savagely crushing
all opposition to his control of the harsh ogre lands of
Kern and Blöde, first sweeping away rival chieftains, then
rebuilding the capital in his image. For this he has had to
deal with the ogre titans, dark, sorcerous giants who have
contempt for his leadership.

VOLUME ONE
THE BLACK TALON

Among the ogres, where every ritual demands blood and every ally can
become a deadly foe, Golgren seeks whatever advantage he can obtain,
even if it means a possible alliance with the Knights of Solamnia, a
questionable pact with a mysterious wizard, and trusting an elven slave
who might wish him dead.

VOLUME TWO
THE FIRE ROSE

Attacked by enemies on all sides, Golgren must abandon his throne
to undertake the quest for the Fire Rose before Safrag, master
of the Ogre Titans can locate it and claim supremacy
over all ogres—and perhaps all of Krynn.

December 2008

VOLUME THREE
THE GARGOYLE KING

Forced from the throne he has so long coveted, Golgren makes a final
stand for control of the ogre lands against the Titans . . . against an
enemy as ancient and powerful as a god.

December 2009

Land of intrigue.
Towering cities where murder is business.
Dark forests where hunters are hunted.
Ground where the dead never rest.

To find the truth takes a special breed of hero.

THE INQUISITIVES

BOUND BY IRON
Edward Bolme
Torn by oaths to king and country, one man must
unravel a tapestry of murder and slavery.

NIGHT OF THE LONG SHADOWS
Paul Crilley
During the longest nights of the year, worshipers of the
dark rise from the depths of the City of Towers
to murder . . . and worse.

LEGACY OF WOLVES
Marsheila Rockwell
In the streets of Aruldusk, a series of grisly murders has rocked
the small city. The gruesome nature of the murders spawns
rumors of a lycanthrope in a land where the shapeshifters were
thought to have been hunted to extinction.

THE DARKWOOD MASK
Jeff LaSala
A beautiful Inquisitive teams up with a wanted vigilante to take
down a crimelord who hides behind a mask of deceit, savage
cunning, and sorcery.

EBERRON

In the shadow of the Last War, the heroes aren't all shining knights.

PARKER DeWOLF

The Lanternlight Files

Ulther Whitsun is a fixer. When you've got a problem, if you can't find someone to take care of it, he's your man—as long as you can pay the price. If you can't, or you won't . . . gods have mercy on your soul.

Book 1
The Left Hand of Death

Ulther finds himself in possession of a strange relic. His enemies want it, he wants its owner, and the City Watch wants him locked away for good. When a job turns this dangerous, winning or losing are no longer an option. It may be all one man can do just to stay alive.

Book 2
When Night Falls

Ulther teams up with a young and ambitious chronicler to stop a revolution. But treachery may kill him, and salvation comes from unexpected places.

July 2008

Book 3
Death Comes Easy

Gangs in lower Sharn are at each other's throats. And they don't care who gets killed in the battle. But now Ulther had been hired to put an end to the violence. And he doesn't care who he steps on to do his job.

December 2008